KU-367-008

In memory of my father, Clifton Edward Sidwell

Pleasing Mr Pepys

An Entertainment in Three Acts

*'Musique and woman I cannot but give way to,
whatever my business is.'*
Samuel Pepys

*Life's but a walking shadow; a poor player,
That struts and frets his hour upon the stage,
And then is heard no more:*
William Shakespeare

Dramatis Personae

As recorded in the diary of Samuel Pepys:
Samuel Pepys – Principal Administrator of the Navy
Elisabeth Pepys – his wife
Deborah Willet – Elisabeth's lady's maid
Abigail Williams – an actress, mistress of Lord
Bruncker
Lord Bruncker – President of the Royal Society
Jane – maid to the Pepys' household
Mary Mercer – Elisabeth's friend
Aunt Beth – Deborah Willet's aunt
Will Hewer – a clerk at the Navy Office

From writs and records of the time:
Jeremiah Wells – curate in training
Hester Willet – sister to Deborah Willet
Mr Constantine – owner of The Grecian coffee house

And featuring the unrecorded lives of:
Piet Groedecker, alias Mr Johnson – a Dutch
spymaster
Bartholomew Wells – a rebel, brother to Jeremiah
Lizzie – a teacher at the Poor Whores School

And sundry and divers citizens of London Town

Act One

1667

Chapter One

September

A METALLIC RATTLE – THE key in the lock. Abigail Williams stiffened her spine as the draught from the downstairs door and the stink of the Fleet River blew round her ankles. Harrington closed the door and she heard him scratch the flint to light the wall sconces. Lighting-up time already. It had been daylight when she had broken into his house. With one hand, she held her skirts closer to her thighs; with the other, she gripped the flat-bladed knife – a small weapon, but the edge sharpened razor-thin. She pressed back against the wall behind the door as the light from the hall flickered across her kidskin shoes.

Harrington's footsteps lumbered up the stairs, his breathing laboured. She tightened her hold on the knife, preparing herself. These breaths would be his last. She found death harder to bear than she used to, now she had seen so much suffering – the plague years, the fire. Oddly, Harrington paused on the threshold of the room, as if he could sense her waiting presence. Through the crack of the open door she saw him standing motionless, his steeple hat a silhouette in the wavering light, his head cocked, listening.

He was an old hand, like her. She repressed a flash of compassion, the foolish urge to call out, to warn him. But then his dark back came through the door and he stepped in front of her, and without even thinking she moved like quicksilver. The knife slid easily across the side of his neck. With the other hand she pushed as hard as she could. He tried to turn, but it was too late, he was already falling, clutching his collar, blood slippery over his hands, hat rolling away under the table.

Experience told Abigail it had been enough. She ran, hoisting up her skirts, down the stairs, flinging the front door open, out into the cramped back alley. Nobody followed her; the passage to Fleet Street was empty. A brownish fog wreathed around her hem. When she finally slowed, she took a rag from inside her sleeve and wiped her blade, wrapped it, and stowed it in the pocket hanging next to her petticoats. She put a hand up to the bare skin at her chest, feeling the hot rise and fall of her breastbone.

She emerged onto the main thoroughfare where the houses were lit with torches, and walked, heart thudding, down towards the King's playhouse. Arriving at the theatre, she saw Lord Bruncker's carriage was where he had left it, across the road. His coachman was leaning against the wall, a smoking pipe in his mouth, waiting. She didn't want to go in the front way – someone might ask why she was late – so instead she made for the tiring house behind.

The stage doorman knew her and nodded to her as she entered. The dressing room was empty, the actors ready to enter by the shutters for act two. From there, the audience sounded like the sea, the swell of all those voices. She checked her face and the satin of her dress for stains: a few dark spots on her sleeve, easily explained away.

Only now did she begin to shake. It was always like this: afterwards the weakness, nausea and trembling would set in. The moment when she wished she could turn back the day, the moment when she remembered their eyes, hollow with their unspoken question. Why?

Legs as unsteady as a newborn calf, she paused, leaned heavily on the trestle table, took out a phial of camphor from her pocket and inhaled. Better.

She arranged her face into a smile. Her performance for Lord Bruncker was about to begin. Her petticoat rustled against the boards as she went along the corridor and up the stairs into the box. On the way she almost bumped into Mr Pepys hurrying up the same stairs with a supply of nuts and oranges.

'For Elisabeth,' he said, obviously feeling the need to apologise for the sheer number of squashed bags hugged to his chest.

She nodded and stood aside, lowering her eyes to avoid his conversation. He could talk the baggage off a donkey. To her relief, he squeezed past and hurried into his own box further along the row.

When she got to her own, the candelabra had been lit, and upon her arrival Lord Bruncker drew out the chair so that she could sit.

'Ah, there you are,' he whispered. 'You're late. You missed the first act.'

She shook her head. 'The traffic through town—'

'Hush, they're about to start again. Have a confit.'

She reached out her hand and smiled, took a marchpane cherry, but dropped it under her seat as soon as Lord Bruncker turned back to look at the stage. She was glad his attention was diverted, so he did not notice her pallid face or that she could not swallow.

The actor who had just entered rapped three times for silence, his face ghoulish from the footlights, which smoked in their holders. The hubbub fell to a hush. But Abigail's thoughts would not lie quiet; she was thinking of Harrington, of how long it would be before they found him.

He should have listened to Piet. Then his mouth wouldn't have had to be shut the hard way. She'd liked him but, in her business, liking was a luxury she was ill able to afford.

Chapter Two

DEB WILLET HUGGED HER sister and turned to glance back through the dark doorway. She'd hated the house for so long, and with such intensity, that she was surprised to see how small it really was. Now she was leaving, it was as if its narrow half-timbered walls had shrunk to doll's house proportions.

Hester would manage without her. She was nearly twelve, after all. Deb tried to prise her sister's fingers from her arm, but Hester clung on.

'I'll write, I promise,' Deb said.

'But I don't know what I'll do … I can't finish my embroidery without you. The butterflies are too hard. Don't go.'

Deb squeezed Hester's hand. 'I have to. See, Aunt Beth's waiting.' She gestured to the carriage, a black berline, where her brass-bound trunk was already stacked behind. Their aunt, a solid black figure in a heavy travelling cloak and jagged hat, wrestled the door open against the wind.

'But when will I see you again?'

'I don't know. Soon. It will depend on the Pepyses. When they let me have a few days off together, long enough to visit.'

'Next week?'

'I told you, chicken, I don't know. Hush now, it's not so bad.'

Hester clung to a fistful of Deb's sleeve, mouth quivering, eyes threatening tears. Deb was about to comfort her again when she heard the bang of the carriage door. She pulled Hester into a protective embrace as Aunt Beth strode over, face pinched with intent.

'That's enough!' Aunt Beth said, throwing up her hand ready to strike. 'I never saw such nonsense in all my life. Making such a scene before the neighbours.'

'It's all right, Hester,' Deb said, thrusting herself between her aunt and her sister. She took hold of Hester by the shoulders and bent to look into her face. 'Listen. I'll come back as soon as I can. Just do as Aunt Beth says.'

'Will you look for Mama?' Hester's voice was a whisper, to prevent Aunt Beth hearing.

'London's a big place.'

'If you find her you'll come and fetch me?'

Deb shook her head, unable to answer.

'But you said we'd always be together. You promised.' Hester wrenched herself away, took a deep sobbing breath. 'You're a liar and I hate you.' She fled towards the house, dark hair flying, shoes splashing mud up her skirts.

'Hester! Wait—' Deb threw up her hands, then let them fall. Hester had slammed the front door behind her.

'Hurry, we've wasted enough time,' Aunt Beth said, ignoring the driver who tried to assist her, and heaving herself up the dainty steps into the carriage.

Deb hesitated as Hester appeared at the upstairs window. Oh, why did it have to be so hard?

'Deb! Into the carriage. Now.'

The carriage was black as ink and drawn by a matching pair of black horses. The colour put Deb in mind of a hearse. And as it was one of the new two-seaters, Deb had no option but to hitch up her skirts and squash herself in next to Aunt Beth. When she craned her neck out of the open door to look back, Hester was blowing her nose into her handkerchief, the fabric flapping like a white moth caught behind the window.

Deb lifted her hand to wave, but Aunt Beth pressed it firmly back. 'Don't pander to her,' Aunt Beth said. 'She's far too spoilt. It will only make it worse. When I return, I'll see to it there's no more of her nonsense.' She leaned over Deb's lap to bang the carriage door shut and the horses lurched into motion.

Deb kept her gaze on her knees, on the dark linsey wool of her cloak. The carriage was cramped and oppressive, with Aunt Beth's bulk taking up most of the room. By the time she looked up through the open square of the front window, and past the driver, the houses of Bromley St Leonard were gone, and her heart pinched with sudden loneliness. The track stretched baldly ahead, and leaves, crumpled like burnt paper, blew across the track under the horses' hooves.

Aunt Beth ticked off instructions on her fingers as they went, but Deb was too preoccupied to take them in, until they creaked to a standstill at the imposing London wall. Their driver leant back to slow the horses. Ahead, a jumble of carts, barrows and horses competed to push through a narrow passage. A gap-toothed costermonger spat a mouthful of curses at a coal cart blocking his path, and the unfamiliar words and his angry gestures made Deb stare.

'Close your ears,' Aunt Beth said.

But Deb was fascinated by the packed roads, the sheer volume of people hurrying down the damp streets, heads bent low against the drizzle. Only then did it sink in; she was really going to live here, in London. Her hands twisted over each other in apprehension and excitement.

'Deborah! Did you hear what I said?'

Deb dragged her awareness back to her aunt, whose lips had compressed into a seam of disapproval. 'Pay attention. You must never walk abroad without your mistress's permission, and never venture into back alleys alone,' she said. 'London is quite different from Bromley or Bow. Do you understand?'

'Yes, Aunt Beth.' Aunt Beth knew London well, for she had a cousin on Jerwen Street.

'And make sure to find a good laundress, one that scrubs the inside as well as the outside of the collars. A lady's maid is not a common maidservant and Mrs Pepys will rely on you to maintain her high standards. Cleanliness is a virtue, as you—'

Aunt Beth made a grab for the front of the leather seat as the horses strained to pull forward in their traces. The carriages began to flow again down Bishopsgate Street and the clatter of wooden wheels and tumult of voices from outside prevented further conversation. Aunt Beth lifted her kerchief back to her nose and kept it there, grimacing at the noise and smoke. Two dark patches already stained the linen where she had breathed in the smuts from the air.

Deb inhaled the faint, sour smell of damp burnt timber. 'Look!' she said, unable to help herself. She pointed at a towering wooden scaffolding where a new building was half-erected, and a wiry man with a hod of bricks teetered like a monkey on the narrow platform.

Aunt Beth did not deign to reply, but her eyes went over to where a gang of men were heaving up buckets on ropes and pulleys, chanting to a rhythmic *heave ho, heave ho*. Although the Great Fire had been more than a year ago, on Deb's left, all that remained were blackened brick chimney stacks, poking heavenwards like accusing fingers. Deb imagined the roar of the flames, and the houses collapsing, expiring into the smoke.

A sharp tap on her knee, and Deb pulled her head back inside, startled.

'It's folly to lean out like that,' Aunt Beth said. 'It's raining. And your head could get knocked off.' She leaned over Deb to snap down the blind, but it was stiff, and stuck halfway. 'I hope you are listening. Maybe the Pepyses will hammer some sense into you. Lord knows, you need it. And don't forget to watch your belongings, London's full of thieves and conmen.' She sniffed. 'And mind your manners. Mr Pepys is very well connected, so don't forget the Willets' good-standing depends upon your behaviour. No followers or young men, no gossip with the servants. You must give them nothing to reproach you for. And in heaven's name don't mention your mother. Whatever is past, is past, do you understand? No matter what *her* reputation, you must rise above it.'

Deb nodded, though the thought of her mother gave her a familiar squeeze of pain. Where was Mama now? Did she ever think of them? Agnes, their maid, had whispered that her mother had come to London, so perhaps she might catch a glimpse of her. But there had been other whispers about her mother too, ones that Deb did not like to hear.

Would her mother even recognise her? Last time they'd seen one another, Deb had been Hester's age, and now she was seventeen and grown so tall. Deb held up the leather blind to peer out, eyes smarting as she blinked away damp and masonry dust.

Aunt Beth prodded her with a bony finger. 'I don't need to tell you, you've fallen on your feet. It cost me a good dinner and a lot of persuading. I had to press the Bateliers to put in a word for you and praise your accomplishments to Mr Pepys. That you have Latin and Greek, and can sing a little. So your education at Bow proved useful for something, at least. The Bateliers have given you a great opportunity, so for heaven's sake don't waste it.'

Mr Batelier was a wine-merchant friend of Mr Pepys, who had also loaned his new carriage to fetch them to London.

'Will Hester be able to go to school now, like I did?' Deb asked. She knew any sort of schooling was unusual for a girl, but knew it had been a condition of her father's; perhaps to make sure she would gain employment and he wouldn't have to be responsible for her again.

'Left! Left, I say!' Her aunt shouted at the driver to turn off the main highway.

'Aunt Beth, about Hester's schooling—'

'Your father and I are in two minds whether it's worth paying to educate another girl.'

'But you promised. You said that if she—'

'We'll have to see. I'll write to your father. And, it'll depend on how you fare at the Pepyses', whether it is worth doing it again. If she's to be schooled, you'll have to contribute. Now you're earning, I'll expect two shillings a week. If you can manage that, then I'll consider it. Lord knows it would be a mighty relief to me for Hester to learn a useful occupation and be out of my way – she's getting far too lazy, hanging about my skirts.'

Deb turned away and looked out of the window. Two shillings. How much of her wages was two shillings? It sounded like a large percentage. She sighed. But there was no point in arguing with Aunt Beth, even though Hester was the least lazy person she knew. The memory of Hester's face made Deb's stomach turn another tumble and her hands grip tighter to the seat. She imagined leaping down and running all the way back, but she knew this to be an impossible gesture. Aunt Beth was insistent Deb was old enough and educated enough to be off her hands, and once Aunt Beth had an opinion, she would beat it into you, rather than take no for an answer.

'Nearly there. Tidy yourself up, Deborah. Put on your gloves.' Aunt Beth hooked up the blind with her finger and peered out of the window to see over the wet rumps of the horses.

Ahead of them the traffic had thinned.

'Hart Street,' Deb said, reading the sign aloud and admiring the painting of a white deer in a forest.

'And St Olave's, here on the corner.' Aunt Beth pointed. 'I expect you to see the inside of it as often as you can. Prayer will keep temptation away. Now, hurry up and straighten your cap.'

Deb tried to tug it down over her thick brown hair, which kept escaping in tendrils from the front.

'Not like that! It's all askew.' Aunt Beth reached over to jerk it down. 'Remember,' she whispered, 'no need to tell the Pepyses anything of your background. As far as they are concerned, your mother died of the smallpox.'

When it suited her, Aunt Beth was quite comfortable with the idea of lying, despite her dire warnings to Deb and Hester of the hell and damnation that awaited them for such a sin. But today Deb did not mind. The Pepyses were her chance, her ticket to a safe future, so she could pave the way for Hester.

But how would her sister fare on her own? Aunt Beth was as cold as a stone wall, and just as immoveable; Hester, the opposite – volatile as tinder. She'd go back for her, Deb vowed. And when she did, she would have made her way in society and Hester would have someone to look up to, and a proper home to come to – one with comfort and laughter and a smiling face to greet her.

A gust of rain startled her. Aunt Beth was calling, holding the carriage door for her to climb out.

Seething Lane. They were here already. Deb climbed out, ducking against the rain. She peered across to the towering Customs House, with its impressive stone frontage, and over broad gravelled pathways and manicured gardens. Beyond stood the offices and dwellings of the Navy Board, the brick-built houses of Henry's reign, and the offices themselves – a weight of masonry that blotted out the sky. She quailed before their bulk.

I will not be daunted, she thought to herself. By the time Deb had glanced around, Aunt Beth was already making strides towards the residences in the west wing of the Navy Buildings. Deb drew herself up tall, smoothed down her skirts, and trying not to run, hurried after her.

Chapter Three

JANE, A BROAD-FACED SERVANT girl with narrow curious eyes, took their cloaks and gloves and hurried away to fetch the lady of the house, Mrs Pepys, while Deb and her aunt waited in the gilded parlour. Despite its grandeur, the Pepyses' residence was gloomy, it being on the north side of the Navy buildings and lacking the sun. The parlour was so full of rugs and furniture, ornaments and pictures that Deb dare not move for fear of knocking something over.

Deb looked down at how the rain had speckled her skirts, and hoped they did not appear too creased from the journey. Aunt Beth had insisted she wore her best-quality grey linen; a tight-fitting bodice with the stiff busk that pushed her chest up high, as was the fashion amongst ladies. A deep kerchief of clean muslin covered the exposed gooseflesh. Feeling a little nervous, Deb tucked the kerchief more securely into her bodice.

She couldn't help staring round at the hotchpotch of pictures and engravings on the walls: square cattle staring morbidly out of a landscape; a limp-necked pheasant reclining on a bed of grapes; maps of foreign towns and Roman ruins. So, like her, Mr Pepys must like history. People's houses were fascinating. They told you so much about a person. All the time the grey London drizzle outside spotted the sooted window with dabs of light.

On a table near the door, three leather-bound books were piled carelessly open, one on top of the other. Deb longed to go and lay them straight but did not dare. Next to them, a blue-patterned bowl of wizened fruit accounted for the slightly sweet, decaying smell. One of the apples was bruised and brown and sported a ruff of white mould. Deb fought the urge to pick it out and throw it away.

From somewhere above, whispered voices echoed in the silence. 'This?' 'No, not this cap, that one! And my best gloves, the ones with the lace!' Deb recognised what must be Mrs Pepys by her slight accent, its rolling French '*r*'s. Aunt Beth had told her Mrs Pepys had been brought up in France.

Aunt Beth pretended she had not heard, but it seemed Deb was not the only one who wanted to make a good impression. When Mrs Pepys eventually arrived, in a froth of yellow silk and ribbon, and wearing the lace gloves, she eyed Aunt Beth nervously. 'Well, here you are at last!' She clapped her hands together. It was a curiously childlike gesture.

Aunt Beth stood ramrod-tall, introduced Deb, and Deb was obliged to drop a polite curtsey. All the while Mrs Pepys flustered from chair to chair, not sure where to sit them down. Her gaze flicked from one to the other, seemingly at a loss how to proceed with the conversation. Not so Aunt Beth, who, to Deb's embarrassment, took charge by detailing all the things Deb would not do – 'No cooking, no emptying chamber pots, no lighting fires, no sweeping hearths. And absolutely no scrubbing floors.' All, of course, were things she had been expected to do at Aunt Beth's.

Mrs Pepys appeared somewhat taken aback at this

list, her finger to her lower lip in consternation, but Aunt Beth was insistent. 'A companion. That was what was agreed. Four shillings a week and her board. And half of that to come to me for the upkeep of her sister still at home. I think you will find Deborah satisfactory. The school always found her a godly child, and her behaviour exemplary.'

Deb looked down at her feet, squirming under the onslaught of her aunt's praise. Aunt Beth's usual word for her was 'contrary', but now suddenly she was 'exemplary'.

But Mrs Pepys fiddled with the lace that fluttered at her throat. 'Of course,' she said, about nothing in particular. 'Quite so.'

'You'll get a servant to bring Deborah's trunk up, will you?' Aunt Beth said.

'Oh. Yes, I'll see if I can find someone ...' Mrs Pepys stood and backed hastily out of the room, calling, 'Will? Can you come?'

A fair-haired young man appeared at the door, nib in hand, collar immaculately starched, and much too neatly dressed to be a servant. He looked harassed at being interrupted.

'Will, this is Miss Willet, who is to be part of our household,' Mrs Pepys said, not meeting his eyes. 'Would you bring her things please – to the upper chamber?'

'Yes, yes. Pleased to meet you, Miss Willet. I'm the clerk, Master Hewer. I work with Mr Pepys. When I'm allowed to get on with it, that is.' He sighed. 'Show me your trunk and I'll bring it up.'

Mrs Pepys beamed round the room in relief. 'Our serving boy won't manage it, you see. And anyway, he's out with Sam.'

After the trunk had been fetched, Aunt Beth

prodded Deb to follow Will up the two flights of stairs to her chamber. Aunt Beth dismissed him cursorily, which made him cover a smile with his hand. Deb smiled back, earning a frown from Aunt Beth.

Her own chamber! Deb was elated. Though she had liked sharing with Hester, their room at Aunt Beth's had been small and oppressive, and she never got enough peace to read and study. Hester was always wanting to *do* something, couldn't be still for two minutes.

Aunt Beth ran a finger over the panelling and examined it with a grimace of disapproval. 'I'll leave you then,' she said. 'Get yourself washed and ready to do your duty.'

'Yes, Aunt Beth. Mrs Pepys seems ...' What? Mrs Pepys gave the impression of a person who could not make up her mind. Even her sleeves did not match her bodice. 'She seems very pleasant,' Deb finished.

Aunt Beth wagged her finger. 'Mind your tongue. It is not your place to make judgements, Deborah. Pleasant or not, they are your employers, and you will behave accordingly. Make sure you please Mr Pepys.'

Deb held out her arms towards her aunt for an embrace, not because she felt affection, but because she supposed that, after lodging with her aunt for six whole years, something more was required. 'Thank you, Aunt Beth. I mean for taking us in. For looking after Hester.'

Aunt Beth gave a snort. 'I'd no choice, had I?' She turned away from the embrace and lifted her skirts, ready to go downstairs. 'If you want to give thanks, make your father proud of you,' she said, turning on the landing to look over her shoulder.

Deb gritted her teeth, swallowed back a retort. To

do that, she would have had to have been a boy, like her brothers. Her father, despite travelling all over the Low Countries these last six years overseeing his exports in wool, had shown no interest whatsoever in visiting his daughters.

'Please, give my love to Hester,' Deb called, hanging over the banister. 'Tell her I'm thinking of her. Embrace her for me, won't you, and tell her I'll write?' But Aunt Beth was gone and there was no reply.

Below her, in the hall, Aunt Beth's thin, reedy voice made effusive farewells to Mrs Pepys. After the bang of the door, the clop of horses' hooves, a jangle of harness, then silence. Deb exhaled, rushed to look out of the landing window.

The carriage was turning the corner, and her old life, along with Aunt Beth, was getting further away every minute. She did not know whether to be glad or sorry. But then she looked up, over the leaded rooftops towards the Tower, its grey stone peaks floating eerily in the mist.

A thrill ran through her. So much history there: queens uncrowned – old Henry's Anne, Lady Jane Grey. And under it, the royal menagerie of lions and bears. She imagined the prowling of hungry wild beasts in the dark caverns behind those walls, wondered whether traitors in the dungeons heard them roar.

Chapter Four

IN THE UPSTAIRS DINING ROOM, Elisabeth Pepys paused over her household accounts, quill aloft. Should she ask Miss Willet to look over them? She baulked at the idea, for though she dare not admit it to her husband, she was in awe of her new maid. Miss Willet seemed altogether too self-possessed, too quiet. She was like a little owl. Those pale grey eyes watching her with sidelong glances; she couldn't tell what the girl was thinking. What she thought of *her*.

Elisabeth squinted over to the silver mirror where she could see the reflection of Deb, who was behind her, wiping over the glassware in the cabinet. And that tight-laced gown she was wearing showed off her figure too closely, Elisabeth thought. It would have to be remedied. Of course, Elisabeth told herself, she was glad to have someone; it had taken her long enough to persuade Sam that she needed a proper companion, not just a common or garden maid-of-all-work. All the other navy wives had lady's maids as companions, except, of course, Lord Bruncker's doxy, Abigail Williams, and she certainly did not count.

It had seemed a fine idea to ask for someone well educated, someone befitting Sam's new station in life as chief victualler of the navy, but the trouble was, this girl was extremely well brought up. Her aunt had made it clear she had standards, and the girl had certain expectations. There were things she should not be asked to do. So now, instead of scrubbing the kitchen grates with Jane, she was polishing glasses that did not really need polishing.

Elisabeth had looked forward to imposing the rules of her household herself, so she had been somewhat deflated to find that the aunt had already done it. When Elisabeth had told the girl 'No followers', Miss Willet had sat down with a long-suffering look, as if she might have to listen to a long list, and when Elisabeth could not think of anything further, she, the mistress, had been left standing like a fool.

Elisabeth brought her mind back to the household accounts, added up the column of figures again, and guessed at the answer, writing it with a flourish. She was aware that she was trying to impress the maid, a quite ridiculous state of affairs. Why, that morning she had felt obliged to get up and get dressed straight away, so Miss Willet could help her arrange her hair. There'd be no more lounging around her bedchamber in her nightgown as she had always been wont to do.

Just at that moment, Miss Willet glanced over her shoulder and caught Elisabeth's face in the mirror, staring. Elisabeth gave her a faint smile. What duties could she give the girl without offending? She couldn't polish glasses for ever. She turned. 'You may stop that now, Miss Willet. I need some diversion. You can read to me.'

'Very well, mistress.' Miss Willet gave the glass she was cleaning another wipe and placed it exactly in its row in the cabinet.

Elisabeth sent her up to fetch one of the French

romances from her chamber.

'This?' Miss Willet asked, from the doorway, holding it up by finger and thumb as if it was something no person of quality would ever want to read.

'Yes,' Elisabeth felt heat rise to her cheeks, 'it is good, is it not, to have a change from the classics from time to time? What are you waiting for? Begin.'

To give the girl her due, she read the romance prettily enough, with no stumbling over any of the words. Yet somehow her prettiness, her poise and her calm manner only served to irritate Elisabeth the more. But Lord, she couldn't get rid of her now, not after she had begged and begged Sam for just such a maid. To outside appearances, the well-educated Deborah Willet was exactly what a lady required. Added to that, Sam's great friend Mr Batelier had recommended her. No, she'd have to pretend to Sam she was in control of this girl, when she felt quite plainly she was not.

Of course, Sam never noticed; he was already describing the new maid to Will Hewer and the clerks as 'our pretty little girl', or 'our Deb', in a proprietorial way, despite her only having been in the house less than a day. It was just that, instead of adding to her status, somehow having Deborah Willet in the house made Elisabeth feel smaller.

Anxious to impress, Deb followed her new mistress as she flitted vaguely here and there in a rustle of ribbon and taffeta, alighting on first one thing then another. First, it was polishing, then reading out loud, but then Mrs Pepys changed her mind again and said, 'You'd better check over my accounts. The sooner you learn household management, the better.'

'Certainly, mistress,' Deb said, exhaling a sigh of relief. She hurried over to the writing desk, but one glance was enough to see the reckonings were in frightful disorder. Deb bit her lip and cautiously picked up a quill.

The balance bore no resemblance to the actual figures, and pence were written in the pound columns. Multiple scratchings out made the pages look like spiders had made nests there. Oh my, what was she to do? Surely Mrs Pepys could not think these were correct? Deb glanced at Elisabeth, but Elisabeth was now engrossed in her novel. Deb had not been given permission, but she could not resist setting the figures in order. She double-checked her calculations and rewrote the columns on a new page in her tidy, precise hand.

'Beg pardon, Mrs Pepys, but would you like me to lay them out for you? In a double-entry system?' she asked. 'I could write out a balance table, then all we would need to do is fill it in week by week. It would be very efficient, and—'

Mrs Pepys appeared at her shoulder and, seeing Deb's alterations, shut the book in front of Deb with enough of a snap to make a draught. 'Mr Pepys is very particular. He likes the accounts the way I do them.' She pushed the book under her arm and hurried away, heels clattering down the stairs to the kitchen. Deb could not help feeling a little hurt.

In the afternoon, Elisabeth handed Deb some crewel-work cushions to embroider, and Deb, hoping to please, stitched meticulously.

Elisabeth watched Deb sewing for about two turns of the hourglass. 'You're very neat,' she said. But it sounded like an accusation. After only a few more moments, Mrs Pepys laid her embroidery to one side and picked up her romance, waved it at Deb. 'What do you think of it?'

Deb swallowed hard. Aunt Beth had taught her they were vulgar things, full of coy heroines and panting hearts.

'Such a lovely story,' Mrs Pepys continued. 'Don't you think so?'

'Yes,' Deb said meekly, aware that this was the right answer, 'very diverting.'

Mrs Pepys waited a moment, expecting more, but Deb could not supply it. She could think of nothing else good to say of it. Deb just held tight to the edges of her cuffs with her fingers. The atmosphere grew strained, but Deb did not know what to do to ease it. Elisabeth stood up with a heavy sigh and left the room without a word.

Deb sagged. She'd failed. She did not know how to make this sort of conversation. Aunt Beth never let them talk of anything frivolous like books or music. She gave an inward groan. Mrs Pepys did not like her. She was certain of it.

In the afternoon, Mrs Pepys took Deb to walk by the Thames. Before they set off, Deb gave herself a talking-to. She would win over Mrs Pepys if it was the last thing she did. The alternative was being reduced to a maid-of-all-work in some backwater of her aunt's choosing. For Hester's sake, she could not afford to fail.

Mrs Pepys seemed afraid to be silent and kept up a constant chatter and exclamation as if to impress upon Deb her immense knowledge of the city – so much so, that, by the time they returned, Deb's head was throbbing with names and places, directions and distances. All the while Deb followed her with eager-eyed attention, nodding and agreeing to everything, and smiling until her face ached.

'Pouf! You've worn me out,' Mrs Pepys said. 'Would you go down and ask Jane to bring us some warmed ale?' She sank into a chair near the fire.

With relief, Deb hurried down to the kitchen, where Jane, the kitchen-maid, was pounding up parsley and butter in a mortar. 'Mrs Pepys requests refreshment please,' Deb said. 'Warmed ale, if you have it.'

'Oh, I'm glad you've come at last,' Jane said, managing to make it sound as though Deb had kept away on purpose. 'It will be good for the mistress to have proper company.' She lifted the copper pan onto the fire and stirred it. 'Mr Pepys is so frequently out, and my mistress will talk on and on. Sometimes it's hard for me to get anything done once she starts.'

'Will Mr Pepys be back again later?' Deb asked, curious about her new employer, who had bustled in earlier for his hat, in a great draught, like a ship caught in the wind. She had caught only a glimpse of a dark periwig, a flapping cravat, and very white stockings beneath a russet-coloured coat.

'I expect so. He's gone back to the Navy Offices. He's dining out today, but if I know him, he'll soon search you out when he comes home.'

She sounded disapproving of him. Mr Pepys had chucked her under the chin as he passed, saying, 'How are we, little Deb?' But he was in a mighty hurry and, as it was a question that hadn't needed an answer, he hadn't lingered to hear one.

'I shall look forward to that,' Deb said.

'Aye, well that'll be short-lived. You'll soon be doing what I do, dodging out of his way. Keep your wits about you, is all I'm saying. And she—' Jane gestured with her head to the parlour, 'she's that mop-headed she don't know the half of it, so don't you go telling her.'

Deb did not reply; what did Jane mean? She distracted herself by taking the tray of heated wine through and setting it down next to Mrs Pepys.

'Tomorrow I may shop for a new nightdress,' Mrs Pepys said dreamily, twirling a strand of hair around her finger. 'My others are simply in tatters, and my dear Mr Pepys hates to wait while I choose. I have a fancy for something of French silk, with that new lace, the *point de Bretagne* everyone's talking of. We shall go together, and to tell truth, we shall be merrier without him.'

'Thank you, Mistress Pepys,' Deb said.

'You may call me Elisabeth.' She pronounced it the French way, with a long 'E', and bowed her head as if it was a great concession. 'And I shall call you Deb, as my husband does. Do you like the theatre?'

'I have never been.'

Elisabeth's mouth fell open. She threw up her hands. 'Never been? *Oh la*! Then we shall have to remedy that. It is our chief entertainment! Three times a week we go, sometimes. I'll talk to Sam and we'll arrange it.'

True to his word, the next afternoon Mr Pepys collected Deb and her mistress from the draper's at the temporary Exchange in a hired carriage, and they set off for the King's playhouse. Brydges Street was so full of carriages all come for the play that they had to get out and walk down the darkening narrow passages and into the theatre. Mr Pepys stepped off to one side to converse with a large, broad-shouldered gentleman.

'That's Lord Bruncker,' Elisabeth said. 'He works with Mr Pepys at the Navy Office.'

Deb stared. Lord Bruncker was about Mr Pepys' age but must have been impressively handsome once. He was tall, dark and lugubrious, unlike Mr Pepys, who was broader and somewhat short in stature, but bristled with a kind of restless energy. The woman who was with Lord Bruncker smiled at Deb with catlike eyes over her fan.

'Is that his wife?' Deb asked.

'No. Nobody important.' Elisabeth shook her head and tightened her lips in a manner that suggested she would like to say more but would not.

Lord Bruncker and Mr Pepys were in animated conversation, so they had to wait for Mr Pepys to catch them up. Deb could not help looking at the woman again, at her mass of sculpted jet-coloured curls, at her pale, almost bloodless skin. She was dressed in a dark-blue silk that shimmered despite the dull day, and a wrap trimmed with white fox fur. She certainly did not need to fish for stares. Despite the stir she was causing, she held her head like an aristocrat. Deb had never seen a more arresting-looking woman; it gave her a pinch of something like envy.

The woman saw her looking and approached Elisabeth, who folded her arms over her chest as if to keep her away. 'Good afternoon, Elisabeth,' the woman said with an amused smile. 'Here again? I've heard the play is very good.'

'Yes, though Mr Pepys has seen it already and says it is the saddest thing he ever saw.'

'Then I wonder that he wants to suffer it again.' The woman raised an arched eyebrow at Deb.

'Oh, this is Deb Willet, my companion,' Elisabeth

said. 'Deb, this is Mistress Williams. She used to be one of the players, but now she's ...' Elisabeth was lost for words. She took a deep breath. 'Can you believe it? This girl has never been to the theatre. We thought it might be amusing to bring her.'

'Quite right.' Mistress Williams turned the full force of her attention to Deb, who realised that, close-up, Mistress Williams was older than she appeared, and the hand on her fan was bony and wrinkled.

'Have you been in London long?' Mistress Williams asked.

'Just a few days.' Deb was shy under this imposing lady's intense scrutiny.

'You'll soon get used to it. And my Lord B is one of your neighbours at the Navy Chambers; he and Mr Pepys see a lot of each other.'

'Miss Willet was educated at Bow,' Elisabeth said, grandly. 'It is always good to converse with someone who knows the classics.'

'Then perhaps she will have something to teach you, Elisabeth.'

Deb reddened; sensed the air thicken between the two women.

'Ah, here come the gentlemen.' Elisabeth glared at Mistress Williams and grasped hold of Deb's arm to propel her forward.

Lord Bruncker and Mr Pepys arrived. 'I was just about to offer your girl a tour of the Duke's,' said Mistress Williams.

'Oh, what a good idea,' Lord Bruncker said. 'Nobody knows the Duke's Playhouse like Abigail.'

'Splendid,' Mr Pepys said.

'Then let her come as soon as the play's ended,' Mistress Williams said. 'That will be the most suitable time. I can show her the new machinery and take her for a turn on stage.'

'Don't give our girl ideas, though,' Mr Pepys said. 'We'd like to keep her a little longer before she turns player!'

Everyone laughed politely, and Elisabeth dragged Deb away until they were out of earshot, then turned to her husband and hissed, 'That woman! Madam Williams! She gets worse by the minute. I don't know why Lord Bruncker insists on keeping her.'

'Because he's pressed for coin, that's why. She has an income from somewhere, and he needs it. I've heard he has another mistress in Covent Garden, but he's always favoured Abigail.'

'She sticks to him like a leech, that's why.'

'Tush, she'll hear us.'

Deb turned to look over her shoulder, and Mistress Williams, still watching, waved. Her gloved hand sparkled with rings.

'I can't bear the idea of her appropriating our Deb like that,' Elisabeth continued. 'You should have said no.'

'I could hardly refuse, could I? Not with his Lordship right there?'

Deb tried not to listen, but the two carried on bickering about it until they were right inside the playhouse. From the narrow corridor, the theatre suddenly opened out into a broad auditorium with green baize-covered benches in semicircular rows. Deb looked about in amazement as the seats filled. She counted the heads and multiplied them by the number of rows. Five hundred and seventy-five, plus the boxes. And everyone so gaudy with their buttons and bows and swathes of embroidery. They jostled in amongst the rustle of satin and silk, and the reek of pomade and stale tobacco.

Lord Bruncker and Madam Williams took their places in a box where the late afternoon light picked them out in a golden glow. Deb thought her mistress, Elisabeth Pepys, was pretty enough and buxom, but Madam Williams had an intense dramatic beauty that kept drawing Deb's eye. She was laughing, regaling Lord Bruncker with a tale that made him guffaw and look in their direction. Deb had the distinct impression they were jesting at Mr and Mrs Pepys' expense.

A rap of a cane three times, and the audience strained to listen. From under the stage the viols began. Deb was totally transported from the moment the first note sounded. How clear the players' voices were! The play was *The Traitor* by Mr Shirley, a tragedy. Deb drank in every word, her hands clutched damply to her skirts; it was as if she had a magic spyhole straight into the evils of the Medici court.

Aunt Beth had given her the impression that the Pepys household would be one of rigid restraint, but within two shakes, here she was in a playhouse, watching a play of scandalous adultery. Never in a month of Sabbaths would her aunt have condoned this.

During the final sword fight between Lorenzo and Sciarrha, Deb had to cover her face. Their bloody deaths wrung gasps from the audience. When it was all over Deb wiped her eyes and clapped her hands together until they were red. She looked to Mr Pepys and found him studying her with a puzzled and tender expression. His eyes met hers, and she lowered them, suddenly wishing he had not been watching her display of emotion. It seemed too intimate to show him her feelings that way.

'Did you like it, my little Deb?' he leant in to ask.

His breath was damp on her cheek.

'I did not know a play could be so ... so real. So much like life.'

His eyes misted over. 'Isn't it the saddest thing you ever saw? But perhaps you are too young to know much about such ways of the world.'

Her legs felt shaky. She did not understand why her heart was hammering so hard. But a sense of loss threatened to overwhelm her. The grieving, keening women on the stage brought back to her the day her mother left them, the day everything changed. Her father's closed face, telling her never to speak of her mother again.

'She's gone,' Father had said, 'and she's never coming back.'

She had not believed him. How could it be true? She'd refused to believe it. Until she pulled open the closet door to reveal a row of empty metal hooks, and it emptied her lungs, like a blow to the ribs.

Mr Pepys interrupted her runaway thoughts with a hand on her arm. She started, looked into his troubled face, this stranger whom she barely recognised.

'Never fear,' he said softly, 'I will bring you again. Next time perhaps we will find a comedy, something with fine music and dancing.'

She blinked. She had been about to cry.

'Oh dear, I told you it was sad,' Mr Pepys said. He took a kerchief from his pocket and pressed it into her hand.

'I'm thirsty, Sam.' Elisabeth's sulky voice broke in on their conversation. She had been talking to an acquaintance and now seemed in a hurry to leave.

'Then we'll walk past The Cock on the way home. Come along, my lovely girls.' And he took them both by the arm, one on each side. His fingers squeezed her hand a little too tightly. Probably being kind, given he'd seen she was moved to tears by the play. Nevertheless, instinctively, she inched further away.

Chapter Five

The next day, Elisabeth was ill in bed with a headache, and she asked Deb if she would take Fancy, her dog, out for a walk. Privately, Deb was relieved not to have to keep Elisabeth company and was looking forward to exploring the city.

Deb had always longed for a dog of her own, and Fancy was an adorable-looking Scottish terrier, with stubby, furry legs. But when Deb approached her holding the collar, Fancy growled and bared her teeth, and Deb had to whip her hand out of the way for fear of losing her fingers. Worse, once on the lead, Fancy gave her a baleful look and sat down stubbornly in the dirt. It took nearly a half-hour just to coax her up Thames Street. Perhaps she had not been walked very often, Deb thought.

Once on the embankment, Deb paused to look at the view, but a volley of hoarse barks in the distance made her turn. A woman with two children pulled them hastily out of the way as a big dog bore down on them in a blur of white. It came with frightening speed, back bristling, teeth bared.

'No!' Deb shouted, as Fancy leapt forward, yapping, tugging at the lead. Deb called Fancy back, but she was too late; the white dog's eyes were fixed on the smaller dog. It opened its jaws wide.

'Get away!' shouted Deb, kicking out with her boot.

The dog clamped its teeth onto her toe as Fancy scuttled behind her skirts. She gave a jerk to free her boot from the slobbering mouth, and the dog dived after Fancy, hackles up. With horror, she saw it set its grip into Fancy's shoulder. Fancy let out a piercing howl, then snapped back. The dog let go.

Deb put herself between them, shielding Fancy as best she could. 'Home!' she shouted, as her boot met the ribs of the big white dog.

'Hey!' There was the sound of running feet, and a man leapt in, grasped the white beast by the collar, and heaved it away.

'I've got him,' the auburn-haired young man said breathlessly. It was only then that Deb was able to properly see the bigger dog, a flabby-jowled bulldog with heaving hindquarters and a short stubby tail.

She crouched down to see if Fancy was hurt but had to snatch her hand away as Fancy, thoroughly excited, snapped and growled at her. Deb was mortified to see her shoulder had lost tufts of fur, and several tooth-marks oozed blood. Deb rounded on the young man. 'Look what he's done! Can't you keep your blasted dog under control?'

She stood just in time to hear the white dog's warning growl as it made to attack again. The collar slipped from the young man's scrabbling hands before Fancy shot backwards out of reach, jerking Deb's shoulder. Deb flailed, tried to keep her balance, but it was no use, and she toppled backwards onto the road, landing with a thud on her backside. 'Of all the stupid—'

The white dog leapt. Deb gave a screech of

warning. But the stranger was quick: he grasped the brute's collar with both hands and dug in his heels, as the muzzle was inches from Deb's nose.

'For God's sake! Get him on a lead, can't you?' Deb cried.

'Are you all right?' The young man was struggling to hang on as the dog still strained to get free.

'Your dog's an outright danger,' she shouted, crawling to upright, trying to recover some dignity over the growls. 'He just went for Fancy, for no reason at all! Dogs like that shouldn't be allowed. I wouldn't be surprised if he was rabid—'

'Here! Chester!'

A skeletally thin man in a long black greasy coat and three-cornered hat was hurrying towards them.

The white dog immediately dropped down onto the pavement, head between paws in submission.

'Thanks, mister,' the man in the black coat said, slipping the looped lead through the collar. 'Here, Ches.' In a moment the dog was following, stubby tail curled between its legs.

Fancy barked at it in a frenzy, ears flapping, full of bravado now the teeth were facing in the other direction.

Deb brushed horse dung from her skirt, keeping a tight hold of Fancy's lead.

The young man retrieved his hat from where it had fallen and pummelled it to get rid of the dirt. Now Deb had a chance to take him in. Tall, rangy, a bit older than her. Pale hands more used to books than labour.

He rubbed his palms together and then smoothed his unruly curly hair. 'Not my dog.' He shrugged. His tawny eyes met hers for a moment before he made her a small bow, replaced his hat on his head and strode away.

- 33 -

Not his dog? Then why had he …? Deb watched him go, chest full of anger. Why didn't he tell her earlier it wasn't his dog? But then, there'd hardly been time. The anger deflated. He'd stopped to help, she realised. She felt two inches tall.

She called after him, 'Wait!' but he was already about to round the corner. 'Thank you,' she called after him. He turned and grinned over his shoulder.

When they got home, Fancy shot inside and promptly pissed on the wainscot.

Elisabeth was in the hall in a moment, wafting her hands at the mess and the smell, and calling, 'Poor Fancy, what's the girl done to you? Come on out to *Maman*, now, good dog!'

But Fancy stayed behind the hall cupboard and wouldn't be coaxed.

Deb felt obliged to get out the pail and scrubbing brush and rub rosemary oil over the floorboards to make them sweet, a task that was certainly on Aunt Beth's 'forbidden' list. But aware of her precarious position as the 'new lady's maid', she knew she must make amends.

All the time she sloshed and scrubbed, she was thinking of the young man. Not many men would have stepped in to tackle a dangerous dog like that. He had a pleasant face, not handsome, and one you might easily forget. Except for his lovely curling hair and nice broad smile.

Still, there was little point thinking of him. She was not going to do anything so foolish as to fall for the first man who crossed her path. Look what it had done to Mama. It had turned her from a rational, sensible woman into someone who couldn't be trusted.

***

Meanwhile, next door at Lord Bruncker's house, Abigail Williams took a note from the messenger boy. She was about to put it aside, expecting it to be a letter for Lord Bruncker, but to her surprise, it was her own name there on the envelope. Despite her worsening eyesight, she recognised the hand: the thick, hurried strokes of the spymaster, Piet Groedecker. So he was here again, in England. The plague and the fire had driven the vermin from the city, but now it seemed they were all coming back.

'Wait,' she said sharply to the messenger boy.

She cracked the seal and unfolded the letter. It was just two lines:

"South side, by St Paul's square, dusk.

Mr Johnson"

'Where does he live?' she asked. 'The man who gave you this?'

'Don't know, mistress,' the boy said. 'He stopped me in the street, gave me two farthing to bring it.'

'Where?' She grabbed the boy by the arm.

'Ow! By the Exchange.'

'Was he alone?'

'Yes, mistress. I haven't done anything, only brought the letter like he said to.'

She dismissed the boy. Poole, the maid, appeared just afterwards, her sleeves wet to the elbows.

'Pardon, mistress, I was washing, I didn't hear the door. Is there anything I can do?'

'No. Nothing.'

Poole gave her a sympathetic look, then dipped her head and slipped away. She knew not to ask any questions. Abigail had made it quite clear that her employment depended on her discretion.

Abigail paced the floor. She did not want to meet Piet. Since the letter had come to dispatch Harrington, she had put Piet out of her mind, as if pretending the Dutch did not exist would make them go away. She sat down and put her head in her hands, rubbed her eyes. She was bone-tired. When night came all she wanted to do was to rest her head on Lord B's shoulder, listen to the comfort of his snores and fall into oblivious sleep. She did not want to deceive him by creeping from his bed and searching his papers. Lately, with no Dutch presence in the city, she had become lax, and, unable to prick herself to stay awake, she had left his correspondence alone.

But now this. She had known, really, that it could not go on. Not while she was collecting her monthly payments from the Dutch. She needed the money for Joan's mercury medicine, if her daughter would even take it, which she doubted. She set aside the thought of Joan. It was too painful and brought too much disturbance in its wake.

Piet's message had to be obeyed, and more trouble would come if she did not go; though she hoped it was not to be another assignment like Harrington. She could not stomach another so soon.

Abigail put on a broad-brimmed hat and tied a muslin over her nose and mouth to keep out the dust. She slipped pattens over her shoes and set off on foot, with Poole following like a limp shadow a few paces behind. On the ground, getting around the city was difficult. There was so much rubble from the fire, and from rebuilding, that travelling by carriage through the centre of town was well-nigh impossible.

She had left Lord Bruncker a note to say she was auditioning for a new play. He would be disappointed when he got home to an empty house. He was getting difficult to deceive, more concerned for her welfare. On a whim, she stopped at the hosier's and ordered new stockings for the winter. She asked for the tops to be embroidered with little bees, a tribute to a private joke between her and Lord Bruncker, whom she always called Lord B, and he in turn jokingly called her his Queen Bee. She imagined his amusement to find the bees next time he lifted her skirts. She liked to surprise him in little ways. You had to work hard, she thought, to keep a man happy.

At St Paul's yard, the booksellers and pamphleteers had begun to re-congregate in makeshift wooden shelters around the ruined crater of the church, so a throng of people had gathered there for the evening printing of the news-sheets. The weight of a hand on her shoulder made her whip round. It was Piet. How had he crept up on her like that? It put her at a disadvantage.

'Well met.' She greeted him with a calmness she did not feel. Even though she'd heard from her network of contacts that her cheating husband was dead, the sight of his pale-cheeked Dutch friend in his high fall-collar always turned her stomach.

'Wait for me over there,' she said to Poole, who melted away towards the crowd at the bookstalls. Piet took Abigail's arm and guided her away from the area of St Paul's and into a low-beamed tavern, where he led her to the darkest recess away from other drinkers. He settled his long frame into the seat, folding his stockinged legs under the table. Abigail marvelled at how such a tall man could still remain so inconspicuous.

A girl appeared with a tray and Piet ordered ale for them both.

'Well? You know why I'm here,' he said. His voice held the barest trace of accent and was almost benign, but his pale, watchful eyes were as cold as oysters. 'You've been suspiciously quiet.'

'It's harder lately, you know it is.'

'So tell me,' he said.

'What did you expect? Your sneaky foxes destroyed the English fleet. Is it any wonder the Navy Board are on edge? Lord Bruncker trusts me, but I still need to be careful; keep up my usual activities, appear in a play every now and then. Not to, would arouse suspicion.'

'We've been concerned,' Piet said, examining his fingernails. 'Lately we have not received a single transcript from you. Perhaps you are getting too old to be of use.'

'I've survived this long because I am wily,' she countered, 'and I've made myself accepted. That can only be done over time. It takes time to build trust – you know that. I'm more use to you now than ever.'

'Hmm. Yet you have sent us nothing from Bruncker's office, or from Pepys',' Piet said. 'You expect me to believe you; that you share a bed with a man from the Navy Treasury and yet you cannot tell us a single thing about how many ships they've commissioned? Or if another war fleet is being prepared?'

'I told you – after the fiasco in the Medway, the English Navy can't afford more ships.'

'One of our other agents disagrees. He says that Charles only made peace to keep our warships in

Dutch waters and stop the French occupying the Spanish Netherlands. That it's a false peace. That he's still rebuilding ships to come against us. We need to know if it's true.'

He placed one of his cool hands over hers on the table; she did her best not to recoil.

'Come on,' he said. 'Bruncker is cheek by jowl with Pepys. He must know something. You should press him more, withdraw your favours. Or is the rumour true, that Bruncker looks elsewhere for a warm bed these days?'

She pulled her hand away. 'No. He's with me nights. Your rumour is false.' She would not let him glimpse how much his words had wounded her.

'I need facts and figures. Proper writs of information.'

'Lord, Piet, these are not petty politicians you speak of. Lord Bruncker's no fool. He's a man of fierce intelligence. Nothing escapes him. Do you really expect me to take chances?'

'You can talk to him, can't you?'

'Yes, but he's obsessed, wants to play all night with his mechanical devices. When he's not, he spends his evenings at the Royal Society, instead of working, and he doesn't bring home as many documents as he used to.'

'Pepys?'

'Pepys is hard to get to. Though he is loose with the ladies, he fears to offend his navy friend by consorting with me.'

The spiced ale arrived and Abigail picked up the horn spoon to stir it. She must rally her forces. She was defensive. Her neck was damp with sweat. Perhaps Piet was right, and she was too old to be doing this any more. Treason was a lucrative but dangerous business. She had a sudden yearning for peace, for a retreat in the country, lush green fields, soft grass. To get away from the stench of burning that still hung over the city.

'If you can't tempt billy-goat Pepys, you must be losing your appeal, my dear,' Piet said.

'Lord Bruncker seems well satisfied.'

'Indeed. Something warns me that little liaison is altogether too comfortable.' He raised his eyebrows at her.

The spiced ale was bitter; she let the grainy liquid wash round her mouth. He was right, though she would not admit it. She had made the fatal error of every spy. She had let Lord Bruncker grow in her affection. It was hard not to like someone who professed his admiration for you every day, and with whom you shared a bed night after night. Lord B, besides being one of the great minds of London, was a very attractive man and she liked him. She did not dare think the word 'love'.

But if she ceased to use her position to gain intelligence for the Dutch, then Piet, or De Witt's men, would finish her. De Witt was a wily politician and his Dutch intelligence service was second to none. Even our own, she thought bitterly. For twenty years she had navigated the dark underbelly of London, the networks of linkmen and forgers, plotters and double-dealers. Not to mention the trepanners; the men who would shoot a hole in your skull and be gone as quick as the wisp of smoke from their pistols.

Piet watched her a moment over the rim of his cup. 'So, you can't get near Pepys himself. Sounds unlikely, given what I know of him. You have not managed to make a friend of Mrs Pepys?'

'I am doing my best,' she said, 'but Mrs Pepys does not like me. She finds me too outspoken, and the fact I am Lord B's mistress offends her stuffy Huguenot morality. Lord knows, I have tried numerous ways to befriend her, but she will have none of it.'

'Well, you must find a way. It is two months since you copied us any useful documents. We need lists of armaments and cannon. The names and tonnage of the ships that are being rebuilt that might come against us. Which hulls are being refitted and whether new frigates are being built at Deptford or Chatham. De Witt's advisers are suspicious of your sudden silence. The word is out that you might have been tempted to give information about our network to the King's petticoat-men.'

'I would never do that.'

He shrugged. 'The De Witts inform me that if we receive no profitable news from you this month, then I am to stop your purse. Of course, you understand what that means.'

She knew. It was not just her purse that would be stopped. She had stopped Harrington's mouth herself when he tried to bleat and run, and he wasn't the first.

There might be a way. A face sprang to mind – Elisabeth Pepys' new maid, Miss Willet. She was someone who looked like she needed to find her way in the world. There was intelligence in her eyes, and self-possession. Educated, too. Did she have enough courage though to spy on her master? Abigail did not know. She sighed. It was a foolhardy notion. She put the idea aside.

'Tell the De Witts that their concern is unfounded,' she said. 'I'll let you have something by the end of the month.' It was a promise she was uncertain she could keep.

Piet saw it. 'For your sake, I hope so. And Abigail, have a care. It does not pay to get close to your subjects. Lord Bruncker may indeed be the paragon you say he is, but remember, he is still your enemy. He is not your paymaster, the Dutch are. He would be the first to shout treason if you were discovered.'

'You think I don't know the risks? After all these years?'

Piet raised his eyes from his cup to look at her. 'I sincerely hope so.'

'How long are you in London this time?' she asked him, changing the subject, to try and lighten the mood.

'I have other business here too, so a month or more before I go back to Holland.' He gave her a penetrating stare, the stare of a bird of prey that made her throat tight. 'There are a few ... loose ends. I must clear them up before I can return.'

Something was wrong with the way he said those words. Her heart banged with fear. She suddenly understood with visceral certainty.

Should she fail to produce what they wanted, he was to be her assassin.

He rose and threw a smatter of coins onto the table before he pressed his steeple hat onto his head and strode away. She heard the jangle of the bell door and exhaled. She reached to gather the coins.

Guilders. Dutch guilders. He was reminding her who paid her. Quickly, she scooped them out of sight, her face burning beneath the white powder.

Chapter Six
October

FOR THE LAST TWO WEEKS DEB had barely had a single moment alone. She had been obliged to accompany Samuel and Elisabeth Pepys into the country to stay with Mr Pepys' tedious relatives. The weather had been unremittingly wet and windy, and the whole expedition had made her mistress even more cross and difficult to please.

On Deb's return, the Pepyses' house seemed even more disordered in contrast to life in the country. The household was chaotic; Elisabeth's attention scattered. People came and went from Mr Pepys' office at odd hours; his boy servant was in and out with messages meaning doors were opening and closing all day. It made Deb feel rickety, as if the ground was unstable beneath her feet. She longed to set everything neat and tidy, to keep it controlled, the way it had been at school, where tradition established the way everything was done. But here, new ideas jostled upon new ideas, one new thing piled upon another. New books, new decorations, new acquaintances.

While Elisabeth dealt with her stack of correspondence, Deb sat down to write to Hester. At least that was one good thing about working for the Pepyses –Hester was at school at last, and her letters to Deb were full of enthusiasm for her new activities and the sheer relief of being away from Aunt Beth for most of the hours of the day.

Deb hesitated, her pen dripping a blob of ink onto the paper. What could she tell Hester? Aunt Beth read all their letters. She did not dare tell Hester she was struggling to find common ground with Mrs Pepys, and besides, what if her mistress caught a glimpse of what she was writing? But Elisabeth was dreamily staring out of the window, quill feather pressed to her bottom lip.

Actually, Deb mused, it was only Elisabeth who did not like her. Mr Pepys was worryingly familiar. A knock at the front door interrupted her thoughts. She went to answer it and found a messenger boy with a letter.

She left him waiting at the door, and as she returned, Elisabeth held out her hand, ready to take the letter.

'Beg pardon, mistress,' Deb said, staring at her own name written in an elegant sloping hand. 'It's for me.'

'You?' Elisabeth frowned. 'I thought you didn't know anyone in London.'

'I don't.' Deb opened it, then stared in surprise. 'It's from Mistress Williams. Mr Pepys agreed she could show me around the Duke's Playhouse. She's wanting to arrange a time.'

'Oh, her.' Mrs Pepys wrinkled her nose. 'You must decline. Tell her we have too many engagements. She's too late, anyway. Mrs Knepp and Miss Gwynn took us round the King's only a few weeks ago. Surely that's quite enough greasepaint and powder for any young woman.'

Elisabeth stood and took the paper out of Deb's hand, and before she could argue scrawled a few words of reply. 'I've apologised and told her I can't spare you this month.'

Deb hid her disappointment. She had enjoyed the last tour, but, more than that, Mistress Williams intrigued her, and she was flattered that she had remembered her and asked for her personally.

Mistress Williams, however, was not to be put off so easily. The next day she called at Seething Lane in person with Lord Bruncker at her side, so Elisabeth was cowed into agreement. After the pair had gone, Deb had to suffer Elisabeth's disapproval, which hung over them all morning like a black cloud. So black, it was a wonder it did not stain the linen, Deb thought, as she kept her head down and hem-stitched pillowcases.

'I suppose you will have to go, Deb,' Elisabeth said eventually, 'though I'd hoped you would accompany me to the Exchange tomorrow. But I know Sam won't be pleased if we offend his Lordship.'

'Will you come too?'

'*Absolument pas.*' Elisabeth jerked as she stabbed the needle into her thumb. '*Ouf!* No, I shall go to my tailor's. I need some new sleeves, and I have no wish to spend time with that trumped-up whore. And I beg you, close your ears to all her gossiping nonsense.'

You're a fine one to lecture me on gossip, thought Deb, considering what went on at Mr Unthank's. The tailor's was a place where well-to-do ladies like Elisabeth picked over the characters of everyone they knew, just as if they were unpicking seams.

Deb hurried light-footed to the theatre through the grey streets, following a scribble of a map from Jane in the kitchen. She was jubilant, partly with excitement, and partly with the freedom of being out and about without her mistress. With Elisabeth, she always felt as if she was doing something wrong, and the harder she tried to make everything perfect, the more Elisabeth found fault in it.

When she got to the theatre, Mistress Williams was full of smiles. 'Miss Willet! Or may I call you Deb?'

Mistress Williams was immaculately dressed as before, but this time in a green silk robe with scarlet trim, her waist nipped in so tight she looked as though she could barely breathe, and sporting a large expanse of white powdered flesh above the neckline. The doorman knew her and let them go through, threading through the benches until they stood gazing into the pit, where wooden stools had been set out for the musicians, each one with a candle-stand beside it.

'How do you like it at the Pepyses'?' asked Mistress Williams.

'Well. Though it is all so different from Bromley. I am not quite used to the city yet, and the way of life. But it is very kind of Mrs Pepys to take me on.'

'Kind? Oh, I think they have a very good bargain.' Mistress Williams smiled and tilted her head to look quizzically at her. Deb blushed and cast her eyes aside and then up to the covered ceiling, where the small open hole designed to provide light, showed rainclouds looming above.

'Keep your fingers crossed it stays fine. Come.' Mistress Williams lifted up her skirts to reveal fine embroidered shoes. 'Take care, these steps are steep.'

Once on the stage they turned to look out over the greasy stubs of candles on the lip of the boards, and out into the rows of benches. The Duke's theatre was a more modern building than the King's. It had been recently converted from an old tennis court, with glittering gilded columns and embossed leather wall-hangings. The back of the stage was festooned with ropes and pulleys like a ship, and iron winding machines stood in the wings for winching scenery onto stage.

It was a bigger playing space than the King's and Deb imagined what it must be like when the seats were full, with all those eyes watching you. The thought of it was disconcerting.

'And the Pepyses, do they pay you well?'

Deb did not know how to reply. Talking about her employers behind their backs went against everything she had been taught. She did not know whether to take offence or brush it off.

Mistress Williams let out a peal of laughter. 'There now! I've made you feel uncomfortable already! It's quite all right, you don't have to tell me. I'm far too inquisitive for my own good; that I know.'

'It's generous of my mistress to spare me a few hours so I could come,' Deb said tactfully.

'Is that so? I'll tell you what I think. I'll wager Mistress Pepys is out of sorts about me bringing you here because she does not think me respectable. Am I right?'

Deb twisted her hand in her shawl, not sure what to say.

'Of course, she's quite correct. An actress is not quite respectable. She sees too much, she begins to think of her own life as a play. And it is tempting to draw in other players to fill the roles you lack.' Mistress Williams moved forward to show Deb the sliding wings or shutters that changed the background, all most lifelike. 'Look, the countryside brought right into town. Deceptive, aren't they, the trees? Is it not well done?'

Deb put out a hand to the painted canvas. 'They're beautiful. And it is such a clever device,' she said. 'That bridge reminds me of the countryside where I used to live, near Bristol.'

'Are your family still there?'

'No, I only lived there as a child. I loved it there. Such a contrast between the city and the wild countryside beyond. Our house was out of town though, on the edge of the moors. People used to come to us for the shooting ...' She tailed off. She should not bore Mistress Williams with her reminiscences.

'Do you ever go back?'

'No.' She paused. 'The house was sold. Recently my sister and I were brought up by my aunt in Bromley. Father moved to Bandon Bridge in Ireland with my brothers. He runs his export business from there.' She tried to keep the bitterness from her voice. 'We write. At least my brothers do.'

'You have lost your mother, then?'

Deb turned away, unable to give an answer.

'Oh, dear. I can see there is a tale there. That was a perfect piece of stage business, your turning away, the hand lifted to the temple in melancholy. The language of the body. It told me that there is a mystery there that needs an answer. Come, let's go down to the tiring house and you can tell me. You've made my day, my dear. I love a mystery.'

She swept away down the steps, and Deb was forced to follow on behind. She hurried after Mistress Williams's swishing green skirts, through the auditorium and to the tiring house where the ladies were to change for the evening performance. A handbill pinned to the wall told her it was to be a comedy by Dryden. As they squeezed past a rail of costumes, Deb saw that the doublets were stained with sweat and greasepaint round the necks. How Aunt Beth would frown if she could see those collars.

In the tiring house, a cramped and untidy closet stuffed with wigs and hats and posies of dead and decaying flowers, Mistress Williams leaned in to examine her reflection in a mirror, grimacing as if she did not like what she saw. She primped her hair, and then pulled out two stools. 'Now, sit a moment and tell me this great mystery about your mother.' She patted the other stool in a confiding way.

'There's not much to say.' Deb was reluctant. She had not talked about her mother to anyone for so long. She looked away, fixing her eyes on the pots of rouge, the charcoal sticks and the 'patches' that littered the table.

Mistress Williams leaned in closer. 'I'm good with secrets, and you can trust me not to tell a single soul.' She smiled and offered a little nod of encouragement. There was something about the way that she gave Deb her undivided attention that disarmed her. 'Where is she now, your mother?'

'She left us.' Deb blurted. 'I've not seen her for six years. Six years.' She hesitated. 'What kind of mother does that to her children?'

'And you've had no word since?'

'Nothing. We don't know what became of her, but a servant said she might have come to London.'

Mistress Williams was still fixing her with her intense gaze. 'And now you're here, will you try to find her?'

Deb's heart gave a little leap of hope. The picture. What could be the harm in Mistress Williams seeing it? She wouldn't be able to tell anything about her from a portrait, and she might recognise her. 'Wait.' Deb brought out a little velvet pouch, and withdrawing the miniature, ran a thumb tenderly over the casing. 'Her portrait. Father had it painted just after Hester was born. But he doesn't know I have it. After she left us, he took all her portraits and threw them on the fire. Except this one; it was in the pocket of his winter breeches, so I took it before he could find it.'

'What extraordinary behaviour,' Mistress Williams said.

Did she mean her, or her father? Deb wasn't sure. 'Please, don't tell Mrs Pepys. It's easier if I just tell everyone she's dead. Of the smallpox. It's what we always say.' She opened the hinged lid and passed the miniature over.

Mistress Williams glanced at it and then her eyes widened and locked on the image. She frowned and raised the picture closer to her eyes to examine it.

'Do you know her?'

'I just thought ...' Mistress Williams swallowed. 'No. I've never seen her before.'

But Deb had seen a flash, something like recognition in Mistress Williams's face, and she wasn't going to let it pass. 'Please, won't you take another look,' she said. 'The maid said she came to London. She would be older now, of course.'

Mistress Williams's eyes rested briefly on the portrait again. 'At first glance, she looks a little like someone I once knew,' Mistress Williams said. 'But portrait painters seldom achieve a good likeness. She has a fine face. How sad that you are estranged.'

'Or perhaps we should be glad.' Her voice was tight. Aunt Beth had forbidden her to talk about it. Mama had shamed Father, she said. The words Deb had been holding back for so long burst out. 'My aunt said that Mama deserved to fry in hell. Those were her very words. "Sin itself" she called her. But it seemed so unlike Mama ... and I couldn't believe she'd just leave us all ...' Deb couldn't finish. She took a deep breath to keep her emotion in check. 'Beg pardon, I forget myself. I shouldn't have spoken about her in that way. I did not mean to be so forward.'

Mistress Williams leaned in towards her. 'Not at all. It is good to unburden the heart.'

Deb placed her palms to her cheeks to cool them. What on earth had made her say these things to Mistress Williams? It was exactly what Aunt Beth had warned her against.

'This servant you speak of, the one who said she'd come to the city, she could give you no more information?'

'Agnes. Yes, all she could tell me was that Mama took seat on a stagecoach to London.' Deb tried to calm herself, as Mistress Williams shut the miniature with a click and placed it on the table. 'But I think it's because Mama was going to have another baby. Hester and I hoped for a girl, because we have three brothers. But then ... she just left in the night. Father got rid of all the staff the day after Mama went. Can you imagine that? Staff who'd been with us for years.'

'What a frightful experience.' Mrs Williams shook her head.

'He laid off every single one, anyone who knew her. He wouldn't talk. Just sold the house, sent us away ...' Oh no. She'd done it again. Mistress Williams must be some kind of witch to get her to talk this way. What must she think of her? Her eyes pricked, but Deb blinked back the tears. She shut her mouth, determined she wouldn't appear a fool.

Mistress Williams patted her arm. 'Don't fret. Here, take this.' She opened her bag and pushed a handkerchief in Deb's direction. When Deb pressed it to her nose, it smelled of camphor and made her gulp for breath.

'There now, blow hard.' Mistress Williams was looking at Deb very intently. It was disconcerting to be listened to like that. Aunt Beth had never listened to her, and nobody asked her questions in the Pepyses' house; it was as if they were all too busy making their own noise to be interested in anyone else's.

'A puzzle then,' Mistress Williams said.

'Mama told Agnes to tell us she'd write, and she was going ... to "the Greek". But she never did write. Not a single word. I've looked after my little sister Hester all these years ...' Her voice wobbled. She took control of herself. 'And as for "the Greek", Hester and I have chewed over it for years, racking our thoughts as to who she meant, but we couldn't bring anyone to mind. I don't think she knew any Greeks, or if she did, it was someone she wanted to keep a secret. Besides, Agnes was insistent it was the London coach.'

'Did you try the King's Post Office?'

'Yes. They could find no address for her.'

'Then if you want to find her, you must put a notice by St Paul's,' Mistress Williams said. 'People still meet there despite the fire. There's a new board there for hiring and firing, under a makeshift cover, and I believe there is also a noticeboard for missing persons.'

'I don't want to find her.' Deb clutched the kerchief in her fist. At the same time, the thought came that she did. She would give anything to see her again. St Paul's Church. Why had she not thought of that? But the idea terrified her. If it came to it, she wasn't sure if she was ready to see her mother again. After all, she could have written, couldn't she? All these years, and not a word.

Mistress Williams was watching her. Deb had the impression she could see into her thoughts. She blew her nose again to cover her confusion.

'Many people still go by the church. I understand you can write?' Mistress Williams asked.

'A notice, you mean?'

'Well, it would certainly be a start.'

'I don't know. It's a good idea, it's just ...' She blew her nose. 'Mrs Pepys might not approve of callers, and my mother might not be ... oh dear. I'm sorry about your handkerchief, Mistress Williams. I'll wash it and—'

'Keep it.'

Deb pushed the scrap of linen inside her bodice. 'You see, Mrs Pepys thinks my mother died of the smallpox.'

'And don't call me Mistress Williams, it offends me – makes me feel about sixty. Call me Abigail.' She took hold of the material of Deb's sleeve with her hand and tugged it playfully. She raised a finely plucked eyebrow. 'Now, take cheer, now you have told me everything, we are going to be great friends, I can feel it. Wait there.'

Abigail swept away down the corridor and returned with a large piece of parchment, quill and ink. She smoothed it out on the table before them, handed Deb the quill.

'Missing,' dictated Abigail.

It would be too awkward to refuse such a grand lady, so Deb wrote out the notice to Abigail's instructions. When she turned, Abigail was watching her with a purposeful expression which immediately transformed to dimpled smiles. 'What a nice, neat hand. And by the way, if you don't want Mr and Mrs Pepys to know about this, let us use my address on the notice.'

'But I don't know how I'll be able to repay you, it's so kind.'

'Not at all. That is what friends are for, is it not – to help each other with small favours?' Abigail tapped her lightly on the arm. 'Now, here is a chit with my address. My own personal address, not my Lord Bruncker's. Copy it down carefully and keep it safe. As soon as I hear anything at all, I'll send for you. And we need say nothing to Elisabeth, need we? It can be our little secret. Now. Leave me the notice and I'll put it up for you.' She held out her hand.

'No, I'll do it.' Deb rolled it up. 'I'd like to see these boards you talk of.'

Abigail frowned and took hold of the parchment. 'But I pass it every day.'

'Still, I'd like to do it myself.' Deb did not let go.

There was a moment while they both tugged, then Abigail released it. 'Very well. I would have saved you the trouble, that's all.'

But Deb could tell Abigail was displeased, just the same.

While Deb was out, Elisabeth was restless. It was good to be back in familiar surroundings, but at the same time it made her uneasy. In London, Sam would find excuses to be up to his old tricks.

This morning she'd caught Sam looking at Deb again. It gave her a suffocating feeling in her chest. After that, she could not stop watching them: Deb's slim graceful wrists as she passed Sam his letters, her pale smooth complexion, and the way she looked puzzled when Sam regaled her with rumbustious tales of court life.

Elisabeth still had not unpacked from the trip to Brampton, so she shook out her day dresses from the trunk and brushed out the creases. Should she fetch Jane? No. She was busy laundering the linens. Deb should deal with them really, but she didn't like to ask her, not in front of Sam. It would feel like a criticism.

She didn't want to seem churlish, even though Deb was young and pretty. Elisabeth glared at the array of gowns on the bed, pummelled at a limp taffeta skirt. It would not do. She would have to have new – something bolder, younger. Something to take Sam's attention.

They should never have taken Deb to Brampton. That's where it all started. In fact, Elisabeth hadn't wanted to go at all, but Sam had insisted on going in order to dig up his gold. Like a dutiful wife, she'd hidden it for him in the grounds when he'd been convinced the Dutch were about to storm London, right after England lost the sea battle in the Medway.

Stupid man. It was all a false alarm – the threatened invasion hadn't happened. But could he leave it be? No. He feared someone else at Brampton might come upon his precious hoard of gold by chance. He kept her awake at nights fidgeting and worrying about it, so he'd insisted on them all going to get it back, even Deb Willet.

Or *especially* Deb Willet.

Elisabeth went over to the fire and stood the iron on the trivet to heat. It was a long time since she'd ironed anything herself, but she was glad of the excuse to do it. The task might occupy her and take her thoughts off Sam. She smoothed a felt cloth over the side table.

Lord, what a fuss he was in when she could not lay hands on his hoard! Of course, the land had changed in all these months, and it was as dark as tar and every sod of turf looked the same. So was it surprising she couldn't point out the place right away? But all through their argument Deb Willet was looking on, supercilious, exchanging glances with Sam, as though Elisabeth was stupid not to remember where it was buried.

Elisabeth had never wanted to kick someone so much in her life.

The worm of jealousy would not lie still. Elisabeth ran the iron over a satin petticoat and replayed their return journey from Brampton in her mind. It had made her fit to boil, the way Sam insisted on seating himself next to Deb.

'Sit here,' she'd said to Deb, patting the seat next to her.

'No, she's better next to me. Otherwise her skirts will be over the bags, and I need to keep an eye on them,' Sam said.

Bags. They'd nothing to do with it. She saw Sam let himself fall 'accidentally' against Deb when the carriage jolted round a corner. Elisabeth fixed him with a stony stare. He saw her pointed look, smiled back sheepishly and stopped leaning so much.

She wanted to wipe that smirk from his good-for-nothing chops. Did he have any idea, she wondered, just how much she saw?

A smell of scorching. Elisabeth looked down. A wisp of smoke curled from under the iron. She pulled the thing away to reveal a triangular brown scorch mark right in the middle of her favourite petticoat. She let out a groan of outrage and threw the iron across the room, where it clanged against the fender.

Deb Willet. *She'd* made her do that. She shouldn't have to do these menial tasks. It was all Deb's fault.

Then she flopped into a chair, head in her hands. What was she doing, hiding from her maid and ironing in her bedchamber?

I do not want to be like this, she thought to herself. Where had she got lost? Where was the bonny, bright young thing she used to be? Sam looked past her now as if she were invisible, his gaze smitten by Deb.

Devil take him.

She refused to fade away. She'd make a fuss until he gave her the coin for a new petticoat, and a new pelisse too, and expense be damned. She'd force him to notice her, if it was the last thing she did.

Deb could not sleep. She imagined the lions in the Tower, prowling restlessly in their cages, their guttural growls to be fed. The visit to Abigail Williams had disturbed her. Why would Lord Bruncker's well-to-do lady want to make a friend of her, a mere lady's maid? Yet it was a relief to have someone to confide in. She'd nursed the grievance so long, it had felt like a part of her, and Hester had never really understood. She missed Hester more than ever. She had gone to put up the notice, for Hester's sake. In Hester's mind her mother had become half-mother, half-saint, and no matter how much Deb warned her otherwise, Hester would not brook the idea that her mother might be anything less.

Strange, the way Abigail had looked at Mama's portrait as if she knew her. And talking of Mama had brought it all back, reminded her of that ever-present hollow in her chest. She took out the miniature again and after lighting a taper, laid it on her lap, though she didn't really need to look at it. Mama's face was engraved on her memory as if the artist had placed his brushstrokes there, instead of on the ivory. She took out the picture whenever she wanted to remind herself that she would never, ever be as cruel as her.

It was deliberate, this act of remembering. Hester's tear-stained cheeks, the moment when Deb had to tell her that her mama was gone, and Hester had to be brave, and it never failed. The old anger rose up in her, dark and bitter as sloes. She would never forgive Mama for what she had done to Hester. To them all. Deb threw the portrait hard at the wall.

'I hate you,' she whispered. 'You betrayed us. I never want to see you again.'

But she woke at first light and was seized by a panic that the picture might be broken. And that her words had been some sort of curse. She scrambled out of bed and picked up the portrait again, hugged it to her heart until the metal case dug a pain in her breastbone.

Chapter Seven

IT WAS SUNDAY, AND curate-in-training Jeremiah Wells had spent the morning feeding the poor of his master's parish in dismal rain, a daunting task since the fire had made homeless men of so many. He'd had to brave a few more snapping dogs, something he was used to in his profession.

The poorer you were, the more dangerous your dog, he thought. Still, at least today nobody shouted at him – not like that young woman a few weeks ago. She'd stuck in his memory, partly because she was exceedingly pretty, but also because she'd yelled at him with more strength than he thought such a delicate-looking girl possessed. And it had given him great satisfaction the way she flushed scarlet when she realised she'd been shouting at the wrong man.

Jem buttered a tranche of bread and lay a nice fat slice of cheese onto it, wondering what had happened to Bart, his younger brother, who shared his lodgings. He was late for supper, as usual.

The thought came too soon, for, as the bread was halfway to Jem's mouth, the door burst open. Bart and his sailor friends clattered in, with their muddy boots, clanking swords, and a welter of dripping hats. So much for his quiet supper and night of study.

Bart's friends had grown rowdier these last months, and they seemed to move as a great rabble –just like a pack of dogs, he thought ruefully.

'We need a favour,' Bart said, as he and his friends crowded round the table, dripping onto Jem's books. 'We've reached the end of our patience. These men were all crew on the *Forester* too, and not one of us has been paid a single penny. Londoners sleep safe in their beds because of us, yet all they gave us was these blasted tickets.' He held out a damp, well-thumbed note and shook it in Jem's face. 'Look! That's not proper payment, is it?'

'What sort of favour?' Jem asked, moving his books to a dry spot.

'These tickets won't feed us,' said Bolton, a cadaverous man in a ragged jerkin, who was looming over him.

'He's right,' Bart said. 'The danger from the Dutch is past. The King's got his blasted treaty signed, so now he's wanting to forget all about us. He's trying to weasel out of paying at all. Now, I remember Crawley introduced you to Mr Pepys from the Navy Board. Have a talk with Pepys, get him to reason with the King. You're a churchman, they'll listen to you.'

'Mr Pepys? But I've only met him once!'

'You know him well enough to get you through the door.' Bart put on his persuasive face.

'Maybe, but I'm not—'

'Mr Wells, my wife hasn't had a decent meal in three days.' Bolton, who had had his eyes fixed on Jem's bread, leaned in to him, took off his cap, shook the drips off it, his eyes soulful. 'She feeds the children first. I can't even afford to give her a scrap of ship's biscuit. Please, won't you try? We fought for our country, not like those filthy

- 60 -

turncoats who went over to the Dutch.'

The man had a point. Their own countrymen had changed sides because the Dutch, unlike the English Navy, would pay. Jem blamed the King. The man had never learned to be civilised, spending all that time hiding abroad in foul company. The country was all at sixes and sevens because of him. What use was he, squandering their taxes on wine and mistresses while the country starved? Good hard-working men like his brother shouldn't need to beg.

Jem sighed and gestured to Bolton, who was eyeing his plate of bread and cheese hungrily. 'Go ahead. There's more in the larder. Fill your pockets if you must.'

Bolton grabbed the tranche of bread and gobbled it down. He and the other sailors hesitated only a moment before they made for the door to the larder.

Jem shook his head at his brother and sighed. 'All right, I suppose I'll have to try, or lose my larder every night. Tell me what you want me to do.'

The next day was fine, and Jem caught a ferry up to Old Swan Stairs and walked to the Navy Offices. He liked to walk, bouncing along, inhaling the aroma of the city; seeing what new buildings had gone up since he last passed by. He loved the bitter aroma of boiling hops as he passed the brewery, the salt-sea smell of fish at a roadside stall, and the tang of the ever-present brackish Thames.

To Jem's frustration, when he got to Seething Lane, Mr Pepys had just gone out. Crawley, an acquaintance from Cambridge whom he had always found insufferable, recognised Jem's voice at the door and sauntered over, running his hand back over his thin greasy hair.

'You after Pepys? He's never in.' Crawley looked Jem up and down with a supercilious smile. 'But he's probably gone for his dinner. He's ruled by his stomach. Sometimes if we're busy we all descend on his house and carry on working so he can eat and work at the same time. Those of us who get an invitation, of course.'

'Damn. Does he live nearby?'

'Only a few steps. Across the yard, and it's the third door round the corner.' Crawley pointed out the directions with an ink-stained finger. 'If you keep your eyes open you might meet Mrs Pepys' new companion,' he said. 'I caught a glimpse of her last week. God's teeth, what a looker!' He blew as if blowing on something hot. 'And old Pepys is delighted with her. Apparently she's very well educated – schooled at one of those new places for girls – though of course that won't stop old Pepys trying to give her a bit more of an education.' He winked.

Jem felt immediately sorry for Pepys' girl, but he took his leave of Crawley and hurried on his way. He was jittery with apprehension about speaking to someone so high up as Mr Pepys, and wanted to get the whole thing over with. He rapped hard on the knocker and the door swung open.

'Oh! Not you,' the girl said.

Jem took a step back as she mumbled an apology. He was face to face with the owner of the little black dog, the girl who'd shouted at him. Her face was flushed, and she looked at him warily with her big grey eyes.

He realised he was staring and whipped off his hat. 'How's your dog?' he blurted.

'She's not mine, she's Mrs Pepys' dog. I was just walking her. Actually, she's recovered well. We put brandy on the wounds.' She lowered her gaze. 'Pardon my rudeness last time we met. It was very good of you to come to our rescue.'

'You looked a bit overwhelmed. I'm used to dogs, so I thought I'd—'

'Who is it, Deb?' A female voice from inside.

'Who shall I say?' The girl raised her eyebrows in question.

'Jeremiah Wells,' Jem answered. 'Assistant to Dr Thurlow. I know Mr Pepys' clerk, Crawley. I'm after Mr Pepys.'

'A Mr Wells,' the girl called back in a loud, clear voice.

'*Pouf*! If he wants Sam, tell him he's not here yet,' came the impatient reply. 'He'd a meeting with Lord Bruncker this morning. You'd better take him back to the offices. And whatever he wants, tell him he'd better not hold him up. Our dinner will be spoilt if Sam's not here directly.'

'Sorry.' The girl exchanged a sympathetic glance with Jem. 'That was my mistress,' she said. 'We'd better see if we can find Mr Pepys at Lord Bruncker's.' She set off at a brisk walk across the courtyard to the other wing. Jem followed, admiring her straight back under its laced bodice, and the way her brown wavy hair was so thick it was escaping from the back of her cap. Up some stairs they went, with her quiet as a mouse, just her leather shoes tap-tapping on the steps and a tantalising glimpse of a slender ankle.

She listened at a big oak door a moment, and then turned, nodded her head, mouthing, 'He's inside all right. With Lord Bruncker. I can hear his voice. Would you like me to knock and introduce you, sir?' she asked.

'No,' he said. 'No need.'

'Mr Pepys can be a bit crotchety until he's had his

dinner,' the girl leaned in to whisper to him, and smiled. Perhaps she was trying to make up for the dog incident.

'Oh dear,' Jem said. 'I need to get him on my side. Maybe I should have brought him a muffin to stave off his hunger.' He grinned. 'No good trying to get a man's attention if his stomach's grumbling, is it? And I won't keep him long, I promise. By the way, I'm pleased to meet you, Miss ...?'

'Willet. Deborah Willet.' She smiled and dipped her head. 'Tell Mr Pepys to come along as soon as he can, won't you? Mrs Pepys gets all of a bother if he keeps her waiting. And it's pigeon pie, his favourite.'

'Sounds very tempting.' He caught her eye, and suddenly his words seemed a bit too forward. Miss Willet fled and he watched her as she whisked downstairs, all flurrying skirts, as if she couldn't get away quick enough.

Jem took a moment to stare out of the window where she was just crossing the courtyard. Miss Willet. So that was her name. She looked so fresh and innocent in her clean blue dress and white neckerchief. He remembered Crawley's words and wished he could save her, keep her somehow from old Pepys' attentions.

'What *are* you talking about?' Elisabeth tutted and shook her head.

'Do pay attention, dear,' Mr Pepys said, through a mouthful of soused herring. 'I told you. You know, Dr Thurlow, vicar of St Gabriel's, one of the ones lost in the fire. They've a temporary shed up now, for the congregation. His assistant came, one Mr Wells. Trying to get me to pay off the sailors' tickets.'

Deb was taken aback. Mr Wells had not looked in

the least like a man of the church when he was grappling with that huge dog.

'It was damned awkward to be put on the spot like that,' Mr Pepys said.

'If the sailors were really starving, then surely the Treasury would give you permission to pay them,' Elisabeth said.

Mr Pepys was glum. He wiped his mouth. 'Not a bean. Can't even get near Clarendon, let alone the King. I tried my best, had a word with Penn, but he was mighty bad-tempered as usual. It's his gout. Anyway, trouble's brewing, he says. The commissioners fear a riot, and as usual they're trying to lay it all at our door. The sailors are plotting to seize their dues from the Navy Offices, so the rumour goes. We may have to go and bury our gold again, wife.'

Elisabeth stood, threw down her napkin. 'Then you must do something, Sam. None of this is your fault! You must persuade the King!'

Mr Pepys laughed at her good-humouredly. 'Don't you think I've been trying?'

'So what about Mr Wells?' Deb ventured. 'What did you tell him?' She was curious.

'Mr Wells?' Elisabeth looked puzzled.

'Dr Thurlow's curate,' Deb said.

'Oh, never mind Mr Wells,' Elisabeth said, flapping her hand. 'What about us?'

'He'd not go, you know, not until I'd listened to maudlin stories about starving children and women who have to pawn their petticoats for a day's bread.' He looked down sadly at his empty plate, speared himself a cut of cold meat. 'Trouble is, he's not the first, and it's becoming tiresome. Any more and I'll have to send for the constable to cool them off in the gaol. Can't do that with parsons though.'

'Best place for them,' Elisabeth said.

'Bruncker and I agreed we'd try to find a trickle of money somehow, keep them off our backs, but it's like squeezing a dry sponge, there's nothing in the navy coffers.' He held up his hands, 'What a to-do. But I don't want my ladies worrying about my business. Come, we'll go to that new play at the Duke's, *The Coffee House*. We need cheering.'

'I've heard it's an insipid little play,' Elisabeth grumbled.

'Best judge that for ourselves, hey, our Deb?' Mr Pepys said. 'Anyway, the King and the Duke of York will be there.'

The King! Deb was entranced by the idea of seeing actual royalty, but going to a play had become awkward. Mr Pepys would insist on wedging himself between her and Elisabeth, and then ignoring his wife for the whole performance. The prickle of trouble was brewing and Deb did not want to be the cause of it. But if Mr Pepys insisted on her company, there was precious little she could do about it. Sure enough, when they got to the theatre, Mr Pepys ushered Deb in first. When his wife did not follow, he was forced to go back for her.

'What's the matter?' he hissed in Elisabeth's ear.

'We should sit in front of her,' Elisabeth said. 'It's not right for my maid to be on the same row as us.'

'But we've always sat together.' Mr Pepys waggled his head in protest.

'I tell you, I'm not sitting down unless she is behind.'

'Just go on in, we're holding everyone up, and you're making a spectacle of yourself.' Mr Pepys was flustered, and he tried to push his wife ahead of him.

But Elisabeth refused to sit in the same row. Deb could hear the whispered argument, and her ears felt as if they were on fire.

'It's not me, Sam, it's you! Do you think I can't see what you're doing? Making a fool of yourself ... with *her*?'

Her raised voice caused Deb to turn away. She felt guilty, even though she had done nothing wrong. But a few moments later Elisabeth sat down next to her with a great fuss, rearranging her skirts, cracking open her fan and fidgeting. Deb glanced sideways at Elisabeth's face to see it was blotched the colour of a beetroot. Mr Pepys was on her other side with an expression like stone.

The King and his party were late, and they had to wait for the play to begin. Mr Pepys did not make his usual jokes, or tell them about the players. Instead, he sat rigidly, and when the play finally started he did not laugh once, which was most unlike him. And when Deb tried to smile at Elisabeth, she lifted her nose and twisted her body away.

Deb could not concentrate. The tension in the air told her that Elisabeth deemed her to be as much at fault as her husband. When they were coming out they paused to get a glimpse of the King, but they had missed him and instead Abigail Williams stepped out to greet them. Elisabeth glowered at her husband and swept past, deliberately ignoring her. Mr Pepys muttered a hasty apology and hurried after.

'Oh dear me, is it something I said?' Abigail Williams asked, smiling.

Deb could not help smiling back. It was such a relief after the frosty atmosphere in the theatre. 'Good day to you, Mistress Williams.'

'Pepys is always at the plays, so I thought I might

see you here. That's why I didn't send a message,'
Abigail said. 'There has been a reply to your notice.'

'Already?'Deb's hand came to her chest as if to still
the jerk of her heart. She ignored the people pushing
past her; she could not move. 'Who from?'

'I didn't open it. It didn't seem right. But I'll be at
home all day tomorrow if you can get away. But
better not mention it to Elisabeth. As you can
probably see, she doesn't much care for me.'

A message, and so soon! Deb could scarcely
believe it. But how would she be able to escape her
duties with Elisabeth?

'And I wondered if you might do me a favour, too,'
Abigail went on smoothly. 'Lord B left his notebook
at your house. He forgot it last time he was there. I
wondered if you'd bring it over when you come.'

Deb hardly heard her. 'What was the handwriting
on the letter like?'

'That? I didn't really notice.'

'Then it can't be from my mother; she had a
beautiful hand. People used to remark on it, she
always used to—'

'Maybe it's from the maid then. The book Lord
Bruncker left behind is a small volume – bound in
white calfskin.'

'Oh.' Deb masked her disappointment. 'But you're
right, it could be from the maid, Agnes. But I haven't
seen Agnes for years. I don't know if we'd know each
other now.' Deb's mind raced.

Abigail laid a hand on her arm and bent to look
into her face. 'Lord Bruncker's book with the white
leather binding – you won't forget it, will
Abigail shook Deb's arm impatiently.

'No, I—'

'And best say nothing to Mr Pepys. Dear Lord B is

anxious he should not appear too forgetful. He's worried he'll be taken for a fool. You won't say anything to embarrass him, will you?'

Deb dragged her thoughts back to Abigail's request. 'No, I promise. I'm just surprised to be hearing something from my notice so soon. I'll come as soon as I can. Thank you, Mistress Williams—'

'Abigail,' she said firmly.

Mr Pepys bustled up, looking agitated. 'There you are! What on earth are you doing? We thought you'd got lost. Come along, Elisabeth's waiting for you.'

'My fault, Samuel,' Abigail said. 'We were just discussing the play. Drab, wasn't it? The Duke's players aren't the same animal at all, now Betterton's sick.'

'Never seen a worse play in my life.' Mr Pepys took Deb by the arm and hurried her away.

As Deb passed under the archway, she turned to wave to Abigail. She was strangely motionless, watching Deb go. Something about her cold vigilance made the hairs stand up on the back of Deb's neck, but then Abigail smiled and lifted her hand, and the moment melted away.

Chapter Eight

DEB WAS UP AT FIRST LIGHT, leaning out of her window, and gazing across the grey London rooftops, which were silvered with rain. The fact that there was a reply to her notice filled her with trepidation. What if it really was from her mother? What would she say? Would Mama even recognise her now she was grown?

And she did not know how she could manage to get away, especially as Elisabeth was insistent that they should go to Unthank's again to have Deb's day dresses altered.

After she had helped Elisabeth to dress, and crimped her side curls with the heated tongs, Elisabeth fixed her with a disapproving look. 'You are almost bursting out of that bodice,' she said.

Deb was embarrassed at how tight her clothes had become, and how much it made men stare. Especially Mr Pepys. She was surprised to have put on weight, since she was always busy and spent half the day picking up things Elisabeth had dropped. Gloves, hats, hairpins – they all were scattered willy-nilly in her wake. If she were ever lost, you'd have no trouble finding her, Deb thought.

Despite Deb's protestations that she did not need new clothes, a carriage was summoned and they put up their hoods and set off to Unthank's. The tailor's was a small cramped shop that smelled of wool and velvet and the sweat of Mr Unthank's underarms. Once out of her wet cloak, Deb fidgeted and held her breath as he lifted up her arms to measure around her chest and waist.

'Something not too showy,' Elisabeth said. 'Navy, or perhaps a dull blue.' A bolt of embossed sky-coloured cloth was thrown onto the table. 'No, no. Far too grand. Something darker.'

More rolls were brought, and Elisabeth exclaimed over their shade and texture, and asked prices, but Deb, who privately thought them all ugly, was silent. To think, the letter was waiting for her at Abigail's, and she had to be here fussing over cloth and trimmings. It made her restless, and she fidgeted with her cuffs. Once the cloth for Deb was chosen, a slate-blue worsted, Elisabeth asked Mr Unthank to bring her some bolder colours for her own new petticoat. A silk of a bilious green was thrown out onto the cutting table, but Deb kept looking to the window, desperate to escape.

'What's the matter, Deb?' Elisabeth asked. 'You look a little peaky.'

Deb seized on this chance. 'Sorry, Elisabeth, I don't feel well.'

Elisabeth paused with a card of braiding in her hand and flapped it at her. 'When did this come on?'

'Just this morning.'

Elisabeth leaned to whisper in her ear. 'Is it your monthlies?'

Deb dipped her head as if embarrassed.

'Oh, poor Deb. I know how that feels. You look quite pale. I'll get Mr Unthank to call a carriage to take us home.'

'No, no. I'd much rather walk. The fresh air will do me good.'

'*Oh la*! You can't possibly walk if you're unwell.'

'I can,' Deb said desperately. 'It's just what I need. And then you can call on Mary Mercer at the linen shop too, as you'd planned. I don't want to spoil your day.'

Elisabeth and Mary Mercer were very close. Mary used to work in Mrs Pepys' household a few years ago. Deb gambled that Elisabeth would prefer an afternoon talking with Mary, gossiping about the court and putting the world to rights, than accompanying Deb home.

'Well, if you're sure.' Elisabeth shrugged, but still looked doubtful.

'Quite.' Deb willed her to agree. 'I'll walk straight down Thames Street to Seething Lane.'

Elisabeth sighed. 'Very well. I suppose so. Mr Pepys will be out for dinner today at Broad Street, so if you're going back, you might as well make sure Jane polishes the cutlery like I asked her to.'

'Yes, Elisabeth.'

Deb gave a brief curtsey to Mr Unthank, tweaked her cloak from the hook and launched herself into the fresh air. She didn't like to deceive Elisabeth this way, not now Elisabeth seemed to be warming to her a little more. She told herself it would just be the once.

She set off in the direction of Thames Street, but after two hundred yards and a quick look over her shoulder, she took a side street and doubled back.

Meanwhile, Abigail had risen at her house in Whetstone Park, and the remains of her breakfast lay on a tray on the table in the window. She wondered how long it would take Deb Willet to come. She'd had to check if Deb had put the notice up. She had removed it, of course. It would not do for her protégé to be running off to find her kin instead of living at the Pepyses' where she could be most useful.

She felt faintly guilty about removing it, and dashing Deb's hopes, but she was used to ignoring that type of sensation. They were just feelings, of no substance, and of no import to anyone else. Only actions really had any importance.

She sat down to forge a letter, forming the characters carefully in a childish print. Forgery was a skill she had learned. She did not bother to blot it but just folded it into a square and watched the blob of cheap brown sealing wax sizzle under the taper. Then she wrote Deb's name and her own address on the outside in the same uneducated hand. She positioned it carefully on the side table and admired it a moment. A dead end – an excuse to bring Deb Willet running; that was all.

Abigail thought of the portrait Deb had shown her at the theatre. Deb would be horrified to think her mother was the spit of one of the women from the whorehouses on Lukenor Lane. The thought of prim, respectable Deb going there made her smile. Just went to show, portraits were wholly unreliable. Painters changed the nose if it was too big, made heavy brows lighter; flattered their sitter.

Abigail shivered, drew her wrap closer round her shoulders, and thrust aside the troubling thoughts of the stews on the south bank. Memories of Lukenor Lane dragged with them the whole sorry business of Joan. And her daughter's predicament hurt. She'd tried everything to get her out of Clement's Yard, but Joan wouldn't listen to her. Called her an interfering bitch. But Abigail knew if she didn't do something to help her soon, it would be too late.

Hope for Joan was the only thing that kept her going. She'd go again tonight, take her the money for the new physic. That part was easy. Persuading her to take it was another matter. The thought made her weary. God help her, she hoped Deb Willet would be easier to persuade than Joan ever was.

A rap at the door. Blazes, the girl was here already. She hoped Deb would have remembered to bring the white book. Lord B had told her Pepys kept his memoranda there, and she was counting on it. Without it, without a sniff of information to keep that snake Piet Groedecker satisfied, hers would be an even shorter road ahead than Joan's.

Deb looked up at the peeling door and checked Abigail's address again. Surprisingly, Abigail's house was an old-fashioned Elizabethan building in an unlikely and unassuming street of warehouses and tradesmen. The windows were dirty and the shutters in ill-repair. Aware of her servant status, Deb decided she'd better go around to the back entrance. A pale, rather slatternly maid eyed her through a crack in the door, then kept her waiting in the rain on the doorstep while she called for her mistress.

'Oh, but my dear, you are drenched to the bone,' Abigail exclaimed when Deb was finally ushered in and up the back stairs. Abigail pulled Deb's cloak off her shoulders and handed it, dripping, to the maid, signalling her to leave them. 'Come along in and get dry.'

She led Deb into a large chamber, where a fireplace flanked by two wooden chairs framed a meagre fire. The room was lofty, on the first floor, with tall windows overlooking the street. It was almost empty in comparison with Seething Lane. There was barely a stick of furniture, no personal possessions at all. No paintings, or rugs or books. Nothing on the mantelpiece. A cobweb swung from one of the shutters. It occurred to Deb that you'd never guess it was a wealthy woman's house, though Abigail was immaculately coiffed as usual, her face artfully rouged.

Abigail seemed to read Deb's thoughts, for she said, 'Do sit. I'm afraid it's not very comfortable here. My other lodgings and all my possessions were lost in the fire, and I'm afraid I must make do with this until my new house in White Hall is ready. And of course I'm so often at Lord B's that I can almost bear its discomforts.'

'I'm so sorry to hear it,' Deb said. 'It must have been terrible.' She sat next to the hearth on the wooden chair that Abigail indicated and spread out the hem of her skirts, which were still soaked from the rain.

'Have you brought my Lord's book?' Abigail asked.

Deb clapped a hand to her mouth. 'Oh my word! I forgot. I'm so sorry, it's just that I was—'

'But I was relying on it. What will I tell his Lordship now?'

Deb was mortified. Abigail had been so kind, and now she had offended her. 'I'm sorry,' she repeated. 'I'll find it as soon as I get home and get it delivered to you. Don't worry. I'll wrap it well against the rain.'

'Will I write a note to remind you?' Her tone was faintly accusatory.

'No. I promise. I'm not usually forgetful. It was just that Elisabeth—'

'He's been fretting over that book all week, almost drove me mad.'

'I know, I'm sorry,' Deb said miserably.

Abigail paced the room, her green skirts swishing on the wooden boards. Deb's sleeves were steaming embarrassingly in the heat. She took a deep breath. 'Might I look at the message now, the one that came addressed to me?'

Abigail turned back from the window. 'Oh, that. Yes. I have it here.' She crossed to a writing desk and fetched a square of folded paper.

A stab of dismay. This was certainly not her mother's handwriting. Deb ran her thumb over the seal, disappointed to see a plain nub of brown wax, with no impression of a signet ring or fob.

'You'd better open it.'

'I'm afraid to,' Deb admitted. 'What if it says she's dead, or that she doesn't want to know me?'

'I'm sure it won't say that.' Abigail reached to pat her arm with a sympathetic expression. 'Would you like me to open it for you?'

'No, no. It's all right, I'll do it.' Deb was still smarting from the fact that Abigail was angry with her. She turned her back to her and slid her finger under the seal until she felt it crack. She unfolded the stiff paper and smoothed it on her lap. Only five words.

"WHITE HARTE YARD
DRURY LANE"

It was just an address. No note. Deb turned the paper over and over in her hands, hoping for the name of who sent it, or some other clue. She looked up. Abigail was watching her expression intently.

'It's an address,' Deb said.

'Let me see.'

Deb handed her the note. Abigail looked it over and shook her head. 'I'm afraid it's not going to be much use to you, Deb. If I'm not mistaken, that's one of the streets that was lost in the fire.'

'But why would anyone send me a message with that address unless it means something?'

'I don't know. There are all sorts of charlatans around,' Abigail said. 'Maybe the messenger just hoped for the tip for delivering it. I did give him a penny because I was so glad, for your sake, to see a reply.'

'Oh.' Deb felt tears prick her eyes. 'Yes, I suppose that could be it.' The disappointment was sharp enough to make her crumple in her seat.

Abigail stood and came over to hug her. 'I know, it's a blow, and hard to have your expectations dashed like that,' she said.

Deb leaned in to her, feeling the whalebone of Abigail's corsets press against her cheek.

A cool hand came down to rest on her head. 'You mustn't give up hope,' Abigail murmured, 'perhaps we will hear better news before long. You can come over again soon, to tell me what you've found and to see if there's been anything further.'

Deb moved out of Abigail's embrace. 'I'll go to White Harte Yard. You never know, there might be something there. I can ask who lived there, at least.'

'Of course, if you think you should,' Abigail said lightly. 'But I wouldn't bother. I think the whole area has been cleared by now for rebuilding.'

'Still, I can ask. It won't do any harm.' Outside, a church bell tolled the hour. Two o'clock! Deb was seized with a sudden panic. What if Elisabeth should decide to go home from Unthank's early?

Deb stood up. 'Sorry, Mistress … Abigail, but I

can't stay. I must hurry back to Seething Lane. It's a
fair step, and I only risked coming because of the
letter.'

'Must you go? It is so cheering to have young
company, and I know we will be great friends. And I
so looked forward to our little chat.' Abigail still had
hold of her hand between hers, and now she pressed
it tight. 'You must come back soon, very soon.'

'Of course, but—'

'Promise me you will.'

'Beg pardon, Abigail, but I must go. Elisabeth
thinks I'm ill. I told her I was going home. If she gets
there before me, I'll be in trouble.' Deb withdrew her
hand and made to leave, but Abigail followed.

'Then, if you really insist, I'll call you a carriage.'

'Oh no, I can't afford one. I'll have to run.'

Abigail picked up a handbell and shook it, and the
strident noise made Deb wince. The pale-faced
servant appeared.

'Ah, Poole. Miss Willet is unwell.' Abigail gave a
conspiratorial glance to Deb. 'Call for a hackney
carriage for her, would you?'

When it arrived, Abigail paid the driver and leaned
in to talk to Deb through the window. 'You'll bring
me Lord Bruncker's book later today, won't you? I do
like to mother him a little. Shall I write that
reminder?'

'No need. I won't forget.'

Abigail pressed her again not to divulge Lord
Bruncker's forgetfulness to Mr Pepys, and then said,
'I'll be waiting for Lord Bruncker tonight at his Navy
Chambers. The sign of the compass. It's only a step
from the Pepyses'. Bring it over to his house between
four and six. Before he arrives.' She kissed Deb on
both cheeks, in a drift of lavender powder.

Deb almost breathed a sigh of relief to be away. Abigail was overpowering. And such a mighty fuss about a book! Lord Bruncker must certainly be a very forgetful man.

The horses clip-clopped their way back through the city. Deb sat on the edge of the seat, willing them to hurry. When she got back to Seething Lane she opened the Pepyses' front door without a sound and crept inside, relieved to see no hat or packages on the side table and no sign of Elisabeth.

Mindful of Elisabeth's instructions, she hurried through to the kitchen to remind Jane to polish the silver. Jane was sitting darning one of her woollen gloves, chatting to a neighbour's coachman, and one of Mr Pepys' clerks, Tom Edwards. She was not happy to be reminded of the cleaning.

She scowled at Deb. 'I'll do them later. There's plenty of time. Mr Pepys told me that after he dined he meant to meet you both at the theatre. So master and mistress won't be back until after four.'

The coachman and Tom tipped their hats to them both and retreated out of the back door.

'You look hot,' Jane said.

'I came home because I'm not feeling well.' The lie made Deb blush even more.

'I wondered why you'd come back. Can I fetch you anything?'

'No, I think I'll lie down.' Deb wanted to look at the letter again, the address that had come to Abigail's house. But then she remembered Lord Bruncker's book.

She made a search of the main chamber but could not see a book bound in white there, although there were several of Mr Pepys' books lying on a stool near the window. Perhaps the book had been packed away. The Pepyses were planning alterations to the windows, so quite a few volumes had been put in baskets already.

She made a hasty search of the rest of the house but could find nothing. Finally, she creaked open the door into Mr Pepys' closet that he called his 'study'. It was dim in there, even in the day, with a fusty smell of wood and paper. Deb realised that this was the scent that Mr Pepys carried round with him, the smell of his study. She liked it, the aroma of learning.

She tiptoed, because he had never invited her into this room where he worked, and she felt like an intruder. She ran her finger along a row of leather-bound volumes, housed in shelves built for the purpose, unable to resist the lure of so many books, but she found nothing white.

Elisabeth never offered her anything of substance to read, but at night Deb sometimes kidnapped one of the master's books if he left them lying in the main chamber. She drifted over to Mr Pepys' desk. A sheaf of untidy papers lay in a pile. She could not read them immediately; they seemed to be written in some sort of code, all squiggles and curls. Just the odd name was legible to her. She was curious though; she loved a puzzle. But she noticed they were not lying flat so she lifted a corner to see what lay underneath.

The white leather book was right there, under Mr Pepys' papers. It was a wonder he had not spotted it and returned it to Lord Bruncker himself.

Deb extracted it, feeling a little guilty. Mr Pepys would not like her being in his office without his permission, she was certain, but Abigail Williams had been so kind to her, she wanted to return the favour. And she couldn't help feeling flattered to be taken up by Abigail Williams, the consort of the most famous mathematician in London.

She scanned the room again. There were no other books with a white binding, so this must be it. A slim red ribbon held the two end pages together.

She was about to untie it when the front door slammed and a voice echoed up from the hall. 'Deb?'

Elisabeth, calling her.

Deb's stomach seemed to drop like a bucket down a well. She left the office door ajar and, hitching up her skirts, ran for the stairs to her room. Two minutes later she was in bed with the book tucked underneath her bottom, the covers up to her chin.

Elisabeth's voice drifted up. 'Ah, there you are, Jane. I was on my way to the playhouse but Mary Mercer told me Betterton's not back and that dreadful Mr Young is to take his role, so I came home. I told Sam he will have to endure it on his own – I simply could not sit through another performance like the last one. How is Deb?'

'Gone to bed, mistress.' Jane's voice sounded sour.

'*Oh la.* I hope she's not going to be a sickly maid. I can't keep her if she goes on ailing.'

A little while later she heard Elisabeth's footsteps on the stairs and lay with her eyes tight shut as she heard the latch lift and the door open. Elisabeth must have been satisfied Deb was asleep because it closed again softly and her footsteps trotted away downstairs. Deb waited another half-hour in bed before she dared get up.

When she went down to the kitchen, Jane said acidly, 'So you've recovered, have you? Now all the polishing's done.' Deb did not dare fetch anything from the larder, though she was hungry. After all, she was supposed to be unwell.

Elisabeth was too busy sorting out books of samples for new drapes to pay her much heed, so Deb risked asking if she could step out again for some air. 'It might help me feel better,' she lied.

'It's late for a maid to be walking the streets on her own. It will soon be dark,' Elisabeth said, laying aside the samples.

'Just a few minutes,' Deb said. 'I feel in need of some air.' It was almost six and she'd promised Abigail she would take the book to Bruncker's.

'No. If you are well enough to walk, you are well enough to play cards with me. You are supposed to be keeping me company.' Elisabeth was suddenly petulant. 'It's not as if you are really ill. You will have to learn to cope with these women's ailments, Deb, if you are ever to run a household of your own. You don't see me taking to my bed every month, do you?'

'No, Elisabeth. I'm sorry.' Deb was chastened, though Elisabeth took to her bed with women's ailments often enough. Lord Bruncker would just have to wait for his book, though it worried her that she was letting Abigail down.

'The cards, Deb.' Elisabeth's voice broke into her thoughts.

Guiltily, Deb leapt to fetch them.

That evening, while Elisabeth was in the kitchen, Mr Pepys came and sat down opposite her in Elisabeth's chair, his serving boy following behind him as usual like a dog.

After a moment or two, he dismissed the boy. 'Those are neat stitches, Deb,' he said, leaning forward to look at the bodice she was sewing.

'It will do,' she said.

'Is that the bodice you were wearing the day you came?'

'You have a good memory, sir.'

'It suited you very well. Showed off your slim waist.'

'Mrs Pepys thought it too tight,' she said, smiling. 'I'm letting it out.'

As she looked up, he caught her eye and reached over to press his hand on her leg. 'Not too much, I hope,' he said. 'I like to see it close-fitting, to see your shape. You have a fine figure, little Deb, don't hide it.'

She felt herself blush, confused by his compliment. It was uncomfortable to be talked of that way. Uncomfortable, but not unpleasant. His hand on her knee was hot through her skirts. He stroked her thigh three times, in a fatherly way, as though he was stroking a cat, then removed his hand. She exhaled, took up the needle again, thought how much younger he might look without his ridiculous wig.

As she stitched she was aware of him staring at her, the noise of his breath loud above the crackling fire. It was odd for him to be so silent. The quiet spoke louder than if there was another person in the room. She concentrated on pressing the needle through the linen with her thimble. A few moments later Mr Pepys leaned towards her, put his hand on her leg again, began to stroke her thigh. Higher.

Shocked, she looked up at him. His eyes were questioning. Should she ask him not to? She opened her mouth to speak, but the noise of Elisabeth's shoes trotting up from downstairs made him leap up in any case and rush over to the window, where he stood as Elisabeth chattered on about flour and dried peas, quite oblivious to the prominent bulge in her husband's breeches.

Chapter Nine

ABIGAIL WAS AT LORD BRUNCKER'S when the parcel came, addressed to her. She untied the string to reveal a white leather-bound book. Praise God. Pepys' notes of transactions from the Treasury. Three days she'd waited and had almost given up. When it didn't arrive as promised, she'd thought Deb Willet had let her down and that she would have to find another way to inveigle the information Piet needed.

It came with a tidily penned message.

> *"Lord Bruncker's book. Begging your pardon for the delay, I'm afraid I could not get away sooner.*
> *Your faithful servant,*
> *Deborah Willet"*

She ruminated a while. There was no doubt Deb could be useful. Having a little 'friend' in Pepys' house was ideal. Deb was obviously a resourceful girl, but was she calm enough? Or bold enough? An accomplice would be a risk.

Abigail sat down at Lord Bruncker's desk near the window and untied the white leather book. The writing was small and cramped together. Damn, her eyes were definitely getting worse. In frustration, she went to fetch Lord B's magnifying lens and put her eye to it. After a few moments of close reading, she paused to let out her breath.

This would save her neck. It might as well be a chest of gold. She imagined Piet's slightly wolfish smile when he realised its value to the De Witts. She flipped through the pages. All the minutes of past meetings in Pepys' close hand – meticulously recorded details of discussions with his fellow navy officers such as Sir William Penn and Sir John Mennes. He had even set down old Penn's stubborn refusal to order more timber for shipbuilding, along with caustic comments about Penn's meanness. Rather amusing, but time-consuming. Nevertheless, she did not dare leave out these bits of extraneous information. Piet became suspicious if she failed to copy the documents exactly, word for word.

So he thinks I'm too old, does he? she thought. Piet had sent her three more guilders only a few days ago – his idea of a warning. We'll see who's too old. She would make Piet think each memorandum a separate paper, eke it out slowly, and wring maximum profit from it. By the time the noon sun streamed in at the window, she was copying feverishly, with the lens held up to one eye.

Lord B had told her Pepys' house was having alterations, so she gambled that Pepys would not miss his book immediately, and if he did, he would assume he had mislaid it. She could even return it to him herself, eventually, pretend he had left it at Bruncker's. As the light faded at the window, she lit a single candle, then another, then another. Grease dripped onto the table. Her hand was stiff with writing, so she clenched and unclenched her fingers before rolling and sealing the documents. She would deliver one of them to Piet's man, Leo, tomorrow.

There was a noise from below, and she heard Poole greet someone at the door.

She thrust the white book down her bodice next to her bust and grabbing her parchments, bolted into the library. She seized the little wooden steps, and jumped up to reach the shelf where there were rolls just like these – Lord B's engineering projects – diagrams of ships that had been gathering dust for years. She slotted her rolls neatly amongst them and leapt down. Just in time, for Lord B came bustling in, velvet cloak smelling of frost and the outdoors, his long nose red with cold.

'What news?' she asked him lightly, relieving him of his cloak.

'An unholy mess, just as I feared. There's to be an inquest into the last battle, to find out why that coward Albemarle was left with only half the fleet against the Dutch. Our best ships lost – the *Loyal London*, the *Royal James* and the *Royal Oak*. Hellfire, even the bloody names are enough to demoralise us all! The navy commissioners want to foist the whole of the blame on us.'

'That's nonsense. How can it be your fault? Prince Rupert went against orders and sailed off with half the fleet. The King says he was trying to prevent the French joining up with the Dutch, but I'm not so sure I believe that, do you?'

'Whatever he was doing, it was a disaster. Weakened our defences, and now, of course, the whole bloody thing has nothing to do with the Prince. Oh no. It's all our fault. And worse than sinking us, the Dutch had the cheek to tow away the

Royal Charles. Rumour has it, she's on bloody display! In some poxy harbour in Holland, as evidence of English stupidity. And of course the symbolism of it is not lost on his Royal Highness, who is mightily displeased.' Lord B flung himself down in a chair, pulled off his wig and scratched his shaved head. 'Infernal thing. It's itching like the devil. You don't mind, do you?'

'No, better you're comfortable. I'll have Poole send it down to Childers. She's better at men's wigs than Poole. She can look over it later, check it for lice.' She poured him a drink from a glass decanter and settled down in the chair opposite him. She wished he had not shaved his beautiful glossy dark hair, but he had insisted, said he could not bear to get grey and grizzled like Penn.

He sighed. 'Oh God, Abigail, what am I to do? I might not survive it. They're looking for a scapegoat.'

'But it's not your—'

'We might need money for a lawyer. A bloody good one. Pepys and I both fear we might lose our positions, even our heads.'

'Surely, it won't come to that—'

'It might. And I want to make sure you are properly provided for if anything should happen.' He put his drink aside. 'Marry me, won't you? Let's stop this ridiculous pretence and live together properly as man and wife. I know I've not always been faithful, but in the end it's always you I want to come home to.'

The words made her dizzy. The agreement was on the tip of her tongue, the relief of it. But then she hesitated, suspicious. Money for a lawyer, was that what he was after? She pushed that uncharitable thought aside. The word 'marriage' must mean he was serious.

She hesitated, and he walked over, brought his hand to her face and stroked her cheek, his expression full of affection. 'What do you say, my Queen Bee?'

He meant it. It made her freeze inside. She could not risk it. Risk him. She took him to a chair, bade him sit. Then she knelt at his feet, took one of his hands in her own, chafed it as she looked into his dear face. 'I can't, you know I can't.'

'But why not? I know in the beginning you were married, but Williams is dead, been dead the last five years. There's no legal reason now why not.'

'It would do you no good, B. I know what they say about me. I'm mistress material, not a fit wife for a man of your standing – a man only two finger widths distance from the King.'

'Blow what people think. I don't care what people think. We've lived together for years. And the King's hardly a shining example of propriety, is he? Look at his flaunting of Countess Castlemaine. Besides, I only want you. You understand me, how I think. You don't mind all my experiments, my research. Damn it, you know never to touch my papers, you know when to leave me alone. And there's no other woman I could talk to of pendulums, or mechanics of ships, like I can with you. Pretty girls are all right in their way, but I need to come home to someone I can rely on, someone with a sharp mind between their ears, not chaff.'

Abigail shook her head. 'You flatter me, my Lord. But I'm too old for change now. I've got used to my own little house, to being on my own. The theatre is a hard taskmaster. I need to learn my lines, and you know how you hate to hear me reciting them. I'd be a very annoying wife.'

A grunt from Lord B. 'Damn it, you're probably

right. Give it up, the play-acting.'

'We're fine as we are, aren't we? I can hardly join the men at your Royal Society meetings at Gresham College, can I? So I need to make my own entertainment, meet my theatre friends, do women's things. And look at me,' she brushed her hand over her fine lace collar, 'I'd not be the sort of wife who'd want to ruin my hands running a big household. Come on, pass me that old sheep fleece of yours and I'll go down and get Childers to fix it up before we go to the theatre. I need to see what the competition are up to.'

She did not wait for his reply but plucked up the offending wig and took it downstairs to the kitchen, where Childers, Bruncker's maid-of-all-work, was crimping a collar.

When she'd handed the periwig over, she paused on the stairs, leaned against the cool dark wall. Never had she imagined he would think of marriage. She had not expected to find him handsome, to even like him, when all this began. Piet had needed her eyes and ears in the Navy Office and she'd needed the money. But over time she had grown to admire B's incisive mind and his unquenchable enthusiasm for the new. He in turn had been astonished that she could listen to his theories without boredom and could easily grasp the concepts that excited him. The fact she was hailed as one of the handsomest women in London was an added delight to him. And, as time went on, she'd found the monetary positions reversed – B had amassed more debts as his fortunes fell, and now he needed to borrow from her. The Dutch, on the other hand, paid her well.

But now her business with Piet was a runaway cart; she was powerless to stop it. If she did not keep feeding the Dutch information, then they would kill her. How much harder would it be trying to manage her clandestine contacts while actually living under the same roof as Lord B?

She pressed her back against the cold distemper, suddenly tired. If she were ever to be uncovered as an agent for the Dutch, it would be the gibbet not just for her, but for him too. Spying on B was a struggle; not because she could not pry his secrets from him, but because he trusted her so willingly.

And there was Joan. How could she possibly explain Joan?

He knew nothing of her, and, of course, she would not reveal her daughter to him. To do so would expose her heart as an entity that still lived and breathed. But every spy knew that to pander to the heart was dangerous. Like a caged bird, she dare not let it fly for fear of losing it completely.

'Abigail?' He was calling her.

She hovered a moment on the stairs in indecision. Time was running through the glass, her eyesight was getting worse, the speed of her responses slower. Agents rarely lasted beyond their thirties, and here was she, well into the next decade. But, maybe, if she could just manage a few more months, then maybe she could risk a flit in the night, somewhere safe, a long way from here. Maybe even the New World. But she would need to buy time to plan, and she would need cover.

Deb Willet could be the godsend she needed after all. Or, more likely, her last chance.

Chapter Ten

Deb was in the downstairs parlour, hem-stitching a chemise and worrying about Mr Pepys. It was a damp stocking of a day, and the fire smoked and struggled in the hearth.

Elisabeth put her head around the door. 'You'll have to go out, Deb dear, we need another loaf, and the oven's not hot enough yet for baking.'

'Have we got company for dinner?' Deb asked.

'No, not today. Sam's going to be at Lord Bruncker's.' Elisabeth sighed and came and sat down opposite her. 'They've to explain to Parliament again why Chatham was undefended, how the Dutch sank our ships.'

Deb hid her relief that Mr Pepys would be out. 'Is all that still going on, then?' she asked.

'Seems so. Parliament must go over it all with a nit comb trying to find someone to blame. Sam's dining with Lord Bruncker to make a plan for their defence. Though the blessed Virgin herself knows how they'll get anything done with that harlot Madam Williams at the table.'

'Is she to dine with them, too?' A twinge of guilt made Deb concentrate harder on her hemming.

'She's always there, sticks to Bruncker like goose-down. I don't know how Sam can bear it. And what on earth can she know of the whole affair? A woman like that? I hope Sam's all right,' Elisabeth went on. 'He was looking for a book he'd mislaid for hours last night, and he says his eyes are bothering him again. He wore his new spectacles last night, and now he's even more convinced his eyesight is failing. Men. The least little thing and it's blindness, or scrofula, or, God forbid, the plague.'

Deb could not help but laugh. In recent weeks, she and Elisabeth had grown more companionable, for when she was out and about in town, Elisabeth seemed to expand; she thrived on company, and was funny and engaging, and often far too outspoken. It made Deb warm to her. But once inside Seething Lane it was as if her husband drained all the joy of life from her.

'Penny for them, Deb?'

'Nothing,' Deb said, 'just thinking.'

'But you've said hardly a word to me all morning! Take cheer, for heaven's sake. It's like looking at a wet winding sheet.'

'Sorry, Elisabeth, I didn't—'

'You can run out and fetch the provisions. It will save Jane a task; I left my list with her in the kitchen. And a breath of fresh air might liven you up. And while you're about it, why don't you bring me more of that pink lining silk from the haberdashery?'

Elisabeth watched Deb from the corner of her eye, saw her fold the sewing into a precise, neat square before going downstairs. Everything Deb did was neat and unobtrusive. In fact, Deb was often so quiet going about the house you wouldn't even know she was there.

Elisabeth let out a long sigh, put her needle and thread aside.

Of course, *Sam* knew she was there, there was no mistaking that; he looked for her first whenever he came home. It wasn't really Deb's fault, it was Sam. He tried not to let it show, but he just could not help himself. His eyes would slide to Deb and then he'd start boasting about all the important people he'd met, and Deb's eyes would grow wide and round.

It made Elisabeth want to prick him hard with a bodkin.

She wondered if she dared to have a word with him, make sure he understood. It was one thing when he consorted with the tradespeople out of the house, she thought; she was quite prepared to ignore the terrible actress Mrs Knepp and the loose-laced bodices and even looser tongues of Doll Powell and Betty Martin. Nobody would take much notice of bawds like them, and besides, they were well away from Seething Lane and proper company.

But Deb was supposed to be her private domain; why, Deb was almost an extension of her person. She was growing a little fond of her too, now she'd understood that Deb's aloofness was masking the fact she was shy. Woe betide Sam if he tried anything with her. A wife would not tolerate looking a fool in her own house.

Deb scanned the address of the haberdashers and realised it was close to where Abigail Williams lived. A note from her had arrived a week ago suggesting she call, but Deb hadn't been able to get away, and another more insistent message had arrived that morning. She dared not hope it might be another reply to her notice. If she was quick, there'd be time

- 93 -

to visit Abigail before finishing her errands.

The weak autumn sun glinted on the rippling surface of the Thames as she was punted upstream.

When she arrived at Abigail's, she rapped hard at the door.

'Who is it?' Poole called, voice full of suspicion.

'Miss Willet.' She heard numerous bolts slide back, and Poole opened the door a mere crack. On seeing her, she stood aside without a word for Deb to enter.

Deb was faintly scandalised to find Abigail was not yet dressed, even though it was nearly eleven of the clock, but wore a faded peach-coloured robe which trailed as she walked so that Deb almost tripped over it. She greeted Deb effusively, like a long-lost friend.

'Do you have news for me?' Deb was eager.

'No, I'm afraid not. I just wanted to have a little talk with you.'

'There hasn't been another reply?'

'No, not yet.'

'Oh.' Deb masked her disappointment by taking off her gloves. She wondered what was so important that it couldn't wait.

Abigail interrupted her thoughts. 'Did you go to White Harte Yard?'

'Last week,' Deb said, handing her gloves to Poole. 'There's nothing left, the yard was gutted, and there are still blackened flagstones where the hearths once were.'

'Half of London's the same.' Abigail turned. 'Some warmed milk with brandy, if you can, Poole. Miss Willet looks cold to the bone.' Her attention came back to Deb. 'And did you find out anything?'

'You were right. There was no trace of my mother or of Agnes. The tenant in the one remaining house had never even heard of my mother and could remember no women of their description. The whole area has been cleared. It's staked out now for rebuilding. The note was just a hoax, designed to part you from your money. How can people be so calculating?'

Abigail shook her head in sympathy. 'It is so sad what we have come to. Since the fire we have had such a rash of petty crime and theft. And who can blame them? People who have lost their homes and livelihoods will do anything to get a few pence. I, at least, had somewhere to go and a nest egg behind me. We must remember how lucky we are.'

Abigail made small talk about the state of the London streets until Poole returned with the drinks. They sat to sip them by the fire. The brandy fumes caught at the back of Deb's throat and made her eyes water. She tried not to stare at Abigail's face, which, without powder, was etched with fine lines. The crêpey skin of her neck was usually hidden by a neckerchief or fur collar.

'Try not to be too disappointed. You have survived without her so far, haven't you?'

'It's peculiar, but I never realised how much finding Mama meant to me, not until I saw White Harte Yard all burned down like that,' she confessed. 'It raised my hopes, made me think Mama must be out there somewhere, and I owe it to Hester, my sister, to try and find her.'

'It's only natural, but I wonder ... whether it might be best to leave well alone.' Abigail's voice was all concern. 'Come and sit here by me, and let me talk to you. I'd like to give you a little honest advice.'

Deb eased herself onto the stool next to the fireplace where Poole was now working a pair of bellows.

'I don't mean to make you despondent,' Abigail

said, 'but you must consider the fact that you might never find her. Surely she would have sought you out herself if she wanted to see you? Besides, anything could have happened. She could have left London years and years ago and gone abroad. And, of course, the plague took many. The best advice I can give you is to forge a life for yourself nonetheless. Like you, I once had nothing, but now I have my own house, my own income. That is freedom.'

'I'll not give up yet. Someone might still reply to my notice.'

'Of course,' Abigail said smoothly, 'and naturally I will send for you the moment I hear anything more. But you must be realistic, make other plans in case nobody replies.'

'I know it sounds fanciful, but I get these strange prickling sensations, as if she's thinking of me. I know she's still alive, I can just feel it.' Deb gripped her skirts, tried not to let her emotion show. 'But I'm older now, and I need to face up to it, to know why she left. What happened to her, and where she is now. I think I can bear it, to know the truth. It was a man, I guess, from my aunt's hints, and my father's anger. But how could she do that? Just walk out on her children without a word?'

'I'm sure I don't know. But love – well, it can send a person to madness.'

'I shall never fall in love.'

Abigail smiled. 'Don't tempt Mistress Fate! The trick is to keep your head. It strikes where it will, like lightning, and mostly with little thought for our convenience. But love or no love, you don't want to be serving Elisabeth Pepys for ever, do you?'

Poole, who was still mending the fire, turned to stare at her.

'That will do, Poole,' Abigail said sharply.

Poole backed away under Abigail's glare and shut the door behind her.

'My beauty may fade,' Abigail said, 'but my pocket is well lined. A woman must make use of her assets while they last. I know you are still young, but it is never too early to put a little money aside. Besides, Deb dear, you have a quick mind, just as I do. Your intelligence is wasted as a lady's maid. How would you like to work for me?'

'Is that why you sent for me?' She was confused. 'But I don't—'

Abigail held out a hand to stay her words. 'Tell me the essential skills a lady's maid needs?' Deb was about to speak when Abigail threw her arms dramatically wide. 'Flattering your mistress, am I right? "Oh, mistress, you look perfectly radiant!" Nodding your head like a simpleton at every word she says. Talking of nothing of substance while wielding a hairbrush – something any fool could do.' Abigail patted her side-curls, pushed out her bottom lip, and suddenly she looked exactly like Mrs Pepys. "Deb, pass me the crimping iron!"'

Deb could not help smiling, despite herself.

'I know, I'm wicked! But do you see? Youth is always the first requirement in a lady's maid, not scholarship. When you get older and less … how can I say … decorative, they'll replace you. But I'm prepared to help you, to push you forward in society, give you something of consequence to do. Something that will use your learning and education.'

Deb was intrigued. 'I'm flattered. But I don't see how I can … I am already working for Mrs Pepys.'

'You would not need to leave the Pepyses. This would be a little side-business.'

'How so?'

'I noticed what a good hand you write. I could urgently use a scribe. Someone to make copies of navy documents. Lord Bruncker likes to have duplicates of his office papers, and then have them bound up in ledgers for future reference. As you have probably gathered, he is often forgetful. He's always misplacing his things. I used to be happy to do it, but my eyes are not as young as they were. It's a strain, all these papers.'

So after all that, it was only copying. Not really anything that required much skill, and Mrs Pepys already kept her busy enough. Deb opened her mouth to refuse, but Abigail jumped in.

'Do say you will. My eyes suffer so.' She put her hand to her forehead. Deb caught the sudden impression of someone small and frail. Deb had always thought Abigail had a backbone of iron.

Deb wavered. Perhaps Abigail was older than she appeared.

'It is only a few things,' Abigail said, 'but they need to be copied exactly. Like all navy documents, one or two are in cipher, but that need not concern you. You won't need to translate, just copy. It's such dull stuff that I used to regularly fall asleep reading it. But your eyes are young and strong. Do say you'll help me. It's only a little favour, for me and Lord B, as friends do for each other.'

Abigail smiled entreatingly at her, and Deb remembered Abigail's kindness in taking her under her wing and letting her use her address on the notice. She would do her this favour in return. After all, she was fortunate, was she not, to have the patronage of this *grande dame*? Besides, the idea of the cipher had piqued her curiosity; she loved anything that played with words or numbers.

'Beg pardon, Abigail,' she said. 'Of course I'm happy to help you. I didn't realise your eyes were so bad.'

'It comes and it goes,' Abigail said, shrugging. She stood and walked purposefully to the desk. 'The first copying will be from this document.' She opened a drawer, pulled out a paper and handed it to Deb.

Deb glanced down at it. It was a letter from Mr Mennes to Lord Bruncker, about a forthcoming Navy Board meeting, but fortunately not in code. She could read every word. There was an official stamp at the top of the paper.

'But you must keep quiet about it, not a word to Mr Pepys, for he and Lord B do not always see eye to eye on navy business.'

Deb swallowed. Keeping anything secret in the Pepys house would be almost impossible.

Abigail was still speaking. 'Can you let me have the copy by Friday?'

'I don't know if I can manage it by then ... I mean, if I've to keep it out of Mr Pepys' sight, then—'

'Discretion is part of our bargain. I am only asking you, my dear, because I'm sure you are *absolutely* trustworthy.'

'I'm really not sure ...' Deb held out the paper to Abigail, hoping she would take it back, but Abigail walked away. Deb had the same tight feeling in her chest as when she used to live with Aunt Beth.

'Friday then,' Deb said uncertainly, and was rewarded with a glowing smile. She was about to tuck the paper into her basket, but Abigail stayed her.

'No, no! Be careful!' Abigail snapped, and hurried to pass her a calfskin folder to put the paper in. 'It must not be marked or creased. It has to come back to me in exactly the same state as it went.'

Deb had the sense that she was wading into deep water, but had no idea how to extricate herself. A maid in her position had to do a lady's bidding, and even though Elisabeth called Abigail a harlot, she was still Lord Bruncker's chosen companion, and it certainly would not do to offend her.

'Now then, you will need to leave me. My Lord B and Mr Pepys and all the Navy Board are meeting me in town for dinner, and I still have to dress.'

'Beg pardon, Abigail. I didn't mean to keep you from your business.'

'You haven't. Thank you for coming. It is always a pleasure to see my little friend.' The dazzling smile again. 'Don't trust Lord B's paper with a messenger. They are unreliable. I'll send for you in a few days and pay you on delivery.'

'If that's best. I'll see what I can do.'

'Remember, not a word to Mr Pepys. Lord Bruncker does not want the rest of the Board to know how forgetful he is, and Pepys' mouth is like a tavern door – never closed.'

Deb swung the basket back and forth on her arm, weaving between the stalls set up on either side of the street. Elisabeth's shopping list was in her hand, though she was not thinking of the list, but of Abigail Williams and the tasks she had set her to do. True, Abigail had done Deb a favour by helping her search for her mother, and it would be useful to have a friend like Abigail if she wanted to continue to look, but now, on closer acquaintance, she realised she found Abigail overbearing.

Deb went in the baker's to fetch the loaf, and then hurried along to buy a rind of cheese and the rest of the groceries. All the time she was thinking. The extra payments from Abigail would mean a possible dowry for Hester. She had worried about whether she was saving enough. But something about the whole business with the copying felt out of kilter. It was not the fact that Lord Bruncker needed copies of his papers, but more the fact that Abigail should employ her secretly instead of Lord Bruncker himself asking a navy clerk to do it. It seemed odd. And the whiff of conspiracy about it made her wary.

She was absent-mindedly staring into a furrier's window, when a growing rumble and commotion behind her made her turn to look. A great tide of people was bearing down on her in a clatter of clogs. As they grew nearer, the other pedestrians pressed themselves back under the jetties to give them room, and Deb was forced to dodge behind a timber pillar.

A heavy-laden coal cart coming up the street towards her stopped, unable to move to the left or right, swamped by the crowd. Deb had never seen a poorer, more unwashed rabble. Instinctively she shrank away. Sailors and their wives, by the look and smell of them, and in a high old temper. The stench of them made her retreat even further, but more and more people poured into the street and soon all she could see were the stained shirts and jerkins of those closest. She stood on tiptoe and craned her neck, looking for a way out, but the cart was blocking the way, and the driver could not reverse his horses.

'Back up,' she heard the shouts. 'Back up, for God's sake!' But the cart was jammed.

More of the crowd pressed forward until there was barely an inch of room on the street. An elbow dug into Deb's side, and somebody trod on her foot as they pushed past.

'What's the hold-up? We've got to get to White Hall by one o'clock,' said a woman in a filthy and battered felt cap who had crammed herself in next to Deb.

'I don't know,' Deb said, trying to give her space. 'I think the cart's stuck.'

There was a sudden surge, the cart creaked into motion, and the flow of people burst forward with a great roar of triumph. Deb fought to stay on her feet, clutching her basket to her skirts. She felt a tug, and the basket almost flew from her grip. A man's sword hilt was caught in the wicker handle, and the owner of the sword, oblivious, charged onwards. Deb clung tight to the basket, fearful of what Elisabeth would say if she lost it.

'Please! Please stop!' She yanked on the handle.

But the man could not feel her tugs and she had no option but to be taken with him. Suddenly, feeling the extra weight dragging him back, the man turned in annoyance, and with a deft flip, he freed his sword. Deb overbalanced and fell backwards. Her head cracked against a pillar supporting an upper storey and then all she could see was a blur of clogs and hems of skirts. A boot came down on her shoulder. Disorientated, she struggled to get up, but another wave of people knocked her to the side.

She clung to the pillar, dazed, and tried to haul her way to standing.

'Oh, Miss Willet! What's happened? Let me help you up.' A pair of strong hands hoisted her to her feet and set her back to upright.

Startled, she looked into his face. It was that young man again – Mr Wells. He seemed to be everywhere, and always when she was at her least attractive. He was still talking, holding out her basket for her to take. He stooped to retrieve the loaf. 'Are these things yours?'

One of the sailors hurrying down the road in the crowd stopped and rushed across, a big bull-like fellow in a knitted cap. He clapped Mr Wells on the shoulder. 'Come on, Jem, we'll be late.'

'I'll be along in a minute,' he said, 'don't wait.' The other man ran to catch up with the throng. 'My brother, Bart,' Mr Wells explained. 'We're on our way to White Hall.'

'My things,' she said, in a panic, searching the ground for the rest of the goods that had tumbled out of the basket. The calfskin folder lay in the dirt. She picked it up and brushed it guiltily with her sleeve.

Mr Wells scooped up a flattened parcel wrapped in brown paper. 'Is this yours?'

'Oh no!' She prodded it gingerly. 'I mean, yes, it's a cheese. Well, it was a cheese. Now it looks more like a flatbread.' She took the limp parcel from his hand and rubbed her shoulder.

'Are you all right?'

'Just a bit winded.'

'There's a boot print on your dress,' he said, reaching out his hand to brush her down.

Their eyes met. The effect was to strike Deb momentarily dumb. An unspoken question hung between them. Something urgent that must be answered at all costs. His hand rested on her shoulder, hot through the thin linen fabric.

She stepped backwards away from him and busied herself brushing her sleeve; anything to hide her confusion and the hot flush of her cheeks.

'I didn't realise it was you,' he said. 'I mean, not at first.'

'Of course it's me,' she said, feeling quite unlike herself. Realising that this sounded foolish, she took a deep breath. 'What's this about?' she managed. 'Why's everyone in such a hurry?'

'It's the sailors. They're going to see if they can get Parliament to pay off their tickets. Bart, that's my brother, well, he persuaded me to try and speak up for them. They're the crews that defended us in the trouble with the Dutch. Maybe you've heard? They've not been paid yet. Tempers can get a bit hot.'

'They look like a crowd who mean business.'

'Oh, don't say that! That's what I'm afraid of. And I'm supposed to be the voice of reason.' He shook his head.

She laughed. 'You don't sound very confident.'

'I'm not. But Bart's very persuasive. He thinks because I've given a sermon every now and then, I'm an expert speaker. Here,' he bent down to retrieve a squashed cone of sugar which was now loose and gritty in its waxed paper.

'Are you a man of the church then?' she asked him, though she already knew the answer from Mr Pepys.

'For my sins, yes. Or, rather, not quite. I'm still in training.' He flashed a smile. 'But I think I've got rather a long way to go.'

They stood a moment in red-faced silence. He was staring at her foolishly, head tilted, as if she should speak.

'You'd better catch up with your brother then,' she said, 'and thank you.'

'Not at all. I have to say it was a bit of a shock. I wasn't expecting to see you down there. When I've seen you before you've usually been upright. With the head at the top.'

Despite herself, she could not help but smile at his good humour. 'Except when I'm mowed down by a savage dog, perhaps?'

He grinned.

'Oy! Jem!' The brother reappeared at the corner, waving his arms.

'I'd like to …' He stopped, mid-sentence, as if the words would not come.

After a moment of awkwardness she filled the space. 'Your brother's waving.'

'Oh. Oh yes. Good day then, Miss Willet.'

He raised his hat and loped off down the street. His heels rang on the cobbles, as he hurried away, cloak flying. He turned once to look over his shoulder at her, before skidding around the corner out of sight.

Her blood was racing, whether from the shock of falling or from meeting Mr Wells again, she did not know. She slapped at her skirts to free them of mud, and tidied her hair, wincing when she touched a bump just coming up on the side of her head. She liked him, she realised. Just as a friend, of course. That was twice he'd had to rescue her, and both times she had made a fool of herself.

Elisabeth's rules were definite: 'no followers'. But surely that wouldn't apply to parsons like Mr Wells?

Chapter Eleven

THAT NIGHT THE WIND GOT UP, making the shutters rattle, and the soot blow down the chimney. It made Jem restless. Bart had gone to the Black Bull with his cronies, so Jem took himself out for a walk to the river. Above him, stars glinted like sparks above the gusting evening smoke.

He took off his hat before he lost it to the wind, and his hair blew about his face so he had to hold it back with one hand. A double-masted schooner took his attention as it was rowed into its berth. It gave him a pang, for he had always wanted to go to sea, and he resented his father's insistence that, as the eldest, he should join the church and Bart should be the one to see the world. But now the idea of being a sailor was beginning to lose its appeal. He definitely wouldn't like to be dealing with intractable men like Pepys.

Ten days ago, when he'd gone to the Navy Offices, Pepys had shaken his head, licked his pudgy finger to separate his papers, and said, 'When the crews are paid is the King's decision. Nothing I can do.'

He'd like to see Pepys try to manage with no pay. He hoped he paid Miss Willet a decent wage. Jem found himself unable to forget Crawley's words – that

Pepys would give her 'more of an education'. The thought made him want to grab Pepys by his cravat and punch him, but he had to content himself with kicking the wall. Today again, when he'd seen Miss Willet knocked flat like that, all vulnerable with her petticoats showing, he'd had the same urge to rush to her defence.

But what a day! The sailors couldn't secure an audience with any of the navy officers. Bart and Bolton and some of the others, already drunk and spoiling for a fight, had taken umbrage and set to looting a nearby pie shop. The atmosphere rapidly turned sour, cobblestones and other missiles began to fly, and in the end the King's soldiers were called to rout them all. Jem had been obliged to duck and dive before he managed to drag Bart away by the scruff of the neck.

Jem stopped to lean over the wall and watch the dark hulks of the barges go by. His thoughts returned to Miss Willet. Crawley was right, though, Miss Willet *was* a beauty. Those strange clear grey eyes. It was odd how their paths kept crossing, as if there were some hidden destiny at work. He thought again of how light she was when he lifted her up. She'd blushed when he looked at her, and it had touched him with something like pain. He was always awkward with women; he never knew what to say to them. But if he could come home to someone like that, perhaps a life on land would be worth it after all.

He looked up at the stars again, his heart straining, yearning for something, something ineffable. In all his studies of theology, he had not found an answer for the yearning the stars gave him. The piercing desire for something out of reach.

When he got home, Bart was in, roughly patching a pair of his trousers. He looked up as Jem joined him at the table.

'I've been thinking,' Jem said. 'I could go and talk to Mr Pepys again if you like.'

'It won't do much good. Like you said, he didn't listen.'

'But I don't mind giving it another try.'

Bart gave a grunt. 'Don't know why you're suddenly taking such an interest. Earlier you couldn't wait to drag me away. But talking's getting us nowhere. If you really want to help, you can join us in the Black Bull on Tuesday. We're thinking we'll try and get a bigger demonstration together – make the King really sit up and take notice.'

'I'd rather try Mr Pepys again first. He's the one who pays you.' He didn't mention Miss Willet.

'Suit yourself. Don't suppose it can do any harm.'

At Unthank's the tailor's, Elisabeth leaned against the cutting table to confide in her friend Mary Mercer, who had come with her to help her choose an eye-catching material for a new upper-skirt.

'Sam's in a terrible state. Mr Kelsey actually had the cheek to accuse him of stealing! Said he brought three wagonloads of prize goods into the warehouses at Greenwich after the battle of the Medway. As if Sam would do that – take goods for himself instead of sending them to the King.'

'That's terrible,' Mary murmured, paying little attention but fingering a piece of velvet brocade. 'Who is Mr Kelsey?'

'I told you last week. The commander of one of the fireships. Of course, Sam said it was all lies and tittle-tattle, that he wasn't stealing anything, just storing it for safe keeping, but now he's going to be called to give a report of himself. And he has to prepare another defence, even when he's done nothing wrong.'

Elisabeth said this with full indignation, but Mary merely looked up and raised her eyebrows. They both knew it would be no surprise if the accusations were true. Mary used to be a maid in their household and, like Elisabeth, Mary knew Mr Pepys' weakness was resisting temptation, in whatever form it came.

'He's done nothing wrong,' repeated Elisabeth, to convince them both.

'Then he has nothing to fear,' Mary said. 'And anyway, your Sam was always a good persuader.' She lifted the fabric to the light. 'This would make a beautiful upper-skirt.'

Elisabeth frowned. Mary did not seem to realise the seriousness of the situation. 'It's not just that, Mary. Sam's convinced that the sailors are conspiring to revenge themselves on him for their lack of payment. Can you imagine! Yesterday, a great rabble of them besieged White Hall and spat at his feet. They narrowly avoided a riot. The King simply refuses to open his purse. I'm frightened to sleep in case they plunder us in the night.'

'Oh dear, what a muddle. Still, at least you have your new lady's maid at last. I've heard she's quite the genteel young lady.'

'She's not like you, though, Mary. She's too quiet. Never converses with me like you did. You were always my favourite. Come back to us, won't you?'

'You know I can't. I'm far too busy helping mother in the shop. And Miss Willet is a gem. You're fortunate to have found someone so lovely, everyone says so.'

* * *

Mary's words haunted Elisabeth all the way home in the carriage. She did not want everyone to think her lady's maid was lovely. She knew she was jealous, but she could not help herself. Sam would keep on looking at Deb like a lovesick swain, and, when she'd taken him to task about it, he'd told her she'd been reading too many romances and it was all her imagination.

Sam could be persistent, she knew. He'd refused to brook 'no' for an answer when he was courting her and had gone against all his parents' advice in his ardent insistence on marrying her. This thought should have comforted her, but it did not. It made Elisabeth feel as though her innards glowed white-hot. What if he became as persistent with Deb? She would have to do something.

Elisabeth went down to the kitchen and asked for a cloth to wipe the windows. 'Don't you be doing that,' Jane said. 'I'll get to it soon as I've finished the tarts for lunch. Or give it to Deb to do.'

But Elisabeth did not go. Instead, she leaned on the table and fiddled with the lappets on her cap. 'What do you think of her, Jane? How's she shaping up?'

Jane gave her a guarded look, the one that meant she was assessing what was the right answer.

'She's a bit forward, isn't she?' Elisabeth continued.

Jane grunted, non-committally, filled a cup from the butt by the back door, and went back to the pastry.

'It's always a risk, is it not, taking on new staff? They don't always settle in,' Elisabeth said. 'You'd tell me, wouldn't you, if Deb did anything … improper?'

Jane looked up again from her rolling pin, with a questioning look.

'You could keep a bit more of an eye on her.' Elisabeth traced her finger across the table before a sly glance from under her lashes. 'That sort of loyalty would be very well rewarded.'

Jane turned the pastry over on the table. She gave a brief nod. It was all that was needed to seal the unspoken contract between them.

Chapter Twelve

November

DEB WAS SURE ELISABETH HAD no notion of what she did when her day's work was over, squinting over Lord B's documents by the light of a candle. Though it irked her, this copying meant she could pay for Hester's music lessons. It still chafed her that Elisabeth refused to allow her two days off together so she could visit her sister, but she wrote nearly every day, and one of her greatest pleasures was Hester's letters in return.

Her copying nights were cut short, though, when Elisabeth arranged for dancing at home with her old dancing tutor. This made it awkward for Deb to retire early as she used to do. Worse, Deb was forced to dance with Mr Pepys, who held her too tight, and then she had to endure Elisabeth glowering her disapproval from the corner.

On one such night after the dancing, Mr Pepys told her to come to his study, instead of the main chamber, so that he could carry on reading while she combed his hair before bed. Deb sagged. She suspected it was because in his own study he could behave the way his wife would never have approved of in their main chamber.

Mr Pepys had taken to making comments as soon as Elisabeth was out of earshot, telling Deb how pretty she looked that day, or how the new slate-blue bodice from Unthank's suited her, so Deb kept herself well out of reach as she prepared the bowl of water and comb.

'My wife has no interest in the day's news.' Mr Pepys thrust the day's newsbook away. 'I can't understand it. When I try to tell her about what's happening at the Treasury, she just becomes irritable. What can a man do with such a wife?'

There was no answer to that, so Deb just shook her head.

'But you listen to me, don't you, Deb?' he said. 'You always hear me out.'

Yes, she thought, *but to be fair, that's because you pay me to listen. And I have little choice in the matter.*

'Now take these sailors and their pay.' He picked up a letter and brandished it at her. 'What am I to do? The King simply brushes me away.'

She carried on preparing the water with the dried herbs as he paced back and forth, his lace cuffs flapping as he talked.

'He will not listen to reason! He's more concerned with who's in his bed than what's in his coffers. And the fact we've lost control – that we can't keep the sailors down – is all over London.' He grabbed a paper from the desk and thrust it in front of her. 'Read this. "King's army called to skirmish on Broad Street."'

She took it from him and scanned the headlines. So much unrest. As if London had not endured enough: civil war; plague; fire – but its citizens must conjure more. The city had a fractious, bristling air, as if the very stones were unable to sleep easy.

'And that annoying parson, Mr Wells, was back, too. I told him I'd send for the constable if he didn't leave me alone.'

Heat rose to Deb's cheeks at the mention of his name. She must have been out on an errand when he came. She couldn't help a tinge of regret. She remembered his tawny eyes, how they seemed to see through her. Mr Pepys suddenly seemed older and fatter and more unattractive.

'Shall I do your hair now?' Deb was anxious to get the combing over and be out of his reach.

He sighed and pulled off his wig. 'Ah, Deb,' he said, 'my pretty peach. Come closer so I can have a little hug. I need one today.'

Deb dodged his open arms and pressed him down into the chair by his velvet padded shoulders. 'Later,' she said, to placate him. 'Let me do your head first.' She dipped the comb in the aromatic herbal water and stroked it through the stubble of his hair, looking out for the tell-tale signs of nits.

'How do you fancy another little outing to the theatre?' he asked. 'They are showing a new play at the Duke's.'

Deb thought quickly. The theatre was fast becoming an ordeal. 'Elisabeth will be too busy this week, what with the alterations. The plasterers have turned everything to sixes and sevens.'

'Of course, you're quite right. It might take a few days to get it back shipshape. Oh, how I wish I had not used that phrase! The Navy Board is causing me a mighty amount of grief right now. There's a man called Carkesse, an abject rogue if ever there was one. Things keep going missing – papers and books. Well, I threw him out of my office, caught him copying documents from my desk, no less, but of course he denies it. It's created a proper stink.'

Deb cringed, thought guiltily of Bruncker's navy papers under her mattress upstairs.

'As if that weren't enough, the scoundrel's accusing me – me! – of underhand dealings, of keeping goods that should go to the King. The cheek of it! Why, the whole thing could blow up into an even mightier scandal.'

'So does he work for the Treasury?'

'Until we can get rid of him. He's a—' He paused as she stepped away and examined the comb. 'Have you done already?'

Deb moved to the window, pushed open the shutter and brushed the flecks of black from the comb outside. Mr Pepys jumped up to follow her, still talking about the rogue in his office, but then he fell silent. Deb was not quite quick enough to get out of his reach. An arm slid around her waist and his lips fastened on to her neck.

'Such a pretty poppet,' he said, breathily. 'You have quite besotted me.'

'Don't be silly, Mr Pepys.'

He pushed her to arm's length, offended. 'I mean it. I've never been so captivated in my life. Here, feel my heart.' He pressed her palm to his chest, and indeed his heart thudded under it.

She dragged her hand away as if it were burned. She did not want to feel that, his blood pumping against her skin.

'Come here.' He wrapped his arms about her, but she wrenched away from him with a quick twist. 'Deb, what's the matter?' He staggered clumsily towards her.

'Isn't that Elisabeth calling?'

Mr Pepys paused an instant, tilted his head to listen. Deb grabbed the basin and fled the room.

At the kitchen sink she rinsed the comb in cold water and struggled to decide what to do. Should she tell Elisabeth? She was sure to blame Deb, not her husband; that was always the way of it with masters and servants. Besides, Aunt Beth's warnings rang in her ears. Any whiff of scandal and they would say, 'Like mother, like daughter.'

She closed her eyes. The image of her mother's face still clutched at her heart. It sobered her; she was both drawn to continuing her search for her, and afraid of what she might unearth. Someone with her mother's reputation could do nothing to help the difficulty with Mr Pepys.

She tapped the comb on the sink, then sneaked away to her chamber to calm herself. She did not know how to avoid Mr Pepys. Abigail's copying, still unfinished, caught her eye. She picked it up but set it down again. There was so much to do, it wore her out, and now this – Mr Pepys.

Given the circumstances, it would be wise to continue cultivating her friendship with Abigail Williams. Maybe she should take that position in her big new house in White Hall, once it was finished. She wondered how long it would take, and whether Abigail would be prepared to take her sooner. It might be a step down, for though Abigail had been kind to her, she could not miss the disdain Elisabeth held for 'Madam' Williams. Mr Pepys, on the other hand, was well respected in society. Aunt Beth had insisted it was a privilege to be working for Mr Pepys. But it did not seem quite such a privilege when you were trapped behind his closed door.

***

The next morning, another letter from Hester arrived, full of exclamations and chatter about her new activities: the crewelwork, the music lessons, the studies of the Psalms, and how she had a new friend, Lavinia.

Deb warmed with pride. Hester's handwriting was neater, and the way she expressed herself more mature – like a young lady. Deb's money paid for all of this. How could she disappoint her now? So there was no question of leaving, not unless she was certain of alternative well-paid employment with Abigail. At the same time, she knew Mr Pepys would be looking for excuses to catch her alone every minute, and she could tell by Elisabeth's watchful eyes that she was already alert to her husband's intentions.

If there was one thing she knew, it was that she must keep Hester at school. If Hester had to go back to Aunt Beth, her aunt would bully her into being a silent shadow of what she could be. She'd end up a skivvy, and Deb wanted more than that for her. Much more.

Chapter Thirteen
December

FOR THE NEXT MONTH, DEB was cautious and lingered over getting Mrs Pepys up before going downstairs, so she did not have to deal with her master's demands for company alone.

The week before Christmas she woke to hear moans. When she went up, Elisabeth was clutching her jaw and rocking back and forth.

'Toothache,' Elisabeth groaned, and demanded a cold compress, despite the fact there was ice on the inside of the windows and it was bitter enough to freeze the ale in the jug. Deb hurried to the kitchen and she and Jane made up a muslin bag of sweet-straw and herbs to ease the pain. The toothache persisted through the day and it was only by giving Elisabeth quantities of brandy that they were able to finally get her to sleep as darkness fell.

To Deb's relief, Mr Pepys was busy and distracted with business and working late with the Navy Board that evening, so Deb spent her time catching up with copying Lord Bruncker's notes for Abigail. Her chamber was bone-chillingly cold, but the week's supply of coals was being used for Elisabeth's fire, and she dare not light another in her chamber. She huddled in her cloak, with her fingers almost blue, cursing she had ever taken on Abigail's work, but determined to get it done.

The next day Elisabeth was no better and had to take to her bed again, leaving Deb and Jane to make all the mince and sweetmeat pies, and to fetch the dry foodstuffs for the Christmas dinner. As if she wasn't busy enough, a messenger boy came with a note.

"The tiring house, Duke's Playhouse, four bells – A W"

Deb screwed up the note and thrust it into the kitchen fire. There was no time for this today. It was the third time Abigail had done this, sent a message demanding Deb should meet her, with no concern for how inconvenient it might be, nor what she should tell Elisabeth. There was never any news from her notice, either, even though she had replaced the old one, which had got torn down.

Whenever Abigail sent a message, Bruncker's boy would only take a reply if Deb paid him, so she had to turn up as requested or be obliged to pay for a reply to decline. Abigail's 'few papers' had turned into thicker bundles week by week, and her insistence on exactitude had started to feel almost threatening.

Deb realised she was being manipulated, and resented it, but thought it wise to keep at least one other door open in case Mr Pepys should prove too awkward and she needed another position in a hurry. After the midday meal, she fetched her folder and put it at the bottom of the basket, glad that at least she would not have to lie to Elisabeth, whose face was now so swollen she could do little but groan in bed, clutching the fresh compress.

Deb skirted a pile of horse droppings as she went, lifting her skirts from the slippery cobbles. The weather was foggy, laced with a cold that sucked the warmth from her marrow, not the crisp white frosty Yuletide she longed for. Everyone seemed to have agues and colds, and the handkerchief peddlers and medicine men were out in force plying a brisk trade.

She took a small diversion as she always did, to pass the makeshift church of St Gabriel's on Fenchurch Street. She could not help being curious to see where Mr Wells was curate. She had passed the rough wooden church several times in the last few months hoping for a glimpse of him, but so far he had eluded her. Today, though, her heart gave a bound as she spotted him just tacking up a parchment to the church noticeboard. She watched him as he hammered in a nail, admiring his broad shoulders and his auburn hair caught back in a black sash. Did she dare? She decided to be bold; there was no harm in being friendly.

'Season's wishes to you, Mr Wells,' she called, waving.

He turned and his face lit up. 'Good afternoon, Miss Willet. How are you?'

'I'm well but Mrs Pepys is poorly.' She explained about the toothache.

'I'm done here, if you would like my protection from wild dogs or rampaging mobs.'

She smiled, a little embarrassed, and found herself wishing she had put on a more becoming dress.

'I'm just trying to gather a bit of a flock for the Christmas services,' he said, pointing to his notice. 'We can't seem to keep a congregation now, no matter what we do, not with our draughty boathouse of a church. Such a shame. St Gabriel's was a fine old building, dated back to the Normans, but since the fire, Dr Thurlow must make do with this pile of old timbers. That, or preach on top of the rubble.'

'Will they rebuild it, do you think?' she asked.

'Doubt it. There's talk of amalgamating it with one of the others – St Margaret's. I've been there on loan for the last two months. Dr Thurlow's in a right stew about it. May I walk with you?'

Deb hesitated. She did not want to say 'no', because she liked him. At the same time, Elisabeth had been more than clear on her rule of 'no followers'. 'So sorry,' she said, 'but not today, I'm afraid I'm pressed for time; I've arranged to meet someone.'

'Oh.' His face fell.

'A lady,' she said, wondering why she was reassuring him. Then, feeling even more flustered and foolish, she blurted, 'But I could come to one of your services if you like.' Elisabeth could hardly object to her going to church.

'Would you? That would be marvellous. There's one the day after tomorrow, six o'clock. I'm preaching, and ... well, I need all the support I can muster.'

'I can't promise, but if Elisabeth doesn't need me to sit with her, I'll come.'

'Be sure to wait for me at the church door afterwards. We could have a stroll together then.'

Deb gave a little bob, realised that that was what servants did, and cursed herself. Jem's eager expression showed he was pleased, and as she hurried away, she was acutely aware that he would be watching. She moved lightly, like thistledown. It was all she could do not to skip. Then she remembered the documents in her basket and was immediately sobered. Somehow she did not think the parson Jeremiah Wells would approve of an actress like Abigail Williams.

At the Duke's tiring house, Abigail was already waiting, dressed in a dark riding habit of damson wool with a jet trim and a hat tied down with a quantity of Seville lace. Around her neck hung another fur, this time as black and glossy as dried ink.

'Come, we won't stay here, we'll go to the tavern where it is warm,' Abigail said.

'I'm afraid I haven't the time. Elisabeth has a terrible toothache and I've all the week's shopping to do. If you could just tell me—'

'A few moments. I won't keep you long. I have some more business I want to discuss with you.'

'Can it wait until after Christmas? I'm already behind with the last papers. Elisabeth needs nursing and I promised her I'd—'

'No, it can't wait.' Abigail said, and set off down the alley, so that Deb had no option but to follow. The alleyway leading away from the Duke's Playhouse was narrow. Half burnt-out timbers of jetty windows stretched overhead. In the gloom, Abigail's dark figure almost disappeared.

Deb resigned herself to it. She hurried to catch up, and Abigail cast her a knowing sideways smile. It grated on Deb, this feeling that Abigail knew exactly how to make her do her bidding. Eventually they came to a smoke-stained tavern which advertised rooms to let. They went in through the back door.

'Do they not find it unusual, ladies coming in here by themselves?' Deb asked.

'They have a room set aside. It is one I always use. I pay them well for it and they know to turn a blind eye to my comings and goings. I shall be meeting someone else here after you.'

The room they entered was cramped and gloomy, but there was a small fire smoking in the hearth. In this unlikely place, Abigail seemed too clean, with her face ghostly pale with ceruse, her twinkling rings. Deb avoided examining the stained cushion on the bench too closely and kept her elbows off the pocked table with its ring-marks of wax and grease; its dinginess and dirt offended her.

'You have my copying?'

'Yes. They are documents about the manning of ships, are they not?'

Abigail stared. 'How do you know that?'

'I worked out the code. It was a simple substitution cipher, but the words have been organised into even lengths to make it harder to find short words like "*the*". And it was clever – sometimes an extra "*t*" has been added to make the word lengths even, especially at the end of paragraphs. Quick and easy to produce, but hard to unravel.' She brought out the papers and pointed at the letter "*p*" dotted amongst the other letters. 'See here. Of course, the "*p*" must be an "*e*" – the most common letter, and from that, if I ignored the false word-spacing, I found "*the*" – the most common word. Then I had the "*t*"s and the "*h*"s. I had to be careful not to confuse the added "*t*"s with the actual "*t*"s. So it went on.'

'Can you read it all?'

Deb could not conceal her pride. 'Except for some of the more complicated names. They aren't easy to translate. You're not angry with me, are you?'

'What does it say?'

'It's a message from Pepys to a Mr Brakes, about Clarendon, the Lord Chancellor and how he has fled.

And it praises Coventry for his administration and—'

'Have you been able to translate any of the other papers?' Abigail interrupted, her eyes hard and narrow.

'No,' Deb said hastily, 'this was the first time I tried.' She crossed her fingers at this untruth. Unwittingly, she was getting to be quite an expert on the affairs of the navy.

'Good. You don't need to translate the things I give you. Better for you if you don't.'

'What do you mean?'

'Just, it is not necessary.' Her brisk manner had returned. 'Especially with the new commission I am to give you.'

'Is it more papers to decipher?' She brightened.

'Perhaps. This will be a little business on the side, apart from the copying. I have found your work most satisfactory, and you are lucky, you have access to certain information, information that I will pay for, provided you are discreet.'

'What information?'

Abigail lowered her voice. 'You must tell nobody, understand? If I confide in you, you must not break my trust. My life, both our lives, could be at stake if you do. Do you understand?'

'Yes.' Deb nodded, but she was bemused. Abigail's sudden gravity intrigued her.

'The King wishes to know what goes on in the Navy Office.'

The King! Deb raised her eyebrows. No wonder Abigail was being so careful.

Abigail's expression showed she was pleased at the impression her words had made. 'Since the war with the Dutch, and the naval enquiry into the Medway affair, I've been helping His Majesty by supplying the

Crown with certain documents. The King suspects that Pepys is taking advantage of him by plundering enemy ships before their contents are inventoried to the Crown. He wants to find out if this is true.'

'You mean, you are sending my documents to the King?' She suddenly understood. So this was why she was transcribing papers. It was not for Lord Bruncker's files at all, but so Abigail could pass them to the King. No wonder Abigail had demanded such secrecy.

A bead of sweat had formed between her breasts, and she pressed her hand to her bodice. It seemed unbelievable that her copying, her penmanship, might at this very moment be in the actual hand of the King himself.

'His Majesty was concerned that Bruncker might be withholding certain information from him and asked me to copy some of the documents. My eyes are not as good as they were and for such a client there must be no mistakes in the accuracy.'

'No. I understand. I hope it is good enough. I have done my best.'

'But the King is not satisfied. He also suspects Pepys is not to be trusted. These rumours – the ones saying Pepys lines his pockets from captured ships, well, they mean that he cannot trust his own officers. You have heard of Carkesse's accusations?'

She nodded. 'Mr Pepys mentioned it.'

'Deceiving the Crown and stealing the King's dues is a serious business.'

'I'm sure Mr Pepys would not wish to harm the King. He is his loyal servant.'

'On the contrary, he was a Puritan in his youth. He had no love for the King's father then. And I suspect none for this young pup on the throne, either.'

Deb remembered Mr Pepys' jibes to Elisabeth, that

the King did not care a whit for the country or the navy – he was too busy bedding Mrs Castlemaine.

Abigail leaned forward again. 'The King simply wants to know whether he can trust your Mr Pepys.'

'What do you want me to do?'

'There are papers at Pepys' house that I want you to copy. A friend of mine, a Mr Evelyn, has heard Pepys writes a diary. If this is true, then the King would like a transcript. He does not want Pepys to know, because it would serve him well if Pepys carries on writing it.'

Deb had a sudden vision of Mr Pepys' cosy study, his rapt face as he played the viol, his urgent scribbling, his heaped papers in disarray on the desk behind him.

'I'm not sure. It doesn't feel right to take his private papers. There might be consequences for other people, and I don't want to be responsible.'

It was as if she hadn't spoken. Abigail leaned in close. 'The King wants copies of Pepys' documents. Anything at all he brings home from the office. They will need to be copied carefully and then returned precisely to their place. But most especially his diary. You will need to be even more careful with that; according to Evelyn, Pepys was boasting he used a personal cipher. And the copying must be word for word, stroke for stroke. There must be no mistakes if the documents are going to His Majesty.'

'But I'll lose my place if they find out! And Mrs Pepys might be something of a fusser, but she has been a good employer.'

'It will be lucrative. The King pays me very well to be his eyes and ears, and in turn I will pay you handsomely when you retrieve the information I need. Besides, as his subject, you have a duty to the

King. Not to help him would be ... how shall I put it? Treason.'

Abigail turned away a moment, took a draught of ale.

Deb did not reach for her drink. Surely Abigail could not mean it? The walls of the tavern seemed to have closed in on her. She balled up her skirt in her hand, seized by a desire to run, but Abigail seemed to read her mind. She fixed her with her glittering dark eyes. 'You have little choice. What the King demands is more important than any personal loyalty. Besides, I want to see you rise in society, Deb dear. Think of it! You will be working for the King himself. Who knows where that might lead?'

'But how will I find the time? Already Mrs Pepys—'

'Her? You'll find a way round her. She's just another stupid French pauper who bedded her way into society.'

Deb was shocked. 'Don't talk about her like that. They are respectable people.' The words were out before she realised the irony of them. 'You're rushing me. I need to think, to order it in my thoughts.'

Abigail shrugged. 'Dig deep beneath any gilded surface and you will find the same dirt. Best choose the thickest gold you can.'

'But what if Mr Pepys catches me doing it?'

'That must not happen. Knowing Pepys as I do, I'll wager he is perfectly aware of you, and there's profit in that, too, if you keep your wits.'

Deb blushed. How had she guessed?

'I don't know how much longer I can stay there. I was hoping that you might be able to—'

'No.' Abigail cut her off. 'You must stay at the Pepyses for now.'

'He's ... he's very insistent.'

Abigail looked at her shrewdly. 'Then you are fortunate. There will be more leverage in it. You will need to make sure every little transaction is an exchange though; that he gives you something you want in return. Something you can gain by ... like his papers.'

Was she suggesting she should sell her favours? Deb straightened her back, set her jaw. 'No. Not that. I can't—'

Abigail smiled, though her expression was cold, her eyes darkening. 'Perhaps you need a little more persuasion.' Abigail drew out the white book from her leather bag and held it out. 'It is no good protesting, for you have already begun. Didn't you guess? Of course, I could always take your copying to the magistrate. Theft from your employer is a hanging offence ...'

Deb stared at it, not comprehending.

'You stole this, did you not, from Mr Pepys' office?'

'Lord Bruncker's book, yes.'

'Not my Lord Bruncker's, no. This book belongs to Mr Pepys.'

Chapter Fourteen

FROM ABOVE, ELISABETH'S GROANS echoed down the stairs, for another day had passed and the bad tooth was worse than ever. Deb scurried up and down with cloves and feverfew. Elisabeth did not deserve such torture, Deb thought, no matter how much she frayed Deb's temper.

As Deb mixed a soothing draught, she brooded over her meeting with Abigail, unable to resolve the dilemma. The churning in the pit of her stomach had left her sleepless and exhausted. To distract them both she tried reading to Elisabeth one of her favourite romances.

'For God's sake, leave me in peace!'Elisabeth yelled after only half a paragraph. Deb went, but left her howling like a woman in labour, coddling her jaw.

Deb was so frightened by how bad it was she decided to brave Mr Pepys in his study. 'I beg you, sir, send for the tooth puller straightaway. She cannot go on like this.'

'Is that what she wishes?' he asked.

'No, she fears it. But something must be done or her face will be ruined. It is the size of a cow's udder now.'

'I had better go and see,' he said. But he made no

move. 'Just a little kiss first, to welcome me home, hey, Deb?' He held out his arms.

'Your wife needs you, sir,' she said. 'Best look to her.' She almost ran down the stairs.

When she got to the kitchen she looked over her shoulder, but he was not following.

'Mr Pepys, is it?' Jane asked wryly. 'I wondered how long it would be.'

'Is he always the same? But why? Elisabeth dotes on him.'

'I don't know. Because he can, I suppose. But it's turned into a sort of weakness with him. The women in the market, the orange girls at the theatre, we all let him touch a bit; we have to, to keep him sweet. Men like him, they're our living, see? I'm warning you, though, Elisabeth's got wise to what he's like, so best if you don't go encouraging him.'

'I'm not—' Deb's protestation was interrupted by Mr Pepys' footsteps coming down the stairs.

They shut their mouths and curtsied, red-faced.

'She won't have the tooth pulled,' he said, 'but she says I can send for Hollier. My boy's already out on an errand. Would you hurry over and tell him to call, Deb? Here's his address.'

So Deb had to fetch Hollier, the chirurgeon, who looked like an old goat with his greying beard and watery eyes. But he could only do what they had already done, which was to lay on poultices and give Elisabeth brandy. When at last she looked to be sleeping, Deb told Jane she was going to church.

'Now?'

'I thought to send up prayers for Elisabeth.'

Jane looked sceptical, but could not object, so Deb bundled on her cloak, pulling up the hood against the freezing rain. But instead of St Olave's, she hastened into the city until she came to St Gabriel's. By the time she got there it was sleeting, and the service had started, but gratefully she slipped inside at the back. She hoped no one who knew the Pepyses would be there. It was most irregular for her to be out at night without her mistress.

She hoped she might be just in time to hear Mr Well's sermon. Her stomach danced a flutter at the thought of him. She told herself it would give her time to think, to pray about the business with Abigail Williams and the King.

The ramshackle wooden church was lit by candles which shivered in the draught, making the whole place like a flickering cavern. Not many had turned out in this bitter weather with the sleet lashing against the roof and water dripping through the gaps between the wooden tiles.

Deb sat near the back and was warmed to see Mr Wells welcome the congregation with a hearty, 'God be with you.' It was a moment before he spotted her, but when he did, his eyes caught hers, and her insides quickened. She had to look down into her lap at her prayer book so he wouldn't see how hot she'd become.

The sermon was on the Good Shepherd, something Deb was rather over-familiar with, but she settled down to listen, watching his animated face persuade her of the usefulness of sheep.

'If you grew up in the country like I did,' he said, his voice ringing out from the pulpit, 'you'd know that sheep are foolish beasts – little sense of direction and no sharp teeth or claws to protect them, so is it any surprise then that they need guidance?' He glanced around to check people were listening. Behind Deb, a woman coughed, but Jem fired on, leaning forward in the pulpit, arms spread wide as if to embrace the meagre congregation.

'How much are we like sheep? Is it any wonder that the Bible repeatedly reminds humans of their need for a shepherd? Sheep are not bad, just lost. They need help to find the right path. The good shepherd doesn't allow his sheep to wander, but instead he feeds his flock with a proper source of nourishment, something that will both sustain and improve them. On what, though? Why, the Word of God of course! For the Scriptures are the only words that are given from the Great Shepherd Himself. Those words are the only words that will satisfy the hunger of the flock.'

Deb was stirred by his speech. He made it sound so simple, this putting yourself in the arms of the Good Shepherd. As if the world was full of moral certainties, not the foggy choices that had plagued her life since she had come to London. She baulked at the idea of deceiving the Pepyses, yet she could not, in all conscience, disobey her sovereign, God's representative on earth.

When the time came to kneel, she groaned under her breath, pressed her clasped hands to her forehead. She needed Mr Wells' self-assurance, his conviction, to know whether she was doing the right thing. Looking at him, it seemed he had not a doubting bone in his body, with his face all glowing and his eyes sparkling with health, and the promise that the glory of the Lord was all his for the taking.

He intoned the Lord's Prayer to the congregation, his eyes closed, face upturned. In the candlelight, she thought she had never seen a more beautiful human being. Awed, at the end of the service she waited for him nervously at the church door.

'I saw you at the back,' he said. 'I'm glad you're still here.'

He was waiting for her to say something. All at once she was too shy to meet his gaze. 'It was a good sermon, Mr Wells … wonderful, I mean.'

An expression of relief lit up his face. 'Really?' he said. 'If you liked it you must come back another day. And it's Jem, to my friends.'

'I don't know if I'll be allowed – Mr Pepys likes us all to worship at St Olave's. He calls it "our little church".'

'"Little church"? Good heavens! It's *enormous*. I can't compete with St Olave's. As you can see, here we need all the faithful we can get. Only three more evening services until Christmas Eve, would you believe? I could do to go out with my crook and round up a few more lost sheep!' His laughter was deep and warm. Deb had been impressed with how he had preached and was entranced now by his good humour.

After the last worshipper had left, Jem threw on a cloak and locked up the hefty wooden door. He thrust the key in his waistcoat pocket, blew on his hands then rubbed them together, and set off purposefully in the direction of the Thames. 'I know the weather isn't ideal, but shall we have a stroll on the bridge?' he asked.

She nodded and they jostled their way past all the other folk trying to pass over the river. The sleet gave way to an intermittent drizzle. When her cloak flapped open, he slipped his arm in hers and she was surprised to feel the heat of his arm through her woollen sleeve. And he'd asked her to call him 'Jem'. It gave her a tingle of excitement. She told him about Hollier's visit and how Elisabeth was in too much pain to want company. In turn, he told her about how he had come up from Cambridge to work with the church on helping the many poor and dispossessed of London.

The way he talked of it made it sound easy and straightforward, the collecting of stale, unsold bread from bakeries all over London, distributing it from a hand barrow. She was amazed he did this. Her aunt had always taught her that the homeless poor were to be avoided at all costs, as if poverty was a disease you could catch.

About a third of the way across the bridge, burnt-out houses gave way to buildings that had escaped the fire, and Jem led her through a narrow alley between the two blocks of houses. From here they could look down to the 'starlings' below, where the water funnelled through in a foaming brown tide. Looking down made her shiver, partly from cold and partly from fear.

Jem put his arm about her shoulders to steady her. 'I love looking down, don't you? Especially knowing that we're safe up here behind these walls.'

They watched the water churn and gush below. Deb's stomach was churning too, but with a strange anticipation. Suddenly light-headed, she stood up to move away, but he caught her in his arms, looked into her face.

A cold spot of rain dropped on her cheek. 'I'd like to kiss you,' he said. 'I've wanted to ever since I first set eyes on you, but I think it too soon, so I'll not presume to ask.'

She pulled away, from some habit of self-preservation, and because she did not know how to answer. Was he asking her, or wasn't he?

'Oh, I've offended you,' he said.

'No, no you haven't.' She was suddenly and unaccountably tearful. She wanted him to kiss her. If he did, it might be like a charm, a touch of holiness that would ward off Mr Pepys. She swallowed, looked away. She did not want to feel so affected by – no, confused by – this man.

'It's my fault,' he said. 'I shouldn't open my big mouth before I've had time to think. I do beg your pardon. I'm not used to female company. Too much sitting in church meetings. You must be cold. I'll walk you back to Seething Lane now, and I promise I won't mention it again.'

The trouble was, she really wanted him to mention it again. She didn't want to go home to Mr Pepys, nor did she want to carry out Abigail's instructions of copying his diary for the King. She wanted to stay out here on the bridge where she didn't have to make any decisions.

And all the while they were walking back, she walked stiffly, Jem's every touch on her arm like a fire burning through the cloth of her sleeve, through her chemise, to make the hairs on her arms stand up as if they, too, wanted to be noticed. She did not want him to take his arm away – she was alight with the touch of him and how it might feel to have her first kiss.

Chapter Fifteen

THE NEXT DAY, IN AMONGST a deluge of letters for the Pepyses, presumably containing seasonal greetings, there were two letters for Deb. One showed Hester's girlish writing, the other Aunt Beth's spiky hand. Aunt Beth rarely wrote, and when she did it was always about money. Deb opened it with trepidation.

> *"19th December 1667*
> *Dear Deborah,*
> *I write to inform you that I can no longer keep Hester at home, as I intend to pay an extended visit to your father in Ireland. I need to see for myself what ails his business. He tells me he has debts. I can scarcely believe this to be true, but so he says.*
>
> *After the New Year, Hester will either have to return with me to her father, which she insists she has no wish to do, or you must make arrangements for her to stay at school. Of course,*

- 136 -

*if she is to continue with her
schooling at Bow then she must
be prepared to take board with
the school, and it will be at your
expense.*

*I asked your father for
assistance, but he denied her.
Things must be bad. He will
only help if she returns to
Ireland, which the foolish girl
refuses to consider. I'm at my
wits' end what to do with her,
because as I told her father, she
is becoming quite ungovernable.*

I await your speedy reply ... "

The second letter was, as she had anticipated, a
hurriedly scribbled appeal from Hester begging to stay
at school. It had an address in Henley at the top, so
Deb scanned it with concern.

*"Oh joy! You can see from
the address that Lavinia has
invited me to stay with her for
their Christmas festivities.
Wasn't that kind of them? I was
simply dreading having to go to
Aunt Beth. She is worse since
you went, the birch always in
her hand, convinced I am on the
verge of some misdeed. I can
never do right by her, no matter
what I do.*

*Now she says I'm to give up
my schooling and must go to*

- 137 -

> *Father in Ireland. Please, Deb, I*
> *can barely remember him, and I*
> *couldn't bear it, to be so far from*
> *England and you. And I know if*
> *I had to have three days on a*
> *ship with Aunt Beth I'd be ready*
> *to throw myself off into the sea!*
> *And just when I was mastering*
> *my Latin declensions!*
> *I wondered if I could come*
> *to you? You could tell Mrs Pepys*
> *I'd be quiet as a mouse, and I*
> *hardly eat anything. I'd be no*
> *trouble if you'd have me."*

Deb folded both letters and put them in the drawer of her travelling trunk. She could not let Hester go to Ireland; that was clear. Father did not want her, and Aunt Beth only kept her under sufferance. No, money would have to be found to keep her at school. And certainly she could not come to London. The very thought of her being under the same roof as Mr Pepys, and subject to his wandering palms, made Deb hug her arms around her chest, as if protecting her own heart would somehow protect Hester.

No matter what happened, Hester must stay at Bow where she was safe, and Deb would have to find the money for her board somehow.

The sun rose smouldering over the city as Deb rinsed out the nit comb and shook it hard, trying to still her nerves. Above, she heard the faint moan as Elisabeth tossed and turned, still in pain. She picked up the tray and knocked softly on Mr Pepys' study door. As yet, she had not been able to muster the courage to try to find out where Mr Pepys' diary was. She kept putting it off, knowing he was sharp and perhaps would see through her clumsy enquiries, and she was scared of being alone with him, of the awkwardness of having to negotiate his desire for her.

But Abigail's word 'treason' had shaken her – she knew what happened to traitors. She'd seen the convict ships setting sail for faraway heathen lands, the dangling half-fleshed bones on the tree at Tyburn.

If finding the diary was the way to fund Hester's schooling, then she had better begin now. She remembered Abigail telling her that a woman must be practical, and line her pocket while she could. Deb could see the sense in it, and reasoning this way gave her the illusion that she had a choice.

She knocked again, louder.

'Come, come!' Mr Pepys, always an early riser, threw open the door, then trotted over and patted the chair next to his, where he had set out some books and maps on the table.

Deb saw that his boy servant was not there, so when she took the chair, she first pulled it away a little more out of reach. Mr Pepys countered by nudging his own chair closer and reaching his arm round her shoulder. Deb felt its weight, just as she felt the weight of her responsibility to the King.

'Elisabeth asks if you will consider new curtains,' Deb began. 'She says the chamber is too draughty, now she has to lie in it all day.'

'Again?' Mr Pepys huffed out a long breath. 'We only just changed them. Never mind that, I've brought you a pamphlet with pictures of the proposed plans for London. You can have first look, before I take it to show everyone at the office.' He tapped his finger on the map. 'Look, it shows the rebuilt Exchange and plans for St Paul's. I have to say, these buildings look mighty fine, don't you think?'

Deb stood again to look, dodging his other hand, which was on its way to her bottom. 'Is that what the Exchange will look like?' Despite herself, she was interested. Plans and maps had always intrigued her, and these plans made the new trading hall look impressive.

'Aha! I knew you'd agree with me! Splendid, isn't it? It's to be designed by Mr Wren, in the Italian style. Bigger than the last, with wider aisles. And see here – the new St Paul's might even have a covered alley for the booksellers to congregate. Come and sit here on my knee, and I'll show you.'

She moved to the other side of the table. 'You must be one of the bookmen's best customers, Mr Pepys. When I came, I'd never seen so many books, not owned by one man. Not even locked in the library at my school.'

Mr Pepys smiled. 'They are my one weakness. I'm thinking of having these new ones bound too, so that they match the volumes I have in the cases.' He pointed to the bookshelves behind him.

'Sir, have you never thought of writing a book yourself?'

'Often. But I have not the time. The Navy Board and the Treasury demand too much of my leisure. So no. Perhaps when I'm old and grey.'

Deb took a deep breath. 'Elisabeth told me you write your pages every day ...'

'Did she? Well, that's true, but it is not for the public. It's a record only for my own interest.'

'What do you put in it?'

'Oh, this and that. The day's events, where I've

been and so forth.' He patted his chest as if to congratulate himself.

'Am I in it?' She gave him her most coquettish look.

'No, my dove. It's things about politics mostly.'

'Elisabeth?'

He laughed, but rubbed his chin, embarrassed. 'No, not really. Only in passing. It's a record of the times. How things are turning out now the King is back. I never thought I'd keep it up, but once I've begun something, well, I can't seem to stop. I call it a chronicle. Though you would have had to have lived through the wars and Cromwell's day for it to have much meaning, and you're far too y—. I mean, you would likely find it dull.'

'It sounds like a fine idea. I know so little about those times, and I'd love to see something you've written. Won't you let me have a little peep?'

The battle went on in his face; he was flattered she was taking so much interest, but was still reluctant to show it to her. Finally, he said, 'I'm afraid the pages wouldn't make much sense to you. I write in tachygraphy.'

'I'm not familiar with tachy—?' she said, although she already knew of the word. She moved closer to Mr Pepys again and traced her finger over the pamphlet in front of them.

He swallowed, his gaze trailing over the front of her bodice. 'Shorthand. I use it for taking notes at meetings and when I need to write something fast.'

She went to stand next to him. 'I've never seen it. How does it work?'

'It's too complicated for you to be studying, Deb. It's not something you will ever need.' He nuzzled his face into her shoulder. 'Now, sit here on my lap, and let's look at these plans.'

She stepped away. 'I could write the lists for Elisabeth. Imagine, me going to the market with my shorthand!'

He laughed.

'And you could write someone a message, and nobody else would be able to read it,' she said slyly. 'Except someone else who could read shorthand.'

She saw him consider this advantage by the way he scratched his forehead where it met his wig. 'Little minx, you've pressed me. Go on then, fetch me that quill over there, and I'll show you.'

She went over to the side table and picked up the quill and bottle. Meanwhile, he had bustled across to a drawer and pulled out a piece of parchment. He laid it out flat, weighted it, and uncorked the ink.

'Shelton's method,' he said. 'Look, this is what we do. Come, sit here.' He hitched her onto one knee where she sat uncomfortably. It felt odd and undignified to have her feet dangle off the ground. She hadn't done this since she was a child.

Mr Pepys dipped his quill into the bottle and drew out a series of signs, more like squiggles than actual letters. 'These are the consonants,' he said. 'And then these are the vowels.' A series of diagonal strokes with little cups beside them. '*Tall, tell, till, toll, tull, teal ...*'With each word his fingers walked further up her thigh. He had made her a child, and she resented it.

She stood his touch as long as she could. Many of the documents she had copied for Abigail were written in a similar way, and she had worked it out without any help, but this was a different and more complex system altogether.

Her attention was brought back with a jolt as Mr

Pepys' hand tried to go between her legs. She slid off his knee, just in time. His hand grabbed for her skirts but she twitched them away.

He caught her by the shoulder. 'Shall I write your name, little Deb?' His voice was breathy in her ear.

'In shorthand?' She spied the advantage immediately. 'I should like to see that. How about ... the cat sat on the mat? In shorthand though, to show me how it's done.' She kept her distance, alert as a stalked deer.

He picked up his pen. Made a few deft strokes on a scrap of paper. Then more. Soon he was scribbling furiously. When he'd done, she saw him add a flourish, his quill sweeping an extravagant curlicue across the paper.

'Come and see,' he said.

She walked over and looked over his shoulder at the unfathomable dark strokes. The symbols were written in short lines, like a poem.

'Can you read it?' he asked.

She shook her head, though she was already running through possibilities, trying to solve the puzzle.

'Just as well.' He stood, took her face between his hands. 'You are beautiful,' he said.

From upstairs came the sound of Elisabeth's muffled voice, calling thickly, 'Sam? Are you not ready yet? You'll be late. They'll be waiting for you at the office. Tell Deb I need more cloves, and my fire's nearly burned out.'

He turned away suddenly, as though a bucket of cold water had soused him from above.

'Coming now, dear,' he called.

Deb curtseyed, aware all at once of her precarious position in the household. 'Your vest and coat are on the hook, sir, and your hot water's on the side. Can I keep this, the note?'

He slapped his hand down on the sheet to stop her taking it. 'What will you give me, my pretty dove?'

Deb froze, but did not let go of the sheet.

'One kiss?'

Deb faltered. She thought of Jem. He'd said he wanted to kiss her on the bridge, and she'd promised herself she would say 'yes' if he asked again. Her first kiss was for Jem. The words were definite in her head, though still she dithered.

'No kiss, no poem.'

Abigail's threats buzzed in her ears. Hester's pleas to stay at school. Her wish not to offend her employer. She hesitated a moment too long. Mr Pepys reached over, pulled her to him and pressed his fleshy lips heavily down on hers. She bore it a moment and then twisted to free herself. His stubble scraped across her cheek.

She jerked away, snatched up the paper from the table and made for the door.

'I'll fetch Elisabeth's cloves,' she said, curtseying as she knew she must, blinking back tears, feeling like a kind of Judas.

When she'd dealt with Elisabeth, she went to her room, rubbed at her mouth with her sleeve. Be practical, she scolded herself. It was only a kiss, no harm done. She unfolded the paper. She hadn't got his diary, but the shorthand was a start. She could search out his diary if she knew it was written in script like this.

All day she kept returning to the puzzle of the shorthand, trying to remember what Mr Pepys had said about the strokes for the consonants and vowels, and making little guesses at the text. Finally it was there in front of her.

Before she had even translated the second line, she recognised it. Shakespeare.

> *"My love is as a fever, longing
> still."*

One of his sonnets to the Dark Lady, with all the connotations of that forbidden affair.

> *"For I have sworn thee fair, and
> thought thee bright,
> Who art as black as hell, as dark
> as night."*

Chapter Sixteen

THE NEXT DAY, A SILENCE. Unnerved, Deb peered out of the window. The dark streets were gone, and snow veiled the rooftops, covering the city dirt and squalor with its virgin white. Her heart lifted. The day before Christmas Eve, she hoped it would last. Elisabeth was in pain and tutted over the weather, giving Deb a long list of errands, but today, Deb did not care; she was mightily relieved to get away from the house, out of Mr Pepys' sight.

She'd woken with the poem running round inside her head. *It's just a poem*, she chided herself. Perhaps it was the first thing Mr Pepys thought of. But she knew she was deceiving herself; she remembered the hungry look in his eyes. She crunched through the streets, feet stinging with cold. She was to go to the wood merchant to remind them to deliver the Yule log, and besides that, there was fetching beans to make a spiced bean-cake, and collecting the bread that Jane would need for stuffing the goose.

She took a deep breath, put her employer from her mind. After the oppressive confines of Pepys' chambers, it was delightful to see all the houses of the Navy buildings with their hoops of frosted greenery set above the doors. Here, in Seething Lane, the willow boughs were hung with nutmegs or with baubles, and one even had carved figures of the Nativity. She was standing staring up at it, admiring the craftsmanship, when a hand came down on her arm.

She jolted and spun round, fearing to see Mr Pepys, but it was Jem Wells, nose red with cold, a beaver-fur hat pulled over his ears.

'I was waiting for you to come out,' he said, 'on purpose.' He opened his mouth and began to sing to her.

'So now is come our joyfull'st feast
Let ev'ry man be jolly.
Each room with ivy leaves is dress't
And every post with holly.'

His voice was enthusiastic but tuneless, so she took up the tune with him and they sang it again together. A passing dame stopped to watch, a smile on her face, and at the end they fell into laughter.

'Merry Christmas, Miss Willet,' he said.

'And to you, Mr Wells.'

'I'm just about to go to meet Dr Thurlow to bless the thresholds, so I wanted to catch you before I went. How is Mrs Pepys' toothache?'

'Better. The swelling's less, but she's tired from lack of sleep these last few nights, so she's resting.'

'That's good. I hoped you'd be on your own.'

'I'll need six pairs of hands though. I've a mountain of purchases to make.'

'I wish I could help, but I've an appointment with a parishioner at eleven. The thing is, Miss Willet, from tomorrow my time will be taken up with services and charitable works, and visiting my parents. They're insisting I go there after the Christmas service to share the family supper, even though it's a few hours' ride.

But to be frank, you've been much on my mind. I wanted to wish you the compliments of the season.'

'Will you be away long?' She tried to hide her pleasure that he had thought of her.

'Not if I can help it. Too many attractions in the city. Like you, Miss Willet.'

She didn't know what to say.

'Here, I have a New Year gift for you – that is, if you'll accept it.'

'Oh, you shouldn't have—'

'It's only a small thing, just a token. Of my esteem, I mean.' He offered her a small woven box tied with a scarlet ribbon.

She took it, noting the sprig of ivy pushed into the ribbon. *Ivy – for binding,* her mother used to say. 'But I have nothing for you.' It pricked her not to have anything to offer in return.

'Perhaps you might permit me ... as it's Christmas ... a kiss under ...'

He was already reaching for her, and she only had time to take a breath of frosty air before his arms came around her back and his hot lips brushed gently against hers. The box was pressed between them, digging into her chest. It was over in a moment, leaving her reeling, her senses all aflame. When she opened her eyes he was gazing down into them and the black of his irises made her feel faint. She opened her mouth to speak but found she could not say a word.

The moment seemed to hang. When he released her shoulders, the iron ring of hooves clopping past seemed too loud, the plaintive cries of the street traders and the scrape of a street sweeper's brush, too coarse.

At the same time, the thought of that other kiss

came. She evaded his eyes, assailed by sudden guilt and shame.

'I've got to go,' she heard herself say. 'I've got far too much to do.'

His face creased in disappointment. 'I'm sorry if I offended—'

'No, oh please, no. You didn't, it's just ...' She tucked the box in her basket, her lips burning. 'Thank you for the gift. But I must hurry. You see, there's all the shopping ...'

'Well, Merry Christmas, Miss Willet,' he said, his eyes suddenly distant and guarded.

'And to you, Mr Wells.'

Deb was aware that they had made exactly the same conversation earlier, but this time it was different, full of hidden tension instead of joy, full of anxiety instead of merriment.

'Goodbye then.' She had to get away, get away from herself, all the conflicting feelings. She blundered up the street, inadvertently knocking into an old gentleman who was passing.

'Beg pardon,' she mumbled, but ran on, head down, without looking back, afraid to let Jem see how much she liked him, afraid for herself, of how much she wished she could have stayed there for ever, kissing him back.

When she had done her errands she peeked in on Elisabeth, but she was sleeping. Deb looked at her curiously, this woman who shared a bed with Mr Pepys. After Hollier's compresses, her face was almost back to normal and she was prettier at rest. With a stab of compassion, Deb moved the coverlet up and smoothed it around Elisabeth's shoulders. She went to peek out through the crack in the shutters, over the snow-covered roofs. Sparrows had made patterns of footprints, like a monk's calligraphy.

At Christmastide she missed them all, Hester and her brothers. And most of all Mama. Oh how she wished she had someone to confide in, someone who'd know what to do about the unwanted attentions of Mr Pepys. She mounted the stairs thinking of Hester, enjoying her Christmas at Lavinia's. At least Hester would have a family Christmas, a Christmas full of cheer like they never had at Aunt Beth's.

In her room Deb shut the door and took out the little reed box that Jem had given her. She pushed away the vision of him hurrying home to his family feast, because it split her heart with an ache of loneliness. Slowly she untied the red ribbon. When she teased aside the straw packing, it revealed a wooden angel, his wings outspread as if he would fly. How had he guessed? It was just what she needed – a guardian angel.

It was beautiful – finely crafted and lifelike, with a string loop to hang it on a garland, so she stood on tiptoe, hung the angel over the threshold, on an empty hook where a picture must have hung. Did she imagine it, or was he looking down on her with a stern expression? Eyes that were telling her he'd be watching her to keep her on the straight and narrow.

Christmas Eve. As soon as she was able, she made excuses to the Pepyses, who were entertaining Hollier the surgeon again. Mr Pepys had promised her an evening off, as Elisabeth would need her for the morning's festivities, but she wanted to try to get away earlier to buy a gift for Jem. The snow had melted and she hurried through the slush to the Convent Garden market. A sweet smell of roasting chestnuts wafted from glowing braziers, and she was relieved to see there were still plenty of stallholders touting for last-minute buyers.

At a stall selling hymnals and pamphlets, she settled on a miniature prayer book, a fraction bigger than her thumb. Of course, such a gift was a little obvious, but she did not wish him to feel she was being too forward or intimate. Besides, this one was charming, with illuminated letters and tiny illustrations of the psalms. After she had made her purchase, she could not wait to return to St Gabriel's for the evening service.

The wooden church was full of Christmas revellers and families bundled up against the cold, but she waited until the service had ended and everyone had gone. A scattering of Christmas Eve bells were already pealing out, but she hardly heard their clamour.

When Jem came to lock the door, she stepped into the porch.

'Miss Willet! I did not see you there. Were you at the service? I wasn't—'

'I've brought you a gift,' she said.

'Oh no, you needn't—'

She brought the tiny object from under her cloak and pressed it into his hand. He turned it over and over, examining it, taking it in. It was then that she saw the mistletoe. A great bunch hanging just above his head, tied up with ribbon.

'Look,' she said pointing to it. 'You're right underneath.' Then, before she could think better of it, she stood on tiptoe and reached her lips to his. She pressed them against him as if she might blot out the other kiss altogether.

At first, he was shocked. He faltered, drew back.

She saw his eyes widen, about to protest. But then they closed. His arms slid around her waist. He kissed her again. The feeling was so exquisite she could barely breathe. It was a long moment later that he let her go. His expression was tender and filled something like admiration.

'Merry Christmas, Mr Wells,' she said.

Act Two

1668

Chapter Seventeen

January

DEB MANAGED TO ESCAPE her duties at Seething Lane to go to St Gabriel's, but after she squeezed into a pew, she was disappointed to find it was dry old Dr Thurlow taking the service. There was no sign of Jem. She wanted to make it quite clear that kissing him had been a moment of madness, and would not happen again.

The thought that she had been so forward made her wince. She could only think it was a weakness brought on by the Christmas spirit. But now Twelfth Night had been and gone, and Deb had not seen Jem since he went to visit his parents. Yet still the kiss haunted her.

She would not think of it again, she decided, and especially not here, in church. She kneeled on the hassock and tried to pray. But the more she forced the kiss away, the stronger the memory of it pulsed through her.

She thought of Jem, too, at night, when she could not escape Mr Pepys. Mr Pepys would nudge her and wink at her while they played cards, his eyes inviting more looks than she wished to return. Tonight it was Mary Mercer and her parents, the Turners, who were cousins of Mr Pepys, and Mr Batelier, who often joined them for a game. None of the assembled company seemed to notice Mr Pepys' obvious attentions to Deb. If only she could fly this stifling chamber with its fug of heat and Mr Pepys' knees always too close to hers. Like a bird in a cage, she was always on show, expected to flutter to order.

Over on the far side of London, in a dark shuttered room in Lukenor Lane, Abigail and her daughter Joan glared at each other.

'What did you do with the money then?' Abigail asked in frustration.

'Gave it Polly for a new skirt.'

'But, Joan, why? It was meant for you – for your mercury treatment.'

'No, Ma. I've told you, I'm not going into the Baths. There's no point. Misery for nothing, that's what it is. Nobody comes out of there. They just get sicker and sicker. Why won't you listen to me?'

'I do, it's just … I want you to get well,' Abigail said, trying not to see the reddish rash of warts that tattooed Joan's skin, the grey shadows under her eyes.

'Pah. You said that about the healing man, and a lot of use he was, with all his abracadabra and laying on of hands.' Joan flopped back against the pillow, her pallid forehead glistening with sweat.

'Now listen,' Abigail said, perching on the edge of the bed and leaning in, 'I happen to know one of the King's courtiers. He took the mercury baths and his symptoms went – just like that.' It was not true, but what else was she to do? She'd try anything.

'Oh, Ma, why won't you face it? What whore ever got better from the pox?'

'This one. You've got to try. It's no use giving up. You've got to fight it.'

Joan let out a ragged sigh. 'It's not an enemy, Ma. It's my own body. And it's tired of all your damn fool cures. Besides, Polly needed a new skirt, her old one was in rags, and she couldn't get no customers. She looks fine in the new one, and business is better already, she says.'

Abigail pressed her lips together to stem her response. She took out her purse and emptied the little heap of gold onto the side table. 'This is for the mercury baths. Not for Polly, or Jess, or any of the others – hear me? The physician expects you on Tuesday.'

'Ma?'

'What?' Abigail retreated inside herself. She knew what was coming.

'Let me go quietly,' Joan said. 'Please. I want to go peaceful, here, where I can hear the girls joshing in the yard, the men coming out of the alehouse. Don't send me there. It's the end for me, whatever you do. You've got to face it, Ma. I can. Why can't you?'

Abigail put her lips to Joan's forehead. 'Get Polly to remind you. Tuesday, ten bells. Look, I've brought you a clean nightdress.'

She pressed the white cambric onto the end of the bed, but Joan turned away. Abigail stood a moment watching the silent lump of her daughter's back, before, grim-faced, heart aching, she gathered her cloak tighter and strode from the room.

Chapter Eighteen
February

'JANE SAYS SHE SAW YOU talking to a young fellow last week,' Elisabeth said, 'in the street near St Gabriel's church. Who was that?'

Deb stood up from the brass fender she was burnishing. 'It was Mr Wells, the apprentice curate.' Her eyes shifted away under Elisabeth's scrutiny.

'And how do you know him? I didn't know you knew any young men. Jane says she saw you when she passed on her way to town, and you were still talking there when she came back.'

'I don't really know him. I answered the door to him once when he came to ask for Mr Pepys. He was only passing the time of day with me,' Deb said, silently aggrieved that Jane should have told tales about her, especially as Jane was always finding an excuse to linger with Tom Edwards.

'You know him well enough to know his name, though.' Elisabeth raised her eyebrows.

'It's on the board outside the church.'

'So what was he saying?'

Deb squeezed the polishing rag in her hands, keeping her face averted so that Elisabeth might not see how guilty she looked. Since his return, Jem had walked out with her on her half-days off, but always well out of the way of Seething Lane and Elisabeth's sharp eyes. 'He was collecting, for the poor. And then we just struck up a conversation ... about the weather.' In actual fact, it had been a long discussion about whether there was any news from Mr Pepys on the sailors' pay.

Elisabeth sniffed. 'When a person is sent out on an errand, I naturally assume they will go straight there and back. I don't expect them to dally with every Tom, Dick and Harry. While you reside under my roof, I'd rather there were no goings-on with young men; after all, they are not paying you for your company. I am the one who pays you for your time, n'est-ce pas?'

Deb picked up the basin of potash for polishing and bent down to finish the fender. If Elisabeth wanted no goings-on under her roof, Deb thought, she'd best look to her husband.

'No, you don't understand,' Bart said, wincing as he dabbed a wet kerchief to a cut on his head. 'Can't you feel it, Jem? It's the beginning ... the beginning of the rebellion.'

Jem leaned his elbows on the table and pressed his head into his hands. 'You're wrong. People have had their fill of wars, and fighting. It will all blow over. And look at you. You're a sight.'

Bart grimaced, felt his bruised cheek with his fingertips. 'Enough with the lectures, you sound like Dr Thurlow. There's always a bit of high spirits on Shrove Tuesday, you know that.'

'Burning down houses? High spirits?' Jem threw up his hands. 'What will those families do, now they've nowhere to go? As if the Great Fire wasn't bad enough, but idiots like you must start another. I can't believe anyone'd be so stupid.'

Bart looked sheepish. 'Wasn't my fault. The sailors have just cause to protest. It's a short step from throwing stones to throwing brands, and it just sort of grew.' He stood and went to wash out the bloodstained kerchief in the ewer. 'We were driven to it by the King. He won't bloody budge. We haven't got a single *sou* out of him. It makes us all sick to see him flaunt himself, frittering away our rightful pay, on ... what? Jewels for his mistress, bolts of gold cloth ... he even bought her two flaming lapdogs! I'll bet they're better fed than us, the whore's bloody dogs.' He flung the cloth into the basin, and water sloshed onto the floor.

'Will you stop griping about the King,' Jem said. 'Those families you've burned out, they're what matters. You should make a collection. For food, warm clothes and—'

'For pity's sake, not that again. That's always your answer. Charity's all well and good, but it's not going to change anything.' Bart stood up and rubbed his forehead in frustration. 'It's like bandaging over gangrene. Useless. What we need is proper action. Political action.' He placed his hands on the table, leaned in. 'Look at your own church. The least variation on the service and you're labelled a dissenter and clapped in gaol. And it's getting worse – the King's banned all conventicles.'

Jem sighed. Bart seemed to thrive on bad news. 'How will complaining help? There are families who have no roof over their heads tonight and it's all your doing.'

'Then will you come with me to Lukenor Lane?' Bart asked, standing up from the table and shoving his face towards him.

'Me? What's it got to do with me?'

'It's your idea to go back there with your do-gooding and your charity. So are you going to come?'

Jem raked his fingers through his hair. 'Why should I? It's your mess, not mine. And Dr Thurlow would burst his garters. He'd see it as me supporting the bawdy houses.'

Bart threw up his hands. 'Hypocrite. You're like all the rest! You won't *do* anything. It's no use any more sticking your head under a blanket. You saw how Pepys and the Navy Board are fearful of displeasing His "holy" Majesty. Please – come with me. Come out of your ivory tower, that's all I ask. Then you'll understand.'

Bart's accusation that he was a hypocrite made Jem uncomfortable. He felt himself weakening. He had always tried to look after his younger brother, even now that they were grown, and as a future curate he felt he should be guiding Bart somehow.

Not that it would be easy, he thought; it would be like herding vermin. Even when they'd been small, Bart had never listened to a word he said.

'All right, I'll come,' Jem said, 'but I'm not promising anything.'

That evening Jem raided Dr Thurlow's charity box, though it riddled him with guilt. He and Bart took turns to push the cart, loaded with a ragged heap of moth-eaten blankets, two sacks of oatmeal and a half-full barrel of dried peas. On the way they were joined by one of Bart's down-at-heel friends, Thomas Player, a hosier. Jem was used to seeing the poorer areas of the city as part of his curate's duties, but Lukenor Lane's warren of filthy dwellings was worse than anything he'd ever seen in his parish.

He averted his eyes from a woman spreadeagled in the dirt, her arms oozing hideous sores.

At his grimace, Bart whispered, 'Ratsbane. They put it on deliberately to draw our sympathy.'

Her rattling pan contained only a few pebbles and a single coin. Jem dug in his pocket but Bart shook his head.

Further down the road, the shocking evidence of Bart's friends' 'high spirits' turned out to be houses reduced to a heap of collapsed timbers and blackened walls. Some families still huddled inside them for shelter, emerging only as they saw them pass.

'A bed-warmer, mister?' called a scrawny young girl, one limp breast poking out of her bodice.

Bart kept his eyes fixed to the cart as Jem shook his head and pushed past.

'I know how to please a man,' the girl whined.

Sorry for her, Jem fished in his pocket again and brought out a coin and, ignoring Bart's expression, he held it out. The girl grinned and reached out to put her arm across his shoulders, but he flinched away. 'I don't want—'

'You've paid for it. Don't you like me?'

'No, it's not that. I'm a man of the cloth. Of the church.'

'Plenty churchmen been through here. Don't you want it?'

He could do nothing but shake his head and race to catch up with Bart, who was straining to push the barrow by himself.

'Come on, you're lagging,' Bart called.

Jem quickened his pace, closed his eyes to the suppurating piles of refuse and horse droppings in the street. The meeting Bart had hastily organised was in a tavern further out of town on the Ratcliffe Highway, so the few miles of pushing silenced their talk. The stench of tobacco and snuff hit them as soon as they opened the door. It was a tiny, cramped place, with barrels for stools and larger barrels for tables, and a smoke that made it hard to see through the gloom.

Pinch-faced Tom Player seemed to be the man in charge, along with a bold-featured woman called Mrs Cresswell, who looked like an overstuffed mattress and was, it transpired, a bawd at one of the brothel houses in Clerkenwell. She'd collected in all the donations and had them set on a trestle to be doled out to the needy. Jem helped Bart and Tom lug their contribution inside, taking great gulps of night air each time he went outside.

'For God's sake, keep it all under lock and key until it's light and we can see what's what,' Mrs Cresswell said, 'or there'll be nothing left by sunrise, and a lot of thieving magpies with fat bellies. Talking of fat bellies, I've got a little scheme in mind,' she said, with a wink, 'to raise merry hell. How's about we write a letter, a public letter, to the King's whore, Mrs Castlemaine, asking her to side with us, her sisters. After all, she's one of us, ain't she?' She raised an eyebrow and waggled her head so that the feathers in her hat shimmied in the light from the lamps.

Guffaws of laughter. The idea of the King's whore was so entertaining it soon gripped the whole assembly. Everyone had suggestions as to what to write.

'Gawd love her,' said another younger woman in a disintegrating red bodice, 'better warn the poor old cow to protect herself. Those sailors and apprentices might come to White Hall next and fire her bawdyhouse too!'

A smatter of clapping hands. Bart and Tom Player grinned at each other.

'Tell her working conditions here are terrible, and ask her to change places with you, Ma Cresswell. Tell her you'll sit outside her house until she can get her royal pimp to make your brothels as well appointed as hers!' said Bart.

Jem nudged his brother in mock disapproval, but could not suppress his amusement, for everyone else was sniggering with glee at the thought of this missive arriving unannounced at Mistress Castlemaine's door. Such good humour was infectious.

'It will need to be carefully done,' a quiet voice said from the back, 'so that there can be no treasonous return on this. We must try to avoid specifically naming the King. After all, we want to gather more support for our cause, not turn people against it.'

Jem turned to see who had spoken. She was a woman of middling age, greying at the temples, her dress a modest, unassuming brown. He wondered if he'd met her before, because she looked somewhat familiar, but he dismissed the idea. He could know no one here.

'She's right,' Tom Player agreed, 'we need to be careful, or—' He drew his finger sharply across his throat.

Paper and quills were fetched, and they gathered round the biggest table and began to draft the letter. Jem found himself contributing with the rest. The woman in brown was insistent that they avoided anything seditious, and passages that were uncertain, she wrote down, to check later.

Mrs Cresswell leapt on Jem's suggestions for wording with enthusiasm. He knew he was a good orator and relished the chance to use his skills. His face ached from grinning. Yet beneath the women's laughter burned an undercurrent of determination, an intent to improve their lot, a steely ambition that Jem admired. To his surprise, for the first time in his life Jem felt as if he was actually doing something useful.

Of course, underneath, the guilt ate away at him; that as a prospective man of the cloth, he shouldn't be hobnobbing with felons and bawds. Mrs Cresswell, well, she might have fallen to the bawd's trade, but it was mighty difficult to dislike her as a person. She'd treated him with such genial good humour, and it seemed to make no difference to her at all that he was a man of the church.

This was where he was needed, perhaps. Maybe God wanted him to preach to them and turn them from their sinful ways. Except that he could not imagine that Mrs Cresswell or the other lady would take the slightest notice of him. Dr Thurlow categorised the poor into deserving and undeserving, and in Dr Thurlow's book, Jem was quite certain these would be the latter.

And yet was it not his duty as a good Christian to save all souls? Perhaps even more so those who had fallen away from the path like lost sheep. Excitement bubbled up inside him. Had he not preached about this very thing himself? Was it a sign?

He gazed across the smoke-filled room, let the voices wash over him. He could achieve much more, though, if he had a woman beside him as a helpmate. A good-hearted woman, one of unimpeachable character, who could act as a shining example in a place like this.

His fingers felt the square shape of the tiny prayer book in his pocket. He was already picturing Miss

Willet. Her face rose up in his imagination, as she had listened to him in church, her grave grey eyes, the slight flush on her cheeks. Since the kiss under the mistletoe, he could not stop thinking of it; though he had not dared ask for another. He didn't know what to say, how to broach it. A kiss was no use without an offer, and he had no living to give her yet, not till he'd finished his training. What would she think of him now if she could see him here? She'd be horrified. And yet she had a spark about her too, an underlying energy. It was tantalising.

What if she rejected him? Of course, he'd hoped she'd kiss him again, but that part of her had been put away, almost as if she was afraid of it. And worse, Mrs Pepys had got word of their meetings and forbidden Deb to see him again. A messenger had brought a short note from Deb to tell him, and it had given him much cause for soul-searching. He didn't want to cause any trouble between Deb and Mrs Pepys.

It was temptation, he knew. To deceive Mrs Pepys by meeting Deb was to stray from the straight and narrow path he prided himself on following.

But still it haunted him, the feeling of her soft pink lips pressed hotly against his.

Chapter Nineteen

DEB FOLDED THE FIRST BATCH of sheets and smoothed the starched edges to make creases. The tip of one finger was stained with ink from copying out papers. She paused, licked it, and wiped it on the underside of her apron, thinking of Abigail. Over the past few months she had searched Mr Pepys' study over and over but found no sign of a diary. Yet she knew it must be there somewhere, because Mr Pepys himself had said he was writing it. On Abigail's insistence, she had searched the bookshelves again, but she had found nothing resembling a diary. In her mind she imagined a slim volume, like the white book she had taken earlier.

How gullible she'd been at first, to think Abigail wanted to be her friend. All servants were prey to their betters, she knew, even when the word 'betters' was the last word to describe them. She was annoyed with herself, because she prided herself on her judgement. In one way, she was not surprised that Abigail was working for the King. His Majesty was well known for his insistent dalliances with attractive women, particularly actresses. Maybe he was tiring of Nell Gwynn, and Abigail Williams had caught his eye.

Deb stretched out the last bedsheet and held it under her chin as she snapped the edges together. Balancing the pile of sheets on the crook of her elbow, she opened the linen press and pushed the sheets inside. She paused to stifle a yawn and rub her eyes, because late-night copying was tiring.

She had never imagined she would become a spy. For this was what she was, she realised. In the absence of the diary, she was still making copies of naval documents: whatever she could easily 'borrow' from Pepys' office. The papers fascinated her, though, and she often wrote out excerpts twice so that she could study them herself after delivering them. The fitting out of warships was a complicated business.

Voices below alerted her to the fact that Mr Pepys was home for his supper, with his clerk, Will Hewer. She shut the linen press door with a bang.

She leaned over the banister to eavesdrop on the burble of conversation, but disappointingly could make out nothing of the words. Since Abigail's assignment, all Mr Pepys' movements seemed suspiciously anti-Royalist. She wondered how she had failed to notice it before, how much Mr Pepys would make mockery of the King.

Still, she reassured herself, it was clear Mr Pepys was a dissenter, and so she was doing the right thing in passing on his papers to Abigail and the King. Trouble was, a niggle of doubt remained, like an uneasy itch that needed to be scratched.

'Deb?' Elisabeth's voice.

Her company was required. She pinned on her best smile, reminded herself of her duty to the King. She must try again to find that diary.

That night, after playing cards with Elisabeth, Sam and Will Hewer, Deb left them early to clear away the supper things, and hearing their voices still engrossed in the game, she took a chance and tiptoed into Mr Pepys' study.

There was a naval chest bound with iron and she pulled it open. It was stuffed full of books and she knew she had already been through each one. Nothing new here. She heard footsteps on the landing. Deb shut the chest quickly and crouched to the hearth with the brush in her hand as if sweeping the hearth. But Elisabeth went past without looking in.

When she'd gone, Deb stood up. From her kneeling position she saw the corner of a small tea chest, pushed right to the back under the table. Just a chest full of discarded linens. She had looked there once before. Still, she should look again. She got down on her knees and pulled out the chest, which was covered in an oilcloth. She peeled it back and opened the chest to see a pair of old curtains neatly folded. As she thought, the old drapes that Elisabeth had taken down from the parlour.

Still, she pulled them out. This time, she was determined to be thorough. Beneath was a thick pile of leather-bound books. She flipped one open.

A ruled page, covered in Shelton's shorthand. She could read enough shorthand to know what it said. *"January, the Lord's year sixteen sixty-eight."*

She was motionless a moment, just staring. Could this be it?

She dug deeper into the chest, feeling the weight of paper. Book after book, pages and pages of it.

But there was so much! And it had all been there, under the desk all along.

Carefully, she slid out a book from halfway down the stack, replacing the top book and the old curtains so that any cursory glance by Mr Pepys would reveal nothing amiss. A shiver of anticipation, mixed with a tinge of guilt sharpened her senses. Scared of being caught, she pressed the volume tight to her chest and scurried across the landing.

Elisabeth and Will Hewer passed the bottom of the stairs on their way to the parlour to fetch the music and instruments. 'Deb, the pastry dishes are still on the table!' Elisabeth called.

Heart pounding, Deb flattened herself back against the wall with the book behind her back. 'Yes, Elisabeth, I'm coming.' She raced up to her chamber and thrust the book between the sheet and the mattress.

All of a fluster, she was clumsy helping Jane clear and wash the pots, knocking the salt crock flying. Vigorously, she applied the dustpan and brush, impatient to get back to Pepys' papers.

Finally, her chores were done and the company departed. Before anyone could demand anything more, she shot upstairs, wiped her hands, prised up the mattress and took out the book.

The room was dark, but she lit a candle and a watery moon shone a pale glow through the window. Deb put her back to the moonlight so it might shine over her shoulder, to help the flicker of the candle.

Below, she could hear the faint tune of Mr Pepys humming a madrigal.

She opened the book at a random page. It was written in his familiar shorthand, but she was more confident now with translating, and the first words came to her easily.

"there I walked."

For the next half-hour she struggled to translate it. When she got to a word she could not fathom, she took out the Shakespeare sonnet and set to work, using the sonnet as a key, one letter of shorthand at a time, and scribbling down words as she recognised them. At one point she was stumped and could go no further. She worried at it for another hour until she had a sudden realisation. The words were in French. At the end of the first paragraph she could barely swallow. She paused to re-read.

> *"there I walked to visit the old castle ruins, which has been a noble place, and there going up the stairs I overtook three pretty maids or women and took them up with me, and I did 'baiser sur mouches et toucher leur mains' and necks to my great pleasure."*

So it wasn't just the events of the day as he had said. The lying rogue.

Her hand came up to her mouth. He was so candid, so frank. His whole life must be there. She felt faint; her head swam with his words. She sat down heavily on the bed, dizzy with being inside Mr Pepys' mind; the voice rang in her head just as if he was speaking to her. She read the passage again, unable to take it all in.

Other pages might have her name on them, she realised. The idea filled her with revulsion; that she might be set down through Mr Pepys' eyes, for other people to read. She knew from even these few pages that it would be a travesty of herself, that to him she would be something quite *other*.

She would have to go through it all, see what he had written about her. And Elisabeth. What if Elisabeth were to find it? His writing his deeds in French would hardly help, considering Elisabeth spoke it fluently, as did she. How could he be so arrogant and so unfeeling as to leave these lying in his office? But then, she guessed, perhaps Elisabeth could not read shorthand? She flipped a page and began to translate furiously, scrawling in her haste.

> *"called on board Lord Bruncker and Sir John Mennes, onto one of the East Indiamen at Erith, and find them full of envious complaints for the pillaging of the ships. But I pacified them, and discoursed about making money off some of the goods, and hope to be the better by it."*

So here it was. The prize goods from captured vessels. The King was right to be suspicious. Underhand transactions were going on in the Navy Office, and this diary could be the breaking of Pepys. The further she read, the more she saw it with utter clarity.

Deb could hardly breathe. She read on, checking back over each word to make sure she had it right, and eventually fascination with the underhand goings-on at the Navy Treasury overcame her revulsion at the contents. Here was the evidence the King sought. Calmer now, she settled herself down with quill and ink to make a fair copy for Abigail. Should she translate it from the shorthand? *Better not*, she thought. Best leave it as it is, with him condemned by his own words. She penned each symbol precisely, blotted it.

The door behind her suddenly opened. An involuntary cry escaped her lips. She shot up, and thrust the book under the papers in one deft movement, her heart leaping in her chest.

'You made me jump,' she said, with a false little laugh.

Elisabeth frowned at her, a candlestick in her hand. 'Are you unwell?' she asked. 'When I went to let little Fancy out just now, I saw a light burning in your room. It seems very late to be up.'

Deb placed herself before the table where she had been working to mask the papers from Elisabeth's curious stare.

'I couldn't sleep,' Deb said, her back rigid, certain that something in her eyes must surely give her away.

'What are you doing?' Elisabeth asked.

'Writing to my sister.'

Elisabeth took a step nearer the table, but Deb placed her hand over the symbols on the document.

'I hope you are not writing anything bad about us,' Elisabeth said, the smiling jest belied by her probing eyes.

'No,' Deb said, 'just news.'

Elisabeth did not look convinced, but Deb could see that she could not bring herself to be so impolite as to ask Deb to show her the letter. Elisabeth's mouth puckered in disapproval and she stood a moment, obviously unwilling to leave. 'Well. No wonder we're going through so many candles. You can write to your sister in daylight hours, surely? I don't want to see lights burning again at this time of night.'

'Yes, Elisabeth. I mean, no.'

Elisabeth hesitated, as if she was about to speak, but then was silent.

'Sorry if I inconvenienced you,' Deb curtseyed, but her hand was clenched around the quill. She made an effort to relax it.

Elisabeth took one last reluctant look at the table. 'Blow it out then.'

Deb snuffed the candle as she asked, but too hastily and wax spilled onto the table and the paper. Elisabeth's own light retreated from the room, leaving Deb to undress in darkness and shadow. She sat down on the bed and wiped her sweating palms on the woollen blanket. That had been close. What if Elisabeth had seen what she was doing?

She lifted the mattress and thrust the copied documents hastily out of sight. In the dark she heard her breath panting, sharp and shallow in the silent room.

Chapter Twenty

IT WAS AFTER MIDNIGHT before Deb thought it was safe to return Mr Pepys' diary to his chamber. She hoped he would not look back over the pages and notice the splashes of wax, prayed he'd be too busy to read back over old entries. But as she crept along the hall to his office, the knocking of her heart was so loud she felt sure Elisabeth must hear it.

Later, she lay tense and still, unable to sleep. It was what Abigail had wanted, and the King would be pleased he had been proved correct, but it would surely mean arrest and possibly imprisonment for Mr Pepys. And only yesterday he had come home in a great gust of good humour, saying that he was the toast of Parliament with a speech he had made about the Medway affair. He was vindicated of all misdeeds, he had told them all. Then he had demanded the best wine and even kissed Elisabeth soundly on the cheek.

In Deb's excitement at her discoveries in his diary, she had not considered the consequences for him and Elisabeth, and for herself, too. She had not thought to find anything, and now she had, she was in a quandary. What would happen to Elisabeth if Sam was arrested? Traitors were executed or consigned to the Tower. Could she really condemn them to that kind of fate? And if the

Pepyses were arrested, then she would have no employment, and when they found out she'd spied on him, no one would ever trust her again.

This thought made her throw off the covers and jump out of bed. She stared out of the window at the looming dark bulk of the Tower, imagining how Elisabeth might feel if her husband were to be incarcerated there, locked up behind that mass of masonry as a traitor. Even though Mr Pepys was an incorrigible philanderer, and Elisabeth was a gossip who drove her to distraction, could she bring them to such a fate? Below, she heard the faint sound of Samuel's comfortable snores, as he slept, unaware of her copying, oblivious to what lurked just around the corner.

She was on the brink of a scandal, and if Mr Pepys were to be arrested, and anything was to happen to her, Hester would need someone else to look to her welfare. She could not leave her to Aunt Beth. She would have to redouble her efforts to find her mother.

'Mama?' The thought was a call. She waited a moment feeling for an answer, but heard only the faint, lonely cry of geese flying down the Thames.

The next day Deb spent the morning helping Jane beat the rugs, so she hurried upstairs at midday to change into a clean chemise. As soon as she entered her room she sensed someone else had been there. Deb was precise with how she laid out her things, but now the ink bottle and pen were askew on the lid of her writing slope. She frowned, lifted them and opened the lid. Her letters from Hester were on the left, not the right.

Elisabeth. The thought made Deb go cold. So Elisabeth had her suspicions – she had been here and was reading Deb's letters.

Of course she should have expected it – she had

heard of employers reading a maidservant's mail often enough. In a panic she threw up the mattress, but exhaled when she saw the papers from Mr Pepys' diary were still there waiting to go to Abigail. She would have to get rid of them, would never be able to leave them unattended in her room.

She tried to remember what was in Hester's letters. Nothing to give Elisabeth concern, she was sure. She had been careful always to speak well of the Pepyses. Yet it was a warning. Her heart pattered fast in her chest. She took out all the letters and read them again just to make sure.

That afternoon, Deb begged an old pillowcase from Jane, cut it in half, and sewed it sturdily to the inside of her petticoat to make a flapped pocket. Thank goodness she was a woman. The bag fitted closely next to her legs where nobody would detect it. She slid all the papers close inside, where she could keep them near. There were few advantages to being female, but this was surely one, that nobody would see the papers under her voluminous skirts.

Later that day, after they'd been to the King's playhouse with the Mercers to see *The Spanish Gypsy*, she took Abigail the copies from Mr Pepys' diary. But she was not a fool. She'd decided to leave out the pages that referred to corruption in the navy, and carefully kept back random pages to give the impression Mr Pepys did not write his diary every day. She had to search hard to find pages that were innocent of insults to the King or Members of Parliament.

If her plan worked, to hide the worst in the diary, she could stay on at the Pepyses' house and Abigail would keep paying her for more information. To do anything else would be like igniting a keg of gunpowder –she could not predict what would happen, nor who would be hit by the blast. Pepys knew so many people, people who relied on him for their livelihood. No, far better to keep things as they were. Though she could not help a frisson of fear. What she was doing was dangerous – to deceive a King.

Abigail took the papers as if they were as holy as the Bible of King James himself.

'Is this all there is?' she asked.

Deb told her there was more, but it was disorganised and would take time to copy. She kept her face closed, and the incriminating parts of the diary she kept tied under her skirts, though it felt unclean to be walking around with Mr Pepys' intimate thoughts just there. She told herself she would get used to it. They were nothing of substance – only words, that was all.

Bart knew Jem would be horrified if he knew where he was, wedged into a dark corner of a private room in The Grecian coffee house, about to meet with a notorious Dutchman who went by the alias of Mr Johnson. Those in the know said his name was actually Piet, but woe betide anyone who used it. Bart poured a dark stream of ale into his tankard and passed the jug to the portly and well-upholstered figure of Graceman next to him. Opposite, sat Skinner, a weasely man in his fifties with a determined face.

Skinner, whom he recognised from earlier plots against the King, was a secret powder expert; formerly one of Cromwell's aides, he was an expert in firearms, although he had spent the years after the interregnum masquerading as a blacksmith. Graceman, however, was an unknown quantity – a newly appointed trustee at the gunpowder mill. He wore the dark-suited doublet of a petty official and looked down his nose at Bart. God willing, Bart would be able to take good news back to the sailors, that the King's days were numbered.

'For sabotage at Chatham to work, we need much better plans,' Graceman said, puffing out his chest with an air of authority, 'proper organisation.'

'Yes,' Skinner said. 'Can't get near the wharf at all at the moment, it's too well guarded. We need a rabbit hole, some way of getting in. Any ideas, Wells?'

'Not sure I can help,' Bart said. 'I'm only a midshipman. I've never been inside the yards.'

Just then, the door to the private room swung open and the Dutch naval commander Cornelis Tromp greeted them with a brief bow. 'Gentlemen.'

Two lackeys followed behind, dragging a large iron-bound trunk through the door. Puffing, they set it down under the table.

Skinner stood to offer the thickset Dutchman his chair, and to fetch one for Tromp's companion, a man so tall he had to remove his hat to get under the beams. This must be Johnson. He was a man with no distinguishing features except for pale eyes and a pent-up power that was so palpable it made Bart instinctively shrink away.

'I have the latest intelligence from my contact,' Johnson said. His English was excellent, with only a hint of an accent. 'Copies of the minutes of the Navy Board.' He patted the leather satchel by his side. 'The English strategy seems to have been less of a strategy and more of a ... what you say? Blind man's bluff. But the main point is, gentlemen, there's a warship being refitted at Chatham, and there are still defences at sea.' He drew out the papers and set them on the table.

'Excellent,' Tromp said without even glancing at them. 'Chance of a skirmish then?'

'No. That's not the aim,' Skinner said, impatiently. 'I was clear about that from the beginning. We want to avoid fighting on the water at all costs. It's essential to channel all men to the city, not have them distracted by petty fighting. We need the sheer numbers of men if our rebellion against the Crown is to stand any chance of success. Your job is to avoid the defences, not engage with them, and to give transport to our men from Ireland. Nothing more.'

'Hear hear,' Graceman said. 'But I'm telling you, the scheme can't fail. I've the promise of five hundred more for our cause in Wexford Bay.'

That many? Bart was surprised. He did not know they had so much support in Ireland.

'Good man. There's enough coin in there to arm them,' Tromp said, kicking the trunk with his boot.

'If your plan is sound enough to warrant it,' Johnson said.

Skinner rolled out a map and traced the route for Tromp and Johnson with his finger. 'From your ships we can row our men up the river. We'll supply the diversion, here at the docks – a big explosion in the yard. Make it look like sabotage by the Dutch, but of course you'll be clear away by then. It will be a feather in your cap, too. The diversion will send the King's army there in a panic, and, with luck, leave the city undefended.'

'Won't the docks be guarded?' Tromp asked, leaning in.

'The King's men are stationed all around the docks, here, here and here,' Bart said, pointing. 'They're nervous, as well they might be. The Admiralty thought your fleet might fire the yards on our last outing, so they've set a guard.'

'Looks like we were right to wait, Tromp,' Johnson said. 'This way, we get the English to sneak into their own yards and blow up their own ships.'

Tromp guffawed. 'True enough. Blast them to kingdom come, won't you, Skinner! Then they'll have no time to make good again, and the trade routes will be ours again.'

Bart shifted in his seat. Having the Dutch laugh at them was more uncomfortable than he had bargained for. His English soul rebelled. But he reminded himself it was for a good cause. This would upset the peace treaty signed with the Dutch at Breda, and no mistake. Mind, it was all a sham anyway. The idea of peace seemed to have made no difference at all to the King – or to Tromp or the Dutch.

'Sounds like a good enough bargain,' Tromp said, pulling on his moustache. 'You blow up your own ships, and we'll bring your rebels in by night. A neat trick, but a shame. I would have preferred a proper dogfight.'

'But you'll stick with our agreement?' Skinner leaned forward.

Tromp sighed. 'You have my word. We'll fetch your troops from Wexford and offload them in the Thames. Then we'll simply lower the boats and sail away. If you wait an hour for your troops to row up-river, and then fire the yard, the King's men will be too busy to come after us.'

'And there is the advantage, too, of surprise,' Johnson said, coolly. 'Nobody will care whether it was the Dutch or the French, or even papists that blew up the ship once the city is overrun by rebels.'

'We've waited years for this! And God knows, it can't come soon enough,' Skinner said. 'Graceman's done wonders. He's rallied the rebels from the north as well as the Irish.'

Graceman smirked, waved away the compliment, took another puff of his pipe.

'Lord, but it would be something sweet to see that second royal head dangling over the gate like his father.' Tromp thumped his hand down, so that the ale cups jumped on the table.

'Sssh. Have a care,' warned Johnson, leaning over the map. 'Remember where we are. We're not in Antwerp now, and people will hear us.'

'We're getting ahead of ourselves,' Skinner said tersely, going to close the door. 'One thing at a time. We need well-drawn maps of the city, plans of the docks in advance, positions of the guards, intelligence as to which ships are still defending the Medway, and how best to deal with them.'

'Skinner's right. It all takes time,' Bart said. 'The word from Chatham is that the building of new ships has been delayed. They can't get the wood – the navy's run out of money.'

'It's important to choose the right moment,' Skinner said. 'We don't want to waste this chance – timing's everything.'

'Have you no mole in the Navy Office to tell us what's going on?' Graceman asked.

'Yes, a woman. Code name "Allbarn". But she's getting a little old and unreliable,' Johnson said. 'I can't remove her, though, not until we have a replacement. A clerk called Carkesse has been working undercover for us for a while, and we thought he might step up to it, but he's turned out to be a proper touchpaper –more of a liability than an asset.'

'A man. Might be better,' Graceman said.

'Not necessarily. A man can't get access to the behind-closed-doors intelligence like a woman can,' Johnson said. 'And it's not so easy to find another woman with enough wit. But I've got someone else in mind, and I'll see what I can do.'

Tromp looked appraisingly at Johnson. 'We need details about the sea defences or the deal's off, and none of you will see my gold to fund this rebellion.'

'I've said, I'll replace her.'

'Good man.' Tromp seemed reassured.

Johnson's face betrayed nothing, but the atmosphere of tension in the room did not lessen. Bart suddenly understood that in this business of double-dealing, Johnson was the one who had manoeuvred the two sides together, and no doubt he was being paid by both parties. You had to be as cool and slippery as water to play both sides this way. And ruthless. Mind, he wouldn't like to be in Johnson's shoes if anything went wrong. The rebels needed the Dutch to bring in the supporters from Ireland, and the Dutch needed the rebels to put a hole in the new English warship, and, once the King was deposed, the lucrative guaranteed trade routes.

It was a good plot. If only it came off.

'Same time on Tuesday,' Skinner said, and all parties stood to shake hands on it.

Bart threw on his cloak ready to go back to his lodgings where Jem would be waiting with his supper. The thought of Jem, his broad open face, pricked his conscience. Why had he got to have a brother in the church? It made him feel like he was always under the eye of God, as if he should continually look over his shoulder.

No matter how much he tried to get him to understand, Jem had never really grasped that if you were a sailor, solidarity between men was the most important thing. That sailors worked as a team, and what one wanted, they'd all fight for. Bart strode out into the night, pondering his brother's sheltered life at university and in the church, and why it was that Jem simply couldn't understand the frustrations of the common man.

The weather was bitter, and ice crunched in the puddles as he walked. Strange to think the city would soon be theirs and they'd be free of the tyranny of the Crown. Unease did not leave him though. Tromp and Johnson were hard men, and he'd taken a dislike to Graceman, despite Skinner's opinion, which seemed to be that the sun shone out of his arse.

Graceman was an oily customer; he'd seen his type before. He'd appeared from nowhere, yet he soon became Skinner's right-hand man. No doubt it was because Graceman had been taken on as foreman at the gunpowder mill, and Skinner had manoeuvred his way in there under his employ. It was unhealthy, Bart thought, this mutual back-scratching.

He stepped around a ladder that was propped up against one of the new houses. Like all sailors he was superstitious. This morning a swinging bucket hanging from a gantry had nearly knocked him flat. It had shocked him, made him aware of his own mortality. He had felt a prayer squeeze out of his lips, with the realisation that his life was so fragile and easily crushed.

He looked up at the light in Jem's lodgings. A stabbing anger rose in his chest at the thought of Jem, blithely unaware, safe in his own little castle, with God on his side, sure of his salvation in the next world, when he had never really lived in this one.

Chapter Twenty-one

Deb had already been to the King's Post Office to ask if there was a London mailing address for an Eliza Willet, and a grumpy, harassed-looking clerk had shooed her away with a 'no'. Now, in desperation, she went back, picked an open-faced old man, and asked politely if he'd look again. Tutting, he disappeared into the ledger room, and after a wait of a quarter hour, he returned, empty-handed.

'No luck?' she asked.

'Worse. Bridewell,' the man said, sucking on his teeth and shaking his head. 'I'll write it down.'

He pushed the paper over the counter towards her, then retreated.

When Deb got back to Seething Lane, she held out the paper to Jane and asked her if she knew where it was. Jane crossed herself, said that it was the poorhouse, and not to mention it again. It was bad luck to even talk of it.

She was still reeling from this, the idea that her mother might be somewhere like that, when she was faced with more bad news. Sickness and plague had struck the west of the city, and Elisabeth feared another summer of death and disease, like the one before last. Mr Pepys had given his permission for his wife to escape to the country.

Deb was numb when Elisabeth told her. *Oh please, no.* The prospect of months in Brampton, with only Elisabeth for company, made her want to tear her hair. Abigail would be angry. And of course there was Jem. How could she tell him? Her stomach contracted with an ache of longing.

'But surely the plague has left London now,' Deb said, 'and you always say it is too dull in the country.'

Elisabeth pouted. 'I don't know what London's coming to. It seems to be one thing following another. People can't sleep safe in their beds for fear a rabble will burn them out, and I'm telling you, my constitution won't stand it a moment longer.' She continued to complain a good few minutes more before finally saying, 'I've got to find some peace and quiet!'

Deb ignored the irony of this, determined to persuade her to stay. 'Perhaps you just need to rest for a day or two. I'll strip the beds by myself, and you can read a little, how would that be? Then tomorrow you might feel differently.'

'I won't. I've made up my mind. I've written to Sam's father to tell him to expect us, and I'm awaiting his reply. It will be a family occasion; Sam's cousin, Mrs Turner, will accompany us.'

'But—'

'We're going, Deb, and that's an end of it.'

Her attempts to cajole Elisabeth to change her mind and stay in London had only made her mistress more resolved to go, and after they'd stripped the beds in silence, Elisabeth thrust the sheets into Deb's arms. 'Take these to the whitster's,' she said. 'Mary Mercer's coming, and the last thing I need is a house full of wet linen.'

***

Elisabeth had furnished her with a bogie to push the bedding down to the whitster's for laundering. Unwilling to leave any evidence of her copying in her room, Deb felt the papers brush against her legs as she walked briskly up Thames Street. Her irritation with Elisabeth vanished as she realised that, with a bit of bending, her route would go past the parish church of St Gabriel's. She'd need to break it to Jem that she would be going away, and she could ask him directions to Bridewell.

She pushed the bogie in through the gate and set it to the side of the path, close to the burial ground, while she went to ask for him at the wooden office attached to the church. Despite the weak sun, an icy blast blew over the burial slabs. She rapped hard at the door, shivering in the cold and damp as she waited for the door to open.

'Miss Willet! What a pleasant surprise.' The words were muffled, and the sight of him made her smile. His cheerful face was half-hidden under a green knitted scarf, but his hands, encased in gloves against the cold, still held a quill.

'Have you a few moments to spare?' she asked.

He pulled the scarf down. 'It so happens I do. Dr Thurlow's not in, he's gone to a meeting with the bishop, and I'm to do his duties today. Is that the Pepyses' laundry?' He frowned, stuck the quill behind his ear. 'It looks too heavy for you. I didn't know you were expected to do such heavy work. I thought it was all tea with the ladies and visits to the milliner, or whatever you do.'

'It's all right,' she said, aware of him gazing at her with concerned eyes. 'Mrs Pepys has a visitor today, and it's too cold for drying unless it's had a start over the fires. I think she wants me out of the way, and besides, I wanted to ask you something.'

He raised his eyebrows. 'Then I'll assist you, and we can converse as we go.' He grasped the handle and pushed the bogie ahead, propelling it forward on its iron wheels as if it weighed nothing at all. As they went, he told her that he was worried about his brother Bart, who had apparently got in with bad company. When they got to the laundry he handed the bundle over to the washerwomen. 'Will you wait for it?' he asked.

'No,' she said, though Elisabeth did expect precisely that. But Deb had other ideas. 'Mr Wells, I wonder, do you know the way to Bridewell, to the poorhouse, please?'

'They don't pay you that little, surely?' His mock astonishment gave way to a grin.

She laughed. 'No, Jane said the church often have cause to send folk there, so I thought you'd be able to direct me. I'm looking for someone – a friend.'

'A friend of yours? In there? Are you sure? It's just ... it doesn't seem like the sort of place where—'

'I know, that's what Jane said. But do you know the way?'

'Better than that – I'll escort you. It will be my greatest pleasure.'

'That would be ... lovely. Thank you, is it far?'

'Only a quarter mile. I'll take you down now, while you wait for the laundry.'

She had not imagined Jem would accompany her, and the prospect was embarrassing. She did not know how to tell him about her mother, and that she would rather go alone. But the grip on her arm was firm.

* * *

Bridewell poorhouse was a long low byre made from cob and plaster, with soot-stained walls and a smell like pigswill wafting from the yard. It had been butted onto the end of a burnt-out stone building as a temporary measure. Even through the metal gate she could see the yard was swarming with people, mostly women, but some old men were leaning up against the walls, clay pipes stuck in their mouths.

'Shall I come in with you?' He'd caught her daunted expression.

'No, thank you all the same, I'll be all right now. And I'll try to get away and come to one of your services on Sunday.' She willed him to go, did not want him to associate her with this foul place.

'Oh no, don't come this week. Not unless you want to be asleep on your bench. It's Dr Thurlow preaching. If you don't mind me giving you advice, go to St Margaret's instead. It's Parson Green, and he's right rousing. Not that you need any rousing, by the look of you ...' He caught his lip. 'I mean, you'll like him.'

'Farewell, then, and my thanks,' she said, and tugged on a rusting bell by the gate. A man in a filthy smock over stained breeches appeared. *He must be the overseer*, thought Deb. She glanced over her shoulder to see Mr Wells stare at her in puzzlement a moment before he disappeared around the corner.

'We've no room,' the overseer said.

'No, I'm not looking for a place to stay,' she said, trying to sound businesslike. 'I'm looking for somebody. A woman called Eliza Caroline Willet.'

He shook his head slowly from side to side. 'No. Don't recognise the name. And we've had that many this last year, miss, what with the fire and all. We're packed to the rafters. I can't help you.'

'The postmaster says an Eliza Willet lives here. Don't you have some sort of record?'

'Aye. They have to sign, but most can only write an *X*. She might have been here, might not. She's not here now.'

'This woman could write her name. Please, can I look at the record?'

'What's it worth?'

Of course. She should have been prepared for this. She turned her back to him so he could not see the contents of her purse, took out a few coins and then held them out.

He pocketed them into his grimy breeches. 'This way.' He swung the gate open. A sea of hollow eyes looked up at her before they shifted as one body towards her, clamouring. Hands clawed at her – 'Please, miss, spare a copper', 'Any loose change?', 'Have a heart, lovely'.

The stench of poverty hit her like a wall. A sudden irrational terror drained the movement from her legs. She felt the pull at her skirts, fingers feeling for her purse strings, but she was overwhelmed, clasped the purse tight to her chest with both hands. At last, common sense returned and she struggled to twist free of the welter of bodies, but she was hemmed in.

A wave of panic made her sway on her feet. 'Help me,' she cried.

'Get out of here!' The man in the smock whipped a cat-o'-nine-tails from his belt and swung it at the mob with a crack. It caught a wrinkled old woman on the cheek. Deb gasped, tears springing to her eyes. The crowd cringed, and the mass of bodies parted reluctantly and gave them room. Deb followed close to the warden, longing to be out of sight.

He took her into a dingy cubbyhole of an office and dragged a mouldering book from a shelf. Deb leaned against the wall, panting, trying to slow her breath.

'This year,' he said, slapping it down on the table. 'The others are up there. They're a bit sooty; the gov'nor pulled them from the fire. Goes back ten years or more.'

'Thank you,' she managed.

It took a few minutes for her to recover enough to begin. From habit, she was already counting back along the shelf in a methodical way. Seven years ago. She had better start there and be thorough.

Did it matter? There wasn't an Eliza Willet here now, the warden said. But somehow it was important to know. To know if her mother had been here. Whether she'd been one of those filthy faces in the yard. She took down the book. It was crusted with soot and the leather binding was furred at the edges with green mould. Just the look of it made her stomach heave. But she steeled herself and prised it open, sighed at the long list of names on the first yellowing page, the long line of badly scrawled 'X's.

When she heard the quarter bell strike, she was still only halfway through the book. She had read hundreds of names but none was Eliza Willet. The enormity of her task struck home. She had hoped to recognise her mother's writing.

She speeded up her reading, her finger scrolling down each page until her nail was thick with dirt, but she dare not miss a single entry. A name caught her eye. Her heart leapt.

"*Eliza Willet.*"

But then she read on, "*aged 23 years*".

Too young. Disappointment flooded through her like an icy tide.

The Eliza Willet in Bridewell was illiterate and was certainly not her mother. The woman had signed it with a clumsy '*X*'.

She slumped against the wall. Had she expected to find her? Not really. But she didn't know what else to do, and it seemed that to do something, however small, might somehow draw her mother back to her. Some unspoken magic. The other, to just give up, now she had determined to find her, was unthinkable.

She sagged, wedged the book back and stood at the office door a moment, blinking at the light. Thoroughness was everything. She forced herself to scan through the rest of the records. Nothing.

The smell of unwashed flesh and filth caught at the back of her nostrils. She dreaded going back through the crowd. It would be her worst nightmare to be trapped somewhere like this. She sent up a silent prayer that her mother, wherever she was, did not have to endure it.

As she stepped into the yard, hand over her mouth and trying not to breathe the foul air, the overseer held out his hand. She was ready with more coins, to drop them so she need not touch his hand, but the ranks of women and children watched silently, accusingly. She bowed her head, ashamed, and the warden escorted her back to the iron gate with his cat-o'-nine-tails flapping a warning.

She fled into the street gulping the air, disorientated. Even the thought that her mother might be somewhere like that made her nauseous. She bent double, knees shaking.

'They didn't search your pockets and keep you in

then?' A quiet voice. She looked up. To her surprise, Jem Wells was still there waiting.

His doubtful expression made her tearful. 'There wasn't room,' she croaked, half crying, half laughing, trying to match his good humour.

'All finished?' He was looking at her with such care that she could not speak. 'Looks like it nearly finished you. You're grey as a goose. Come, let me give you my arm.'

He held out his arm and she fell against him. They made slow progress back to the laundry. He felt sturdy and solid, well attached to the earth. She leaned on him, feeling the comfort of his touch, and his other arm came around her shoulders to support her.

'I don't mean to pry,' he said, 'but it seems like an odd place to spend your free time.'

She remained silent.

'You can tell me, you know. I'm trained to it. We're taught to listen and let God make the judgements, not us.'

'I'm sorry, but I can't tell you. But I do thank you, nonetheless.'

'You disappoint me. I thought my parson's manner was improving. Perhaps I'm not as good as I hoped.' He smiled ruefully at her, and she had to smile back. A trickle of heat seemed to flow from him, fizzing in her blood, melting the hard stone that was lodged in her chest. 'Here we are.'

They were back at the laundry already. Over the tang of the urine used for bleaching, the clean smell of soap and lavender drifted over them like a blessing. The sheets were folded into a heap on the bogie, and Jem took charge of it straight away, which was a relief as it was heavier damp. He insisted on pushing it right to the Navy Chambers and hauling it round the back to the kitchen gardens so she could ask Jane to help her spread it out to finish airing in the faltering sun.

'Miss Willet, I know you are not allowed to meet me, but I wanted to say how much I've enjoyed your company. Perhaps I could call on Mrs Pepys and—'

'No.' She felt the pages of Mr Pepys' diary against her legs, and in her ears echoed Abigail's voice saying 'treason'. Jem knew nothing of all that, and she couldn't let Jem become involved with the Pepyses if they might be arrested as traitors.

'I mean, I've got to go away. Mrs Pepys is taking me to the country for a few months.'

'Months? What for?'

'She's afraid of these plague rumours. I'm sorry, Mr Wells.'

'It's Jem. Please. I keep telling you, you must call me Jem. I'd hoped...' After a quick glance at the windows, he reached for her hand, '... never mind. Come and find me at the church when you're back. Mrs Pepys can't object to prayer, surely. And if you're tired of poorhouses I can show you the madhouses instead. Or the plague pits. They might be full by then. Anything, if it means being with you.' His expression was serious. 'I didn't mean it, you know, about the plague pits.'

She smiled despite herself. 'You really know how to court a lady, don't you?'

'I like you, Miss Willet. You're not afraid of life.'

'Tush.'

'A parson needs someone who's not afraid. Someone who's prepared to go into places like Bridewell.'

'But I *was* afraid,' she said. 'It was unspeakable, I

couldn't even—'

'Exactly.' He lifted Deb's hand and pressed it to his lips. His touch made her heart race and skitter. She hoped her hand was clean enough to kiss. 'Don't forget,' he said. 'I'll be waiting. You can write, care of the vicarage.'

She hitched her skirts and hurried away, through the rows of fruit trees, flustered at the way her thoughts whirled so fast she couldn't catch hold of them. She would write, she knew that already. And he had hinted … was she imagining it? The thought came that she liked him, more than liked him. That being with him gave her a pain in her chest that was sweet and sharp together.

Was this the way Mr Pepys felt about her? The thought of Mr Pepys made her stop dead just outside the kitchen door. She had managed to evade her master's attempts to get her alone, but his eyes were always on her, his glances too lingering. It was as if the more she evaded him, the more it inflamed him.

She turned to see Jem still watching her. He had no idea, she thought, no idea at all. Full of guilt, she steeled herself and went inside.

Chapter Twenty-two

THE DAY AFTER, JEM SET OFF to the chapman on Fetter Lane, for today was the date when the news-sheet was to be printed – the one he'd helped Mrs Cresswell and the other 'ladies' to write.

'Sold out,' the chapman said when he got there. 'They're hot as hell, those. You'll get one by St Paul's though.'

Jem strode quickly through the lanes towards the ruined church, taken aback to see a great gaggle of people gathered by the printers' stalls already. All seemed to be holding a copy of the flimsy news-sheet. There was a deal of laughter and people returning to buy a second one. One young cloth-worker in a threadbare jerkin was so overcome with mirth, he wiped tears from his eyes and began reading aloud.

'Listen to this! *"Should your Eminency but once fall into these rough hands ...",'* he declaimed in a parody of a woman's voice, *'"... you may expect no more favour than they have shown unto us poor inferior whores!"* Can you imagine King Charlie-boy's face!'

'Do you think Lady Castlemaine will reply?' asked his lantern-jawed friend.

'Agree to be the patron saint of her sister whores? Do me a favour.'

'I can tell you one thing,' the chapman said, 'that printer had better watch his arse. It's going to cause a right stink.'

Jem's stomach dropped. What had seemed like a jest was now an unstoppable sensation. He bought his copy and took it home to read. Now it was in print, in black and white for all to see, it was bolder than he had ever thought. He could be in trouble. The paper lampooned the court as the whorehouse of White Hall, and the writers offered to venerate the King's mistress, Lady Castlemaine, as their sister prostitutes in Rome and Venice venerated the Pope.

Oh, merciful heavens. The reference to Barbara Castlemaine's Catholic leanings was sure to provoke an outcry from the court.

Everywhere he went there was talk of this paper. His brother Bart pounced on him the minute he came through the door, a dog-eared copy in his hand, jubilant.

'It's working!' Bart crowed, brandishing it in front of him. 'It's catching quicker than the pox! More will join our cause after this, I'm sure.'

'Not without trouble though,' Jem voiced his worry. 'They'll be coming after those who wrote it.'

'Fiddlesticks. They can't pin a thing on us. We took advice. Lizzie ran it past Bates the lawyer.'

Nevertheless, Jem thought, it was hardly the sort of thing a curate should have got himself involved with. He cursed himself. What would little Deb think, if she knew he'd been responsible for such a thing? Even the language of it. He hoped she'd never get to hear of it. Of his involvement. It was a good thing she was going out of London. But all the same, he could not help feeling a little proud of his own contribution.

* * *

Jem could not resist going down to the tavern on the Ratcliffe Highway to see how the so-called *'Poor Whores' Petition'* had been received there. Over the last few weeks, before it came out, he had gone to Lukenor Lane more and more often, carrying his printed copy of the Bible, his tracts and his collecting box.

Strange, but the Bible and the tracts had never seemed to come out of his bag. He wanted to preach to the people he met, but found in the end that his wooden collecting box was far more use. He was always opening it to fish out a copper or a token to give to a man that needed it.

His friends in the tavern were celebrating.

'Ah, my favourite parson! Come have a sup with us!' boomed Mrs Cresswell, pulling out a stool for him. She jammed her pipe back between her lips and sucked appreciatively.

There was no room at the table, but the quieter lady he had seen before smiled towards him and beckoned, and he went to join her at her table.

'We haven't been introduced,' he said. 'Jem Wells. You were here when we were writing the petition, weren't you?'

'Yes,' she said. 'I'm Lizzie. I run the school next door.'

'A school? I'd no idea there was a school near here.'

'It's not a proper school. Just a room above a shop. But it's where I teach the children their letters and the girls their manners.'

'How many children?'

'As many as I can cram through the doors – twenty, thirty maybe? Those that can have a few hours away from trying to scrape a living. Often they might only come once a week. It makes teaching hard. But better a few hours than none at all. They learn numbers and letters, that's all. There's no time or staff for more.'

Already an idea was forming in Jem's head. Now here was an enterprise where he could help. 'Can I see it?'

She laughed. 'There's nothing much to see. We have only a few slates, one sand tray for writing, and a few tracts for copying. If you want to, though, I'll take you for a look.'

He stood and she dipped her head. 'We'll catch it before the light goes, if we're quick,' she said.

She led the way through an ironmonger's shop, telling him to watch his head as there were pails and scuttles hanging from hooks above. He ducked past them and followed her up the stairs.

The room was bare except for a table strewn with slates and some papers with proverbs written out, which the children were copying. There were no benches such as he had when he was schooled, no globe or lectern for teaching from. He could not believe anyone could teach anything here.

'You see?' she said. She picked up one of the slates where the letters '*a*', '*b*' and '*c*' had been copied out in rows. He could not help but notice her hand was puckered and red, as if it had been burned.

She saw him staring. 'I can still use it. I'm lucky.'

'Is that from the fire a year back?'

'Yes. I used to have work in a printer's shop – cleaning, and parcelling up orders. It burned down. I lost everything. My son died after the fire. The smoke … he wasn't strong.' She put down the slate, looked at her bad hand as if she had just remembered what it looked like.

'Oh, I'm sorry. I did not mean to pry.' He was suddenly awkward, but Lizzie scrubbed her hand on her skirts as if that might erase the scars.

'It's all right. What's that they say? That strife helps one endure? Mrs Cresswell took me in. Nobody else would help me. I had nowhere else to go. And I couldn't work, I was too consumed with grief. I did not see how I could go on when I lost Thomas. I lived for that child.'

'Have you no other family?'

She paused; a fleeting expression of pain was immediately masked. 'No.'

'It's just that you seem ...?' he was too embarrassed to voice his thought, 'too much of a lady to be here.'

She smiled, shook her head as if she understood. 'Come, the light is waning. Let's make our way down before it gets too dark.' As they went down the stairs she paused and turned back to look over her shoulder at him. 'Men like you may call them "whores", but they're good-hearted here, kinder than the folk where I come from. In their line of work there are often children, and their prospects are bleak. The school is my way of repaying them. They gave me hope and a reason to live when I had neither.' They emerged onto the street. 'Look at me, Mr Wells. I'm too old and plain to be much use in the bedchamber. A governess is the best I could ever have hoped for. So why not for many, instead of only a few?'

'I can help,' he said, suddenly, surprising himself. 'I can raise some funds for your school, even teach, if you'll let me.'

'Are you not a working man?'

'I'm a curate in training. But my parish burned down and is being joined to another. Besides, it seems like a sign. That I should do something.'

'A sign?' She looked amused. 'A fine offer, Mr Wells, and I'd be a fool to refuse. When can you come?'

A clap on the shoulder made him jump.

'Bart!' he exclaimed.

His brother and his friends were a little the worse for ale already, and corralled Lizzie and Jem back through the tavern doors into the fug from the fire and the sharp, sweet smell of snuff and hops.

Some of the men had found themselves women. A blonde doxy sprawled in a sailor's lap, her shift unlaced under her bodice, and too much mottled flesh showing. Jem averted his eyes. 'Don't you find it hard,' he asked Lizzie, 'living here?'

'You mean, do I approve?' Her eyes appraised him. 'You should try it yourself. People judge too easily. Try living here, Mr Wells, with no servants, no work, and no means of finding any, then you'd understand. People are never what they seem on the outside.'

'I don't think—'

'Why not? If you want to be a good parson, then a week of living here would give you more of an education than any university.'

He squirmed under her gaze. 'I'll think about it.' He was wondering about Deb Willet, and how it would appear to her. It was one thing to visit the poor, but quite another to actually become one of them. But Deb was in the country, so perhaps he should. After all, a week could not hurt. And he was keen to do what he could for the school.

'I'll do it,' he said, suddenly reckless. 'Just tell me where to lodge, and I'll do it!'

Her grey eyes glittered. 'You're a fine young man, Jem Wells. You won't regret it.'

He was already regretting it. To agree to live with felons and whores. Whatever had possessed him?

Chapter Twenty-three

April

'IT'S A DISASTER. Couldn't you dissuade Mrs Pepys?' Abigail had said, when Deb went to her house to tell her she was to go to the country. 'The King will be displeased.'

'There is little I can do,' Deb said. 'I suppose I could take some documents with me and copy for you while I'm away, but it would be most unwise. Elisabeth is already suspicious. She searches my room, and once she almost caught me copying, but—'

'What?'

'It's all right. She saw nothing.'

'Fool. You must be more careful.' Abigail flounced back and forth, swishing her skirts. 'Lives are at risk. The security of the country is at risk. You made an agreement.'

'And I have honoured it,' Deb said, clenching her fingers. 'But if I am to remain employed by the Pepyses, I must surely behave as any good servant should.'

'There are pressures on me from certain quarters. I need more from Mr Pepys' diary.'

'His diary seems rather dull and uneventful to me. Is Mr Pepys still under suspicion, then?'

'The King is not a trusting man. He fears plotters everywhere, and who can blame him? Since the plot that killed his father, he has nothing but chronic distrust for everything and everyone. The treachery of the Fifth Monarchists has made him nervous, and now there are riots amongst his people and a trade embargo with the Dutch. He fears another attack from any quarter, even from within his own ministers. No, he suspects everyone of underhand dealing, even my Lord B and your Mr Pepys. That is why he pays us – us and a whole network of others to act as his secret eyes and ears.'

This thought made Deb uncomfortable. Who else was in this secret network of spies? But she reasoned with herself that if it was work for the Crown, it was good work, even though she was making the King believe that Mr Pepys had done nothing wrong. Of course, she knew this to be false, and a sliver of unease remained as a tightening in her throat – that she was actually daring to hoodwink the King.

The last few weeks of frantic preparations for the excursion were done, with Elisabeth satisfied at last with how Deb had packed her valises. They were to travel with one of Mr Pepys' cousins, Betty Turner, as well as Jane. Mrs Pepys did not trust the cook at old Mr Pepys' house. In their absence, Mr Pepys would eat out, but a daily woman, Bridget, would come in to look to his needs.

On the day they left for the country, Mr Pepys caught her in the passage with the bags, trapped her against the wall and forced his kiss on her again. Quickly, she turned her head so his lips slithered over her cheek. She was ever ready with a nimble dodge and an excuse as far as he was concerned, but he was becoming wise to her tricks, and like a hound after a fox, she could feel him moving in for the kill.

'Will you miss your big bear?' he asked, but a door slam warned them of Elisabeth's approach and, to Deb's relief, he scuttled away.

Later, just before she got into the carriage, he pressed a whole ten shillings into her hand and enjoined her in all seriousness to 'look after Elisabeth'.

In fact, the excursion to the country was a relief. Deb certainly did not miss Mr Pepys, nor did she miss the pressure of Abigail's demands. Elisabeth and Jane were better company with no men to answer to; more open and at ease, and with the warmer weather and the casting off of cloaks and heavy woollen skirts, they all felt lighter. After the dust and soot of London, the country air was reviving.

The cousin, Betty Turner, seemed used to old Mr Pepys' querulous demands, and it was clear she was fond of him, whereas Elizabeth found him a trial. Betty, who had bad knees, was happy to keep the old man company whilst Elisabeth explored the countryside with Deb and Jane. One day they took a blanket and sat on the grass amid the purpling bluebells, watching the birds drifting above them against the pale sky. Elisabeth told Deb of her childhood outside Paris, of how she rode in the forests, lived for a time in an Ursuline nunnery.

'Ah, I was such a happy child,' Elisabeth said. 'Childhood is indeed a precious thing.'

'Did you and Mr Pepys not wish for children?' Jane asked, emboldened by Mrs Pepys' confidences.

Elisabeth frowned at her impertinence, but then shook her head. 'We wish, yes, but they do not come.

And now I fear I am getting beyond it.'

'You need to get Mr Pepys to wear cool Holland-linen drawers,' Jane said, flapping her skirt up and down to make a breeze, 'my auntie swears by it.'

'Tush, Jane! I can't see my Sam in those! He likes his plain wool.'

'Well, have you tried making the bedhead lower than the foot?' Jane asked.

'To tell truth, we have tried everything,' Elisabeth said, and she looked so woebegone that Deb could not help but lay a hand on her arm, and Jane too patted her mistress's skirts in comfort.

Elisabeth pressed her lips together, and her eyes glistened. She turned her head away as though she might cry. 'It's me. He blames me. He says nothing, but I know he does.'

'Perhaps this healthy country air might do the trick,' Deb said.

Elisabeth took Deb's hand and squeezed it, but Deb could tell by her expression that Elisabeth was not convinced. How sad to long for a child so much and be denied. Deb vowed she would try even harder to befriend her mistress.

Jane was sweet on Tom Edwards, the clerk, and talked about him every minute. They were hoping to be wed soon, and the thought of it inevitably brought Jem Wells to Deb's mind again. The ache would not go away. She reprimanded herself for such feelings, but they came just the same. She had told Jem not to reply to her letters lest it upset Elisabeth, but it was harder than she had imagined to write to him and receive no reply. The thought of him made her suddenly anxious to move.

'Come on, Jane,' she said, jumping up. 'I'll race you to that tree.'

'You won't. You'll win. My legs are too short for running.'

But Jane grudgingly stood, and Elisabeth called the marks. They set off and Deb did win after all, but Elisabeth clapped her hands with the fun of it. And in the following weeks something arose between the three of them that felt like friendship, though, of course, Deb and Jane had to mind not to overstep their place.

They were to travel onwards to the West Country to meet up with Mr Pepys, who wanted a tour of the druidic monuments and the old Roman city of Bath, so Deb asked if she might write to her Uncle Butt who was still in Bristol. Uncle Butt was her father's cousin and a little intimidating. Since the break-up of the family and her mother's disappearance, she had not set eyes on him or his family, and she was not sure how she would be received. Still, there was nothing to lose. Her uncle might know the facts of why her mother left them, might even know where she went, and she was determined to find out, however uncomfortable the truth might be.

Chapter Twenty-four
June

So MUCH RATTLING ABROAD in a hot carriage; so many towns with their shops that were all the same; and Elizabeth would make the driver stop at them all. Deb was restless with nothing to occupy her mind. Surprisingly, she found that she missed the stimulation of the copying, but most of all her heart ached for Jem.

Mr Pepys came down to meet them in the West Country as Deb dreaded that he would; but to her relief Elisabeth watched him like a hawk. When they got to Bath, a letter was waiting for Deb from her Uncle Butt. Deb explained that Uncle Butt was a wealthy Bristol merchant trading sherry sack and sugar with the Indies.

Mr Pepys was enthusiastic about the idea of inspecting Deb's family, even if they were only cousins, and she said she would try to arrange it. Though, if she remembered him rightly, Deb thought wryly, Uncle Butts would certainly give Mr Pepys a run for his money. She left the Pepyses at the lodging house and went in a hired hackney to her uncle's house close to the Bristol quay. She was surprised to find when she got there that Aunt Lillibet was in bed and suffering from a complaint of the stomach.

'Deborah! What a turn-up! My, how you've grown,' Aunt Lillibet enthused, sitting up in her lace bed-jacket, her thin hair scraped back under a frilled cap. 'Quite the young lady.' She pulled Deb towards her and pressed an effusive kiss on both cheeks.

Deb leaned away; Aunt Lillibet smelled overpoweringly of sulphurous medicine. There were several bottles of greasy-looking elixir on the table next to the bed, and a bloodletting basin.

Aunt Lillibet patted the bed to indicate she should sit. 'Uncle William will be back soon. He just had a few items of business to attend to. Have you heard from your father?'

'He's well.' She masked her feelings about him. 'My brothers write to me and tell me how he does. He's not much of a writer himself, he's far too busy. His wool exports from Ireland are less lucrative than they were, but I expect he'll weather it as usual.'

'You must miss them all.'

'We keep in touch by post,' she said, 'but I haven't seen either of my parents for more than a year. In fact I haven't seen my mother for more than five years.'

'You've heard nothing from her? Not in all this time?'

Deb shook her head. A lump seemed to have formed in her throat so she could not utter a word.

Aunt Lillibet reached out and placed a wrinkled hand over her fingers. 'That's shocking. I know it is none of my business, but, Lord knows, I thought they'd repair the rift somehow. But your father can be as stubborn as a mule. William says he was always the same, even as a child. And if William were here I wouldn't even be speaking of it.'

'Has he talked with my father then?'

'Yes, he sides with him, as men do. They can't bear the idea that they're not in control.' Aunt Lillibet tapped her hand on the bedsheet. 'I told him, a girl needs a mother's hand, and he should let her see you once in a while. None of it is your fault, though it was a terrible business, your father turning your mother out like that. Though I have to say, he can hardly be blamed. But I heard your father tell William she'd gone to her brother in London. Did you not think to ask after her there?'

'You mean Uncle Jack? But I thought he had gone to Holland. Was he in London then?'

'Yes. Though I dare say he didn't want anyone to know. Not since he was involved in that plot to keep New Amsterdam out of English hands. He was staying at The Grecian, the coffee house at Wapping.'

Deb let out a cry of recognition. The Grecian! So that was it. A coffee house. Why hadn't she thought of something like that? She obviously hadn't remembered it rightly; she'd thought they were talking about a person, not a place. And Uncle Jack – yes that would make sense. 'Aunt Lillibet, why did my father send my mother away? What had happened to make him so angry? I don't understand.'

'Has nobody told you?' Her aunt looked discomfited. 'It's not really my place ... but I guess you've a right to know ... from what I've gathered, she cuckolded your father. But he never speaks of it, and I've only heard whispers, not the whole story. William doesn't like me to even mention your mother's name. I think he's frightened I might do the same to him – that infidelity's catching somehow, like the plague. And there were rumours,' her voice dropped to a whisper, 'that the baby was ... that he was not your father's. But I don't think I should betray his confidence ... it's really up to him—'

'A baby?'Deb asked, grasping Aunt Lillibet's hand. 'You mean she'd had the baby before—'

The bang of the downstairs door made Aunt Lillibet snatch her hand away and sit up in bed, arrange her ruffled cap over her sparse grey hair. 'It's William,' she whispered. 'Best you don't say anything about what I've told you, he'll be angry—'

Moments later, Deb's Uncle Butts arrived and there was no more chance to speak. Though she was glad to see his familiar face – fatter and with a bigger, more extravagant wig than her father, he had the same long family nose and pointed beard.

He exclaimed on how much she had grown, and how wonderful it was to see her, but Deb's mind was elsewhere, thinking of Aunt Lillibet's words about her mother. No wonder Aunt Beth had thought her mother scandalous. Who was the man who had dared to belittle her father, the man who had ruined their lives? She had known all along that it must be this, but she had not wanted to admit that Mama could have been so stupid. And a baby? The thought was too disturbing to think on.

She hoped, at least, that her aunt was right about Jack. Uncle Jack, on her mother's side, had always been known as the black sheep of the family because he held dissenters' views, being a staunch Presbyterian. He had fled to Holland and Mama used to sigh over him and wish he would repent. Deb had no idea he was back in London, though her mother must have had word.

As soon as she returned to London, she'd go to The Grecian coffee house and find out where they were now.

Elisabeth was not happy to be going back to London, but Sam was insistent he had had enough diversion, and was needed at the Treasury. On the way, the carriage jolted and jounced, and flies from the horses kept getting in through the open windows. She flapped her fan at them and stifled her annoyance with her husband. He *would* keep telling Deb the latest scandals – the King and Lady Castlemaine, Lord Carnegie, whose whore gave his Lordship the pox, and the Duke of Buckingham, who had installed that slattern the Countess of Shrewsbury in his house. They always said Paris was bad, but it was *nothing* to London – a city full of whores just waiting to pull a good man down.

And when Sam wasn't telling Deb about whores and doxies, he was simpering across the carriage at her like a fool, as if these exploits were some great joke. It was enough to make any woman scream. It was clear from everything he said that he had spent the entire time they had been away in the country, not at work as he should have been, but *gallivanting*.

She glanced over. Ever since they had met Deb's relations, Sam was looking at Deb in quite a new way. 'Well, your family seem very nice people. Very nice indeed,' he had said to Deb, after the odious Butts had showed off his enormous wine cellar, and glass cabinets full of blindingly polished silver plate.

Elisabeth's heart had shrivelled in her chest with jealousy. Her own family were the cause of much shame – continually impoverished and the source of much annoyance to her husband. Now Elisabeth stared out of the window at the darkening landscape, dreading returning home. Back to her empty life in London, with nothing to do except envy other women their babies and give the servants instructions.

It was better when it had just been her and Sam, when they were poor, and she did the cooking herself, and he came home every night asking for a cuddle with his hot broth.

On days like this, the terror of losing Sam was just too much to bear, as if it would consume her, this tearing feeling in her chest. She had the urge to flee, back to France, instead of staying in the black wart of London, which disfigured the country with its whoremongering King. A king who gave every man a God-given excuse to behave just as His Majesty did.

Sam was still telling Deb about the scandals of the court. Elisabeth gritted her teeth. If that pricklouse laid one finger on Deb Willet, she'd see to it that he never walked again.

Chapter Twenty-five

THE DAY'S TEACHING WAS DONE, and Jem picked his way over the creaking duckboards which covered the running slime of filth in the road and into the yard. The first time he saw the dilapidated tavern where he was to lodge, the lanterns swathed in red silk by the door, he had protested.

'Not here,' he said to Lizzie, but she had taken him firmly by the arm. 'You wanted to see how we live? Well, Clement's Yard is the best place to see it.'

Even now he could not quite believe he was actually lodging at Mrs Cresswell's bawdy house, in the same house as Lizzie herself. He passed two of the scantily clad, white-faced girls by the door, who giggled at him and said in chorus, 'Evening, Mister Wells.'

His curt nod in reply brought gales of laughter in his wake.

He passed through the tavern and up the uneven wooden stairs to the end of the corridor. Groans and a woman's hoarse cough came from behind the plank doors as he passed, but he studiously ignored them. He was not used to being laughed at, especially by women, and it made him feel foolish.

Once inside his own room he shut the door firmly behind him. None of the doors had locks, to his surprise. 'What's there to steal?' Lizzie had said. 'And besides, we trust each other.' Jem went to pick up his Bible, which lay open on the floor by his pallet. But he had no mind to read it; he was too tired and cross.

What was he doing here? He had asked Dr Thurlow for a week's leave, to do charitable work in Lukenor Lane, and to his surprise it had been granted, eventually, but only after he'd done another month's stint preaching at St Margaret's. He almost laughed, remembering how full of zeal he'd been when he arrived. Now he was exhausted. In only two days he had discovered that he could never be a teacher. His ideals from the hallowed halls of his own education simply did not apply here in the rookeries of Lukenor Lane, where violence was the language of every day and discipline meted out with a cane would be laughable – too mild to even provoke surprise.

How Lizzie stood it, he had no idea. Her pupils came and went, most of them barefoot and riddled with lice. Her weapon was kindness, and she was patient with them all, even though writing out a single chalk letter might be the most that any of them would ever achieve.

He unbuttoned his coat and took it off, but some instinct of self-preservation made him reluctant to take off his breeches. Hauling the rough, thin blanket up to his chin, he lay down, hearing the straw rustle on the hard wood. He shifted to try to get his hip-bones comfortable and thought ruefully of his well-furnished chambers in town. This room was empty save for a weighty chair, probably from old Henry's time, which Lizzie had somehow found for him. Its solidity was unsuitable for a room which had only been partitioned from the next by a thin wall of wattle and daub. A wall which panted and sighed along with Polly, the whore next door.

A week, he'd said he would stay. God's truth, but it would be a long week.

He took out Deb's letter which he had brought from his lodgings. It told him of her journey towards the West Country. She described the sight of Wells Cathedral, and told him it was his namesake, and she hoped he would one day have the chance to see it for himself.

He pressed the letter to his cheek to try to catch a scent of her, and he itched to reply. Over the weeks, he had received several letters, but she had told him not to write back, for fear she would lose her position. Thinking of her made him hot and fidgety, and not at all like a churchman. Instead, it gave him an ache that made him want to hit something. Groaning, he put the letter to one side, closed his eyes, and before long, fell into a restless slumber.

He was woken by a hand shaking him by the shoulder. Bleary, he sat up, tried to slap the hand away.

'Mr Wells, you've to come quick. Lizzie says to fetch you.'

In the gloom he made out Polly from next door, hair hanging loose, a sack wrapped round her shoulders over her grubby chemise.

'What's the matter?'

'Someone's dying. We need a vicar.'

'I'm not a vicar.'

'What's the bloody difference? You're something aren't you? A churchman?' She pulled at his shirt to try to rouse him. 'You've to come quick.'

'Let go, I'm coming.'

Polly held out his coat for him to put his arms in. 'We need you respectable. It's our Joan, and she's going to have a proper send-off. We owe it her.'

Polly grabbed a lit taper from the rush-stand and led

him downstairs, clattering down in her wooden clogs. The taper blew out instantly in the air outside and he heard her curse, but she did not slow, just wound her way a half-mile, through the dark wasps' nest of alleys until she came to a brick-built house with lights like hot eyes at the windows. Over the door swung a sign showing a metal bath with a pair of naked winged feet hovering disembodied above the painted steam.

Polly did not knock but burst through the door with Jem at her shoulder.

What he saw inside was a scene from hell.

He instinctively covered his nose to block out the stink of metal and sweat. Steam belched from copper vats over four huge fires. In one of the baths flopped a naked man, his body cratered with sores, what was left of his ravaged face red with heat. Jem had heard of this, the mercury baths, a treatment for the French pox, but had never stopped to think of the reality of the words. He passed another bath where a woman with her sleeves rolled to her wet armpits was wiping a man over and over. Jem averted his eyes; he did not want to see what she was wiping. Nobody paid them any attention as Polly hurried them through the coiling blanket of steam to a back room.

They stumbled their way past the paraphernalia of the sick; the cloths and basins, the bloodletting bowls and chamber pots, but what made it even more difficult was the crowd. Twenty or so young women, packed close together, in various states of disarray, one even with a grizzling baby at her breast. Jem was relieved to see Lizzie, the face of sanity, stand up from where she had been kneeling to greet him.

'Thank you,' she said. 'It's Joan. She won't last much longer. We sent for her mother, but she might not get here in time.'

Jem looked at the waiflike figure on the bed. Lacking hair and her cheeks hollow, her nose eaten away, her skin silvered with mercury, she looked like a corpse already. Jem stared in horror. He could go no nearer.

'Courage,' Lizzie whispered. 'It is her soul that needs your prayers, not her body.'

'What do you want me to do?'Jem dithered.

'For heaven's sake man, what do you think? Say a prayer, and quickly. Tell her who you are, and if you believe it, tell her there's a better life waiting than the one she's had here.'

He looked around him for inspiration but was met by the expectant stares of the gathered women. Lizzie pushed him forward. 'Take hold of her hand.'

Jem took the cold clammy hand in his. 'I'm Jeremiah Wells,' he said. 'I'm a curate ... from St Gabriel's ... come to pray with you.'

The girl showed no response, her breath was fetid, rasping and slow. He could think of nothing, was frighteningly hollow, completely unprepared. He grasped onto the first words that came to him. *'I pray you, Good Jesus, that as you have given me the grace to drink in with joy the word that gives knowledge of you, so in your goodness you will grant me to come at length to yourself, the source of all wisdom, to stand before your face for ever. Amen.'*

On cue, the rest of the women mumbled 'Amen'.

'Don't he look nice in his smart breeches?' He heard a woman's loud whisper.

'Wish Joan could see him, an' all. A blooming parson praying over her. She'd have laughed so hard she'd 'a' split her sides,' another said, but her voice was crock-full of tears.

A slight movement in his palm. The girl twitched her hand.

He squeezed it harder, feeling the birdlike bones of her fingers. 'God bless and keep you,' he said, but he was hanging on to her now, holding her to life, willing her to stay. As if she could read his mind, her hand tightened a moment. A great exultation rose in him, and he squeezed the hand for all he was worth. The hand fell limp. There was silence.

Jem squeezed again, but there was nothing.

This couldn't be it, could it? Just this? He looked up to Lizzie, who leaned down to listen at her lips. She shook her head.

The girls gathered in the room did not cry – there was not a sound – but many made the sign of the cross before trooping out.

Jem shifted in his boots, unsure whether to stay or go. The atmosphere in the room tied him there, and the gnawing sense of having failed somehow.

'I'll sit with her until they come to bury her.' Lizzie's voice broke the tension. 'You go.'

'No, I'll wait with you. I couldn't sleep now in any case.' He sat down opposite her.

She shot him a grateful look. 'Bede. A man who believed in miracles. I've always liked that prayer.'

'It was the first thing—'

The door behind them opened. They turned. A handsome woman in a full-skirted green dress took one look at Lizzie's face. 'I'm too late.'

'Sorry, Abigail, she could not hang on any longer. Mr Wells, here, said a few words.'

The woman looked dazed. 'Mr Wells?'

'Our pet curate.' Somehow Jem did not mind this description. He stood to give the woman his chair, but she did not take it.

She went to the bed, knelt and took the still-warm body in her arms, stroked her white forehead and the scanty strands of hair. 'She used to let me do this when she was a baby. But she wouldn't let me since. She'd be angry with me if she could see me, wouldn't she, Lizzie?'

'Probably,' Lizzie said, 'she was always a wildcat, your Joan. But she's at peace now.'

'At peace.' She looked to Jem. 'The pain will be gone?'

Jem nodded, though he had no idea what might be happening, what heaven might await a girl like Joan. Yet he could not think of her in the fires of hell either. It did not seem fair.

'She was so pretty. Will she be pretty too?'

Jem could not answer. The woman was too large for this scene. She was too well-dressed, too bright, her clothes too fine. Only her eyes were the right size, searching for an answer from him for her own pain.

'Lord forgive me,' the woman said to him. 'She didn't want to die here. Fool that I am, I bullied her into it. I thought there was a chance ... but it was too late. And she wanted to die near the folk she knew, in Clement's Yard.'

'It's all right, Abigail,' Lizzie said. 'Clement's Yard came to her.'

During the long night, Jem sat with Joan's mother, Abigail, and with Lizzie. In the morning Abigail left to make the funeral arrangements.

'She must be made of steel,' Jem said. 'Her daughter dead, and she did not shed a single tear.'

'She could always hide her feelings. She's an actress with the Duke's players. Lord Bruncker's lady. She and Joan used to live here, after her drunken husband tired of her, got a new wife, and threw them out. They lived just round the corner, plied the usual trade. But then Abigail got taken on by Davenant's men, and as she

- 221 -

moved up, little Joan moved down. Wouldn't listen to her mother, though Abigail tried often enough to get her out of Clement's Yard. I taught Joan for a while, but it was no good. She was one that was too clever for learning.'

'You taught her?'

'She was sharp, but she wanted the quick way. She'd no time for sitting still, always needed to be on the move. She'd pilfer, and run rackets or bets, and always thought she knew best. Wouldn't have it that her mother could help her, and it used to be torture – to see Abigail leave her behind, drive off in her fancy coach, her back ramrod stiff as if she didn't care. Broke her heart, I wager. But Joan was adamant. "A whore's a whore," she said, "however you dress it up, and I don't know any other life but the yards."'

'You mean she chose it? She could have got away from it all?' He was incredulous.

'It was her home, where she was queen of the roost. You saw all those round her bed paying their dues to her; she had friends in the Yard; she was well liked, respected. Invincible, they used to say. That was until the pox got her. It was one of the King's men, I think, who was responsible. Her friends warned her, watch out for the King's petticoat-men. They're the dirtiest, despite their fancy lace breeches and French manners.'

Jem was silent. His chest felt as though it was caving in.

'It wasn't her fault. It's a risk they all take. Goes with the occupation. Just like sailors at the mercy of the weather. Joan was a good woman, lived her life her own way, valued only her own opinion. Don't suppose any god could ask for much more.'

Jem turned away; her words had brought up a great well of emotion. Abigail Williams's tears came then, but not from her eyes, from Jem's.

Chapter Twenty-six

THE STINK OF THE CITY gave Deb a shiver of excitement. She had not realised how much she missed the bustle and hubbub of the streets, and, though she did not want to admit it to herself, how much she had missed Jem Wells.

She allowed herself a moment to dwell on him. It had been months, and now summer was here, and there wasn't a single day, or even an hour, when she had not thought of him. She couldn't help it; it was as if all her thoughts had gathered in a magnifying lens, all focussed towards him, with a light so hot it could burn. She hoped something would have resolved itself and his brother would have been paid by now. It made her feel guilty to be employed by Mr Pepys, who worked for the Navy Board, when Jem's brother was still awaiting his pay.

And now it was her first day off. She hurried to St Gabriel's but was disappointed to find Jem was out, so she decided to continue to The Grecian coffee house in search of Uncle Jack. It was a long way downriver, so she had to catch a boat, but once alighted at Wapping Old Stairs she found it easily enough. She was nervous, but the smell of roasting coffee beans drew her along the street to a sagging half-timbered building with an unevenly tiled roof, which was almost dipping into the river at the back.

At the door, a liveried man, sweating in a tied wig, waited to take the pennies from the customers. 'Beg pardon,' she asked, 'but may I speak with the proprietor?'

'If you're another wife that wants to tell him to close down, no you can't.' The doorman scowled at her.

'No, nothing like that. I'm looking for someone. Jack Gates, and his sister Eliza Willet. The proprietor might know them.'

'Women aren't allowed.'

'But—'

'Wait.' He put a hand up to stay her words. 'All right, all right. I'll ask if Mr Constantine will see you. Name?'

'Deborah Willet.'

He called a boy from inside who touched his cap and scuttled away back into the dim interior. How on earth he stood the stench of roasting beans, she did not know. She had almost given up hope of anyone coming when a swarthy man in a flamboyant lace jabot emerged from the door. This must be Mr Constantine.

'Miss Willet?'

She nodded and he beckoned her through the door with a curl of his index finger. She followed him into the dark, past a group of staring men in rough smocks and up some uneven gloomy stairs.

Mr Constantine sat down in a captain's chair and pointed to the chair opposite. She sat, trying not to stare at the ship's wheel hanging on the wall and the bare-breasted mermaid figurehead. The noise of voices below sounded like sailors crammed in the hold of a ship, and when she glanced down, she saw that smoke sifted up between the floorboards to drift round her ankles.

'Now, they say you are looking for Jack Gates, the bone-setter.' Mr Constantine's black eyes were not unfriendly, but businesslike. His accent was unmistakeably foreign, but perfectly intelligible.

'That's right. He's my uncle.'

'Who said you could find him here?'

'Another relation, my aunt. I just want to know where they are. They're my only family in London. Do you know them?'

'I know Jack Gates,' he said guardedly. 'But he's long gone. He lived upstairs, in my lodging house. It wasn't a coffee house back then, see, just a sailor's tavern with rooms. He was a regular – backwards and forwards he went, between here and Rotterdam in the Low Countries. Sometimes a month, sometimes half a year at a time he stayed. Last time was a few years ago. Afore the fire anyway. Then he disappeared. I suppose back to Rotterdam.'

'You don't know an address?'

'No. Sorry.'

'Do you remember if there was ever a woman with him, his sister?'

Mr Constantine laughed as if his cheeks would crack. 'Was there ever a woman, she asks! Jack Gates, he was never without one. Gentleman Jack, they used to call him, for he was well-spoken. I'd hear them – creeping up the back stairs and then the banging of the bed. Round here, it's easy pickings for a gentleman. Specially a good-looking cove like Jack with money in his pocket.'

Deb let her gaze drop downwards, abashed, but then persisted. 'My mother's short, and they say she looks a little like me. Oh, and I don't know if this is right, but it's possible she was expecting a baby or might have had a baby with her?' If Aunt Lillibet was right, it was worth asking.

Mr Constantine shook his head, but then he paused, rubbed his jaw. 'Wait – something comes back. There *was* a woman with a baby. Jack told me she was his sister, but I thought it was another of his doxies, you know? One he'd got in the family way. I remember because I thought it was strange, that he didn't just throw her out. And the baby, oh it was a horrible sickly thing. There were complaints about the crying. Day and night it cried, and the gentlemen didn't like it. I told Jack she'd have to go somewhere else. Next thing I knew the woman and the baby were gone and I thought no more of it. But it was a long time ago.'

'About five years since?'

'I'd say so. Lord love us, I'd forgotten all about it. Strange what you forget, isn't it?'

'She never came back?'

'No. Seen *him*, though – last time about a year ago. Downstairs, supping alongside old Skinner and his cabal of cronies. Then there was that sea battle with the Dutch. Afterwards, anyone suspected of being a sympathiser scarpered. Like the rest of them, Jack Gates just did a flit in the night. He's not been back, more's the pity.'

'Then where will I find this Mr Skinner? He might know where my uncle is now. Do you have an address for him?'

Mr Constantine narrowed his eyes and scrutinised her. 'I can't just give out a customer's address like that. It could make trouble. You must give me yours and I'll ask him to contact you.'

'Oh. I see what you mean. Have you a nib?'

He waved his arm towards the table by the grimy window. Conscious of his eyes fixed on her back, she picked up the ragged goose quill that lay there, dipped it in the ink. "*Mistress D. Willet, Care of Samuel Pepys*", she wrote, then scratched down her address in Seething Lane, forming the letters slowly to make sure it was legible.

She blew on it and handed it to Mr Constantine. He glanced once, then looked again, this time more closely. He frowned. 'You stay with Mr Pepys? Mr Pepys of the Navy Board?'

'Yes, that is he.'

Mr Constantine walked away. He took out a pipe, tapped it with his fingers and sucked on it without lighting up, seeming to come to a decision before replacing it in his pocket. She sensed a shift in the atmosphere, something indefinable. When he turned back to face her, his face was grim. 'Empty your pockets,' he said.

'What?'

'Jack Gates, he never paid his bills or his notice. If he is a relation of yours I'll take some of what he's owing.'

'But you can't—'

Her words died in her mouth. Constantine strode towards her so that she had to back away towards the wall. A barometer behind her swung as she stepped back into it. He was speaking, but she could not take in the words. It was as if a baited bear had suddenly turned and was snarling at her. She readied herself to run, but he was a big powerful man, and his men were downstairs barring her way out.

'If you work for Pepys, I dare say you have been paid, unlike some others I could mention. Your purse, Miss Willet.'

- 227 -

Shakily, she took out her purse and shook the coins and tokens out onto her palm. 'Please, this is all I have. Take it, but leave me enough to get the wherry back up to Tower Hill.'

He brought his face so close to hers she could see the black hairs in his nostrils, the furrows between his brows. 'Do you think sailors' wives have the luxury of travelling by boat? My tavern went under because sailors were never paid their dues. Thank Christ for coffee is all I can say. Pepys is a lapdog. Too scared to stand up for the sailors to the King. All bluster and no bloody action. You can walk.' He scooped the coins off her palm with his hand and counted them. 'More than four pounds your uncle Jack Gates owes me. Your coins don't cover the debt. I'll send you the bill. If it is not paid within one month, then I will send the debtor's clerk to fetch goods to the value.'

'But you can't! It's not my fault—'

'You're his relation. You should pay. Is it fair I should be out of pocket? No. And besides, Mr Pepys withholds payments from our sailors, doesn't he? Your uncle's debt will drop when all our sailors are paid. Tell that to your Mr Pepys.'

After she had stumbled back out into the light, Deb waited a moment by the wharf, breathless with shock. She leaned on a wooden rail, peering down into the murky grey water sliding past below. What was she to do? She certainly could not tell Mrs Pepys that she had actually been inside a coffee house. And it was even more certain that she could not afford to pay Mr Constantine four pounds.

Curse Uncle Jack. Her mother had always said he was a ne'er-do-well. 'His own worst enemy' was her phrase. But she would have to find the money somehow, or Constantine would send his men to the house. Why had she given him her address? That had been foolish. Now he knew she worked for the Pepyses and he might come and threaten her again, and Deb could just imagine Elisabeth's horrified face if Constantine or a debt collector arrived unannounced at Seething Lane.

Unless she could find her uncle, she would have to pay off the debt. It gave her a pressure in the chest, as if something was squeezing her stays too tight. Deb inhaled the damp woody smell of the water and set off to walk downriver. Without her purse, she was vulnerable, as if her last protection had been stolen from her. She had trusted Mr Constantine, but he had changed in a heartbeat when he read Pepys' name. Now every man seemed unpredictable, a threat. She kept her head down and walked as quickly as she dared without drawing attention to herself.

A safe distance away from The Grecian, Deb stopped to lean on the railings and massage the stitch in her side. Passing barges ferried loads of timber and bricks to put London back together again. She sighed, knowing Mr Constantine probably would not give her note to Mr Skinner, not seeing as he seemed so against Mr Pepys' household.

So Uncle Jack was in Rotterdam. Perhaps Mama had gone there with him, too. But no, she had left before that, Constantine had said. The thought that her mother had actually been at The Grecian, but that she'd missed her, swamped her with despair. Where had she gone after that? Had she stayed in London, or had she eventually followed Uncle Jack?

She stepped aside to let a woman pass. She was pale-faced and thin, carrying a squirming bundle of what looked like old clothes. The woman gave no smile or thanks but trudged past with hollow eyes. Only after she'd gone did Deb realise the bundle was a baby. Constantine said he'd remembered a baby.

She imagined her mother, cast out from The Grecian as well as from her home, all because of some passion she could not resist. Why could she not resist it? She should have been strong, thought of her children. But perhaps the new baby meant more to Mama than her other children. Deb braced herself, pushed the hurtful thought away. Perhaps she should give up. She did not know where to start looking for a woman and child.

She took out the miniature and stared at it, at the pale oval face with its composed smile. Then she hurled it, watched it arc into the river. Immediately, she regretted it, but it was too late. She would never see her mother's face again.

Chapter Twenty-seven

'GOOD MORNING,' JEM SAID, holding out a wooden box with a slot in the top of it. 'I'm collecting for the poor of this parish.' He dropped his voice to a whisper. 'I bumped into an acquaintance of mine, Crawley from the Navy office, and he said that you were back. I couldn't wait any longer.'

Deb half closed the front door behind her and frowned at him, but her eyes were laughing. 'Wait there, I'll get a donation.'

'No, don't go.' He put his hand on her arm, then slid his fingers down until they brushed hers. The touch was delicate, but intoxicating.

'Who is it?' Mrs Pepys demanded from inside.

'Collection for the poor,' Deb shouted.

'Again?' The voice was disgruntled. 'Oh, *d'accord*. Fetch my purse and I'll find them a few coppers.'

Deb hurried indoors into the dark of the house, and after a little searching found the purse in the fruit bowl on the dining-room sideboard. Thinking fast, she withdrew a scrap of paper from the drawer and wrote Jem a quick message. In the parlour, Elisabeth pouted and emptied her purse to fish out a few farthings. A few moments later Deb was back on the doorstep. She slipped the coins into the box.

'Here,' he said, and passed her a note.

'Snip-snap!' She handed him a scrap of paper in return.

He laughed. 'We think alike. You look well,' he whispered. 'The country air suits you. And I've so much to tell you.' She had been thinking the same, and her cheeks were stiff with smiling. It was so good to see him.

'Deb?' A voice from inside. Mrs Pepys wanted her.

Jem grimaced to show he'd understood, before he backed down the few steps and crossed the street, narrowly missing being run down by a dray-cart because his eyes were still fixed on her face.

'Watch out!' she cried, her heart jerking in her chest.

As she watched him go, her attention was caught by another man across the street – a man in a dark cloak with a slouch hat pulled down over a straggling wig. It could be the man from The Grecian – Constantine's man – but she couldn't be sure. Something about his furtiveness alarmed her. She had not had time yet to do anything about Uncle Jack's debt. She hurried inside, shut the door. Immediately, Elisabeth began to talk –about how airless and cramped the house was after the country, and she must have new decorations to brighten it up. Deb was to write for samples and order quotations.

She was forced to pen the orders and listen to how Mr Pepys was too mean to buy them their own coach, and that Elisabeth deserved better than a hired hackney. As soon as she could get away, Deb ran upstairs to peer from the upstairs windows. The courtyard and the surrounding streets were reassuringly empty. The thought occurred to her that perhaps the man had been sent by Abigail or the King to check on her return. She remembered Abigail telling her about the network of spies, and it filled her with foreboding.

I'm imagining it, she thought, shaking her head at her own foolishness. He was probably just a passer-by who had happened to glance up. She put him from her mind and took out Jem's message. To her surprise it was a tract of poetry, written in his long sloping hand. Of course, she knew he had been to the Merchant Taylor's School, and had been a Fellow at Cambridge, but she had not known he was a poet.

"For dearest Miss Willet, in case you are regretting leaving the peace of the country for the soots of London, with my great affection."

'Dearest'. 'With great affection.' Her heart seemed to flip in her chest.

Eagerly she scanned the poem. Elaborate and full of metaphorical references, it was a poem likening Paradise to a garden in which all moral virtue was contained. It thrilled her that Jem, who was always so ready with quips and jests, could also be such a deep thinker. But then, she thought, he was training to be a curate after all. She pressed it to her chest. How different it was from the poem Mr Pepys had given her.

Jem's poem was all innocence, with its emphasis on sowing and reaping moral virtue, but it gave her a queasy feeling that she might not be good enough, might fail to match up to his expectations. She vowed she would do her best in future, to be the unsullied embodiment of everything Jem Wells might wish a young lady to be. She would wear crisp white linen and avoid any contact at all with Mr Pepys.

Her note to Jem had simply said, *'I'll be at church on Sunday at the morning service.'* Elisabeth was sitting to have her portrait painted that day and had grudgingly given Deb the day off.

When Sunday came she was in a ferment of anticipation. She wore a dazzlingly white neckerchief and kept straightening her straw hat over and over, tapping her cheeks to make them rosy. After the service they emerged into bright sunshine and Jem suggested they catch a wherry out towards Richmond for a stroll in the country. On the way he took hold of her hand and encouraged her to lean back against him, letting the noonday sun warm her heart as her head rested against his shoulder. His hand crept gently around her waist, sending tingles through her body like the currents of the water.

As they approached the landing stage, she asked him, 'How is Bart? Have the sailors received their dues yet?'

'He's just the same,' he said, handing her out onto the jetty. 'He twisted my arm and persuaded me to help them. He's got me involved with his little group now. I'm giving help to some of the poor women in Lukenor Lane. There's a school where they educate the children—'

He paused, looking to her reaction. She was trying to make sense of it. 'Isn't that where ...?' She licked her lips, unwilling to say the word 'whore'.

He took her arm and steered her onto the path away from the other passengers. 'Yes, but it's such good work, Miss Willet. They have nothing, and worse, they turn to sin to try to solve it. While you were away I went to live amongst them, saw how they have to scrape and scrounge to get by.'

'I don't understand. You lived *there*? But why?'

'I've got a plan, to set up a mission in that parish, somewhere sailor's wives can go if they're in trouble. Somewhere with a physician, and a midwife, and ... oh, there's so much I need to tell you. But I'll need a woman to help me, a woman who could set an example. A woman like you, Miss Willet.'

Deb could not catch up with his words. She could make no sense of them. Was this a proposal? And what was this talk of living in Lukenor Lane? She could not believe he could be serious. But she had no time to think, for he was speaking.

'You remember that news-sheet, the one there was such a fuss about, that was addressed to Lady Castlemaine—'

'Oh yes, a scandal wasn't it?' Deb said, trying to find her feet in the conversation, and anxious to impress upon him her disgust at such vulgar news. 'Mr Pepys showed it to me when I got home, though I was quite shocked he should give it to me to read. Such uncouth language. That someone should have the brazen cheek to publish such a despicable thing. The King should find out who did it and deal with them.'

Jem stopped. He withdrew his arm from hers. He was looking at her in a puzzled way.

'What's the matter?' she asked. The sun beat down on her shoulders.

'Don't you think it appalling that the King should set such an example, to openly flaunt his whore at court, with no consideration whatever for the poor Queen? That he should expect our sailors to fight his cause yet pay them nothing – not even a dry pea – for their trouble?'

She was flustered. He was frowning at her in a way she had never seen before. A wasp settled on her arm and she flapped it away. 'I know nothing of the court, the ins and outs of it, I mean,' she said, still trying to find an even keel, 'but dissenters are never satisfied, are they? And I have to say, though the King has his weaknesses, when Cromwell ruled us I got the impression life was a deal more uncomfortable than now. I can't remember much, but Mr and Mrs Pepys are quite convinced of it. Look at how he closed all the theatres and stamped on any sort of entertainment. People are grateful that the King is back, and that news-sheet was monstrous cheek. It did nothing but stir up trouble.'

Jem looked away out over the river, staring at the opposite bank.

She touched him on the arm. 'Jem?'

He turned, a sharpness in his eyes. 'And you think the King's rule better? A man who sets us no example? He is king in name only. As far as I can see he is a dissolute, cruel, unthinking man, who cannot see the nose in front of his face. He is bringing the country to ruin. A man like that is unfit to rule decent men like us.'

Deb stopped dead, as if her boots had glued themselves to the ground. His words struck deep inside her. Her family had been staunch Royalists. It had never occurred to her that Jem might have different views to her own. She did not know what to say; there seemed to be no answer to his statement.

'Let's not talk of him,' she said finally. 'Look, those ducks over there – aren't they sweet?'

He grunted an assent, but she could see he was still thinking. He twisted his hat in his hands and did not take her arm again, but walked ahead, striding forward as if he wanted to get somewhere fast. She followed a little behind, struggling to keep up in the heat, her skirts flapping hot around her ankles. A wave of feeling wanted to burst from her chest but was stuck at her throat.

Eventually she stopped in the middle of the dirt path, stared at Jem striding away, his broad shoulders hunched. He turned when he did not hear her footsteps following. She did not move, just stood, hands hanging limply at her sides. A trickle of sweat ran down to her eyebrow. His face was unreadable, like a mask. She had never before seen him without a smile.

'I think I'd like to go home now.' Her voice sounded tight and small.

He walked back towards her. 'Oh. If that's what you want. I thought we could ... but no, I see it is impossible.' He sighed. 'Very well,' he said.

They walked side by side, silently, as though a wall of glass was lodged between them. Several times she opened her mouth to speak, but then dare not.

Back at the jetty there was a family group waiting to get the boat up to town. They had a basket of provisions and the two children were laughing and jesting, tickling each other, full of noisy excitement. It reminded her of her smaller brothers and made her even more miserable.

When they finally got to Old Swan Stairs, Jem put out his hand to help her to dry land, but his eyes stayed resolutely away from hers.

'I'll find a hackney and make my own way home,' she said.

'If you're sure.'

'I'm sorry,' she said. 'I don't know what I've done, but I'm sorry.'

'There is nothing to be sorry about,' he said briskly. 'We just see life differently, that's all. Goodbye, Miss Willet, I hope to see you in church again.'

No. Not this, not this icy politeness. Tears blurred her eyes, but she did not want him to witness them. She had no money for a carriage; Constantine had taken it all. Still, she hurried away as fast as she could, not daring to look back, her hand pressed to her nose.

Chapter Twenty-eight
July

OVER THE FOLLOWING WEEKS, DEB could not get Jem out of her mind. It was a torture. This was it, this was love, she realised, this feeling that your insides were being torn apart by wild dogs.

She replayed their conversation over and over in her head, trying to find the moment when things shifted. At first she was inconsolable, then angry. What was clear was that while she was away he had changed. And worse, he was a man who disliked the King. So he would be even less enamoured of her if he were to know that she was working for the King's agent, Abigail Williams.

As if sensing some sadness in her, Mr Pepys was even more attentive than usual, and his hot, pawing hands made her want to scream. Abigail had asked for her to listen to Pepys' talk and note down anything about plans for re-equipping the navy. Deb was still copying tracts from his diary, the earlier years, but also couldn't resist reading his daily entries, scouring them for references to her. When she found her name, it was always about how he had touched her.

There was never any reference to how she might feel. It was as if she was just another of his household furnishings, or a book, to be brought out from the cabinet when he wanted entertainment, and it hardened her towards him. Soon she thought nothing of it, this stealing of his diary.

Until one night when she crept down to his study and the door would not open.

She jiggled it again and rattled it as hard as she dared, but it would not give.

'It's locked.' Jane appeared at her shoulder, the week's laundry bundled in her arms.

'Why?'

'There've been burglaries round the corner in Crutched Friars. The master fears for his books. He's worried about thieves.' Jane gave her a pointed look. 'Don't know why you're up. You haven't to light the copper at this hour like I have to.'

Deb watched her go, feeling a little guilty that her life was not as arduous as Jane's. But this feeling was replaced by relief. If she couldn't get to the diary, she would not have to translate it any more.

But then the second, more disturbing thought came. Maybe Pepys was suspicious or had missed his papers. She turned cold. She would have to tell Abigail, and she did not know what would become of her if she displeased the King.

Chapter Twenty-nine

'I'M SORRY, ABIGAIL, BUT I CAN'T bring you any more of the diary.' Deb rushed to explain the problem. 'It's more difficult now. Mr Pepys locks his office at night and keeps the key with him. And he's become much more troublesome.'

'What do you mean?' Abigail stood up from the chair in Bruncker's apartment. 'I need those transcripts.'

'He wants to touch me and ... Abigail, is there no chance I could work for you and Lord Bruncker?'

'The King relies on your information. In time, perhaps we could see about alternative employment. But for the present, it's essential you keep your live-in position. Now what did you mean—?'

'But I'm not sure how long I can keep Mr Pepys away. He gets more urgent every day.'

'But surely that's to your advantage?'

'Copying his papers from the navy and the office is one thing,' Deb said, 'but I don't like copying his diary. There could be things in there about ... well, it's personal.'

'Good. The more personal the better,' Abigail said. 'That kind of information can provide leverage. Just copy as much of it as you can. I dare say he has hung himself already, but that need not concern you. The

King demands all of it, if possible, but you must take the utmost care – if Pepys finds you out, then His Majesty would be most displeased. Now, I expect the documents as usual.'

'But I've told you, he locks his office against thieves.'

'Then you must get the key.' Abigail wafted her arm in its draped sleeve, as if that objection was of no importance. 'The King looks ill on those who refuse to do his bidding.'

'You don't understand,' Deb protested. 'Mr Pepys keeps it in his pocket. How can I?'

Abigail made a gesture of impatience. 'You have just told me he is enamoured of you. So use your guile. Coax him. Use what charms you have.'

Her charms had not been enough for Jem Wells, thought Deb, bitterly.

The weather was sultry and still, the dust hanging heavy in the house. Twilight had fallen, so Deb went to Elisabeth's chamber to light lamps, turn back the sheets and lay out her mistress's nightclothes. When she'd smoothed the counterpane she went to open the window and let in a little air, putting off the moment when she would have to go to Mr Pepys and try to persuade him to give her the key. Elisabeth came in behind her and began to wash with the hot water Deb had left out for her, but Deb's attention was hooked by something else.

A little way down the street a carriage was parked. She made out the silhouette of a person inside. She stared. Was that the same man she'd seen before outside the house? She shut the curtains with a rattle, suppressed a shiver.

'I can manage, Deb. You may go,' Elisabeth said.

Deb nodded and withdrew, and walked slowly

down the broad staircase.

From downstairs in the main chamber she heard Mr Pepys singing. He had a new espinette which he was just learning to play, and she could hear the pluck of its strings. The song was plaintive and sad, which was most unlike him; perhaps his eyes were bothering him again.

'Deb, I can't bear it!' Elisabeth yelled to her from the landing. 'Tell Sam to stop that infernal noise! I won't be able to catch a wink of sleep with his plinking.'

As soon as she entered the main chamber Mr Pepys stopped playing, swivelled on the stool. 'Blasted thing. It's too hard for me to read,' he said, pointing at the tightly written music propped above the keys.

'Are your eyes so bad?' she asked.

'So bad I can think of little else. What will I do if I can no longer read? My work, my pleasure, everything depends on my eyesight.'

'Shall I read to you a little then, instead? Then you may rest your eyes.'

He sighed. 'Come and give me a hug. I need some consolation from my pretty maid.'

She went over, her heart thudding, knowing that whatever he wanted of her, she must not lose sight of getting the key to his office. When she got close, he reached for her and drew her close to his chest. She expected him to do more, but instead he turned to look up at her, his expression troubled. 'What shall I do, Deb? I fear I am going blind. How shall we live if I can't use my eyes?'

'Perhaps you just need to rest them more. You use them too much. Give me the key to your office and I'll fetch something soothing to read.'

When he looked up to answer her, his face was haggard. 'I don't feel like it. I've never felt so glum in all my days.'

'It'll be soothing, to be read to.'

'No. I just want my hair combed. No book.'

His downcast face made her feel worse about what she had to do. She fetched a basin and ewer, poured water over the teeth of the comb as she thought how to get the key. Once he was seated, she took a deep breath. 'Mr Pepys, I must confess something to you,' she whispered.

'A confession, is it? Tell me more.' He turned, but she pushed his head back around to the front.

'You might not like it.'

'Tell me. Tell your old sad bear. It can't be that bad.'

'When you are in bed, I take books from your office, so I might have something to read before I sleep.'

He swivelled around, then he laughed, his eyesight forgotten. 'Is that all? I thought you were going to confess to a murder, or felony at least. Tush, girl, I would lend you what you'd like, happily, you only need to ask. What sort of thing do you like to read?'

'It's hard to know in advance,' she said, wiping the comb on the washcloth, 'but I like to choose one to help me sleep. And you have so many. It is hard to decide.'

'I know what you mean. We are alike. I, too, find pleasure in having the right book for the right mood. And I don't know why I bought Elisabeth that Merchant Taylors' book, it's—'

'But now you lock your study, so I can't get in.'

'Oh. Wait a minute—' He took hold of the lace at the front of her chemise and ran it through his fingers in a teasing manner. 'You mean to tell me you sneak about the house at night in only your nightclothes? Into my study?'

A sharp tug, and the bow at her neck fell loose. His other hand fumbled with the knot. He ran his tongue over his lips, but she kept on talking, breathless.

'Yes, sometimes. I was wondering, please would you leave the key out for me.' She lowered her gaze.

'The key, is it?' He pulled her towards him by the strings of her chemise, his eyesight forgotten.

Deb tried to make a joke of his attentions, pulling the strings from his fingers.

He fumbled in his pocket and drew out the key, dangled its bronze weight before her. She leaned to take it from his hand, but he smiled and swung it out of her reach, and instead he caught her round the waist with a well-padded arm. He was smiling now, his eyes alight.

'Try again,' he said, a hand squeezing at the top of her breast where it pushed out of the top of her stays.

Curse it. He was too excited by this game.

She made another lunge for the key, but again he swung it away. As she made another bid for it, her fingers just brushed the tassel on the cord. Between her legs was the heat of a hand snaking up her thigh, past the lace of her petticoat.

She leapt to the side. He mustn't find the pocket beneath her skirts. She hitched them to one side, feeling the crackle of the papers beneath the material. She held them tight away from his searching hands.

He took her hitching of skirt to be an invitation, and his hand slid up again to the soft part between her legs. Deb forced herself to ignore it, kept her eyes on the key. His other hand went slack and Deb closed her fingers around the cold metal. A quick tug and she had it. They tussled a moment, in mock fight, before she jumped up. He made a lunge for her, but missed. He was laughing.

She could not help but smile back, panting, triumphant. 'You can have it back in the morning.'

He held up his hands in a gesture of defeat. 'You win,' he said. 'You have the key to my study. And the key to my heart too, little Deb,' he said, eyes moist. 'I'm mad for you. I can't sleep, can't work for thoughts of you. *If ever man lov'd woman, I ... you ...'* He did not finish.

She stood a moment and watched his face crumple, as though he too had just realised the enormity of what he'd just said.

'I love you.' He was almost in tears.

'No, sir.' Deb backed away. 'No, you don't.' She kept her hands crossed on her chest, the key pressed to her heart.

In the dark of the night, long after Mr Pepys had retired to bed, she was creeping out of his study, when she bumped into Jane.

'What are you doing?'

'I could ask you the same.'

'I'm always up this early. Today I'm to get the grates cleaned.' Her look was accusing and full of blame, as if it was Deb's fault. 'You've no need to be up. You should be abed.'

'I was just taking some things back to the master. Books.' She was still fully dressed and with a volume of Mr Pepys' diary tucked into her skirts.

'At four o'clock in the morning?'

'I couldn't sleep.'

'Mr Pepys doesn't like us in his study. How did you get in?'

'He gave me a key.' She held it up.

'Why?'

'No reason.' Deb slipped the key into the keyhole and locked the door.

When she turned to go, she was nose to nose with Jane, who was still standing there in her apron, arms folded, her expression sceptical. Deb squirmed under the directness of her gaze.

'If I were you I'd spend more time seeing to my mistress's demands than those of her husband,' Jane said. 'Don't say I didn't warn you.'

Chapter Thirty

August

WHENEVER DEB WAS IN THE ROOM, Mr Pepys had the
hangdog look of a lost soul, and it made her feel
guilty. Love, he'd said. She feared now that he would
force her, and she knew that openly rejecting him
would be like rejecting his household, his lifestyle,
and all that went with it.

So she was even more apprehensive when she was
informed she was to accompany Elisabeth and her
friend Mary to see the fortune-teller on Norwood
Common. Mr Pelling, an apothecary friend of Mr
Pepys, was to loan his carriage for the excursion.
Although she knew fortune-tellers were charlatans,
what if some of her secrets were revealed to Elisabeth?
What if the gypsy told Elisabeth about her liaisons
with Mr Pepys? She told herself not to be so foolish. It
was all nonsense, this stargazing and casting the
bones.

Copying at night for Abigail and the King had
taken its toll, and the incessant August heat wore Deb
down; she had never known a summer so hot. On the
way to Norwood, in Mr Pelling's carriage, she was so
sleepy at his dull conversation that she fell into a
doze, but she sat up sharply when Elisabeth's fan

rapped her on the knee.

'Are you listening?' Elisabeth's voice was cross. 'Mr Pelling was talking to you!'

Deb apologised and tried to look attentive.

They struggled out of the coach. The Great Fire the year before had made the common overcrowded. Makeshift dwellings had sprung up like mushrooms. Barefoot, half-naked children ran in amongst the stalls begging for change, and bluebottles buzzed in clouds around the trestles where a few frazzled women were selling cloudy ale and sweating cheeses.

They made quite a procession. Elizabeth and Mary traipsing after the strutting Mr Pelling, and Deb following Mary and Elisabeth, holding a fringed parasol over their heads against the burn of the sun. The two women ignored her, their heads close together, giggling over something in whispers and flicking their fans open and closed. She both hoped and feared Elisabeth would not make her have her fortune read, too. There was a tension in Deb's heart all the time now, like a lute-string.

She did not want her secret life exposed, but on the other hand, perhaps she could ask if the gypsy could see any end to Mr Pepys' attentions, or to this work she was forced to do for the King. At the back of her thoughts was always Jem. Perhaps she might ask the gypsy if Jem could ever think of her again with affection.

Mr Pelling shepherded them past the brightly coloured awnings on the booths advertising "*Fortunes Told*, or *Your Fate in Your Hand*".

'What about this place?' Deb asked, longing for any sort of shade, and pointing to a tent with a large queue of other well-dressed ladies.

'No, no. My wife, God rest her soul, absolutely

swore by Marina-Rose Sadira. She's a *bona fide* Romany. We've to look for the sign of the "Rose on the Waters",' Mr Pelling said, signalling them forward.

The sign turned out to be a large flap hanging over the doorway, with a peeling red rose floating above a badly painted sea. It looked shabby, and Deb was immediately sceptical. There was no queue, so after a slight disagreement over who would go first, Mary lifted the canvas flap with her finger and went within. Elisabeth could not contain her nervous anticipation, which resulted in more batting of her fan and making cow eyes at Mr Pelling as they waited. Lord knows why. Mr Pelling was middle-aged and paunchy, with eyes like boiled oysters.

'Deb, you could go and purchase refreshment. *Mon Dieu*! I'm almost melting in this heat.' Elisabeth drew her hand across her brow.

Armed with a few coins, and warnings to watch her purse, Deb set off to find lemonade. When she returned, Elisabeth was inside the tent, and Mr Pelling was impressing Mary with the gypsy's predictions of how prosperous he was to become, and that he was certain to be made chairman of the Apothecaries Guild.

Unable to be so impolite as to interrupt him, Mary was anxiously waiting, almost simmering over with excitement, her hair plastered to her forehead with sweat.

Deb uncorked a bottle and offered it to Mary, but she waved her away as Elisabeth burst out of the tent, flapping her lace-cuffed hands in agitation. 'You'll never guess! I'm to become well known at court, she says; do you know, she was uncanny.'

Deb stifled a smile. The gypsy probably told everybody that.

But Elisabeth was still gushing it all out, breathlessly, hands waving, face pink with pleasure. 'She had two decks of cards and she spread out the both of them, and you'll never believe this, but she knew all about Sam. She said I was married to a good man, but that I had no children, nor would I have any, but she said, too, he would be famous one day for his words, but I can't believe that, he's far too busy, he—'

She paused to take a breath, and Mary, unable to wait any longer, grabbed her moment. 'I'm to meet a dark stranger, the cards said. The knave of clubs. And I'm to marry within the year!'

This news was met with silence.

'Impossible.' Elisabeth looked affronted that Mary had been given such good news. 'But who? Did she say who?'

'No,' Mary said. 'Fancy! I'm to be married after all. What a pity she couldn't get a name. Just that he was dark and tall. Can you think of anyone, Elisabeth? Oh! It couldn't be Simpson's boy, could it? He hardly says a word. If it's him, my mother will be thrilled, and she said—'

But Deb did not wait to hear more. She put the two bottles down on the ground, took her chance and lifted the curtain. The tented booth was airless, with a pinkish light from the red paint on the outside and a fire smoking in an earth pit despite the August heat.

'Come along in, then, if you're coming,' a voice said, through the smoke and gloom.

Deb approached the table, expecting to see a swarthy gypsy with a tremendous hooked nose and perhaps a necklace fashioned from coins, or a shawl covered in stars. But no, this woman was singularly unprepossessing, somewhere in saggy middle age, her hair grey and thinning. Her plain homespun bodice was dark with perspiration, and she was wiping her lined face with a scrap of linen.

Deb sat down where the woman gestured she should.

'Yes, pay me now, get it done with. A silver farthing.'

Deb fumbled in her almost empty purse. This was the last of her monthly wage. She'd been saving these few coins to help pay off Jack's debt, but recklessly she pushed the coin across the table. The woman's hand shot out and took it.

'What do you want to know? Love is it? Or fortune?'

'I don't know. Both.'

The gypsy sighed, pushed her damp hair off her forehead. 'Cards or palm?'

'Cards, please. I've always liked the look of them.'

The woman shuffled the cards with a practised hand, but then paused, blew air over her upper lip to cool herself. Moments later, she slapped the deck on the table and pushed the farthing back. 'Look, maid. I'm going to give you your money back. I can't stand it in here another minute. It's the heat.'

'But I—'

'I've been here since ten this morning and told the same old story twenty times over. Nobody really listens. They grab onto my words, all the time thinking it can't be true. I'll do you a favour. Don't ask me what your fortune is, because none of us know. Only the Almighty, and he's not telling.' She pushed her stool back, and stood, stretched her back.

Deb stood too, 'Please wait. I need to know something. That's why I came. And Mrs Pelling said you were the best.'

'Did she? She's not the lady that just came in, is she?'

'No, Mrs Pelling's no longer with us. That was my employer, Mrs Pepys.'

The woman reached out for Deb's hand, turned it palm up in her bony grasp. 'Not for long,' she said.

Did she mean Mrs Pelling or Elisabeth? Deb was confused. 'Are you going to read my palm? I thought you said cards,' Deb said.

'Your face told me I need to look at your hand.'

Deb squirmed to pull away, but the gypsy caught her by the wrist. 'Hold still. If you want to know answers, I'll give you them. But listen, mind.' The woman sat again, dragging Deb down with her so she had no option but to sit, too.

The woman brought her face close to Deb's palm and began to speak in a monotone, as though reciting a liturgy. 'You've lost family, people close to you, and you'll lose more.'

A shiver ran through Deb's body; the gypsy had hooked her attention in an instant. She pressed her calloused thumb hard into Deb's palm. 'That lady who came in before you, is she a relation?'

'No.' Deb was disconcerted. 'I told you. She's my employer. And what did you mean when you said not for long? Why? Will she not be keeping me?'

The woman held her hand tighter, looked over Deb's shoulder into the distance. 'There's a shadow over her. Your life together will soon be over.' She laughed. 'Sounds good, doesn't it, the shadow? Like what you're expecting?'

'Are you jesting with me?'

'Aye. And no. Does it feel true to you? It's you who has to find the truth in my words.'

'Sometimes I think Elisabeth doesn't like me very

much. And her husband, my master—'

'If you care for her, tell her ... tell her not to go abroad. Of course, she won't listen. But tell her, won't you?'

Deb was perspiring now. The woman was right, it was far too hot in there. She felt queasy, like seasickness. Guiltily, she thought of Elisabeth's happy face. If the woman spoke true and she was to leave Mrs Pepys, it could only be because Mr Pepys had found out she had copied his diaries and betrayed him. Elisabeth would be devastated. She tried to withdraw her hand, but the gypsy gripped it tight, turned it over.

Deb took a gasp of air. She had been holding her breath. It brought her to her senses. She would not believe any of this woman's nonsense. Gypsies were renowned charlatans. She fought for self-control. 'My mistress is waiting. I haven't the time to—'

'Look inside yourself,' the woman said. She ran a nail down the palm of Deb's hand. The gesture was at once threatening and intimate. It produced an involuntary frisson up Deb's spine. 'Your lifeline is split, one side to the dark, one to the light. You must be careful. Dark forces will always be with you, tempting you.' She looked up at Deb with complicity in her eyes.

Was she mocking her? Deb pulled at her hand again but the woman was wiry and kept hold.

'You've paid me, my love,' the old woman said, 'so you might as well listen to what I have to say.'

The old woman's eyes nailed her, as a pin fixes a butterfly. The gypsy's face wavered, blurred, lost its outline. The features shifted, melted, bloomed into a newborn baby; moments later it became sharp, snouted like a fox, flowered into a beautiful soulful young woman. Face gave way to face, all of human life, shifting and dissolving, looking out at her through those gypsy eyes.

Deb let her hand flop. Her head swam.

The words came as if from a great distance. 'You will bring a deep hurt to someone you care for. There are papers, a writ. There will be some dealings with a prison; I can see bars. And ink. No wait, not ink. I see—'

Deb leapt up, disorientated, jerking on her arm. 'Stop it. I don't believe you. You're frightening me on purpose.'

The gypsy clung on a moment more with surprising strength. Then suddenly she released her. 'Have it your own way. Got more than you bargained for, did you? Ha!' She laughed. 'You saw something though, I can feel it. Saw who you really are.'

'You're nothing but a fraud. You said so yourself—'

'Your choice. You can choose to believe, or not.' The gypsy pulled the silken tablecloth from the table and shook it out in a great draught. 'I'm closed,' she shouted. 'Tell that to the queue – if there is one.'

Deb stumbled backwards, hitched up her skirts and ran. But the way out was not easy to see and she blundered round the edge, frantically searching for air. Finally, she found the flap and burst outside. The sudden sun made her blink, cover her eyes.

Elisabeth's eyebrows shot up. 'What did she say? You're as pale as a ghost.'

'Nothing. She said I'll have five children.' It was the first thing Deb could think of.

'Five! And with no husband on the horizon yet either,' Mary said, tutting.

'Well I hope that doesn't mean you'll be leaving us, Deb,' Elisabeth said. 'I've only just got you trained to my liking.'

Deb did not dare say a word. She wanted to discount the gypsy's words, but all the way back home in the carriage they ran round and round her head. Her conscience told her that something about her work for Abigail Williams was wrong, but she had fallen in too deep before she realised.

Oh, what was she to do? She needed her employment; she did not want to risk losing her position with the Pepyses, despite Mr Pepys. How would she pay Hester's school fees? And the gypsy said she'd seen a prison. A small voice inside her whispered, what if it was true? She could not condemn Mr Pepys to that. Or what if the prison were her own?

That night, as she sat writing to Hester again, she tussled with it in her mind. Hester had told her she was to stay with Lavinia's family for the summer holiday. She had just found herself telling Hester to be *'good and obedient'*. Deb put the nib down, shook her head at herself, a stab of guilt and hypocrisy stopping her mid-sentence. The gypsy's strange, shifting eyes came back to her.

She re-read her letter. Naturally it mentioned nothing about her spying for the King, or Mr Pepys' unhealthy obsession with her. Nor did it mention Mr Constantine, Uncle Jack, or the debt she still had not yet paid. Maybe she could tell Hester about the gypsy. She would tell it entertainingly and dismiss it all as nonsense. But still she hesitated, quill poised, because there was something about the encounter that prickled her.

With a spurt of determination she described Elisabeth's new gown and the play at the Duke's. There. It was done. She signed off quickly with endearments and blew on the inky marks to dry them. But her shoulders sagged. It was a fiction, the life she was describing to her sister.

Her body was restless, as if things around her wanted to shift and move. Deb paced and paced, hearing the creak of the cold floorboards under her bare feet as she went. She was afraid, she realised. The gypsy had painted a future she did not want to own, and she dare not continue the way she was: living all these lies.

All the next day and night she went through her duties by rote, with no appetite for anything, lying awake, fretting in the heat of the night. Becoming involved with Abigail Williams had been a mistake. She would have to extricate herself, beg Abigail to find someone else. It was a gamble – what if she were to denounce Deb as a thief, or worse, a traitor to the King?

Chapter Thirty-one

WHEN SHE KNOCKED ON ABIGAIL'S DOOR, Deb was hot with trepidation. She was supposed to be out buying fish – Elisabeth hated the pungent smell of the fish market in summer and always sent Deb. She had left Elisabeth wrestling with the flageolet with her music teacher, Mr Locke, and the piercing squeaking sound had left Deb even more on edge.

Abigail was out.

Poole, the maid, was used to Deb coming to Whetstone Park twice a week with the papers, so she invited her in to wait and showed her in to the drawing room. Without Abigail the room was echoing and bare. A vase of drooping roses had dropped most of its dead petals in front of the fireplace. The sun slid in through half-closed curtains, striping the floorboards, filling the room with the fusty smell of hot drapes.

Poole brought Deb a cold mint tea and she took a sip, but she was too apprehensive to drink much. She put the glass down; it was slippery with her perspiration.

She went over to the little desk and paused with her fingers on the brass handle of the drawer, curious to see what Abigail would have asked her to copy next. She opened the drawer for a peek. Another vellum of ciphers lay there, on top of some other papers. Unable to resist a puzzle, she lifted it out for a closer look. The paper was similar to the last one she had copied – impenetrable. Frustrating.

She tilted it this way and that, counting the repetitions of numbers that could be '*e*'s or '*t*'s, but there were not enough for it to be a straightforward translation, so, impatient, she went to put it back. Why waste her time? She would not be doing this again anyway.

A folded square of parchment on the top of the remaining pile caught her eye. It was a letter addressed to a Dr Allbarn. She took it out, to see there were several more, all opened. Who was Dr Allbarn? Abigail had never mentioned him. The rest of the papers seemed to be in a foreign language. Dutch?

As she stood puzzling, raised voices reached her from below. It was Abigail, shouting at her maid that she should not have let Deb in. She froze with the letter in her hand.

Abigail's footsteps approached along the hall. Deb tried to push the papers back in and shut the drawer.

The door flew open and Deb took a step back.

Abigail surveyed the scene in one glance: the open drawer. 'What are you doing? That's my correspondence.'

'I was looking to see what my next assignment would have been.'

'You had no business to look in there. My desk is private.' Her tone was icy.

'It doesn't matter, because I have decided not to work for you again.'

'And why is that?' Abigail came nearer, her manner threatening.

'It feels dishonest. And I don't want to get Mr Pepys into trouble.'

'So soft now, Deb? What has brought this on? Neither of them gives a jot for you. I've heard Mr Pepys say so.'

'That's not true! Mr Pepys ... he ...' She couldn't say it. 'Mrs Pepys was right all along. She told me you had no scruples, and not to have anything to do with you.'

'She said that, did she?' Abigail's expression hardened.

'You deceived me, tricking me into doing the King's spying for you. You twist the truth, so I never know what's right. I thought you were my friend, but you've just used me. I shan't be coming here again, and I will do no more of your ... work.'

Abigail's mouth quivered a little, as if she might speak, but she let the silence hang. She strolled over towards the desk, shut the drawer softly. She turned. 'Oh yes you will.' Her voice was quiet, but definite.

'No. I'm resigning. I mean it; I'm not coming back.'

Abigail moved swiftly in front of the double doors. Deb made as if to pass her, but Abigail put out an arm to prevent her. Her body had become as rigid as stone. 'Do you think I've trained you all these months for nothing?'

'Trained me?' Deb shook her head. 'I don't know what you mean.'

'Oh come now. You are not a fool. You've known all along that the copying is not just that, haven't you?'

Deb took a step back, swallowed, thoughts crowding in on her. Was she right? She had not wanted to acknowledge those fears even to herself. She held the basket in front of her chest like a shield.

'You cannot stop now, Deb dear. You know too much. The papers you copy go from me to another agent. To someone who takes them on board the ships bound for Holland. And from him to the Dutch court.'

'The Dutch?' Deb faltered. 'But you said ... surely the papers are for the King?' Abigail said nothing, just watched as the facts filtered into Deb's realisation. 'But then ...' Deb's voice dropped to a whisper, 'it's treason.'

'You did not think to question it, a girl of your education?' Abigail's voice held the trace of a sneer.

'I trusted you, I thought ...' She shook her head, unable to take it in. 'How do I know you're telling the truth now?'

'You know because if you can break a cipher you are intelligent enough to know the difference between truth and lies.'

The words hung a moment. Deb summoned her resolve. 'I won't do it any more. Whether it's for the King or the Dutch. We're finished. Let me pass.'

'If you wish. But let me warn you that, with a word from me, the Dutch spymaster will soon locate you. The stab in the night, the powder-shot in the back, the sudden push on the bank of the Thames. All easily arranged. You know too much about me, about what we do. You had your fingers in my drawer, did you not?'

Deb's stomach seemed to drop five fathoms. She retreated back into the room; she needed to think. But the thoughts ran round like rats in a trap. She'd been duped. And yet somehow she was not surprised. She cursed that she had foolishly ignored her own instincts.

The stab in the dark. She imagined Hester alone, with no one to encourage her, no one to look up to. A life without love. She sat down, put her head in her hands.

She raised her eyes to find Abigail watching her with a look almost of pity.

'That's better,' Abigail said. 'You've seen what it means. I knew you'd see it my way in the end.'

Chapter Thirty-two

FOR THE NEXT FEW WEEKS it was as if it had all been a bad dream. Life went on as usual: the making of beds; the answering of the door to callers; endless shopping at Unthank's. Deb made no deliveries of Pepys' journal to Abigail, for she could not bring herself to get the key to Pepys' office. She pretended the whole business with Abigail was a bad dream, procrastinating, telling herself she was too busy to go to Whetstone Park. And she kept well away from Mr Pepys and hurried into another room if he appeared.

Today, Elisabeth had sent her shopping, which involved a long walk, since the Great Fire had burned down a lot of businesses. She was wary of going out, frightened that Abigail might send someone after her. She glanced left and right, as she walked briskly towards the Exchange. It was a while before she paused to cross the street and became aware of someone fast approaching behind her: a flash of black coat, a pulled-down slouch hat.

Abigail's threats came back to her, filling her with cold dread. The thought of the sedate, overstuffed interior of Seething Lane suddenly seemed like a sanctuary. She quickened her step, tying the strings of her purse round her neck and tucking it down inside her bodice out of sight. A glance over her shoulder and she was disconcerted to see the man still following, closer now, so she could hear the ring of his heels. Panicked, she broke into a run. A thud of footsteps behind her. She sprinted in and out of the alleys, hoping to lose him, not daring to turn until she came to a cobbler's shop with its door standing open. She dived inside, relieved to see a man hammering there.

'There's a man following me,' she panted, 'a footpad.'

The cobbler put down the shoe and, armed with his hammer, followed her outside to look. The alley was empty. There was no sign of the man in the black coat. She exhaled a sigh of relief. She had lost him. Knowing she appeared foolish, she felt obliged to spend a long time purchasing a pair of bootlaces and thanking the old man for his trouble.

Looking to left and right, she emerged onto Thames Street, and seeing no sign of 'black-coat', she took a shortcut between two buildings, intending to get to the market to buy the hooks, as she'd promised, and then catch a ferry. Her heart was still beating so fast it made her faint.

Outside a haberdasher's she leaned on a window frame and stared in through the window, breathing hard. She did not notice the rows of bobbins, the rainbow colours of the cards of braiding and threads. What if Abigail's spymaster was following her?

She was contemplating this when another face appeared behind hers in the glass. She froze, unable to move. The man's arms came either side of her head, trapping her to the glass.

She whipped round. It was the man who had

followed her, but now he was so close she saw the rheumy eyes, the pockmarked, prominent nose. Constantine's man.

'What do you want?' she said, glancing sideways, searching for an escape route.

'Mr Constantine told me you keep Mrs Pepys' purse. I'm to relieve you of it. A bad debt, he said.'

'No, please. I'm to buy goods for my mistress.'

'Then your mistress will have to go without, like the rest of us.'

As a party of gentlemen passed the end of the alley, Deb saw her chance and dodged to the side. But the man was too quick for her. He twisted her arm behind her, shoved her back until her ribs pressed against the wall.

'Help me!' she shouted, but a sweaty palm clamped her mouth shut, and the passers-by who glanced down the alley turned aside and hurried on.

Black-coat probed down her bodice for her purse, drew it out, and tugged hard at the thong about her neck. The leather was sturdy, and Deb winced as it cut into her neck. There was a glint of something metal, and a knife appeared at her throat. A ripple of silver as the knife sliced across the cord and he yanked the purse free.

'Did you think I'd slit your throat?' He laughed. 'Not this time. I'd want a hand up your skirt first.'

'Let me go!'

'Not yet,' he said, leaning close to her face. 'Constantine said to warn you. He wants his account settled. Either that, or the sailors paid.' He traced the point of the knife down her bodice until the tip lodged over her heart. 'You need to sweet-talk your Mr Pepys. Word is, he has an eye for a skirt like you. But if he won't play, I'll take payment in kind, if you like.'

Deb stayed still, tried to act calm. 'I'll get the money,' she said.

He pushed the purse into the pocket of his greasy coat. 'One week you've got,' he called. 'Or I'll be back. Mr Constantine, he don't like to be kept waiting.'

Chapter Thirty-three

Elisabeth pulled Sam's suit from his closet and held it out at arm's length before examining it through his magnifying spectacles. She was looking for signs of Deb. That girl was always on her mind these days. Hadn't she given her a whole five shillings last week, and what did the careless girl do? Lose her purse. Elisabeth dare not mention the missing money to Sam. He might take a birch to her the way he had their last maid, Dolly, and with Deb, who knows what might happen then? *Oh la*. It would surely give him an excuse to touch her on the *derrière*.

The Medway affair had kept Sam busy and away from the ladies, but these days he had too much time for dalliance. With Sam, it was a disease and she must guard against it; an outbreak could happen at any time.

Elisabeth scrutinised her husband's collar again for Deb's wavy brown hairs, but found nothing except a greasy stain from yesterday's meat pie. Jane said that Sam had given Deb the key to his office. Ever since Elisabeth had found out this titbit of information, she'd wondered if Sam sneaked away at night to the office while she slept. She tried to try to catch him at it, but found herself wide awake as Sam snored on.

She had now given that task to Jane.

It did nothing to allay her fears. Something was happening between him and Deb, she was convinced, even though she had found no shred of evidence for it.

Yet.

She bundled the suit back in the closet, not caring any more that it would crease. Deb could iron it again, she thought. Serve her right.

She pulled open her closet door and trailed her hand over her skirts, screwing up her nose at the pungent balls of camphor hung there to keep the moths off. Tonight, Sam was intent on taking his 'girls' to Bartholomew Fair, and worse, he'd arranged tickets for a tented play, because he knew that Abigail Williams was to be in it. Another trollop if ever there was one.

Elisabeth pulled out a beribboned brocade skirt, made a whimpering sound and then shoved it back. There was nothing showy enough to keep his attention. Not when it was Deb he really wanted to take to the fair, she thought bitterly. She, Elisabeth, was expected merely to drag along behind, the convenient excuse he made to himself for going at all.

Bartholomew Fair was the biggest event of the year, but Abigail Williams was not in any mood for celebration, or for being on stage. Joan's death had sapped the colour from everything. What was the point of working like this, Abigail thought, pretending to be someone else? She was already just a façade. And what damn use was money, now there was no Joan to fritter it away?

Piet had been to see her and given her one last warning. She'd seen nothing of Deb Willet for two weeks. The fact she could not control Deb's behaviour with verbal threats was worrying. The intelligence to Piet had run dry again, and he was a snake who could strike at any time. Worse, if Deb did not deliver, and that state of affairs continued, Abigail would have the unpleasant task of silencing her. She had never had to do that to another woman.

Abigail pushed impatiently through the throng, with gnawing frustration at her slow progress, tiptoeing her way through the squelching mud from yesterday's rain. Past coffee traders dressed as Turks, past the rouged and painted ladies with songbirds in cages, past the stalls of glistening jellied eels and hot pies. Every stall boasted a drum or a horn to attract attention, and the cacophony of rattles, drums and fiddles made her poor head throb like the devil.

Any sort of serious acting would be more or less impossible in this noise, she realised. Fortunately, the play was *Marry Andrey*, one she knew well and could perform in her sleep. In the tented tiring house, she ignored the other actors' chatter and banter as she changed into her scarlet gown. She skewered her feathered hat into place by feel, as there was no mirror. At the canvas door, she took a quick peek, and sighed to see the benches already packed with rowdy revellers.

Lukeman, who was to play her husband, peered out of the tent over her shoulder. 'Looks like a good house.'

She ignored him. 'Courage,' she said to herself, sliding a flask from her hanging pocket. She tipped it back, drained it, grimacing at the sudden fire in her throat. Then she hurried up the makeshift stairs to the raised platform.

Concealed behind a painted flat, she looked down

at the audience from the wings, despising them for liking something so low. She was glad Lord B could not see her; she had not confessed to him what play she was in. She remembered when she could command everyone's attention on the fine stage at the Duke's, but now she was hardly ever offered anything but these potboilers. She was getting old, she realised, losing her glamour.

The liquor began to warm her, numbed her thoughts, turned the world soft and fuzzy.

She heard her cue, took a deep breath, and swept on-stage. She was partway through her simpering act, cajoling the audience with quips and asides, when she spotted Mr Pepys on the second row. She felt her face heat with annoyance, that he should see her in such tripe.

A quick glance, and then she saw her. Deb Willet, wedged between him and his wife. Deb's eyes were fixed on her. Abigail's lines kept coming, but Deb's scrutiny disconcerted her. She dropped a line and floundered for a moment until Lukeman prompted her, hissing, 'What are you playing at? It's "*No, my Lord, I won't.*"'

After her line she was supposed to go to fan herself at the side of the stage. She cracked open the fan and flapped it before her face. From the corner of her eye she saw Deb push away Mr Pepys' hand when it strayed onto her lap, and Mrs Pepys' expression turn as sour as cheese. With difficulty, Abigail dragged her thoughts back to the script.

At the end, she smiled, and catching Pepys' eye, bowed extravagantly to him. He stood to clap and cheer, but Deb was still and silent, as if stuck to the bench. Nor did Mrs Pepys deign to applaud. Abigail made for the wings to watch them go, but was near enough to hear Mr and Mrs Pepys arguing on the way out in hushed whispers. Abigail caught the words 'hussy' and 'dreadful' and had to shut her ears to it, bile rising in her chest.

So Deb Willet was too above her to applaud, was she? She should try it, making people laugh when inside you felt like weeping. The sight of Deb still sitting there staring at the stage filled Abigail with steely rage. The girl would have to be made to follow instructions. At least if she wanted to survive. Abigail hurried down the steps from the stage, still in her gaudy costume and greasepaint.

'You should have delivered last week.' Abigail could not keep the anger from her voice.

Deb recoiled, looked for help from her master and mistress, but they had gone on ahead.

'I saw you in the audience,' Abigail said. 'You're late delivering. And I warned you I wouldn't stand for it.'

'I know. I was busy.' Deb's eyes shifted to the muddy, flattened grass at her feet. 'Elisabeth wouldn't give me time off.'

'Don't give me excuses.'

'Deb!' Samuel's voice calling over the hubbub of the street.

'You want honesty?' Deb raised her chin, looked at her with the same defiant look Abigail used to see on Joan's face. 'I told you. I don't want to touch your underhand business ever again.'

'You don't know what's good for you, do you?' Abigail said. 'I'm trying to help you.'

'I know that spying's no good for me,' Deb said.

'Keep your voice down, for God's sake!' Abigail took hold of Deb's shoulder, to steer her somewhere more private, but Deb jumped back as if she'd touched her with a burning brand.

How could she get Deb to comprehend? She was just like Joan, stubborn. Didn't know what was in her own best interests. She'd have to make her understand; that was all. In one swift movement Abigail swept the hatpin out of her hat and deliberately thrust it deep into the flesh of Deb's upper arm.

Instinctively, Deb's hand shot up to clutch her arm, face frozen in shock.

Abigail withdrew the long steel needle and leaned down until her mouth was near Deb's ear. 'Either you work with us, or against us. There are no half-measures in my line of work. If you lie to me again, next time, the stab will be to the heart. I expect you to deliver tomorrow.'

Deb looked down at her sleeve. A tiny hole in the material oozed blood where her arm throbbed. When she looked up, Abigail was already gone, the scarlet silk of her costume swallowed into the crush of people.

Deb could not think. Even her thoughts had scattered, hidden themselves for fear. She peered over the heads of the crowd for Mr Pepys, afraid they'd leave without her. She scurried across the street and waved frantically to her mistress, who was standing by the coaches and scanning the crowds.

'Where've you been? We've been waiting.' Elisabeth's voice was filled with disapproval.

'I thought I saw someone I knew,' she said. Her voice sounded reassuringly normal, despite the shivering that would not stop.

'Who?' asked Mr Pepys.

'Just … a friend from school. But I was mistaken.

And then I could not cross, there were too many carriages.'

'You're cold,' Mr Pepys said.

'No, I—'

'We've been standing here for an age.' Elisabeth was not placated. 'You should have told us where you were going.' She turned to Mr Pepys and gave him a look that clearly meant: *see what a bad maidservant she is.*

Deb tried to make an excuse. 'I thought you were talking to—' She saw Elisabeth's forehead crease into a frown, thought better of it and hastened to apologise. She dipped her head. 'Beg pardon, Elisabeth.'

'I should think so, too.'

Mr Pepys cast her a sympathetic look as soon as Elisabeth's back was turned, tried to hook his arm in hers, but the gesture made her feel worse, not better.

She had not realised Abigail's acting skill. Abigail was a professional, Deb realised. Skilled at becoming someone else. Not someone who did a little spying for the money, but a spy who would be quite ruthless in pursuit of her aims. Deb licked her lips; her mouth had turned dry as parchment.

The next morning Deb examined her arm. The puncture was deep, but it had stopped bleeding, and she hoped it would not fester. That any woman could do such a thing in cold blood made her feel faintly sick.

Constantine's debt preyed on her mind; she could not endure the thought of having to watch for his man as well as Abigail or her maid, Poole, following her. So she counted out her savings, laid it out in rows of tens: the farthings and halfpennies, the few half-sovereigns –all the money that once had been meant for Hester's schooling. The coins she had earned from spying for the King, except that now she knew she had not been spying for the King at all, but for the Dutch.

How could she have let herself be duped so thoroughly? Bitterly, she got out a pouch for Mr Constantine. Enduring Mr Pepys had all been for nothing. She was going to lose it all. As if reading her thoughts, Mr Pepys called her from below.

A sudden rage against him made her smash her fist down on the pile of coins so they flew up and clattered away, rolling over the floorboards. It was his fault that Constantine was to take her money: Constantine had turned against her the minute she said she worked for Mr Pepys.

'Deb?' Mr Pepys' cajoling voice again.

She scrabbled to gather the coins together again. Life was suffocating her in every direction she turned. She did not want to work for Abigail Williams. She did not want to play the 'lost key' game any more. And the thought of letting Mr Pepys trawl his fingers on her bare skin, just to get a few papers, sickened her.

But she thrust the money back out of sight in her drawer and slowly descended the stairs. She was in too deep –Abigail Williams and her mysterious spymaster would kill her unless she supplied them with the information they craved. She was afraid, deep in her bones.

At noon the following day Deb took her savings and went to The Grecian. Constantine's man was leaning up against a wall, a pipe stuck between his lips. He took it out lazily as he saw her coming.

'There's an end to it,' she said, handing him the purse. 'My uncle's debts are paid.'

Black-coat thrust the pipe back in his mouth, took the purse, felt its weight.

'I'll wait. You can bring me a receipt,' she said.

He raised his eyebrows and grinned through his yellow-stained moustache, in a way that made Deb instantly alert. He's going to pocket it, she thought, with sickening certainty. He swung away inside, and a few moments later she was aware of someone else watching her.

She looked up and saw the burly figure of Constantine gazing down on her through the open window. 'There'll be no interest on this debt, if you get Pepys to pay our sailors,' he called.

Interest. She should have known. It wasn't the end at all.

She waited another half-hour but no receipt came. She dare not go inside and was close to weeping from the unfairness of it all. 'You're a damned fool, Deborah Willet,' she told herself.

Two weeks later, the bill from the school at Bow arrived, and she knew she could not pay it unless she carried on copying more of Mr Pepys' diary. As soon as the Bateliers, who had been supping with them, left, she waited in the parlour for the inevitable sound of Mr Pepys calling her name.

The bells tolled a mournful clang outside, and she was reminded of how they had rung the bells for the plague-ridden to put out their dead. Perhaps it was because she felt sullied already. Last time, he had made her strip to the waist before he would give her the key to his study.

'I like a maid that loves her books,' he'd said.

As if she would really do that – let him paw her breasts – just for the sake of a chapter of Homer. But if that's what he wanted to tell himself, if that was the role he had cast her in, she would not enlighten him. Anyone else would do the same if the alternative was a knife in the heart.

She passed Jane on the stairs again with the coal scuttle as she went down. Jane was often on the landing as she went down at this time of night, Deb noticed. The fires seemed to need an inordinate amount of attention, and always when Mr Pepys called for Deb.

The door clicked shut behind her, and Mr Pepys was already holding out his arms. As he reached for her she was only dimly aware of the clank of the coal scuttle being put down, and the echoing tread of footsteps going upstairs to Elisabeth's chamber.

Chapter Thirty-four

October

THE DOOR FLEW OPEN. No warning, just the gape of the hall and a draught of air.

Elisabeth, her hand as if frozen to the handle.

Of course, Deb jumped up like a cat from a hot trivet, but even the way she did that, the way she hitched her bodice back on her shoulders and smoothed her skirts flat to her knees with such haste, must have told Elisabeth all she needed to know.

'What are you doing?' Elisabeth's voice was small, barely a voice.

'Nothing, my dear,' Mr Pepys protested.

'But I saw you, you were ...' She couldn't choke out the words. Her eyes swivelled back to Deb, whose cheeks flared fever-hot.

'I was just helping Deb with ...' Mr Pepys looked to Deb for an answer.

With what? What could he have been helping her with? Deb floundered, searching for any excuse, but none came. The nit comb, still unused, dug into her hand, but her muteness said it all.

The bang of the door sliced through the silence. Then a clang and clatter of the coal scuttle and a cry. Elisabeth was gone. Sam cast Deb an anguished look and hurried after his wife. He said not a word to Deb, as if she did not exist. It was so quiet Deb could hear her own heartbeat; dust motes swam in the draught and the light from the lamp.

Then, below, angry whispers. Mr Pepys saying, 'No, my dear, no!' and then the sound of sobbing.

Deb's soft private parts still tingled where his hand had been.

Elisabeth's face was seared into her mind as if printed there with ink: her shocked eyes, the way the pupils turned small as if to shut her out, the flutter of the skin of her throat, a vibration where words would not come. The feeling of hurting her made Deb's insides shrivel in shame.

It wasn't as if she had anything to show for it either. She had not managed to persuade Mr Pepys to give her the key before they were interrupted. She sat down again, but then stood. She could not bear to sit on that chair, the one with the view of the door. Instead, she walked to the windowsill, put the comb down. Outside, the night was black and dense and empty, except for a few pinpricks of light from the torches on Tower Hill.

She peered out of the door. The coal scuttle had disgorged the coal onto the landing. Nobody came back. Would she be dismissed? If she was, where would she go? Visions of the poorhouse assailed her thoughts. Not there, please God, anywhere but there.

The room seemed different from before, as if the furniture itself was accusing her, the pages of the books whispering what she'd done. She tiptoed out and up to her chamber, but she could not sleep.

Downstairs, Elisabeth's voice echoed up to her, railing, 'I've gone back ... back to the true church! They'll forgive my sins and then when I die I'll be in heaven, a papist heaven, far away from you and your lies and false affection, and you'll be in hell, boiling in hell, do you hear me?'

Muffled endearments from Mr Pepys.

'... I tell you it's too late ...' More sobs.

Deb put her hands over her ears but could not block it out.

'How could you? On a Sunday? How could you prefer that slattern to me, your own dear little wife?'

Deb did not sleep all night, torn between listening and not listening to the sounds from below. The next day, nobody called for her to dress them. She missed Mr Pepys' cheerful morning talk and Elisabeth fussing over her collars and cuffs, and how best to dress her hair. Deb slunk down the back stairs to help Jane churn the milk. The way she felt, it might turn sour straight away. Jane looked at her with a smirking, satisfied eye, unsurprised at her sudden uncalled-for appearance in her territory. Did she know? Deb did her best to ignore her, nonetheless expecting a call for dismissal any moment from Mr Pepys.

But he went off to the Navy Board as usual, determined to brush the whole thing to one side as if it had never happened. When she gave him his hat in the hall, he whispered, 'It was just a hug, nothing more. Just the once.' His eyes pleaded with her.

She nodded; what else could she do? But the complicity made her feel small, as did the fact that she still had to fetch and carry for Elisabeth. Elisabeth's eyes were puffy and her manner tight and too brisk. Deb did not know where to put herself, wanted to hide but was not allowed to. All through the day Elisabeth refused to meet her eyes but kept up a pretence of haughty indifference.

When Mr Pepys came back at midday, she was forced to dine with them as usual, with the worm of it all eating away at her.

Elisabeth spoke in a hard voice. 'The salt, please, Deb, *if* you don't mind.'

And Deb had to pass it over, careful not to touch her hand. The relaxed atmosphere had gone, to be replaced with a misery as tangible as the London fog. Mr Pepys himself was nervous, eyes shifting from one to the other. Once, he tried to squeeze Elisabeth's hand under the table when he thought Deb wasn't looking, but Elisabeth snatched it away, her eyes threatening tears.

The afternoon dragged on but still Deb was not sent away. She heard them arguing over it in the night, and again the next day. Elisabeth would not speak to her except to give orders.

Later that day, Elisabeth set her to wiping over the glasses in the dining room, but when she went to collect one from the main chamber, Elisabeth said, 'My friend Mary Mercer is coming this afternoon. You will not be required to attend me.'

'Do you want me to finish the—'

'No. Just ... just get out of my sight.' And she threw the glass down at Deb's feet where it cracked, instead of breaking.

Deb wanted to pick it up. She half stooped, ready to, but Elisabeth yelled again, 'Get out!' so she had no option but to retreat.

Outside the door she heard Elisabeth weeping again. She wished she would stop. Deb clutched her hand to her stays; the sound echoed inside her, a sound she would make herself if only she could. But she did not weep. Instead, she went to her room, tidied everything over and over, trying to set things in order. Blood, phlegm, the hot and cold, the dry and bitter. The humours she must control if she was to stand another day in Seething Lane.

Chapter Thirty-five

Dᴇʙ ᴡᴀs sᴇɴᴛ ᴛᴏ ᴛʜᴇ ᴘᴏsᴛ ʜᴏᴜsᴇ, probably to get her out of Elisabeth's sight, but on the way back she rounded the corner to find her way blocked by Jem Wells. He'd obviously been waiting for her on the corner by St Olave's.

Her spirits soared at the sight of him, then immediately plummeted. How could she even speak to him now, since what had happened? She lowered her eyes, intent on going past without greeting.

He stepped out directly in front of her. 'Have you got a few moments to talk?' he asked.

'Sorry, I can't, I've got to get back,' she said, trying to manoeuvre past him, not daring to look into his face.

'Please.' He caught hold of her arm. 'Can't we start again? At Richmond, well ... I was a complete boor. My feelings were hurt and ... and I was angry. I've worried and prayed about it for weeks, until my conscience has driven me practically to bedlam. I've just been waiting for a chance to beg your pardon.'

'It doesn't matter.' She avoided his gaze, shrugged away.

'Please, Deb, wait. My mouth ran away with me. I should never have begun to talk politics before a lady. I promise I will never do so again. What can I do to make amends?'

'Nothing, I—'

'You see, the thing is, I've really missed your company.' He squashed his hat between his palms. 'Put a poor man out of his misery, won't you, and let me walk out with you again?'

'It's too late. I'm sorry.'

His hurt expression was like a stab between the ribs.

She hitched her skirts above the wet, and stepped off the cobbles and into the road to get by, stumbling in her hurry to get away.

Heaven knows, she wanted it. Wanted to feel his arms around her, like a shield against the world. But she was realistic. Would he be so interested in her if he knew what she really was? If he knew she'd let her master's hand wander into her most private places? Let alone that she was a traitor and a spy for the Dutch. The ugly facts stood like a wall between them.

She speeded her step until she was half running, head down, in a kind of lope, the loss of dignity superseded by the urgent need to get away. Even then she couldn't resist turning to look over her shoulder. He was still watching her, his hat scrunched into one fist.

Goodbye, Jem. The sense of loss was so needle-sharp it took her breath.

Nearly a week later, into November, and she still had not been dismissed. After taking her master's shoes to be resoled, she slipped into the house quietly, anxious not to come across Elisabeth. She could not bear another confrontation. As she crossed the hall, Deb stopped, listened. A familiar, abrasive voice was coming from the main chamber. It couldn't be. Of course, she knew from Hester's letters that Aunt Beth was back from Ireland, but the sound of her here, in the Pepyses' chambers, still startled her.

No wonder Elisabeth had been so keen to be rid of her that morning.

She paused, motionless, as she heard Elisabeth say dully, 'No, it is nothing Deb has done. I am no longer able to keep a woman, that's all, so we must part with her.'

Deb pressed her hand to her chest. So she was to be let go after all. Her first thought was that the gypsy had been right. Her second was that Elisabeth had not told her aunt what Deb had done. A sudden welling-up of gratefulness pricked her eyes. Elisabeth had saved Deb from shame, and from Aunt Beth's wrath. She could quite easily have done the opposite. It must be embarrassment that drove her mistress – after all, what woman would want people to think she could not keep her own husband happy?

Her aunt's clipped voice. 'It is so disappointing. I had hoped this would be a permanent position. How much notice do you intend to give?'

'Oh, I ... I don't know, a week, I suppose,' Elisabeth said.

'Is that reasonable? It is not much time for her to find something else.'

Deb clung to the newel post on the stairs, willed Aunt Beth to be quiet, in case Elisabeth should lose her temper and tell her everything.

'A month would be more suitable,' Aunt Beth continued. 'References?'

Deb winced.

'I ... I suppose so.' Elisabeth sounded empty, tired.

'Well. There's not much more to say, is there?'

Aunt Beth's frosty voice. 'I find your behaviour unspeakable. You should have made sure you had the means at your disposal before taking on a live-in servant. I bid you farewell, Mrs Pepys.' There was the noise of a chair being scraped back.

Deb bolted from the hall and up to her room. A few moments later she heard the door bang so hard the handle rattled. She peered out of the window, saw her aunt's upright figure stride away, climb into the Batelier's carriage and drive off.

Her days at Seething Lane were about to end. No more plays, no more nights of cards and conversation. No more chats with Elisabeth over upholstery and decorations, no more discussions over wallpaper and curtaining, lace and ribbon, or the right way to tie a bow. That night, Mr Pepys insisted Deb should sit down at the table for supper, and she could not refuse. He mooned at her with his big sad eyes whenever Elisabeth turned her back, shaking his head as if to say to her, 'I did try, but it's no use.'

Though she thought she would not weep, her body defied her, and she was mortified to find that when Jane brought the soup, a tear squeezed out and she had to knuckle it away before it dropped into her bowl.

Elisabeth glared at her, affronted, as if she had no right to cry, and indeed she did not.

A few days on, and ... oh, torture. Still Mr Pepys had not told her to go. What was he waiting for? She could not bear it. It made her want to scream. Instead, she scurried about her daily tasks in an agony of expectation, fearing the axe at any moment, and even more afraid when it did not fall.

Days passed. The decorators were in the house and

she hid away with them, sewing hems for the curtains and ironing cushion covers over and over. The men sensed something was the matter in the house and did not engage in their usual jesting and back-slapping. The household was muffled, as if bereaved.

I've done this, thought Deb – wiping the hallway table for the tenth time – made their marriage a dead thing. She circled the house from safe hiding place to safe hiding place, from the cupboard under the stairs to the outside latrine, afraid to enter any room where Elisabeth or Mr Pepys might be languishing.

She could not endure yet another frosty supper with them, so when she heard Mr Pelling, the apothecary, was to eat with them, she decided not to go down. The cutlery clinked below, and Mr Pepys' monologue gave every impression of him being his ebullient self.

She cursed the King, the Dutch, and Abigail in turn, could find no will to do copying work. Instead, she darned the same stocking again and again, until the patch was puckered and too thick to wear. After the door closed on Pelling, she heard Elisabeth climb the stairs in silence. Even the tap of her shoes made Deb feel guilty. Deb could not sleep. Does Mr Pepys sleep, she wondered?

The next morning, head aching, she buried herself under the bolster so she might not hear what Mr Pepys said when he bade goodbye to Elisabeth. His leaving spurred Deb to drag herself out of bed and begin to dress. She was only half into her bodice when her door flew open and Elisabeth stood there like an apparition, hair in disarray, eyes burning white-hot with anger.

Before Deb could react, Elisabeth's hand shot out and grabbed Deb's sleeve. Deb stumbled to follow as

Elisabeth hauled her out of the room.

'Slut! Tell me the truth!' Elisabeth cried, followed by a hard slap on Deb's cheek.

'Let go!' Deb squirmed, tried to fasten the laces of her bodice together, but Elisabeth hung on to her sleeve, pulled her, protesting, down the stairs.

'Admit it. It's been going on for months, hasn't it?'

'No, we were just—'

Slap.

'Swear it on the Bible!' Elisabeth dragged her into the main chamber. Deb heard the seam of her sleeve rip under Elisabeth's force.

'It was just a hug,' Deb protested, pushing her sleeve back on her shoulder.

'Liar.' Elisabeth's hand swept out to slap her again, but Deb dodged and she missed.

Breathless, Elisabeth gathered the heavy Bible from the table in both arms and pushed it towards Deb. 'He told you to say that. I just want the truth! Is it too much to ask after all this time, just to have the truth?' She tried to give the Bible to Deb, but Deb stepped away.

They both stared down as it dropped on the floor with a thud, and lay between them like an accusation.

'I did not mean to—'

'Did not mean? I saw you. In the chair. He had his hand up your skirt. I saw your legs, all your ...' Elisabeth could not say the word. She dissolved into sobs. 'Why can't you admit it?' She collapsed to the floor in front of the door, skirts puffing up round her, her face reddened with grief. 'Have I been so bad a mistress? Don't I deserve that much?'

'Oh please ...' She wanted to tell Elisabeth to stand up, but a catch in her chest stopped her voice.

'How long?' Elisabeth demanded.

'A month or two.'

'I knew it.' Groaning, Elisabeth scraped up fistfuls of skirt in both hands.

The Bible still lay askew on the floor. Deb bent down to retrieve it and put it back on the table. She took a tentative step towards Elisabeth, intending to help her to her feet. 'I'm sorry ... I'm sorry, I never meant—'

'Don't you dare to touch me.' The intensity of Elisabeth's voice made it barely audible. 'You whore. How could you? You were employed to be my friend. My *friend*, do you hear? And yet you do this. You are despicable.' Trembling, Elisabeth hoisted herself to upright and went out. Her draught caused the door to slam behind her, like a full stop.

'I thought it would blow over,' Mr Pepys whispered. He had finally told Deb to go, and now she was about to leave his office.

'The milk is spilt, sir; it's best I find somewhere else.'

'But where will you go to?'

'I have friends who will help me.'

'But who? Where will I find you?' His eyes were clinging, like a dog who'd lost his master.

'I'm not sure if it's a good idea that you do.'

They both turned to the door. Elisabeth was coming upstairs. Mr Pepys leapt away, gave her a brief nod, and hurried out onto the landing.

'It is done?' Elisabeth asked. 'She's going?'

'Yes,' her husband said.

Later, Elisabeth came in to where Deb was working with the decorators. She laid out a pile of coins on the table and pointed to it.

'A month's notice. But I want you out sooner than that. I have ordered a coach for the morning. You must tell it where to take you. I don't want to know.'

'Elisabeth, I—'

'No. Don't dare say a word ... I can't bear it.' The quiver of her side-curls showed she was shaking.

The decorators ignored their conversation with a studied indifference. Deb heard the slap of their brushes against the wall. She picked up the sewing she had been doing but saw no point in it any more. She dropped it on the floor where she stood and leaving the coins lying on the table, went up to her bare room. The angel above the door gazed down at her, wings pinned to the wall, wooden arms outspread in a shrug that seemed to say, 'I don't know.'

Chapter Thirty-six

DAWN. DEB LAY AWAKE until she heard Jane's footsteps stop outside her door. A scraping sound, and a letter was slid under her door. Deb lit a taper to read it by, shivering in the cold.

Since she must have displeased the Pepys, Aunt Beth wrote, finding another position was to be Deb's responsibility.

> *"I know what your mother did was not your fault, but the stink of a bad reputation sticks. Mistress Pepys must have heard tell of it, and perhaps that is also why I have not found another mistress willing to take you. Your sister will not be continuing at Bow now that you are unable to provide for her. Your father's business has had some difficulties; sales are dwindling. He certainly cannot afford the fees, that much was clear when I visited, at least not now that your brother Robert is*

old enough for schooling.

I wish you well in your search for another position. You had your chance, and must make your own way now. I will arrange for Hester to come back to me as a maid-of-all-work until she is old enough to find an alternative. I would not want this to be a permanent state of affairs, since she has not a fit temperament for such a position. As you know, she's unruly and wilful. Let's hope her schooling has had the desired effect ..."

Deb looked at the words and a stone seemed to lodge in her throat. What was she to do? The thought of Hester going back to Aunt Beth, when Aunt Beth so clearly did not want her, was unthinkable. There must be some way to keep her sister at school, to give her a chance at life. And it was clear she could not come here, to London, not now Deb had been dismissed. With regret, she realised she should have taken the money Elisabeth had left her. She had been too proud. A pride she couldn't afford. And now it was too late.

There was little choice left in the matter. Deb sat at her familiar table and picked up a quill, one whose nib was almost furred from her nights of copying, and wrote a note to Abigail begging for assistance. It stuck in her gullet that she must crawl to Abigail, but it had to be done, for Hester's sake, if not her own. She would need a place to stay, and an income, and Abigail could offer both. She could think of no one else. Only Jem, and she had far too much pride to ask him.

When the letter was sealed, she slipped it into her pocket and began to pack her portmanteau and her chest of drawers. She flattened out her whale-boned bodices on the bed and folded them, smoothed out the skirts, feeling how much wear was left in the cloth. A Brussels lace collar that Elisabeth had given her as a gift one day at Unthank's caught her eye, and she lifted it closer. Now it appeared too flimsy and transparent, her hands coarse and red under its white silk. She left it on the bed, did not pack it, for the sight of it filled her with remorse.

She thrust Jem's angel to the bottom of the trunk. What had she become? Just the empty body Mr Pepys described in his diary, she supposed. A girl who was just a stuffed bolster of straw one might lie on. She had despised her mother for what she had done, but was she, Deb, not as bad? The gypsy had been right: the dark side of her was always there, calling. She was like a fish swimming against that tide. She shut the lid on her portmanteau, surveyed the bare room.

But when the time came to go, there had still been no reply from Abigail. It was a stark choice – the streets or the workhouse. She could not go to the workhouse. The stench of Bridewell came back to her.

Anything but that. She would have to go to Abigail and beg.

Will Hewer avoided her eyes as he put her trunk in the carriage.

Deb leaned forward to the driver. 'Whetstone Park,' she said.

The windows of Seething Lane stared glassily after her, but Deb was certain Elisabeth was behind a curtain watching her go.

Chapter Thirty-seven

DEB'S LETTER LAY ON TOP of Abigail's work desk, where she had torn it open first thing that morning. Abigail went to pour a drink, but found only a dribble, the last of the rum in the bottle. She'd had a sleepless night dreaming she was saving Joan from a sinking ship. She'd fought her way out from the sheets dry-mouthed and wet-eyed, and now this.

She shoved the empty bottle away. When had she drunk that? Her mind was soft, as if she'd lost her edge.

So Deb had got herself found out, had she? Oh, how she wished she were younger. She could have played Deb's part to perfection, teased Pepys just enough to get what she needed, without giving too much of herself away.

But what to do? She could not let the girl loose in London, to go Lord knows where with her mouth a-flapping. How could she sleep easy if Deb was taken on by another employer? Yet a disturbance in her territory could not be borne. Her arrangements were too complicated to take account of someone else. She had it all sealed tight, rigidly timetabled, her comings and goings to the theatre and Lord B, her meetings with Piet. She came home as one thing and went out as someone else. Another person in the house would loosen it all, like unlaced stays.

Abigail walked to the bedroom. If Deb was to be silenced, it would be down to her. But then she would be back to the old problem. Piet would expect information from the Navy Office, and she was expected to supply it. He had no idea she wasn't already doing so. She had never told him of Deb's existence.

It was as if she was forcing her way through mud. It was a conundrum too much for her to unravel. Even now, months later, she still couldn't seem to think, except of Joan. It haunted her, those last days, how little Joan had weighed in her arms. A fledgling, dropped from its nest. And her heart still hurt, with a tearing feeling that would not stop.

She pulled open the window; the air was sharp and damp. Joan was gone, though she could not quite believe it. She did not want to follow her. Put like that, it was simple after all. She could not displease Piet, or she would be the one in the river. Deb must come here and be her eyes and ears as usual.

'Poole!' She ran to the stairs and called down. She should have replied to Deb straight away. She hoped she was not too late.

Deb did not relish the idea of arriving unannounced at Abigail's, but she did not know where else to go and still feared one of the spymaster's men would come after her. Better in the lion's den where you could see the lion, than lost in the jungle where it might leap on you unawares. Besides, already the November wind blew biting through her cloak, and she dare not sleep on the street with no shelter.

Abigail must have been expecting her, though, for

after the carriage drew up, she opened the front door herself. Her face was white with leading, even more of a mask than usual; dark charcoal was smudged round red-rimmed eyes. Deb wondered if she was drunk, but could smell no alcohol on her breath. Nevertheless, there was something sad and adrift about her that she could not place.

'Where's Poole?' Abigail said, looking in the carriage.

'I don't know. I haven't seen her.'

'But I sent her to fetch you.'

'We must have crossed. You got my letter then?' Deb asked.

'You should have been more careful. Did they catch you at it?'

Deb looked down. 'Just a few days, I need, till I can find something else.'

'You have references then?' Abigail's tone implied she knew she hadn't.

'A chit saying I worked there.' Deb was defiant.

Abigail nodded, as if it was what she expected. The driver, anxious to be off, dumped her trunk before them on the damp pavement.

'Drag it into the hall,' Abigail said. 'Poole will help you bring it up later.'

Deb paid off the gig and driver, and when it was out of sight, they waited in the front vestibule. Deb had never been in through the front door before.

'Watch.' Abigail rapped on the knocker of the inner door, a staccato pattern of knocks. 'Four singles, two close beats, two singles,' she said. 'Have you got that? If I'm out, Poole will know it's you.'

Abigail unlocked the door with a weighty key, then slid the bolt home behind them and mounted the wooden stairs to the first floor with Deb close behind.

The door to the main chamber was also locked. Abigail examined the lock, before saying, 'If you go out, make sure you are not followed home. Be observant. It's not the obvious ones you need to look out for. Often they are a false tail – there to keep you from spotting the real danger, the one who is unobtrusive.'

They climbed the second set of stairs past the living quarters to the top floor, where Abigail led her to the wooden shuttered window. She threw it open to reveal a loading gantry and another set of stairs on the outside of the building. 'You can get out of here if you need to, down to the tannery yard, if there's trouble.' She shut the wooden doors again. 'Give me a hair.'

Deb did not think she had heard correctly, but then Abigail gave a tug and withdrew one of her own long black hairs from the nape of her neck. 'Watch,' she said. She tied the hair carefully around the latch of the shutters and pulled it taut. 'It's what I do. Now, do the same to the chamber door when you go out. If Poole doesn't answer, or the hair's broken, you'll know someone has been in. And they may still be in here.'

'Is it really necessary? I mean, I don't think I—'

'You can't be too careful. If you expect to live here, you must abide by certain rules. I have found them useful, and I am still here to tell the tale.'

'What about when you have visitors?'

'I have none, and neither will you. My visitors are received at Bruncker's or I meet them in town. You were my only visitor, and I had my reasons for that. I do not want Pepys or anyone from the Navy Office to know you lodge with me, so you must make sure you are not watched, and never bring him here. Often I will be at Lord Bruncker's and Poole will escort me. It means you will be alone, so you must be vigilant.'

'What about your new house? Will you be moving there soon?'

Abigail laughed, a sharp humourless sound. 'There is no new house. There never was.'

'But—'

'It is a ruse. I use it when I need to breed confidence in gullible people.'

Deb coloured.

'Bring no one here, and keep little. Be ready to move on to another safe place if we need to run.' Deb's sense of unease grew. This amount of vigilance could only mean that it was somehow necessary.

'You'll find all you need,' Abigail said, gesturing around. 'And I'll give you more unobtrusive clothes, things that are more shapeless, that don't draw attention to your looks.'

'I only have a few dresses. Mrs Pepys chose them.'

'So I see.' She looked Deb up and down with disdain. 'Poor woman never did have any taste. For this work you sometimes need to look poorer, or to be so bold and fashionable that nobody dares challenge you. You're the nondescript type. I've a grey skirt and bodice I'll loan you.'

'Thank you,' Deb said. 'It's kind of you to take me in when I've nowhere to—'

'Kind? I've no use for kind.' The thought seemed to make Abigail angry. 'Who was ever kind? It's business. There'll be documents to copy as before, and we still need Pepys' intelligence. You'll be able to entertain him at the Black Bull tavern.'

Entertain him. She had thought she was clear of all that.

'Naturally, you will be paid less. You are not as

valuable as you were, now we can't have such easy access to Pepys' diary. Still, you must get what intelligence you can. My contact wants to know which ships are being rebuilt at Chatham, and which at Portsmouth or other docks, for some scheme he's involved in. He's particularly interested in the hundred-cannon ship that Pepys mentioned to you. Try to find out where that's being refitted.'

'I understand,' Deb said.

'Poole will take a message to tell Mr Pepys where to meet you.'

'Yes.' She had no intention of meeting Mr Pepys again, but she was in no position to argue.

'Ask him the layout of the yards, what's being refitted, how many artisans live on site, the hours they work in the roperies and the sailmakers and so forth.' Abigail was throwing on a wrap as she spoke. 'Try to persuade him to take you there, if possible. And you must ask him what day they inspect the yards. The day and the time of the weekly inspection. Have you got that? It's most important.'

'Yes.' She knew better than to ask why these details were needed. Abigail never told her and she drew her own conclusions from the evidence she copied.

'I'll be at Lord B's. When Poole returns you may use her as a messenger.'

Deb nodded.

Abigail gestured to a shut door. 'And my chamber – it is strictly private. You have your own chamber here.' She walked along the hall and pushed open a door to reveal a servant's quarters at the back. The damp and Spartan room told Deb all she needed to know about her status there. 'I need the yard inspection times by Friday,' Abigail said.

Deb had lost all sense of time; she'd forgotten

what day it was.

'I have an appointment to dine with Lord Bruncker.' Abigail brushed down her full taffeta skirts and adjusted her veiled hat. Deb noticed the hatpin on the brim, skewering it tight to Abigail's hair, and could not help staring now she knew how that pin could be used.

'The spare key.' Abigail dropped the cold weight of it into her hand. 'Don't lose it.' She did not bid her goodbye, but Deb could hear her red heels clack all down the front stairs, the shunt of the bolts and the other key turning in the lock.

When she was quite sure she had gone, Deb let out her breath and took stock of her surroundings. Without the presence of Abigail, and with the fire unlit, the house was dank and she could see dust on all the surfaces. It did not seem to be a home, just a collection of random possessions, as if nobody had ever really lived there at all.

She wondered if she should clean it. Abigail had not made her household duties clear, only her spying duties. She did not know how to be Abigail's maid. She was a different beast entirely from Elisabeth Pepys, and besides, something in Abigail's manner had shifted from feigned interest in Deb to a ruthless contempt.

After an hour or so, she heard the strange pattern of knocks and went down.

'Who is it?' she asked warily from behind the door.

'Poole.'

She was almost glad to see her. She explained that Abigail was out at Lord Bruncker's. When she and Poole had lugged up the trunk, it sat in the middle of the floor, making it feel even more like a waiting room. This chamber was nothing like the Pepyses' cosy parlour, full of half-read books, portraits and maps on the walls, soft cushions and rugs for comfort.

After Poole disappeared downstairs, Deb dragged her trunk, scraping on the boards, to her chamber. Suddenly exhausted, she sat down on the hard pallet bed and examined a patch of creeping mould on the whitewashed wall. She was stuck here, she realised. Elisabeth had thrust her a hastily scrawled paper that merely stated the dates of her employment and no recommendation. The lack of words said more than any reference could.

Where had it begun to go wrong? Was it the moment she met Abigail? Or the moment she set foot in the Pepyses' house? Once things started to slide, it was hard to claw them back; they were sand sucked away by the sea. One thing dragged another in its wake. She had hoped to set an example Hester could follow, one as far away from her mother's ruinous reputation as possible. Yet here she was.

Hester. Deb groaned. Hester must never know. Deb could pay for her board and schooling just the same, if she did Abigail's bidding. Her own chances and reputation might be lost, but she would make sure her sister kept hers, and what's more, that Hester would never find out how. A resolve hardened in her.

Very well, if she was a whore and a traitor, she would be one that survived.

And if Abigail Williams could hide her true profession, then so could she.

Chapter Thirty-eight

Abigail MADE DEB WRITE to Mr Pepys, and Poole brought the return message to Deb asking to meet him at his tailor's. From there they took a ride in a hired coach. She was surprised to find she was glad to see him – his familiar jovial face, his beaming smile. He was full of questions about her new employer, but Deb simply told him it was a Dr Allbarn, and led him to believe he was a dull but dutiful physician. Frustratingly, Mr Pepys would not be steered to a conversation about the docks or inspections or anything to do with the navy, no matter what enticements she tried.

'I need diversion,' he said. 'The office is a mighty trial. Let's not talk of that now. Show me where you live, little Deb, where we can be private.' He emphasised the word 'private'.

'I'm sorry, Dr Allbarn won't permit callers after hours, and I must be back soon.'

'Big bear misses you. I've been half-mad with it,' he said, trailing his finger along her bare collarbone.

'And Elisabeth?'

He frowned, was silent, playing with the embroidered pocket of his waistcoat. The coach rattled across the cobbles.

'I love *you*, Deb,' he said, in a sudden gush. He took hold of her hands. 'Don't you care for me at all?'

'Of course I do,' she said. It was true, she did. He was the closest she had to a friend. But she did not want to be his lover. It was all so complicated, and then there was Jem. Jem – she dare not even think of him.

Mr Pepys pressed his lips down on hers, but she pushed him off. 'Someone might see us, through the window,' she said.

His answer was to pull down the blinds and lift her skirts.

'No,' she protested. 'I just want to talk.'

'But I'm mad about you. The house is so quiet. There's nothing left to look forward to.' His eyes were wet and soulful as he tried, again, to creep his hand up past her stockings to her bare thigh. 'You know you like it, Deb. Just a little kiss.'

'No,' she said, loud and definite, pushing his hands away.

'But why?'

What could she tell him? That he was deluding himself. That he could not love her, because he did not even know her. What could he know of the real Deb? The Deb he loved was a figment of his imagination. He wanted a grand 'amour' and as his inferior, she was supposed to supply it.

'But you're all alone in London,' he went on. 'I want to protect you. I don't know where you are, and I worry that someone will hurt you.'

The coach drew up again at his tailor's. He would not let her alight until he'd warned her to take care, and to make sure she kept away from predatory men. Somewhat impertinent, she thought, coming from him. She resisted the urge to snap at him but threw open the carriage door in silent frustration. She still had no definite information and knew this would mean more threats from Abigail and no pay, but she just could not stomach being alone with him any longer.

He made a lunge to detain her with a kiss, but she was already out and brushing down her skirts. He pressed her into agreeing to meet him a few days later at Herringman's booksellers. She agreed, only because it meant he would leave, and it would go some way to appeasing Abigail.

Strangely, though, at the appointed hour at Herringman's, Mr Pepys did not arrive to meet her. It was unlike him, and Deb wondered if he was unwell. She puzzled over it, whether she had made a mistake with the day or time. But one early morning in the following week, the answer came in the form of a steady rap at the door.

Abigail was at the window in an instant, to peer out onto the street.

'It's a young man,' she said, frowning. 'Quick, see if it's someone you recognise.'

Deb held back the curtain to look out. The neat and well-suited figure was unmistakeable. 'It's Will Hewer,' she said.

'Hewer?'

'Mr Pepys' clerk.'

'Oh, him. How does he know where you live?'

She remembered he'd been there when she gave the driver instructions. 'I don't know. It must be something about Mr Pepys.'

Abigail paused for a moment, considering. 'Then you'd better go down, but don't on any account let him in. I don't want him to see me here.'

The knock came again, harder and more insistent. This time Deb hurried down and undid the bolts to open the door.

Will cleared his throat with a little cough. 'Beg pardon, Miss Willet. I hope I don't disturb you in your duties with the good doctor, but I brought this.' He held up a letter. 'From Mr Pepys.'

'Do you know what it's about?' she asked, a sudden impossible hope flaring that she might have been forgiven and Elisabeth wanted her back.

Will looked away, seeming to read her thoughts. 'There's been more bother between Mr and Mrs Pepys. She found out he's still seeing you – someone saw you in a coach together. He says ... he won't be coming to you again. I think it wise to let matters cool, Miss Willet. Like he says in the letter. Mrs Pepys'll not have it, any kind of ... meeting between you.'

He held the letter up in front of her. 'Please take it. It's more than my life's worth to take it back. And before you ask – no, I can't deliver a reply.'

So that was the way things were. She reached out for the letter, knowing Abigail would be watching her from the window. 'Is Mr Pepys all right? Not unwell or anything?'

Will's eyes flashed. 'What do you think? Of course he isn't all right. His work's suffering and it's brought him to ... well, he's just not himself any more. And Mrs Pepys, she weeps and weeps. It breaks my heart to see how she takes on. Please, do as he asks. The whole house is at sixes and sevens because of you. Just stay away, that's all I ask.'

Deb reached for the letter, silence hiding her conflicting emotions.

Will shifted from foot to foot, growing redder and

redder. 'It should never have started,' he burst out. 'It wasn't fair on Elisabeth.'

'I didn't mean for it to be ...'

He stood waiting, frowning, stubborn, expecting her to finish, but she could not. He was right. What was the point? After a moment's awkward silence, Deb said, 'I can't stay, my new mist ... master, is waiting.'

'Apologies for keeping you,' he said with sarcasm. 'Farewell, Miss Willet.' His words had a finality about them.

From habit she dipped her head towards him before going back inside and closing the door. In the dim hallway she unfolded Mr Pepys' letter. She knew his handwriting so well, yet it was odd to see a letter actually intended for her and signed 'Samuel Pepys' with an inky flourish. She ran her finger over it, over the flamboyant letters, the sheer confidence of it.

There could be no more meetings, he said. She was not to go near him again; their affair was at an end.

'Deb?' Abigail called.

Slowly she climbed the stairs. A sharp pinch of regret had lodged in her chest – not for him, but for Elisabeth, who, she was sure, had made him write it.

'What did he want?' Abigail asked, looking at the letter. 'Is it information from Pepys?'

'Yes.' Deb was still digesting the impact of the words.

'I don't want his servants here. If Pepys and Lord B find out that we live in the same house, it could be a risk.'

'It won't matter now, because he won't be back. Pepys doesn't want to see me again.'

Abigail pounced on the letter and twisted it from her hand before Deb could stop her. Her expression did not shift as she read. Finally, she screwed up the letter and cast it down on the floor. 'You know what this means?'

'What?'

'You don't understand, do you?' Abigail threw up her hands in annoyance. 'You don't matter, don't you see? Nothing is important to Piet but the information. A spy is not a person, but a conduit. When intelligence flows through, all is well, but if it stops flowing, you're useless. Nobody cares who you are. You are utterly disposable. It is the bargain that you strike whenever you turn traitor.' She was tight-lipped now, her words staccato as if she was firing them at Deb. 'That's the thorn in the handshake. But you haven't just put your own skin at risk, have you? The Dutch intelligence office doesn't know you exist. How am I to explain it to them, the sudden drying up of information?'

Deb couldn't answer. Abigail's agitation seemed to fill the room. Even the silk of her skirts seemed to crackle as she paced the floor. She took hold of Deb by the wrist. 'Did you refuse him? What did you do to stop him wanting to see you?'

'Nothing, Abigail. Will said Elisabeth—'

'I took you in because you were Pepys' whore. Why else did you think I would take in a girl like you?' Abigail's face was close to Deb's, so close she could see the black pupils of her eyes.

Deb struggled to release herself. The word shocked her, as if she had been kicked by a horse. She struggled to make sense of it. 'Don't call me that.'

'You're worthless to me.' Abigail thrust Deb away. 'What am I to do with you now?' She pressed her hand to her forehead. 'How am I supposed to find out which ships are being built in which yards without access to Pepys?'

'Go to Lord Bruncker then! He knows as much as Pepys.'

'Bruncker never writes anything down himself. He thinks it beneath him to act like a clerk. There must be someone else who wants to get his hand up your skirt. One of Pepys' friends. His clerk, the one who just came, what's his name?'

'Will Hewer?' Deb shook her head to free it of the idea. Not Will, the idea was appalling. 'No, I couldn't. He dislikes me. He has a fondness for Elisabeth and I—'

'You'd better think of something. Or there'll be no bed for you here. Take it or leave it. You can sell yourself my way, or take your chances in Bridewell or on the streets with the other whores.'

'Don't call me that,' she said again.

'You did it with Pepys, didn't you?'

'No! It was only a hug,' she shouted.

She ran to her room and slammed the door. Why had she said that? It wasn't true. But she wished it was. With all her heart, she wished it. She had not let him take her; that was true. She was still a virgin, but it had been far more than a hug, she knew that.

She sat down hard on the bed; her legs were shaking. She could run, but where would she go? The poorhouse? No, she would go stark mad in there, and Hester would surely find out. She could not bear it if Hester had to set foot in such a place. She had not had the courage to tell her sister what had really happened – how could she? Instead, she had written and told her that she had a new position with a Dr Allbarn who was a well-respected chirurgeon with a flourishing practice. Lies, lies, lies. It seemed all she could do now was lie.

Pepys was one thing – he had some affection for her, and she for him – but she couldn't be a cold-blooded whore. Not that. She used to look down on the mollies on the street with revulsion, thought them beneath her, another sort of woman altogether. Nothing to do with her. She crossed the road if she saw one propping up a doorway. The shame of it, to have to sell herself so openly.

Jem Wells's face sprang into her mind. She looked up to where she had pinned his wooden angel over the door. The sight of it depressed her. There was no guardian angel watching over her, she thought bitterly, only her own conscience.

'What are you looking at?' she said to it.

Then she pushed the thought of Jem down, back to the place inside that nobody could touch.

She took out paper, began to make a list of Pepys' associates. If whoring was to be her business, then she would choose wisely, make it pay; give as little as possible, take as much as she could.

Chapter Thirty-nine

December

DEB CLOSED HER EYES IN ANGUISH, the letter dangling
in her hand. It was from Hester; she was coming up to
London with Lavinia, whose father was buying her a
viol. They had offered to bring Hester to town with
them, and they would drop her off at noon in three
days' time, at Dr Allbarn's address. Hester was looking
forward to meeting Deb's new employer and seeing the
fine mansion where she lived.

Deb sat down, stood up, sat down. Obviously Hester
could not come to Abigail's house. She did not want
Hester anywhere near Abigail; it was too dangerous for
her to even meet her. Nor did she want Hester to see the
strange emptiness of where she lived, the echoing
chambers, the down-at-heel street. She thought quickly
and then penned Hester a note to tell her Dr Allbarn
was busy with patients, that she had the day off and
would meet her outside the temporary Exchange.

On the day, Deb dressed in her blue woollen dress,
the one from Unthank's that she often used to wear at
the Pepyses'. Even though it was a dull shade, it was of
good quality. It made her feel conspicuous to be
wearing it again, as though everyone was staring at her.

'Deb! Deb!' A lacquered and gilt carriage was pulling

in, and there was Hester waving excitedly from the window. It had barely drawn up to the kerbside when the door opened and Hester leapt out in a flurry of skirts and petticoats and threw herself into Deb's arms.

When Deb had kissed and hugged Hester tight, and brushed away her tears, she was introduced to Mr Hartley, and to Lavinia Hartley, his daughter. It was clear right away that they were people of a certain class. Lavinia's damson-coloured dress was well cut, of the finest warm worsted, and her fur muff was lined with velvet. Mr Hartley greeted Deb with polite reserve and surreptitiously looked her over, as if to determine whether Hester was really a suitable friend for Lavinia.

Deb bridled under their scrutiny and took on her best Abigail Williams impersonation of hauteur. 'My apologies that I cannot entertain you today,' she said. 'Dr Allbarn has a very important client this morning, from White Hall, and cannot be disturbed.'

'From White Hall? You don't mean from the royal household?' Hester was wide-eyed.

'I'm afraid I am not allowed to say more. Dr Allbarn does not discuss his clients,' she said, and let them draw their own conclusions as to the royal, or otherwise, nature of his business.

The Hartleys looked suitably impressed and arranged to meet Hester again by the carriages at three o'clock after they'd been to the music shop.

'Only a few hours.' Hester was rueful.

'Come, let's go inside out of the cold.' She put her arm in Hester's and they wove their way under the jetties of the new houses towards the bustling market.

Hester had grown taller. Deb took a sidelong glance at her. She was no longer a child, but a young, self-confident woman with the sort of raven beauty that drew men's eyes. The sight of her made

Deb expand with pride.

Inside the market they found a stall selling warmed milk and honey, and they seated themselves on the little stools set around makeshift tables. When they had their drinks before them, Hester chattered on about her life at school, her friend Lavinia, and how Lavinia had a brother who was simply the most handsome man she'd ever seen. This news discomfited Deb. She had not realised how quickly Hester was growing up. Soon she would need employment and a dowry, and Deb was now in no position to provide either.

'Deb?' Hester tapped her arm to get her attention.

'Sorry, just daydreaming.'

'You look tired out. Is it hard with Dr Allbarn? Does Mrs Allbarn work you long hours?'

'No. Not at all. He's a very good employer.'

'What's his house like?'

She twisted the lace on her cuff. 'Well, it's large, and lofty, and … well, what you'd expect really.'

'What about Mrs Allbarn?' Hester leaned forward, face alive with interest. 'I'll wager she's less untidy than Mrs Pepys! And the other servants, how many staff are there?'

'A lot. I haven't counted.' She was at a loss, so she tried to turn the subject. 'But tell me about your music lessons. You say Lavinia plays the viol?'

Hester told her about how they sang choral music for the church services. 'But this is lovely, isn't it? I hope to come and visit you much more often. Lavinia's father is a magistrate and he's often in town for business, and he says he can bring us. In fact, I meant to ask, I mean … I wondered if there was room for me at Dr Allbarn's? After all, I'm nearly fourteen and I don't want to stay at school any more, not when I could be here in London with you.'

Deb's thoughts raced. 'There are no vacancies where I work, and besides, you need to finish your education.'

'But that's stupid. I know you pay my fees, and they cost you dear. If I was working, you wouldn't have to do that any more, and we could be together every day.'

Her sister's bright-eyed enthusiasm only made Deb feel worse. The idea of seeing Hester daily made her realise it would be impossible to keep her uninvolved.

Hester saw the indecision in her face. 'Have you got used to your new London life without me? Is that it? Don't you want me with you? I suppose that's why I can't come to the house; I'm not good enough for your fine doctor.'

'No, that's not it at all … look, Hester, you must stay at school. Learn as much as you can while you can. A good education is your chance – don't throw it away. I'll send for you when there's a suitable vacancy, I promise.'

'Lavinia's leaving school at Christmas. Her family think she's old enough. She's going to tutor two small children. She promised me we'd explore the city together, and I want to be in London, like her.' She pouted. 'Bow is so unfashionable … and so dull.'

Good, thought Deb. A dull life was a safe life; the duller the better. 'Be patient, Hester. You're too young. Just complete your schooling like a good girl.'

Hester slammed her cup onto the table so the other customers stared at her flushed face and angry eyes. 'Don't treat me like I'm four years old! I'm nearly fourteen! Fourteen! It's selfish of you not to help me. If it was the other way round I'd help you. I thought you'd be pleased: saving you your hard-earned wage and offering to come and help.'

'You don't understand. London's not all it seems from the outside. There are dangers you don't know about—'

'Dangers? Don't be so old-fashioned. Deb, I cannot bear that stuffy schoolroom a moment longer, not while you are shopping at Unthank's and going to the theatre and living the life of a lady.'

Too late, Deb realised that in censoring the reality of her circumstances, she must have given the impression in her letters that life was one long round of luxury and entertainment. She could think of nothing to say.

Hester took her silence as refusal. 'Well, if you won't help me find employment, I'll ask Lavinia if her father knows of anything suitable. I'll show you I'm not too young. I'm old enough now to do it without you.' She stood, flung her cloak about her shoulders and marched away, head up high in her neat little hat.

'Hester! Wait!' Deb leapt up to follow, but the bearded man at the counter stepped out to stop her.

'Thinking of leaving without paying, were you?' he said.

'No, of course not …' She fumbled frantically in her purse for the few remaining coins and tokens, her eyes fixed on Hester's back as it disappeared into the crush of the crowd.

When she reached the end of the row of stalls, she looked about helplessly. There was no sign of Hester's navy blue cloak and hat anywhere. Deb was forced to wait outside the Exchange until Hester deigned to return. Deb walked listlessly up and down, seeing nothing of the stalls in front of her but ruminating miserably on what to do.

What would happen if Hester came to London? It would all come out then: her sullied reputation, the strange clandestine life she had been forced to live. If anyone discovered Deb was a traitor, and working for the Dutch, then, if they lodged together, her sister, too, would be a suspect.

More than an hour later, Hester appeared, face tear-stained and red. 'I'm sorry,' she said, and burst into fresh tears. 'It's just ... I'd dreamed of it so many nights. Us both living and working together, like a proper family. I felt sure you'd say yes.'

Deb's heart melted. 'Sorry, Hester love, I can't. Dr Allbarn, well, he's not easy. In fact, he's a bit of a tyrant. You wouldn't want to come to him. But I'll find you something as soon as I can. I promise.' The lie made her sick to her soul. Quite apart from the fact Dr Allbarn didn't exist, by omission, more deception seemed to be closing round her, choking her. Hester only wanted to save her trouble and money, and for them to be together. What sort of sinful creature had she turned into, that she could tell such outright lies to her own sister?

Just then, Lavinia and her father arrived and Deb and Hester were forced to put on brave faces as Lavinia chattered on about her new viol, which even now was being loaded carefully into the waiting carriage by a liveried servant.

Deb reached out to hug Hester, and in her anxiety held her too tight, so that Hester pushed her away as if she was embarrassing her.

'I'll write in a few days,' Hester said. 'But I meant it, about coming to London. You always told me families should stick together. And I've missed you so much. But look at me, Deb. I'm grown now, and you can't keep me at school for ever. Once the New Year is over, I'll be looking for a position near you in the city, with your blessing or without it.'

Act Three

1669

Chapter Forty
January

NEW YEAR'S DAY, and everyone was going to church. Deb had chosen St Olave's, the navy church, deliberately, but she had to be cautious. The Pepyses would be sitting upstairs, in the carved wooden boxes reserved for senior staff of the Navy Board, but she was still careful not to go in until the last minute and then to sit downstairs, at the back behind a pillar, in her nondescript grey dress, her bonnet pulled carefully down low over her eyes and her hair tucked up out of sight.

She fixed her eyes on the monument to the side of her, a painted wooden altar carved with armorial insignia, and their skulls nestling together like plums in a bowl of fruit. On the altar, the carving of the rich merchant stared solemnly at his wooden wife, over coffins of their children. She thought of her mother then, wondered what had become of her, if she ever thought of her and Hester. It was a bitter thought, and she swallowed it back.

Just for a moment she wished that, instead of here, she'd dared to go to the little wooden church where Jem preached. She remembered his eyes searching her out, the special look he gave her. Did he still look out for her? She hoped so. But there was no point thinking of him; she had left the straight and narrow path for one of sin and shadow. She was in Abigail's pay now, though it was little enough, just food and board, and a few coppers for fares. Only when she supplied information would she get paid more. Besides, only a few weeks ago, Abigail had threatened to send every trepanning-man in London after her, unless she made a new navy contact, and Deb knew Abigail well enough to believe it.

Deb scanned the crowd in desperation, looking for any of the clerks. Up until now she had prevaricated, fearing to come into contact with Mr Pepys. But Mr Pepys had kept to his word, and had left her alone, and Abigail was insistent she should cultivate someone else from the navy who might spill the information she needed into a woman's ear.

Just before the service began, a great crowd of people pushed their way in, and she had to shuffle along the bench to let them sit. She recognised one of the workers from the Navy Offices at the end of the row. It was Hal Crawley, from Pepys' office. He had been to Seething Lane for dinner on a few occasions, and had sat next to her and breathed unpleasantly down her neck. He pulled his cap off his greasy hair and sat with bowed head. He would be worth a try.

She watched him covertly, saw his leg twitch restlessly as the parson began preaching about the new year and the renewal that Jesus brought. So, not an overly religious man then, just paying lip-service. Something about her gaze must have alerted him, and he raised his pale blue eyes to hers, before they moved down to her chest and then back again to her face. He recognised her, dipped his head.

One of his friends nudged him and whispered

something, and she forced herself to smile back brightly, to meet his eyes. At the end of the service, as she went out, she almost bumped into Elisabeth, flurrying out of the door in a billow of velvet cloak. Deb shot backwards into the gloom again, but only just in time, for the portly figure of Mr Pepys was close behind, his hand reaching for his wife's shoulder to propel her out into the light. How it gave her heart a cold ache to see them.

'Not going to wish Pepys the compliments of the season then? Miss Willet, is it not?'

She started, dragged her eyes away from Mr Pepys' back. Crawley was hanging back at the church door, his hat in his hand, revealing a greasy rim where it had been on his head. His words were polite, but his manner suggestive.

'A Happy New Year to you, Mr Crawley,' she said, with a small curtsey. So he was interested.

'Aye, I hope for a better one, with no more trouble from the Dutch.'

'They certainly caused a deal of trouble for you in the Navy Offices,' she said, attempting a smile.

'Terrible. Lost most of our ships,' he said. 'And money still owed on them for the building. Could take years to replace them.' He sucked on his teeth, ready to complain more, but she interrupted him.

'That has always fascinated me, the building of ships.'

He narrowed his eyes, laughed. 'A strange passion for a woman.'

'It's working for Mr Pepys,' she said earnestly, trying to convince him. 'He talked of it often, and it made me interested. The craftsmanship of it. I'd love to see a ship being built. Mr Pepys is always talking of the docks at Chatham.'

'But I heard you've left the Pepyses'. Did it not suit you?'

'Unfortunately Mrs Pepys decided she did not need a lady's companion after all.'

'Or perhaps Mr Pepys found you a little too interesting.' He smirked slightly, and it made her want to kick him hard where it would hurt. She quelled the urge and instead put on a pleasant face and tried again to turn the conversation to the docks. She put on her little girl voice. 'It is a shame because Mr Pepys had promised to take me to see the ships, and I've always wanted to see a ship up close like that—'

'A promise was it? Well, we can't have you disappointed, can we? I'll take you, one day, if you like.'

'I'm free tomorrow. My master Dr Allbarn has given me a day's leave with it being New Year and all.' She snatched the chance while she could. But he frowned. She could almost read his suspicion. Young women probably never behaved in this way towards him.

She tried another tack, made her tone casual. 'But Will Hewer said he might take me sometime, so perhaps ...'

'As it happens, I'm free tomorrow too,' he said. He glanced over her shoulder to where Pepys was chatting with some other solidly built citizens, their breath steaming round them in the freezing air. 'Though there's not much to see, and it will be mighty bitter out there on the water for such a long journey. Are you sure you wouldn't rather I took you to see some entertainment? A play, or some music? Somewhere warm?'

The thought of being inside, pressed up too close

to Mr Crawley, was not one she relished. But this was business. She repeated her desire to see the docks. After a little cajoling, he agreed to take her out to take a tour of the yards. 'Nine bells then, at the Old Swan Stairs,' he said. 'We'll take a wherry.'

The next morning was another dismal and cold day, the sort that leaches away your heat from the inside out. She had dressed warmly, but, more importantly, modestly. She was treading on a knife-edge inviting any sort of intimacy with Crawley, but Abigail's words had hit home. Unless she could supply the right information, she would simply be another missing woman – one that vanished into thin air, one that no one could ever trace.

Crawley was waiting at the wherry dressed in a too-shiny coat and breeches under a thick woollen cloak, with his face scrubbed red and his chin shaved raw except for his wisp of a beard. He had a cold and kept blowing noisily into his kerchief. On the journey he insisted on paying and then on sitting close to her so that he could take hold of her arm at the least opportunity, to point out sights, or to shield her from spray whenever another craft came too near. He kept up a tedious commentary on types of watercraft, but she feigned bright-eyed interest. At one point, he said, 'Your hands must be frozen, let me hold them,' and she had to let her cold hands sit between his warm moist ones. It was all she could do not to shudder.

The trip downriver took most of the day, by which time her teeth were chattering and she was wondering why she had ever thought it a good idea. But at Gillingham Water they disembarked at Queen Stairs, and Crawley steered her towards the fortified gatehouse. She tottered slightly because her feet were numb and her legs stiff, but Crawley used it as an excuse to drape an arm about her shoulder.

He had his navy papers ready, but the gatekeeper recognised him. 'Mr Crawley. Raw day, ain't it? This your missus?' he asked.

'Not yet,' Crawley said, giving her a coy look, 'but I have hopes.'

She smiled with tight-closed lips, folded her arms across her chest. *Not unless I'm six foot under*, she thought.

Once through the gates, Deb really did take an interest. She let Crawley's commentary wash over her, determined to commit the layout to memory. She made an imaginary map of everywhere they walked, past the mast ponds where timbers were soaking under a thin sheet of ice, past the sailmakers' sheds, the wheelwright's shop and the block and tackle makers.

Crawley stood her inside one of the covered slipways, where an enormous hulk of a ship was sitting in dry dock waiting to be fitted out with cannon and sail. 'What's this one called?' she asked.

'It's a refit of the "Duke of Something". A forty-nine gunner.' She watched the men hammering and splicing wooden pegs. 'But the biggest one's in Portsmouth, so I've heard. I wouldn't mind seeing her. A hundred cannon. That would give the Dutch something to stick between their teeth.'

'Indeed, yes,' she said.

Just then one of the shipwrights appeared to greet them, a cheerful man with a brown twill apron over his woollen winter doublet.

'How fares it?' Crawley asked.

The shipwright talked about how work had been held up through lack of funds. 'But we've just heard there's money for cannon now. Blooming nuisance, too. Foreman wants everything finished before the inspectors come, and it will be a rush. That's why we're all here now when we could be at home with our families enjoying a New Year dinner. Still, truth be told, I'd rather be here than cooped up at home.'

Deb perked up. 'How long before it's inspected?'

'What do you reckon, Crawley?' the shipwright asked.

'A fortnight, I'd guess.'

The shipwright turned to Deb. 'They come regular, see, about every six weeks. Men from the Navy Offices.' He gave a disparaging glance to Crawley. 'Supposed to make sure she's seaworthy before they arm her.'

'I see. How do they tell?'

'They don't.' He laughed. 'Useless buggers, making a nuisance of themselves, upsetting our routine. They stand here in their fancy clothes, and most of them don't know a mizzen from a mainmast. But we have to kowtow to them while they say "Carry on, men".' He spat in disgust. 'Crawley'll tell you. He has to write up the notes.'

'Is that right?' She looked at Crawley with new interest. 'It must be a painstaking task. Do they ever find anything?'

Crawley shifted from foot to foot, uncomfortable. 'It's mostly just routine.'

'They tell us to change this or that, but we take no notice. It's a fiddle, that's what it is.'

'What day of the week?' asked Deb.

'Dunno. Mondays, I think. They go to sup afterwards at the Three Tuns. Why do they do it, send those dusty old men from the offices, Mennes, Huyton—?'

'Come on, Miss Willet,' Crawley said firmly. 'Let's leave the man to his work.'

'But I'm interested. It's fascinating.'

'Hush up, won't you? D'you want to make a fool of me?' Crawley dug his fingers in her arm. She nodded to the man, and let Crawley lead her away. That was enough. She had something to give Abigail. She suggested they should make ready to leave on the next boat.

'But you haven't seen the carpentry shop where they do the fitting out. If you like ships, that's the most interesting part of all.'

So she was obliged to follow him. Everywhere they went the men stared at her; a woman in the yards was deemed an entertainment, as this was almost exclusively the domain of men. The only other women they had seen were in the hemp house and the ropery where the sails were sewn and the rope-ends plaited off, and when she went in there, the scathing but envious look on the women's faces was even harder to bear.

She endured the stares and the catcalls as she passed, but the effect was to make Crawley ever more puffed-up and pleased with himself, until, as they came out of the ropery, he pulled her towards him and fastened his wet lips over hers. She was taken by surprise and it was a moment before she could free herself and push him off.

'Mr Crawley!'

He pressed her back against the wall and tried again, but this time she was ready for him and dodged out of his way.

'What's the matter?' His expression was offended. 'You like me, don't you?'

'Please, not so quick,' she said, gasping at the air

and moving quickly to put a bale of rope between them.

He raised his arms in a gesture of frustration. 'What? It was only a little kiss.'

'You are too forward, Mr Crawley,' she said frostily. 'I shall walk back to the wherry by myself now, if you try to take advantage.' Outrage suited her purposes now. She had seen what she wanted to see. She would remember enough to pacify Abigail. 'Now, escort me properly as a gentleman should.' She held out her arm.

He was cowed by her imperious manner, something she had learned from Abigail. If you acted as if you were a lady, then people believed you to be one. And she might need him again. He was her only contact in the navy, and she would try to keep him sweet if her stomach could stand it.

When she got back on dry land she reassured Crawley she would meet him at church the following Thursday, then went the long route home, in the deepening dusk, determined he should not know where she lived. It was second nature now to check behind her, check the hair on the door, keep watchful.

Once inside Abigail's house, she lit the candles, and fearing she might forget if she didn't pen it down, drew up a map of the docks. Carefully, over three sheets of vellum, she marked out the names of the ships, what all the buildings were, and where there were the King's men on guard. She placed arrows where there were unfenced areas, or places where it would be easy to go unnoticed, and where an unskilled labourer would be able to blend in without arousing suspicion. She inked a picture of where the site of Upnor Castle was, complete with its turrets, and where the reels for the chain lay that were to hinder ships passing up the channel. She had not been told what the information was for, though she guessed it was for the Dutch. She put that out of mind. It was probably better if she did not know.

Deb rubbed her hand over her face in weariness, when it was done. Abigail would thank her, for the plan was detailed and clear. The outing with Crawley had served her well. She'd need to do this over and over, she realised – use men to get what she needed. It wasn't so much now that she valued her chastity, but that she could not bear the deception. Crawley had thought she liked him, and even a sorry whelp of a man like him must have his own hopes and dreams.

She went to look out of the window, and there saw a man and his wife following the link-boy's lantern, strolling arm in arm, intent on each other's conversation. It was a life that was forbidden to her now. Nobody would be able to be close to her; she could not risk her own neck, and she could not risk theirs. She pressed her forehead against the icy glass, closed her eyes. It hit her like a punch to the guts.

She had sentenced herself to a life of loneliness.

A moment later, a hackney carriage drew up, its lamps glowing like eyes in the dark street. The driver alighted to open the door for Abigail to climb out. The sight of her initially filled Deb with the desire to smash something. Without her, she would never have got into this situation; she would still have been at Mr Pepys' house, curled up by the parlour fire, talking about chemises and the right width for ribbon with Elisabeth. She pressed her balled fists against the glass. But then she saw Abigail's furtive look behind her, a sharp, suspicious glance up and down the street. In the dull glow of the carriage lamps, Abigail's features were haggard but she drew herself up, gave imperious orders to the driver to take the carriage away. In that moment, Deb understood.

She sank into a chair, head in her hands. Abigail did what she did because she had no choice.

It was as if she was looking in a mirror. Abigail's life was her life, her life as she would be in another twenty years. If, like her, she could actually manage to survive.

Chapter Forty-one

ABIGAIL WAS PLACATED by the maps of the dockyard, and encouraged Deb to see more of Crawley, a prospect which Deb found wholly unappealing. Next to Crawley, the memory of Samuel Pepys seemed courteous, fatherly, even endearing. Every day, Deb did as Abigail suggested, wound a single imperceptible hair around the door and shutters. She led a secretive, ghost-like life now, mostly locked inside Abigail's chambers. She went out only to buy food, to carry messages, or deliver documents to the post. And at Abigail's insistence – to meet Crawley.

In the daytime, the warehouses in the street below hummed with activity; they were used for storage by a tannery and its associated trades. There was a saddlery, a vellum maker, a furrier. They made goods for export, and bales of furs and boxes of parchment were stored there. On the rare occasions she went out, nobody paid her any mind; she tried not to draw attention to herself, and kept a maid's demeanour in her grey homespun and dark cloak.

One night at dusk, after she had been to buy new parchment, she returned home to see that the hair on the door was broken. She was sure Abigail was still at Bruncker's. She stood a moment in the dark vestibule staring at it. The door must still be locked; after all, she had the key. Could it be Abigail back already? But Abigail would have replaced the hair. No candlelight shone at Abigail's window.

She did not know what to do, whether to run away, or wait to see if anyone was there. She put her ear close to the door, straining to hear any sound from within, but could hear nothing. Perhaps the hair had just broken by itself. The wind, maybe. But she knew that was unlikely. She waited another few minutes, before taking courage. If it was a burglar, she would give them a chance to get away. She put the key in the lock, but was shocked to feel that it was unlocked already.

She made a great noise of rattling it about, slammed the door hard behind her and made her footsteps loud upon the stairs. But still there was no sound. She must have been imagining it. There was nobody here.

Until, at the top of the stairs, she saw the light. There was a candle lit after all, in the main chamber.

'Abigail?' she called.

Silence.

The man turned as she came in. He was long-boned like a greyhound, but with watchful pale eyes. He was holding one of her maps of the docks in his hand. 'Careless,' he said, 'to leave these papers lying around.'

'Who are you? How did you get in?' she asked, squaring her shoulders despite her thudding heart.

'With this,' he said, holding up a ring of what looked like iron toothpicks. 'Most people call me Mr Johnson.' He dipped his head.

She took a sharp intake of breath. The spymaster. She quelled the urge to run. 'What do you want?'

'Have you any refreshment? Some small beer perhaps?'

'I don't know. I'll look.' But she did not move. 'What do you want of me?'

'I wanted you to know that a locked door would not stop me if I had a mind to enter.' He smiled, a mild smile that was more mockery than humour. 'And I will not be leaving until we have discussed the business I have in mind, so we should make ourselves comfortable.' He sat back down on the bench by the table, extended his long legs.

'I will give you a quarter hour,' she said.

He gave a near silent laugh and shook his head. 'You will give me as long as I decide, as it is I who pay your wages, though perhaps Abigail does not see it that way. She left in a carriage for Lord Bruncker's, did she not? So she will probably be gone overnight. Poole went with her, so we're quite alone. Now, give us a little more light, won't you?'

Deb struck flint to the rushlights on the mantel, concealing her trembling hands, one eye fixed on Johnson. Finally, she asked again, 'What is it you want?' She still did not sit, but stood warily in the centre of the room.

'Abigail did not tell me you existed. Only through having you followed did I realise it is you who supplies her information.'

Deb's thoughts raced. She had seen nobody following her. Not since Constantine's man. The thought of it weakened her.

'And here's the proof.' He held up the map she had been working on. 'You might do better to keep it out of sight in future. As you might imagine, I am not the only agent with a set of skeleton keys. And many of them, especially the English, are much less polite than I.'

Deb waited for him to go on, her hands clasped tight in front of her chest.

'I notice you have some attention to detail, that you know some little tricks Abigail has taught you. The door?'

Deb felt herself redden.

'She's arrogant,' he went on, 'to bring someone else in. You are a risk to which she subjected us all, without consultation. Abigail should watch her step. She is becoming, how do you say, a liability?' He crossed his legs, looked down at his fingernails. 'There is always danger, of course, when an agent becomes too close to the subject's interests and begins to neglect her duties. As I feared, she is too involved with Lord Bruncker. She may be selling our secrets elsewhere.'

'So what is that to me? I know nothing. I just do what she tells me.'

He gave her a sharp look, as if he did not believe her. 'Her loyalty is in question and we want you to help us find her other contacts.'

'What if I was to say "no"?'

He smiled. 'I would not advise it, now we have met. There was a man named Harrington once, he said no. He is no longer with us, of course.' He smiled again, seeing the expression on Deb's face. 'But we treat our agents well. They have the best protection, and a fine lifestyle.'

He wasn't offering a choice, Deb realised. She would have to do as he asked. She hardened herself once more. 'Let me think a moment,' she said. 'I'll fetch some beer.' The kitchen door stood open. She went through and reached into the food press to bring out a pitcher. She gathered her wits. Running was too risky.

As she poured, she thought how strange it was that she had become so calm. Her hand was so steady on the jug that the ale streamed out precisely into the tankard. Johnson was asking her to play Abigail at her own game, and there was a power in that, though it would not be easy, because Abigail was as sharp as a rapier and would easily sense something amiss if she wasn't careful. But why should she not? At least then she would be free of Abigail's threats and have the spymaster's protection.

She set the tankards down on the table. 'Tell me what you need,' she said.

'There is an operation planned for the Chatham docks in six weeks' time. A small act of sabotage. And as you have no doubt surmised, Abigail is supplying us with certain information – maps and so forth. I assume it is you who supplies her with this information from your contact, Crawley. We do not want this intelligence compromised at any cost. We simply need you to watch her. After all, you are close to her, you see where she goes.'

'But how? She has told me we are not to be seen together in case it arouses suspicion.'

'As I thought, she is trying to hide your existence, thinking to pass your work off as her own. Once an agent begins hiding from her paymasters, then who knows what other deceptions lie beneath? You will work directly for me now. You can use the code name "Viola" in our correspondence. Here is a name and address you must use to contact me.' He held out two pieces of paper. 'My holding address – I have someone in the sorting office who will put it aside for me, and then deliver. You must memorise it and then destroy it. The other paper is the master sheet for the cipher you must use if we need to send a coded message. It is not the same code used by Abigail's "Dr Allbarn". Sign your communications with "Viola".'

Battling to keep up with this volley of new information, she took the papers from his hand, and scanned them quickly.

'You can send the names and addresses of Abigail's contacts separately in batches labelled as if they are a list of customers and their physic. I want to know names – everyone that Abigail Williams mentions. We need to know who she meets, where she goes, who her contacts are.'

'And my payment,' she asked, 'what about that?'

He smiled. 'You have a bold spirit. I think we will do good business. You will keep whatever Abigail is paying you and I will give you an extra ninepence a week if I get the information I need.'

'It is not what I am worth, but I suppose I have no choice.'

He looked at her appraisingly. 'Value depends on demand. I believe you lost your previous employment because of an indiscretion.'

'I took a necessary risk, yes.' She did not bow her head, but looked back at him as if she were his equal.

He gave a grudging nod. 'Then we are in agreement. You can begin now.' He slid a piece of paper before her. 'Names, Miss Willet.'

She nodded, and sat down. A sup of ale eased her dry mouth. She uncorked the ink and dipped her pen.

> *Edward Skinner – blacksmith,*
> *Thomas Player – hosier,*
> *Hal Graceman – foreman, gunpowder mill,*
> *Mrs Behn – actress,*
> *Leo Berenger – printer*

The list grew with the scratch of her nib over the paper. Her memory was acute and she knew most of the names to whom she had delivered post or messages. Finally she was done. With a flourish, she added *Mr Johnson – apothecary*.

He read them, barked out a laugh at reading his own alias there.

A moment of silence. With one fluid movement he was behind her, the cold muzzle of a gun hard against her temple. The click of him releasing the catch made her jerk away, but his other arm pinioned her easily by the throat.

'Beware, Miss Willet. It does not pay to be too clever.'

Deb stayed absolutely still. A pulse twitched in her neck.

'Better.' He released her and thrust her away with such force she sprawled on the floor.

'Get up,' he said, sheathing the pistol in his belt. His voice was casual. 'Pass me the list.'

She stood slowly, brushed the dust from her skirts, and with her eyes fixed on him, pushed the list across the table. He rolled it and tied it with a leather thong before putting it into his bag.

'I'll see myself out,' he said. 'By the way, Miss Willet, talking of Mr Harrington – it was Abigail Williams who removed him. She is experienced in – how shall I say? –"disposal". So, in your own best interests, it would be wise to make sure she suspects nothing of our acquaintance.'

Chapter Forty-two

ON THE OTHER SIDE OF LONDON, Abigail picked her way down the ruins of the freezing dark alleys towards the vestiges of St Paul's. The cold February weather suited her because it gave her an excuse to lace herself tight into stiff clothing and unforgiving boots. Since Joan's death, she sometimes thought it was only the clothes that held her together.

Adjusting to living so close to someone else was difficult. Deb was always watching, and Abigail hadn't quite managed to force her from the role of favoured friend into the role of servant. In Deb's presence, Abigail had to put on another face when she got home, instead of slopping into a chair to grieve for her daughter. Often, seeing Deb there – so like Joan with her youth and her girlish figure – tears had threatened to overwhelm her. But, afraid Deb would see weakness, she had held them back.

She sniffed, speeded her step. No point grieving. Joan's death was a release, she kept telling herself. At least this time she could pray without guilt, glad her daughter was free from suffering. But she had seen so many deaths, and all of them too early. Who had prayed for those other men's souls, she wondered? She had never considered herself as a murderer, but now the thought of her victims haunted her.

The knowledge that Joan had been too proud to accept her help still chafed. That perhaps she would still have been alive, if ...

If. If. No point in dwelling on 'if's. Lock it away in the invisible cabinet in her head, the one she would never open. Lock it up, along with all the other hurts from her past: the confusion of being a child-bride; her first husband's taking her by force; the terror of birthing Joan at sea.

Abigail turned her collar up against the knife of the wind. Maudlin thoughts and too much sentiment. Joan had been a weakness. Like Lord Bruncker.

She hardened herself, hurried towards the printer's shop where Leo Berenger worked as an apprentice. Leo's Huguenot family had fled to England from France to escape religious persecution, and, when he was desperate for extra money, she had introduced him to Piet, who realised a printer's apprentice could be an asset to his work. Now Leo had become an expert forger, and a reliable, if naïve, linkman for the documents Deb copied, the ones that needed to be delivered to Piet by hand.

Under the sign of the book and needle she saw a light burning within the frosted window, and the doorbell tinkled as she went inside. Leo was there, eyeglasses perched on his nose, face close to one of the enormous iron presses he was setting up with print. Fortunately, his elderly employer was nowhere to be seen. The room was hot with the lamps and smelled of the iron in the ink and of the rabbit skin glue boiling in the pot over the fire.

'Mistress Williams.' The young man with the receding hair stood up, squinted at her. 'Haven't seen you in a while.'

'How's my favourite apprentice?' She held out a map of the gates to the shipyard. It was one Deb had drawn from descriptions by Crawley. 'Something else to go to Piet.'

'Just a moment.' He went back to his typesetting.

Abigail drummed her fingers on the counter impatiently. Usually he jumped to serve her, and she rewarded him with the full force of her charm.

He rubbed his hands down his apron and said, 'I'll take it this time. But I have to warn you, things have changed.'

'What do you mean, changed?'

'I'm getting married next week.'

'I didn't know you had a girl,' Abigail said. 'Who is she?'

'I'm not saying.'

'I'd hoped to wed you myself.' She made a mock pout at her own jest, then laughed. 'What's so special about this girl anyway?'

He inserted another piece of paper into the press, but then stopped. 'She's not like us. She's just an ordinary milliner.'

'Sounds interminably dull.'

'I'm serious. She's, well ... good, and wholesome – knows nothing of spiery, or plots, or double-dealing, or a stab that comes in the night. Once we're married, there'll be children, and I don't want to be the sort of husband that leaves her to fend for herself.'

She raised her eyebrows. 'Heavens! You have caught it, and no mistake. Does Piet know?'

'Do you think I'm stupid? Of course not. But every time I act as his courier, I take a risk, just as you do. You know the feeling – like seasickness – that you can never rest easy. It's like I'm drowning in it all. I just want to be free of it, to be an honest man—'

'Nonsense. You won't stop,' Abigail said. 'Nobody does. They know it's not worth the risk.'

'Harrington thought it was. I forged his papers. He just disappeared one night, took ship and went to France. If he can do it, then so can I.'

She picked up a seal from the bench and turned it in her fingers. 'You didn't hear about Harrington?'

'No, what?'

'It was in all the news-sheets. Sorry, Leo, but he never made it to France. They found him at his lodgings with his throat slit.'

Leo paled. 'You jest.'

'It's true. Don't do it, Leo. I'd miss you. It takes time to build trust, and with you I always know my copies are going into cautious hands, that there will be no ... accidents.'

'Likewise. It has been good to have friends, but I want a real life now.'

'You know that this could be the most dangerous task you've ever undertaken, don't you? To stop?'

He paused, wiped his hands with a cloth. 'I know.' He searched her face. 'I'm fond of Lord Bruncker and his treatise on mathematics, and he's been a good client of ours. A straightforward client who just wants his papers printing. And I shall miss you. You took an interest in me and introduced me to Piet, when I had nothing, so I owe my livelihood to you. And of all of them, you are the most ...' he searched for the word, 'the most reasonable. But this is my one chance, to be free of it. To live without always looking behind me.'

'When will you leave?'

'I don't know. As soon as the weather improves, as soon as I can find the courage. And as soon as I can persuade my girl she wants to live in France. She won't be happy, but what can I do?'

Abigail shook her head. 'Be careful, Leo. Be careful who you talk to.' She held out the papers, and he took them.

'I've talked to no one,' he said. 'Only to you.'

Elisabeth took the gloves from their box. Soft leather, with enough gauntlet to keep the wrists warm; they were for Sam. At last she had been given a proper household allowance of thirty pounds a year from him, and this gift was what he had agreed she should give him as her thanks. The allowance was guilt money, of course, she knew that, and it didn't make up for the boiling feeling she still nursed inside.

She reached out to touch the gloves where they lay on the bed. The shape of them, so much like hands, brought back the image of Sam's hand on Deb's thigh. She stifled a groan, banished the thought and hurriedly wrapped the gloves back in the calico cloth. She must not think of Deborah Willet. She tied the string in a fierce bow. If she was careful and hummed madrigals in her head, she could almost get through a whole day without tears.

Later in the afternoon she went down to see if Jane was back with the list of things she'd sent for, and for some company. Though she hated to admit it, it was lonely with nobody to talk to. Not that she would want another lady's maid – oh la, certainly not. Except for dear Jane, of course, she was loyal; after all, it was Jane who'd told her about Sam and Deb.

Jane looked surprised when Elisabeth went down to help her unload the baskets from the market. Carefully, Elisabeth transferred the eggs from the bag into a punnet lined with straw, and then cut the yellow slab of butter into quarters. She picked up the wooden butter mallet ready to shape the pat for the table.

'Everything's there,' Jane said, stowing the baskets. 'Except I couldn't order more rush-matting, like you wanted. The weavers are behind. It will be a month, they say.'

Elisabeth sighed. 'The old ones will have to last a bit longer then. Though they are more hole than mat, I must say.'

'We haven't had new since Deb was here.' Jane paused and twisted her hands in her apron. 'Talking of Deb ... Netty, the Mercer's maid, thought she might have seen her with Mr Pepys again, in a coach.'

Elisabeth felt a great drench of cold run over her.

Jane gabbled on. 'Netty thought Deb still worked for you, but I told her Deb had left, and why. Still, it was probably months ago. I told Netty she must be wrong because Mr Pepys had written to her, finishing it.'

Elisabeth felt her expression drop, her face turn hot with humiliation. She had not imagined that she would become the subject of wider servant gossip. 'If I hear that you have been discussing Mr Pepys and that ... that harlot with anyone else, I mean *anyone*, you will no longer be working for me. Is that understood?'

'Yes, mistress, but I thought you'd want to know, you asked me to—'

'I do *not* want to know.' Her voice rose to a shriek, but she tried to bring it under control. 'Not now she is no longer working for me. It's gossip, evil, malicious gossip.'

'But Netty said—'

'Enough!' Elisabeth pounded the butter mallet down onto the table. Jane shot back away from her, hands shielding her bodice.

Elisabeth slowly raised the mallet. Underneath it,

the punnet oozed broken yolks and shell. She lay the mallet down quietly and said, 'If anyone calls, I do not want to be disturbed.'

'Yes, Elisabeth.'

'Yes, *mistress*.'

Jane gave her a shaky curtsey. Elisabeth stalked away, feeling as though her heart was like those eggshells – impossible to put back together. Only when she was in her own chamber did she allow it to sink in. Inside her, something turned cold and angry.

Where was he? God help him if he was with her. After all he had said about it being finished, after everything they had been through. It wasn't over at all. It would never be over, because for it to be over she would have to trust him. And she could not.

Elisabeth was unsurprised when Sam denied it all. He begged her to come to bed, but instead she huddled next to the fire, feeling the blaze scald her cheeks as her back froze. Sleep was impossible. She was exhausted with lying awake, night after night, picturing him with Deb, wondering what she could have done to make things different. Deb's face with its cool eyes and enigmatic smile floated before her, tormenting her.

Elisabeth pushed the coal tongs into the fire and watched them heat until they glowed red. If she pressed them against her hand, maybe the pain would stop this pain in her chest. From across the corridor she heard a sound. She listened above the hiss of the coals.

A snore.

The bastard was actually sleeping. Her pain had affected him not at all. She grabbed the tongs and was across the corridor in two strides. She dragged the bed-curtain open and thrust the tongs inside. 'You liar,' she cried. 'Liar! You never tell me the truth. Tell me where you were today.'

Samuel's eyes shot wide-open now, and he scrabbled upright like a startled rabbit.

Elisabeth poked the red-hot tongs menacingly close to his face. 'Were you with Deb?'

'No,' he said, shifting himself further away, 'God's truth I wasn't. Put those things down. I've told you, I was with Mennes at the Treasury Board.'

'You weren't. If you were with Deb, I'll—' she stabbed the tongs towards him, but Sam parried her arm and after a tussle the tongs flew from her hands. A clatter, and there was the acrid smell of singed wool as the hot metal shrivelled the pile on the rug.

Sam fended off her flailing arms as she beat at him with her fists. 'What the hell do you want?' he said. 'I give you everything a wife could need. Look at the house – new curtains, new rugs. Our portraits painted even! What is the matter with you?'

'I don't care about those things. I just want to know where you are. I want to know you're not with her. You promised me. "No more," you said, and I believed you. But they're talking about us everywhere, Sam. The Mercers and everyone, they're all telling tales about you and that—'

'You mustn't believe it all, it's just gossip. Take no notice. It's just words. Words can't harm you. I swear to you, I was at the office. Come now, love, quieten down and get into bed.'

Elisabeth could not. She shook him off and stooped to pick up the tongs, now a dull grey. She stared at the scorch mark on the rug. 'Ruined,' she said. But it was not the rug she meant. She took the tongs back to her room, and later she heard Sam snore again, but her anger was spent, replaced with a dull despair.

In the small hours of the morning, aching for comfort, she climbed into bed next to him. He did not stir. *What has happened to us?* she thought. She reached out to touch the linen of his nightshirt, but his sleeping back was like a boulder, immoveable, impenetrable.

A wave of rage made her grit her teeth. She would like to get hold of Deb Willet, reach her fingers into her chest and pull out her heart, then maybe she would know what it was like to feel this way.

Hours later, Sam turned, fumbled to embrace her. 'My own dear wife,' he said. 'I never meant to hurt you.'

She wept then, shameful tears. It happened whenever he was tender. Tenderness pierced through her resistance like a hot needle through wax. And she was ashamed that she let his words touch that deep place inside her again, the place he could so easily bruise.

After a while she let him talk her round with his soft, sly words; agreed that she had no evidence, no evidence at all, that he had done anything wrong. She pretended that she had forgiven him, because what else could she do?

But, inside, the shame was like the grind of a millstone, turning, turning.

Chapter Forty-three

ELISABETH WAS NOT THE ONLY ONE who could not sleep. Night after night in the draughty house in Whetstone Park, Deb stared up at the cobwebs on the ceiling, not daring to close her eyes. The pressure of her life was beginning to take its toll. Every sound outside made her fearful she was being watched. The fact she had been followed once by the spymaster's men and not caught sight of a soul had agitated her. When she went out, she wrapped her winter cloak around her as if swaddling herself tight would help make her invisible.

After Johnson had gone that first time, she had removed all trace that he had ever been there, washed and dried the ale cups, assiduously replaced the hair on the lock, opened the window wide in case a trace of his smell might alert Abigail. But still she fretted, all eyes, watching the doors and windows, afraid that he might return while she and Abigail were sleeping.

Living with Abigail was not what she had expected. Abigail was often out for days at a time at Lord Bruncker's, but when she was at home she drooped into depression. Unless she was in a play, which was seldom, she did not bother to put on her public face, to dress her hair or paint her lips. The flamboyant actress had gone; she could have been anyone, in her drab house-dress. Deb saw in her the same unease, the same inability to rest, as she felt herself. Some deep, drowning sadness hung round Abigail too, like a miasma, and its dank emptiness filled her with foreboding.

Deb watched her, made surreptitious notes of where she went and the messages that passed through the house. When Abigail gave her letters to post, Deb paused at the trestle table in the post office to copy down the names and addresses of Abigail's contacts and then she sent them to Piet Groedecker. She knew that was his real name, but it amused her sometimes to see the letters from Abigail addressed to 'Mr Johnson' at Noon Street, because she knew they were for Groedecker, and of course she often added letters for 'Mr Johnson' of her own.

The chill of February came and went, with iron-hard ground and frost stiffening their outdoor cloaks. Abigail treated her with the same indifference, not as a servant, not as a friend, but with her fake courtesy, learned from the stage.

A few of Abigail's letters were for Lord Bruncker. The next time Piet appeared, again unannounced, he told Deb he was particularly interested in these, and to intercept any of this sealed mail and scan it for useful information. She became adept at gently breaking open the letters and then adding more wax to reseal them, and she forced herself to be immune to Abigail's intimate and often bawdy exchanges with Bruncker. Bruncker seemed to be a man who wanted to put his ardour on paper.

One morning, Deb was watching Abigail through her open chamber door as she applied patches and rouge and fastened a large sparkling brooch at her throat.

'Why are you staring at me?' Abigail asked.

Deb went to lean on the door jamb. 'That brooch suits you,' she said.

'No. You were examining me, like a chirurgeon. Don't do that, it makes me uncomfortable.'

'I'm just trying to learn from you, how you make yourself up.'

She gave a sharp rasping laugh. 'I know what you're thinking – that I'm putting on my public face, and that really I'm an old woman.'

'You look well.'

'It's a front, as well you know. I've been an actress all my years and I can't stop now.' She applied some drops to her eyes from a glass phial and blinked. 'Making myself up. That's a fine term for what I do. There is no real Abigail Williams, just a series of roles. Lord Bruncker is the only one who gets a glimpse of the real me.'

'It must be good to have someone you can trust that way.'

'Yes. He is the only one.' She added dark powder to her lashes. 'Except for Leo, and you, little Deb.' She turned and pinned Deb with a look. 'I can trust you.'

At the moment where their eyes met, Deb's blood ran cold. *She knows*, she thought.

'And I you,' was all Deb said.

But Deb saw Abigail tie a hair on her chamber latch just the same.

The next day, Deb broke the hair on Abigail's chamber and went inside to look through Abigail's papers. She paused. A strong scent, like ...? Lavender. She scanned the room for anything unusual, but could see nothing. A cry of frustration. Too late. A fine mist of face powder had been sprinkled over the floorboards just inside the door. Abigail must have done it on the way out. Crafty vixen. It was designed to catch her footprints, and she'd just stepped there. She froze, unable to move forward or back.

Devil take it. Her heart thumped as if her blood had turned to glue. She'd been right; Abigail knew she was watching her. She remembered Piet's warning and stepped back hurriedly, looking down at the telltale footprint in the powder.

Apprehensive in case Abigail should return to check on her, Deb cleaned the floor and her boot with a wet cloth, then had to wait for it to dry before she could replace the powder. She searched Abigail's room for the lavender powder but could find none. Curses, she must have taken it with her. Deb found some powder of her own and put the pot up to her nose. A scent of something sweet; roses? Not lavender anyway. But it would have to do. Carefully, she tapped out a fine cloud of rose powder. It hung in the air before settling onto the floorboards in a grey sheen. Please God, let her not notice the difference in smell. Then she teased a hair from Abigail's hog's-bristle hairbrush and retied the door.

A few miles away, Jem Wells had just come home and was pouring out more small beer for his brother and his friends who had descended on the house for a meeting. Bart had decided that since the public's interest in the poor whores' petition was waning, it was time to stage another protest for sailor's pay.

The table was littered with tankards and the remains of an eel pie. As usual, Bart had brought his hosier friend, Tom Player, along with Joseph Bolton and several other sailors Jem recognised. But this particular day there were two new friends of Bart's:

Graceman and Skinner. Jem didn't much like the manners of Graceman, who had ignored him and sat in what should have been his chair at the head of the table.

'Will you join us?' Skinner asked Jem. 'We need to muster as many men as we can. There's men from York and another group will be making their way from Ireland, but we're desperate for more city men.'

'Wait a minute,' Jem said. 'All these others, are they sailors?'

Bart looked sheepish. 'No. But we've broadened it out now. We've got so much support we thought it would be good to ask other men to join us. All those old soldiers of Cromwell's that have been deprived of their position or livelihood and are for our cause.'

'Soldiers? But it *will* be peaceable, won't it?'

Jem saw Skinner and Bart exchange glances. 'There's been enough talking,' Skinner said. 'It's time for action.'

'But I thought this was to be a peaceful protest,' Jem said. 'Once soldiers are involved it could turn into a battle. We don't want that.'

'It's our chance, Jem, don't you see?' Bart caught hold of his wrist where it lay on the table. 'We've got the whole country behind us. There are pockets of men all over England that feel the way we do, men who want rid of the King for good.'

'All we have to do is organise them,' Skinner said. 'That's what Mr Graceman is doing. We'll march on White Hall and they won't know what's hit them.'

Jem withdrew his hand, bewildered.

'Mr Skinner, here, he'll set a diversion, something that will occupy Parliament while we go to take the King hostage,' Bart said.

'What?' Had he heard them aright? 'You're talking

about a rebellion.' Jem stood up, disgusted, looked down at the eager faces looking up at him. How could he have been so stupid not to see it before? He turned on Bart. 'Why didn't you tell me this was what you were planning?' He looked at his brother's lowered eyes and suddenly saw it all. His stomach dropped. 'They'll be armed, won't they?'

'It's time, Jem. Time to birth a new world.'

'No. Not with fighting! Not with more bloodshed and more families mourning their dead.'

'Then how else? Tell me that? Didn't you go yourself to talk to the Treasury Board and get nowhere?'

'If Mr Wells will not join us, then we should not press him,' Graceman said. Then he turned slyly to Skinner and said, 'But we will remember who our friends were once it's done, won't we boys?'

Jem was taken aback. 'Get out. All of you! I'll have no dealings with lawlessness and fighting.' The men were reluctant, but Jem bellowed, 'Out.' They got to their feet with surly expressions, picked up their hats.

Jem turned on Bart. 'How could you? I'm a man of the church. A curate in training! You knew I could not condone this, yet you think to bring them here.'

'But, Jem—'

'Get out!' Jem shouted at the men hanging around his door.

'We'll be at the Black Bull,' Bolton shouted over his shoulder. Jem slammed the door behind them.

'You fool.' Jem stood in Bart's way. 'What do you think you're doing? Those men are villains. I can see it just by looking at them. Do you want to get yourself killed?'

'It's you who's a fool. Why did you have to do that? Ordering them about like a lord of the manor?'

Bart was flushed with anger. 'I'll never live it down! You've humiliated me in front of my friends.'

'It's treason. I'll not have them in this house.'

'Don't I pay equal rent? I have a right to bring in whoever I choose.'

'I'll not have plotters or criminals under my roof,' Jem said.

'They're not criminals.' Bart snatched his hat from the table and put it on. 'They're fighters for justice and freedom.'

Jem sat down, put his head in his hands. 'Oh, Bart, why? Why must you do this? It's asking for trouble.'

Bart thumped his fist on the table. 'Because I've still not been paid. It's all right for you with your fancy stipend and Father's bloody backing. But I've got creditors from here to Wapping, and they're short on patience. And yes, I know, we tried pamphlets and soapboxes, and even the poor whores' petition and it got people's attention, but nobody could *do* anything. Graceman's got a scheme that could work, and I'm sick of waiting. I'm going to help him.'

'Not from this house, you're not. I won't have those wretched dogs over the threshold again.'

'It's all right, your perfect holiness, you need know nothing about it,' Bart said bitterly. 'Now you've thrown my friends out of my own house, I'll join them at the Black Bull. They're the ones who actually care enough to do something, instead of just spouting their mouths like gargoyles from the pulpit. Don't wait up.'

'I don't know what to do,' Jem said to Lizzie. 'They're firing each other up, stirring up the old grievances.'

It was a few days later, after the poor whores' school had finished for the day and the last child had just grabbed his cap and run bare-footed down the stairs.

'There's nothing you can do.' Lizzie shrugged, and she started to collect and stack the slates. 'If I were you, I'd just keep away from the whole business.'

'But shouldn't I warn someone?'

'Who? The King?' She smiled, carried on stacking.

'Ha, ha. No, of course not, but I can't just watch it happen.' He began to straighten the new benches into neat rows.

'It would put Bart in danger if the word got out. I'd just keep quiet.'

'I suppose so.' He stood up from the bench he was lifting. 'It's just all the innocent people that don't know what's coming.'

'London's survived worse. Look at the last few years. War, plague, fire. And still she rises from the rubble.'

'There could be bloodshed.'

'Bart strikes me as a man who can take care of himself.'

'No, not Bart. I need to warn someone. I mean ...' He stopped, thinking of Deb Willet, felt himself redden.

'Who?' When he didn't answer, Lizzie paused, leaning forward, her hands on the teacher's desk. 'Ah. I see. There's a girl, isn't there? Someone you're close to.'

'No.'

'I had a feeling there might be someone. Is it anyone I know?'

'No. Well, there was a girl I was fond of – once.' He shrugged. 'But we had a disagreement.' He sat down, stretched his heels away from the low bench. 'And I feel I should warn her, tell her to get out of London, but I don't know how to … well, how to tell her what I know.'

'Just knock on her door and explain. She'll understand you're not like Bart.' She sat down beside him. 'Where did you meet her? What's she like?'

'She used to come to my services at the church. She's cultured and well bred, and well … in short …'

'She's pretty, and you found yourself smitten?' He saw her repress a smile.

'I suppose so. But we had a disagreement. I mean, I'd hoped she'd be able to see why I come here, how necessary my work with you is. But she's an entrenched Royalist. She thinks our pamphlet to Lady Castlemaine a travesty.'

'Is that what you argued over? Our pamphlet?'

He shook his head. 'You know, I thought she would be of my persuasion.'

'And it shocked you to discover a woman might have her own opinions?'

'No, but—'

'Politics is all in the mind. Don't let it set you apart. The human heart beats just the same, no matter what thoughts divide us. If you still like her, you should find a way to mend it. Perhaps she just needs time to adjust to the idea, so that you can both come to a compromise.'

'I tried to apologise once, but she brushed me off. And it is not so easy any more, because she's moved, and I don't know exactly where she lives. But I can't bear the thought that something might happen to her because of my brother, not if I could have prevented it.'

'Where did she used to live?'

'She was maid to Mrs Pepys, but she's left there now.'

'Then go to the Navy Offices and ask him for an address for her. And while you're there you could gently warn Pepys that more trouble with the sailors is brewing, and suggest they prepare themselves. That's the best you can do. And as for your brother, you should sit down with him over a table and talk it out. Use your curate's powers of persuasion.'

Lizzie did not know how stubborn Bart could be, Jem thought. And if he went to see Mr Pepys he might not be able to keep his temper. He'd met his old acquaintance Crawley from the Navy Office; he was drinking in the Bell Tavern, and Crawley had told him with great relish that Deb had probably left because Mr Pepys had tupped her. It couldn't be true, he knew that, but just the idea of it choked him.

'What's her name?' asked Lizzie, interrupting his thoughts.

'Deborah, but people call her Deb.'

'Nice name. I like the old biblical names. Used them for all my children, Thomas, Hester—'

'I didn't know you had children, Lizzie. I thought you were a widow.'

'I just let people assume that. But no, I'm married. Alas, I'm estranged from my husband and family.' Lizzie turned her face away. 'Have been these last seven years.'

'That must be hard.'

He saw her swallow, press her hand to her chest. 'Their father won't allow me to see them or even tell me where they are. I write, but have never received a reply, though I can't say I blame them. My sons don't want to know me.' She shook her head. 'It all happened a long time ago. My children will be grown now, and I missed my chance to mother them. They'll have no need of me after all this time. It still hurts, though, to think I missed their growing up.'

'Whatever caused the rift,' Jem said, 'I'm sure it can have been none of your fault.'

'Then you are naïve. It was more my fault than anybody's. I was young, and wilful, and in love. It was like madness, and I couldn't see the consequences. But you must talk to your Deborah, see if things can't be mended. Don't let it go on until it's set as cold as stone.'

She went to the desk, scrubbed at it too hard. Jem had the impression she was trying to rub out the past.

'There's not one day goes by when I don't curse myself,' she said. 'I lost my youngest son in the Great Fire, and after that I hadn't the heart to confront my husband, to fight him to see the rest of the children.' She paused, sighed. 'Grief does that. Wears you down. It all seemed like too big a mountain to climb. But I'd give anything to see their faces now, though I wouldn't impose on them. I know it's too late. They will think me too much dropped in society. But never a day goes by without thoughts of them, and the ache that goes with it. It's why I do this.' She gestured round the room. 'The children are all substitutes for my own. I'm not so stupid that I don't know that. So if you think I'm good, it's only self-preservation, not charity.'

'It's fine work, and I'm sure your children would be proud to see you.'

'But they never will.' The words stung like a slap. She picked up a rag from the bucket and wrung it out. 'Pass me those slates.'

At the Navy Office the next day Jem tried to reason with Mr Pepys. 'I beg you, sir, think again. If you don't do something soon, there will be trouble. You will have a rebellion on your hands, and don't say I didn't warn you.' The sight of Pepys sitting smugly in his leather chair, his well-coiffed wig and the waistcoat straining against his heavy stomach, made Jem want to strike him.

'Good Lord, are you threatening me?'

'No, sir, just plain speaking.'

'A good deal too plain for my liking.' He thumped a fist on the table. 'Newman will show you out.'

Jem had almost reached the door when he remembered to ask for Deb's address. He bit back his anger, tried to put on a neutral face. 'Miss Willet, who used to be maid to your wife – she used to come to my church sometimes. Do you happen to know where she lives now?'

At the sound of Deb's name, Pepys frowned and looked up from his desk. 'She's working for a Dr Allbarn in the west of the city, but I don't know the exact address. Why? What's it to you?'

'No reason, just some charitable work she might be interested in.'

'Charitable work? Our Deb?' Now he did look flummoxed. Jem gave him an icy glare, bowed sharply, and withdrew.

If Pepys wouldn't listen, he supposed he should try to speak to Lord Bruncker, warn him that if they didn't want a rebellion, they should act now. Bruncker was just finishing a meeting with Mennes, but the clerk invited him in to wait in the vestibule while he went to see if Lord Bruncker was available yet and had time to see him.

Jem peeped round the door into Bruncker's office. It was full of the good oak furniture that sailors like his brother would never be able to afford, polished so highly that it gave off a treacly sheen. An imposing leather-covered desk was flanked by two gleaming upholstered leather chairs. The desk itself, with its silver inkwell, was littered with correspondence. Weighty letters, stiff with red wax seals, in amongst rolls of what looked to be architectural plans.

Jem could not resist walking over to try out one of the chairs. The leather was so new it squeaked, so he stood again and glanced at the papers on the desk. He was peering at what looked like a plan of a ship, when the door opened and Lord Bruncker strode in, casting him a disapproving look down his long nose. Jem jumped away, aware of how rude it must appear to be caught perusing someone else's private papers.

'Good afternoon, sir.' He stood up straight and held out his hand in greeting but Bruncker did not take it.

'What's so urgent it could not wait?' Bruncker said, glaring. 'Some sort of charity? Be quick, man, I'm busy.' He didn't sit, but stooped to sift through the papers on his desk.

Jem began to explain to him about his fears for a rebellion and why he had come. He was only halfway through his speech when Bruncker flapped him down.

'Tush, lad, we know all that already. We've told the sailors often enough, we're in the hands of the King. We're doing what we can. And if we weren't constantly interrupted by people like you, we would be able to get on with it that much quicker.'

'But, sir—'

'Now stop wasting my valuable time, and get back to ministering to your parish. If they're as poor as you say they are, they certainly need your charitable assistance more than I do. Good day.'

Bruncker ushered him to the door while he was

still protesting. Outside the door, Crawley jumped back and wiped his hands down his breeches. The nosy dog had obviously been listening.

'Show Mr Wells out, would you, Crawley?' Bruncker said.

'Yes, sir.' Crawley bowed low to him and led the way.

If Crawley's head bent any further it would scrape the ground, thought Jem. After the door shut behind him, Jem turned and threw his hat at the door in frustration. For the first time, he could understand Bart's embitterment. These well-to-do men in their fancy offices had no idea at all of life in Whitechapel or Lukenor Lane, nor the depths that sailor's wives must stoop to just to put bread on the table.

When he got back to his house he could smell tobacco as soon as he got in through the door, and Bart and his friend Tom Player stood up guiltily from the table. Jem sighed and slung his cloak onto the back of the door. No doubt they were plotting again. Player gathered together the sheaf of maps and papers on the table and stuffed them into his bag.

'Evening, Mr Wells,' Player said. 'I'm just on my way out.'

Jem watched Bart whisper to him on the doorstep, before he disappeared into the dark.

'Don't worry, I won't be here long,' Bart said, tapping the embers of his pipe onto a plate. 'Just getting a change of clothes and then I'll go out to eat.'

'You can eat here with me. I've been to see Mr Pepys and—'

'No thanks. If my friends aren't welcome at your table, I'd prefer to join them. Tom's found me new lodgings, so I'll be out of your way as soon as the lease is signed.'

Jem was taken aback. 'You don't need to do that. You don't need to move out.'

'I know I don't need to, but it's what I prefer.'

'Come on, Bart, let's try to be civil with each other. I believe in your cause. I just don't believe in violence, that's all. Why do you think I spend so much time at the school with Lizzie? Because I'm educating the poor to pull themselves up out of poverty, that's why.'

'Lizzie Willet is a fool. She was perfectly capable of managing that school without any help from do-gooders like you. Now you're taking it over and the poor woman—'

'I'm not taking it over!' He paused. Something had just registered. 'What did you say her second name was?'

'Willet. Why? What difference does it make?'

'Be quiet. Let me think.' Lizzie Willet's daughter was called Deborah. And hadn't Deb once told him that her sister was called Hester, or was he imagining it?

Bart was waiting for Jem's reply, but when none came he threw back his head, blew a sigh of annoyance, and stomped off to his chambers.

Jem sat at the table and tried to remember all the things Deb had told him about her family, and all the things Lizzie had told him about her daughter. It was all fitting together. How stupid of him not to realise before. He'd never thought to ask a surname. The children just called her 'Missus', and everyone else knew her as Lizzie; no one had titles in the rookeries of Clement's Yard. The strange affinity and familiarity he had felt for her from the very beginning began to make sense. Could it be he'd been helping Deb's mother every day?

He got out a map of the west of the city, already

looking for the churches still standing there. Dr Allbarn. That's what Pepys had said. Deb lodged with Dr Allbarn. He could check at the churches to see if Dr Allbarn was part of their congregation. And he could ask at the Royal Society. If he was a physician then someone there would surely know him. Jem was in a ferment of excitement, could not sit back down.

This new information made him see both Deb and Lizzie in a new light. He rolled it round in his mind. On one of their walks after church, Deb had confessed she was searching for her mother, but was reticent about her family background. 'I don't want Mrs Pepys to know about my family,' she said, 'so keep it to yourself.' He'd thought it was because she suspected Pepys to be of a different political persuasion from her parents. But now he wondered.

Lizzie had said her husband had disowned her, but not why. Whatever had gone on in the past, he should go and tell Lizzie he thought he knew her daughter. Hadn't she said she'd do anything to see her children again?

But he'd go to Deb first because it might be the news that would mend things between them. He imagined her pleasure and his heart lifted. Tomorrow he'd go and find out where Dr Allbarn lived, and, with luck, persuade Deb to see him so he could give her the good news.

Chapter Forty-four

ABIGAIL OPENED HER CHAMBER DOOR and looked down at the floor. The film of powder was undisturbed. She breathed out, chided herself. She was on edge all the time, as if some feeling was ready to burst out, like a cask of fermenting wine ready to explode. She found herself rattled over small things, seeing demons where none existed. Sometimes she thought that Deb was more intelligent than she gave her credit for, and on occasion she'd thought Deb was actually watching her, instead of the other way around. Something was out of kilter, and experience had taught her never to just dismiss these things.

Abigail sighed, hitched up her skirts, tucked them in the waistband and fetched a besom and dustpan to clear the floor. This was a task she did not ask of Poole, since it was designed to catch her too. Abigail coughed, wrinkled her nose; the smell seemed sicklier than usual. When it was done she went to her dressing table, slid the pins out of her hat. She was never without them, their heavily jewelled finials masking their effectiveness as a weapon.

She reassured herself; she had not seen Deb do anything out of the ordinary, and she seemed obedient enough. Abigail shook her black hair loose, scrutinised the wrinkles on her forehead. They seemed deeper these days – not that she could see them as clearly now; her eyes had grown some kind of milky film, and she could make out little now without the aid of a glass.

She froze, alerted by a noise below, but then relaxed. Deb. She knew it from her tread. She was back from her meeting with Crawley already. Abigail took her time peeling off her gloves before her mirror, and when she eventually went through, Deb was sitting near the window dutifully writing notes.

'How is Lord B?' Deb asked. As she sat back, Deb's elbow knocked one of her quills to the ground.

Without thinking, Abigail bent down to pick it up. It was then she caught the smell. She froze, inhaling deeply. That was the same smell that was in her room. It lingered on Deb's skirts. Something floral and sweet, but dry, like rose petals.

A smell that was not her own. That could only mean one thing. Deb had been in her room.

'Are you well?' Deb asked, when Abigail did not stand up immediately. 'Is it your back?'

Abigail rose, all her senses honed as sharp as a blade. She kept her voice light. 'I'm not as young as I was, that's all.'

She stood and went back to her bedchamber. There she rummaged in her bag and took out the brass compact of lavender face-powder. She dabbed in a finger and brought it to her nose. The scent of this was quite different; sharper and fresher.

The consequences whirled in her head. She sat down on the bed to think. Lord B had complained to the post office only last week that some of his letters had been opened. Until now, Abigail had assumed it to be someone at the post office, for it was common knowledge that agents operated from there. But now there was a more sinister answer. It could have been Deb.

Still thinking, she rose from the bed and walked back through to the parlour. The bitch. She was spying on her. On her own instigation, or Piet's?

The answer came as Deb turned to look up briefly, questioningly, and smiled at her.

She was not as scared as she used to be.

Deb no longer feared her. She should have noticed it before; and it was so obvious, now she'd seen it. If she was not afraid, it must mean she had protection. Deb went back to writing, leaving Abigail looking down on the top of her head, at the pale skin where the hair was parted.

After all she'd done for her. Taking her in, putting up with her filling her space – a girl who wasn't even her daughter.

Abigail curbed an overwhelming desire to smash something heavy down on the back of that head. She had trained herself never to act in the heat of the moment. She drew herself taller, took a deep ragged breath. She came to a decision. The time had come. She rang for Poole.

'Fetch me a carriage,' she said. 'Round the back, something unmarked, unobtrusive.'

'Yes, mistress.'

She fetched her outdoor things.

'Where are you going?' Deb asked.

'B's.' Abigail draped a fox fur around her shoulders.

'To Lord Bruncker's? But you've only just come back.'

'Supper and then on to a friend of his,' Abigail said, tersely.

***

Deb watched from the window, bemused by Abigail's sudden departure. She was hovering by the back gate waiting for the carriage, her body restless, her hand twitching at the fur around her neck. She usually waited inside, out of the cold. Deb was uneasy. When the carriage arrived, all Abigail's movements, the way she fumbled with the door, showed an agitation.

'Berenger's,' she heard Abigail say.

She's up to something, Deb thought. But she knew she could not follow, for the carriage was already gone in a clatter of hooves.

Leo was working late, as he often did, by the time Abigail got to the printing house.

'I need a document making,' she said, slapping her gloves down on the table.

'Oh yes?'

'A letter of safe conduct. I need to get out of England.'

'You too? What's the hurry? Is something afoot?'

She ignored him, traced her fingertip on the wooden counter. 'Are you still planning on leaving?'

He nodded. 'Soon. At the end of the month. The passage should be easy then, when the spring blusters have passed.'

'Then I shall travel with you.'

He blinked, opened his mouth, but did not speak.

'We will travel together,' she said. 'You will supply the papers so I can pass as your girl's mother.'

'No.' He stepped back from the counter, one hand up as if to ward her away. 'Sorry, Abigail, but I have to say no. I don't want Rachel to be involved in any trouble.'

'No one will know. You know me, I'm a good performer. We'll be a close family group travelling after a wedding. What could be less suspicious?'

'But Rachel knows nothing of my life, except that I

am a printer by trade. How will I explain you to her? Besides, what if her mother wants to visit?'

'You'll think of something. Don't tell me you don't know how to lie? Not after all this time.'

'No, Abigail. I wanted to be free of all that, and how will Rachel ever be able to trust me if she sees I am lying to get you to France? The whole point of it was to leave it behind, to make a new start.'

'And you shall have it.' She gave him a taut smile. 'After we are in France. I need a new identity, one that can't be questioned. Do this one thing for me, won't you, Leo, as a favour for an old friend? You would be in the poorhouse if it wasn't for me.'

He had the grace to look a little discomfited.

She tried again. 'You know how I always used to say I have a sixth sense, that I can read the signs? Well, I know I'm being watched. I have a bad feeling about it. It's always been me doing the watching. So I need those papers.'

'I can't. I can't risk Rachel knowing anything. It's too dangerous. For her, I mean. You'll have to travel alone.'

'Alone? You know that would look suspicious – a woman on her own. And they will be looking for me.'

'Why? What have you done?'

'Nothing.'

His eyes said he did not believe her. 'No. I'm sorry, Abigail, but the answer's "no".'

So that was the way. She must press him harder. She picked up her gloves and slid them on. 'You disappoint me. Of course I could tell Piet of your plans. He would not be quite as desirous of your safe passage as I am.'

Leo's face lost its colour.

'Think about it. You have until this time tomorrow night. If I don't have your agreement by then, I'll go to Piet.'

His eyebrows lowered, and he crushed an oily rag in his fist. 'I trusted you. Tell me I was right to trust you. Abigail? Please?'

She turned her back on him.

'So you're like the rest after all.' Leo's voice was bitter. 'But I tell you, if you have the gall to threaten me, what's to stop me doing the same?'

She whipped round. 'That wouldn't be wise. You have too much to lose. They might think Rachel is involved.'

'Why would they think that? She's never—'

Abigail raised an eyebrow. 'A word in the right ear ...'

'You two-faced ... you would, wouldn't you? Condemn her to save your own skin.'

'Think about it, Leo. Only a few papers. Surely you can do that for an old friend.'

The look he gave her was one of hatred and contempt. It hurt her but she masked the sting.

'Dusk tomorrow,' she said.

After Abigail left Leo's, she walked down to the Thames and stood a while watching the trade barges up and down the river. Her city. She had called it 'home' for so long, knew every inch of its byways and thoroughfares. But the fire had destroyed most of what she knew. And now the pox had destroyed the only thing keeping her here.

Leo would do it, she was certain. Threats worked as long as you knew you were able to carry them out. In practice, she rarely had to. Her conviction alone was usually enough to persuade people. She liked Leo; he was a nice boy. But too nice, too easily persuaded. It made her despise him.

A barge passed, its lights reflected in the murk of the water. She had travelled this water so often, but now she'd be leaving. She could not say farewell to B, or tell him anything, for fear it would bring him harm. How strange the paradox of the human heart, that it could attach itself to one soul and not to another. Apart from her fierce, uncompromising love for Joan, Lord B was the only person she had ever cared a whit for, perhaps because he was an intellectual, a man with no time to waste on foolish ideas, a man whose mind was as sharp as hers. In other circumstances, she mused, he would have been the perfect spy.

He had sneaked his way into her heart over time, and the thought of leaving him was a pain she did not want to contemplate. But she must go now, and she must be traceless. Travel as one person, and then assume a new identity on the other side of the Strait of Dover. She had done it once before and she could do it again. But her timing would need to be impeccable; she could not risk Piet finding out before she got away.

She picked up a pebble and threw it into the water. It sank without a ripple under the greasy grey tide of water. Deb Willet was too dangerous. Unlike Poole, who was illiterate and knew none of the details of Abigail's invisible business, Deb knew about her meetings with Berenger, and Piet would soon trace Abigail through him.

Deb would have to be silenced.

Abigail felt a rush of something that could have been dread or could have been excitement. It was good to feel something at last. Since Joan's death she had been numb. She had known all along that it must come to this, but now the time had really come. Her new life was so close. *Carefully does it*, she thought. *No mistakes. Leave no traces.*

Chapter Forty-five

April

DEB CONTINUED TO MILK CRAWLEY for the information which she now knew went from Abigail to Piet. Piet had told her she must carry on just as before, so not to arouse Abigail's suspicion, but that was easier said than done. She found Crawley repugnant, and it was harder and harder to keep his amorous advances at bay.

During one of Piet's uncomfortable, unannounced visits, he told her that some of Abigail's contacts, particularly the printer, Berenger, were giving the Dutch cause for concern, and she must stay vigilant.

'She came back from Lord Bruncker's and put a new padlock on her door,' Deb said to him, 'so I can't get access to her chamber like I used to.'

'Ah yes. I remember. She has never shown you how to pick a lock.' Piet strolled over to Abigail's door, took out his batch of skeleton keys and juggled them in his fingers. 'This one should do it.'

He slid one of the prongs into the lock and twisted. After a moment of feeling with his fingers, the lock clicked. He locked it again, and gestured for her to try.

After several attempts it was still immoveable.

'No. Listen with your fingers,' he said.

After a few more minutes of jiggling and manoeuvring, she felt the ratchet of the mechanism give. He plucked off the padlock and told her to turn the handle.

'Ah, better.'

She paused on the threshold. 'She put powder down last week, to see if I'd been in. Then, a few days later, the lock.'

'That old trick. I hope you didn't fall for it.'

Deb shook her head.

'Good girl.'

Between them they searched the room, but there was nothing untoward. She did not like the look of Piet's long pale fingers handling Abigail's shifts and nightdresses, though he was very careful to replace everything exactly as it was.

When they'd done, he slipped the pick from his key ring, passed it over. 'Check it regularly,' he said. 'Copy anything you find to Mr Johnson.'

Deb soon learnt the feel of the lock and checked Abigail's room every day. A few weeks later, when Abigail was out at the theatre with Lord Bruncker, Deb opened the door to see a leather trunk, dragged out next to the bed. It was a large one and contained woollen undergarments and two of Abigail's least fashionable dresses. Her heaviest fur-lined cloak lay on the bed, with a leather overcape and kidskin gloves.

She was going somewhere.

Deb searched the leather compartment in the lid of the trunk. She was surprised to find a bone rattle, of the sort that might belong to a baby, and a baby's bonnet, both yellow with age. Abigail had never mentioned knowing any children. She pulled out travelling papers, a pass for safe passage, and a ticket to Boulogne. The papers claimed to be for a Mrs Taverner, travelling with Leo Berenger, a printer, and his wife Rachel. Leo Berenger, she knew, had already had correspondence with Abigail, and was the man Piet had mentioned.

Deb slid everything back. Why was Abigail leaving? Should she tell Piet? If she said nothing then Abigail would be gone, out of her life. If she didn't tell him and he found out she had hidden it from him, she did not know what he would do, but it would not be good, that much was certain.

Even the thought of him made her prickle with unease. She could not afford an enemy like Abigail, but she could afford one like Piet even less.

She left everything exactly as it was, relocked the door and wrote a brief note to 'Mr Johnson', signing herself as 'Viola', telling him that Abigail was planning to travel to France disguised as a 'Mrs Taverner'. She gave it to a boy to take to Noon Street.

Abigail did not return at the end of the play so she must have gone on to supper again with Lord B. A few hours later a note came back with a messenger boy.

> "*Gault's coffee house, six o'clock.*
> *Johnson*"

It was dark when she got there, but Piet was already waiting in the shadows, away from the glare of the wall sconces. She slid into the seat next to him, from habit, so they could both face the door.

'Did you find any coin in her belongings?' he asked.

'No, and I did look everywhere.'

'So someone else must be financing her move. Certainly not us. I can't think that she's got business with the French, so it looks like she's about to squeal and run. She's probably planning on outing us to the King. That's if she hasn't already. She'll have to go.' He took out a long object in an ivory case and placed it onto Deb's lap.

She picked it up, but before she could look closely he pressed his hand down on hers. 'Keep it out of sight. It's a razor. Quickest and easiest.'

Deb did not understand.

His hand gripped hers tighter. 'You're the one who can get nearest to her. Poison is too unpredictable, and a pistol too noisy. Stand well back, come from behind, and aim here.' He tilted his head and pressed on his throat just under the ear. 'One deep cut should be enough.'

'But I can't—'

'Or if you're so squeamish, while she sleeps.'

Deb could not take it in. But something about it must have registered because she could feel her breath coming quick and shallow. 'It's impossible. She's gone to Lord Bruncker's. She might not come back.'

'She'll come back for her trunk.'

'She's a light sleeper, she'd never—'

'Know this: she will have plans for you.' His words were sharp and incisive. 'She will not want to leave you to testify against her. You're a loose end, Miss Willet. Agents hate loose ends. You are not the only one with one of these.' He picked it from her lap, slid it open to reveal the glint of the blade, and with a quick movement caught her by the wrist.

The blade was a hair's width from her skin. 'If I were you,' he spoke into her ear, his breath hot against her cheek, 'I'd watch your back.'

She wondered if she could run, get out of London.

He seemed to read her thoughts. 'I wouldn't. Remember Harrington. As I said, agents hate—'

'Yes. Yes, I understand.'

He snapped the razor shut, closed her hand over it. 'I'll arrange for you to move on, to another safe house. Send word to Noon Street when it's done and I'll send someone to deal with the mess. Tonight. Quicker the better.'

Chapter Forty-six

JEM WAS FRUSTRATED. Easter was his busiest time of
year, and it had taken two weeks of sleuthing,
between his usual duties, to find any information at
all about Dr Allbarn; nobody seemed to know him,
and he had had to hand over a substantial bribe to
one of the clerks at the post office to find the address,
something that offended his conscience.

Restless, and unable to resist, Jem had sent a boy
with a message to Lizzie saying not to expect him
again today, but that he hoped to have some good
news for her and would come tomorrow. After he had
skimped his duties – the palm crosses, the
parishioners' Easter feast – he was forced to walk to
Whetstone Park because he could not find a decent
hired horse, so it was late in the afternoon by the time
he arrived at Dr Allbarn's.

The house was shoddy and down at heel, not at all
what he was expecting from a man of physic. He
knocked and waited, and a grubby-looking servant
opened up, peering out of the crack in the door, her
eyes suspicious. She looked up at him silently a
moment before speaking.

'The doctor's out.'

'It's Miss Willet I've come to see.'

'Wait there.' The door shut in his face. Within, her iron-heeled clogs clumped upstairs. He took a step back to look at the house. A face appeared at the window, blurred, but he could just make out Deb's features.

He heard footsteps coming downstairs again. The maid opened the door. 'She's out.'

'Please. I know Miss Willet is at home because I saw her at the window. Give her this note, won't you.' He scribbled a quick line with a stub of graphite.

> *"News of your mother. Please*
> *come down.*
> *Jem."*

Then he thrust a threepence at the maid along with the note. 'She'll see me if she reads this. I'll wait.'

Deb read the note and read it again. Was it true? Did Jem have news of her mother? She looked out of the window and he was still standing there. The sight of him gave her a wrenching sensation. Her feet began to move towards the door.

'Will you go down, miss?' Poole's expression was disapproving.

'I'll just see what he wants.'

'But Mistress Williams—'

'That will do, Poole.' Deb straightened her collar, smoothed the wrinkles from her bodice.

When she opened the door he came forward to greet her eagerly. 'Miss Willet! Deb, I mean ... forgive my intrusion, but I had to come. I could not in all conscience keep it to myself. I think I know where your mother lives. I met a lady who says she has a daughter called Deborah, a lady by the name of Lizzie

Willet.' When she did not immediately reply, he said, 'Isn't that wonderful?'

She felt herself maintain a distance. 'Nobody's ever called her Lizzie. It must be someone else. My mother is Eliza Willet.'

'I'm sure it's her. She has a voice like yours, something of the West Country. And your eyes. Though she has lighter colouring than you. She's a very charitable lady. Shall we go in and I'll tell you all about it?'

'No.' She was too hasty. 'That is, Dr Allbarn won't allow it.' Deb was still trying to take in what Jem had said. She could not accept it. An inner resistance prevented her, for she was in another world now, one where curates and a charitable lady would not fit.

Jem kicked at a stone by his feet, disappointment etched into his features.

'Where did you meet this woman, this Mrs Willet?' Deb asked, unable to help herself.

'She runs a school. On the north bank, near Lukenor Lane. Children whose mothers have no prospects of better employment and no hope of escape. I'm helping there. She's got so much patience. I wish I could be as good with the children. They're fortunate to have her.' He paused, concern in his eyes. 'Are you all right? You look pale.'

Deb knew she had lost weight, that there were dark circles under her eyes from lack of sleep. His scrutiny made her defensive. 'It can't be her. She would have a child with her, my half-brother.'

The words did not seem to disconcert him in the least. 'I'm sorry, but I think I'm right in saying the child died. Lizzie mentioned a bereavement. And sons, and another daughter named Hester.' He paused, let the name sink in.

Deb swallowed. A gaping chasm had opened inside her. 'Coincidence, merely.'

'Deb, it has to be her. She told me she was estranged from her family by her husband, that she'd give anything to see them again but he won't let her near them. She doesn't know where any of you are. He won't tell her.'

'It's not her.' Deb spoke with finality.

'How do you know? You said—'

'Begging your pardon, Jem, but this woman can't be my mother. My mother went abroad.' She heard her voice crack as she clutched at the dwindling straws. 'She went to the Low Countries with my Uncle Jack. It must be someone else.'

'But Deb, she's desperate for news of you! Cannot I tell her something, give her some small hope that—'

'It's not her, I say. And please – do not mention me to this … this woman. Now leave me in peace.'

She saw his confusion, his hurt eyes, and it twisted inside her. But she stepped away from him, shut the door, bolted it loudly from the inside before she could change her mind. Then she stood in the hall, propped against the panelling, tears coursing silently down her cheeks.

Her mother was in London, not Antwerp. She had been here all along. All the time she was at the Pepyses'. And now Deb was at Wheststone Park, she was even closer. Yet it might as well have been another country for all the difference it would make.

Jem had spoken of her with affection. Good, and charitable, Jem had said.

But Deb had known her as a 'woman of sin' for so long, she could not let herself believe it. So what, if she was good and kind? She'd left them, hadn't she? Without even a goodbye.

Deb was not ready to drop the image of her mother that allowed her anger. At the same time, she wanted to run to her there and then, bury her head against her skirts as she did when she was small. Instead, she tightened the grip on herself and hauled her leaden legs up the stairs, twitched back the curtain. Jem was still staring up at the house.

When he saw the curtain shift he raised his arms, in a gesture of surrender. As he turned and walked slowly away up the street, she kept her eyes fixed on his back. *Curse you,* she thought. She could not help resenting how things for him were so straightforward, how he was bathed in an aura of goodness that only made her feel more black beside him.

He was not for her, she told herself. She dropped the curtain over the window. She would never be able to repay him with anything but a soiled reputation. Her dream of building a respectable life for herself seemed laughable now. Here she was, a spy and a whore and a traitor. By comparison, her mother's affair seemed mild. When Abigail returned, she was to murder her in cold blood. If she did not, her own life might be forfeit by one of Piet's men. She would be the killer or the killed. Either way she was better to be completely alone in the world. She could not risk it, that she might bring Jem or her mother into danger.

She took a kerchief from her pocket and wiped her eyes. Crying would not keep her alive. Only tenacity and a sharp mind could do that. She picked up her skirts and took herself to the desk. She must stay calm. Forget about everything else but survival. And in case things did not go to plan, she needed to write to ask for Hester's forgiveness.

Chapter Forty-seven

ABIGAIL WOKE AT LORD BRUNCKER'S, late. Their evening at the theatre had been poignant, for she knew it was the last time she would sleep here, that soon she would be in France, with a new identity and a new life. She would sail with Berenger and his girl at dawn tomorrow. Lord B had kissed her, and she had clung to him a moment too long, so he huffed at her and pulled away.

Now he had already gone off to a meeting at the offices; he'd said he'd be with Mennes for luncheon at Saul's and that he'd see her again in the evening. An engagement she would not keep, but would send an excuse – a headache perhaps. She had already told him she was going away for a few days on a theatrical tour. He had no idea it was one from which she would never return.

She drew the sheets up to her chin, savoured the feather-filled mattress, the satin embroidered coverlet, the bed-end carved with pomegranates. She would miss the safety of this six square foot of land, screened from the outside world by its velvet drapes, for tomorrow night she would be on a ship with a hard plank berth, an uncertain future ahead of her. Fortunately, she spoke French; her former husband, bastard though he was, had taught her the rudiments. After a few more precious moments in bed, she rose and dressed and opened her satchel. Inside was a sheaf of documents, mostly correspondence from Piet and from his lesser associates.

She lay them out on the table to check them. All were there: the information about the proposed plot in Chatham dockyard and the rebellion against the King. She owed it to Lord Bruncker to inform him of this. Another scandal of navy negligence, of English sabotage right inside the dockyard, would finish his career, and she could not do that to him.

It was intelligence for which she would not take a penny. It would be her parting gift to Lord B – little enough information considering the constant sly trickle that over all these years, had seeped out of his correspondence and through her pen.

Using a forged hand, she copied extracts from letters from Graceman and Skinner, the explosive suppliers. The correspondence mentioned Piet, under his pseudonym Mr Johnson, and a number of others, including the Dutchman Cornelis Tromp. They had trusted her to supply the plans of the docks. She was careful to leave out anything that might incriminate herself, or anyone that might lead to her.

And as for Piet, she could not risk betraying him to the English authorities. He would be only too willing to give them her identity, too, if she handed him over.

She dressed in her best clothes and took a sedan down Cheapside towards Dowgate and Cloak Lane. After so many years, she was leaving nothing to chance. She could have sold this information, she knew. She'd learned early on that goods were never as valuable as information. You could sell your goods, you could sell your body, but all these were subject to decay and the difficulties of limited ownership. Far better was to sell the invisible – it would never run out and would always retain its value.

But she was doing this for love. A word she could not even speak. She was surprised at how excited it made her to think Lord B would never know where the intelligence came from. She examined the address on the front of the letter: *John Mennes, The Navy Offices, Sign of the Ship, Seething Lane*. She could not take the chance of anyone seeing her with the letter, so when they arrived at Cloak Lane, and the General Post Office, she asked the bearers to wait, and she handed the letter to Poole.

'Find a lad. The stupider the better. Give him a farthing to take it inside.'

Poole dipped her head, and Abigail watched her slide away into a back alley towards the laystalls and the docks. After a few minutes, Poole re-emerged with a barefoot lad of about five years old. She watched Poole bend to point out the way and hold out the coin on her hand.

Abigail watched her letter go inside the building. *Good.* Information about the plot would be on Mennes's desk in the morning. She had chosen Mennes deliberately, because Lord B had told her he was an old fool who loved to gossip, and she calculated he was the most likely to panic and tell people. When Poole returned, she gave her the rest of the day off, told her there was no need to return to Whetstone Park until the following evening.

'What ails you, mistress?' Poole asked.

It was the first time Poole had ever asked a direct question. Abigail swallowed. Poole pinned her with a shank of a gaze that did not falter.

'Nothing, Poole. I'll see you tomorrow night.' The

lie stuck on her tongue. Tomorrow night, Poole would find the house empty. Except for the blood-soaked body of Deb Willet.

Poole caught something of her thought. 'God keep you, mistress,' she said, as she made a curtsey, but her tone was a warning.

The approach to the hiring stables was wet; a fine drizzle made the streets misty, and the bearers' feet splashed in the puddles as they went. She climbed from the sedan and ordered a coach and two horses to collect her and a trunk the hour before dawn and take her to the London Docks. She should be able to dispose of Deb Willet at night while she was sleeping. By the time Poole found the body, Abigail Williams would no longer exist and 'Mrs Taverner' would have sailed in her place.

Now she needed a drink. Dutch courage. The irony of the name made her smile.

Chapter Forty-eight

Bᴀʀᴛ ꜱʟᴀᴍᴍᴇᴅ ᴛʜᴇ ᴅᴏᴏʀ as he went out. He had argued with Jem again and was angry that Jem refused to see things his way and insisted on trying to tell him what to do. His brother's solicitous concern over his welfare only irritated him and made him want to do the exact opposite. The wind gusted an icy blast, nearly removing his hat, which he held on to with one hand as he made his way to meet the men at Player's house for a final check through the plans.

Still, it would soon be over and Jem would see that he had been right. A whole new order was coming, and he, Bart, was at the heart of it. His father had fought for this; he and all the other good men who had been lost in the Civil Wars – the 'great shaking' that had brought England's aristocracy begging to its knees.

Bart walked briskly, still feeling a discomfort in his chest from the rift with his brother. The two of them had just crossed wordlessly on the threshold, unable to breach the gulf that had arisen between them. So far, Bart had not moved out. He tried to keep out of Jem's way and avoided being in the house when Jem was there, though Jem had laid in wait for him to give him another lecture nearly every day. Bart deliberately kept what he was doing a secret. Jem would try to stop him, and it was far too late for that. Everything was planned, right down to the quantity of gunpowder, which they had obtained with difficulty and at considerable expense through Graceman, who was the foreman at the gunpowder factory.

A squall of rain made him wipe his forehead as he made his way towards the alleyway by the bank of the Thames where Tom Player lived. He went over the arrangements in his head as he walked. There was to be a meeting point at the Black Boar tavern close to the city gates, and Skinner was to muster one cohort of men to the north at Charterhouse Square before Graceman would co-ordinate the main march of men down to Aldersgate. The groups from the south would either come up by boat with Tromp's Dutch schooners or muster in the Bear Garden near the old ship *Liberty*, forming up on the other side of the river before crossing the bridge. Bart, along with Bolton and a man called Rigg, was to be in charge of the actual sabotage of the ship at the docks.

The street where Player lived was busy with night hawkers, being close to the Old Swan Stairs, so Bart slipped into the alley unobserved. A sharp knock and the door swung open to let him in. The men were sitting around a small table by candlelight, maps and plans spread out before them, weighted down with their tankards of ale. It was going to be a long night, and no sleep whilst they made their last-minute preparations. Bart nodded to Tom Player and Joe Bolton, but he could see they were restless. The draught from the wind outside made the candles quake and flicker. Bart sat and removed his cloak, noting that Graceman and Skinner had not yet arrived. He was anxious to know how many men

Graceman had recruited, and whether the word had yet arrived as to how many were assembling at the Irish docks.

Mr Johnson's woman had supplied them with a good map of the layout of the docks, and along with intelligence from one of the mast-makers, they knew the interior layout of the ship. They had procured fine doublets and breeches to make themselves look like gentlemen, paid for by the Dutch. Papers from Berenger the printer proclaimed that they were *bona fide* inspectors for the navy. Tomorrow, Monday, they would arrive late in the day at the usual inspection time and ask to look over the ship. The satchels they carried would contain the fuse. The mast-maker was to set the barrels in advance. It was straightforward, but all knew the penalties, and the delay was making them nervous.

'Any word from Johnson?' asked Bolton.

'A runner came to say Dutch ships are ready in Ireland for Graceman's men. Two more as escorts wait in the mouth of the Thames. They will move once they see the Irish ships and fire a shot to time the explosion. I told him you should be able to see the smoke from White Hall, there's that much powder!'

'Where are they? Graceman and his lackey? We've been waiting an hour.' Tom Player voiced everyone's thoughts. 'I hope nothing's happened. If the authorities have wind of us, we'll all be in trouble. I say we give them another half-hour and then send someone to ride out to Skinner's, see what's afoot.'

The tension in the room seemed to increase with the whistling of the wind. They were ready, primed like matchlocks ready to be fired, but there was still no sign of the other two men. The clock candle flailed until it had burned down another notch.

'I can't stand it. I'll go to Skinner's, see what's

happened.' Bart leapt up.

'I'd better stay here in case they come,' Taylor said. 'But there's a hiring yard at the end of the road. You'll need a nag. Skinner's in Cateaten Street.'

'I know it.' Bart found the hiring yard, paid twopence for a hired horse and heaved himself up. Clapping his heels to its sides, he rode as fast as he dared in the dark towards Skinner's house, a brick-and-timber built monstrosity that had unfortunately survived the fire. There was a light burning there. Bart cursed. So the devil was in after all.

He threw himself down and hung the reins over a post. Had Skinner forgotten the time? He couldn't have, surely?

He thumped hard on the door. Nothing. A movement in the window alerted him. Someone had snuffed the candle. 'Skinner?' he yelled. 'Graceman? Are you in there? Open the door.'

Had they turned lily-livered all of a sudden? Bart tried the door, but it rattled against its bolts. Frustrated, he strode around the back. All was locked up, but he'd seen a candle burning, hadn't he? He pulled on one of the shutters at the downstairs window, and to his surprise it gave. A hard tug and he saw that there was only a leather curtain to keep out the weather and not glass. The window was narrow and he assessed it. He might just be able to ...

A few moments later and he fell head first onto the floor of the kitchen. Some pans clattered from the table as his cloak brushed past. By the time he stood up, Skinner was there, a candle held querulously before him.

Bart pushed him backwards until he was against a cupboard nailed to the wall. 'Where's Graceman? You've kept us all waiting. What are you playing at?'

Skinner's eyes looked left to right looking for escape. 'It's not my fault,' he whined.

'What? What are you talking about?'

'Graceman. He's gone.'

Bart grabbed him by the shirt and almost lifted him off the ground. 'Where? What is all this?'

'He's run away. He didn't do anything. He let us down.' Skinner wrestled himself free. 'There's no men, nothing. He led us all a merry dance, puffing himself up, pretending he had all these contacts. It was all nonsense, the lot of it. He couldn't organise shit in a stall. So now he's gone.'

Bart let go of Skinner's shirt, the feeling in his chest so much like a physical pain that he could hardly stand, let alone speak. 'No. I don't believe it.' Seeing his face, Skinner backed away. Bart looked wildly round the room. 'Bastard. Where's he hiding?'

'When he didn't come here, I did what you did – I went to his house and found his wife there, distraught. He's got debts, mountains of them. She knew nothing about any rebel troops, nothing about any of it. He took the final trunk of money, from Tromp. Left her there with nothing. Loaded all the trunks of coin into a carriage and went.'

'When?'

'Last night. He could be anywhere by now. She told me he's an inveterate liar. He does it everywhere he goes. Half the country's after him.'

'But you said—'

'I know, I know. I believed in him, and now I feel such a fool. And I was too afraid to come and tell you …'

Bart sat down heavily on a kitchen stool, his head in his hands. 'No soldiers from Ireland?' He looked up, beseeching.

Skinner shook his head. 'Nor from the north. And no arms. I told you. He's done nothing. Except talk,' he said bitterly. 'He was always a fine one for that.'

Bart stood up. 'Are you still with us?'

'What do you mean?'

'Do you still stand for our cause? I'm not giving up, Graceman or no Graceman.'

'You can't. What will you do?'

'Do it alone, muster who we can. The barrel's already set, we're ready for it. We'll take the King ourselves.'

'It's madness. Suicide!'

'There's fifty men I know by name.'

'But not enough to take London.' Skinner was backing away.

'Then we'll just blow up the King's ship—'

'You're mad! What's the point?'

'I don't know. I don't bloody care! All I know is, we've got to do something. Are you with us or not?' Bart put his hand on his sword. 'You'd better be, after causing all this trouble, or I swear to God I'll run you through.'

Skinner stared, wild-eyed. Licked his lips.

'Speak, man.'

'With you.' His voice was a croak.

'Then fetch your cloak. You can explain to the rest of the men where Graceman is.'

Chapter Forty-nine

DARKNESS HAD FALLEN by the time Deb heard a carriage draw up. A wave of apprehension made her nauseous. As she heard the door open and Abigail's footsteps creak on the stairs, she pushed the razor in its ivory case deeper into the hanging pocket under her skirts.

'Such a day!' Abigail said, throwing down her bag onto the table as usual. Her eyes flicked left and right around the room.

Deb detected the smell of liquor. 'Have you been at the theatre today again?'

'The theatre?' A pause. 'Oh. Yes, but Lord B was not feeling well, so I will be staying here tonight.'

This information made Deb's throat tight. She would have no excuse, then, for not doing as Piet had ordered. 'What ails him?' she asked.

'A stomach upset. Nothing to worry about. But it will be nice to sleep in my own bed for once. He snores so. It's a wonder I get any sleep at all.'

Deb watched Abigail take off her gloves. Her hands shook a little; Deb wondered if she was cold. 'How was the play?'

'Oh, it was good. Well done.'

Deb cast about for normal conversation. 'What did you see?'

- 387 -

Another pause. '*The Mock Astrologer*. That one. It's on again.'

The conversation stalled, and Deb sought something else to say. 'Shall I ask Poole to cook us something? There are eggs, I believe, and a meat pasty.'

'I dismissed Poole. I did not think you'd need her, as I am here, so I gave her the evening off.'

The fact that Poole was not to be in the house made Deb even more uneasy. She wasn't hungry but went to fetch food from the larder all the same. Abigail did not eat, but she sliced the pasty into smaller and smaller pieces, pushed them round the plate. Now Abigail was in front of her, the whole idea of killing her seemed fantastical. She was so much *here*; besides, it seemed inconceivable, the fact that she was offering food, giving life with one hand knowing she was about to snatch it away with the other.

Finally, she decided she would retire to bed, and Abigail, too, yawned. Was it her imagination, or was the yawn just a little too long and forced? Abigail went to her room and closed the door. Deb's hands were hot and damp. Through her skirt she felt into her pocket; the ivory of the razor case was smooth and cool against her fingers.

For distraction, she tidied away the supper dishes and wiped down the table, and after blowing out the sconces in the hall, locked the front door and the parlour door as they always did at night. Just as she was about to go to bed, Abigail appeared again in her nightdress, candle in hand. 'Did you bolt the doors?' Her words gave Deb a start.

'Yes,' she said. 'The parlour door needs oiling again.'

In her nightclothes Abigail looked smaller, more

vulnerable. Her hair, unpinned from its careful arrangement, showed grey at the crown where the dye had grown out; without powder and paint her face was pinched and wan. Deb swallowed, almost pitied her. She knew then that she could not kill this woman, not while she was sleeping.

'Make sure to blow out your light,' Abigail said. 'There was another house burned in Sackhall Street – someone knocked over a lamp.'

'I will. Goodnight, Abigail.'

'Goodnight.'

Deb took the candle into her bedchamber, slid the razor from her pocket and opened it, but just the sharpness of the edge made her head swim. Abigail seemed to be no threat in her nightdress, but Deb remembered Piet's words and knew not to trust her. She placed the razor under her pillow. Still, sleep was impossible, and her ears strained for any little sound. She could not do as Piet asked – too many fears gathering like crows: fear of blood, fear of God, fear of seeing someone die.

Her heart sounded too loud, the thump of it too close to her throat. Maybe she would hear Abigail leaving. She imagined the scrape of the trunk being moved, the relief of hoof beats trotting away. Then she could convince Piet that she had tried but been too late. But there was no sound, only the late-night screech of an owl, the hollow pealing of the single bell as one o'clock came and went.

Two o'clock went, and three. Deb blew out the candle, but lay tense between the sheets. Surely if Piet was right, and Abigail intended to harm her, she would have taken her chance before now? She was too fanciful, imagining Abigail's watchful manner.

Abigail had dismissed Poole just to be kind. Tomorrow they would breakfast as usual, and Abigail would confess she was leaving for France and say 'goodbye' to her as any woman might.

Deb let her body sag a little. Piet's instructions seemed like a bad dream, not part of real life at all. Her thoughts became hazy, her eyelids heavy as lead. She was dozing, seeing pictures of the past, of her mother and her brothers at home in the apple orchard, her father's angry face. She was about to shout back at him, when she heard a noise.

A very quiet click.

She lay motionless, lest the sheets rustle and mask any more sounds. Was that the noise of footsteps? The soft pressure of bare feet on floorboards? She held her breath. Her fingers crawled for the razor under her pillow, and closed round the ivory casing, careful not to touch the sharp edge. There was a barely perceptible rattle as the latch was lifted. Deb wanted to speak but found she could not.

The door swung open to reveal a candle lit in the main chamber. Abigail was there, paused on the threshold, listening as if to gauge whether she was asleep.

'Abigail?' Deb found her voice.

'I can't sleep. I wondered if you were awake too.' Abigail came in clutching a knitted blanket around her shoulders and sat down on the bed. Deb relaxed.

'No, I—'

There was a sudden movement, and the blanket pooled on the bed. A flash of silver. By instinct Deb shot backwards and to the side, grabbed a pillow to her chest. The blade of Abigail's razor missed her shoulder by a hair's width.

'Don't come any nearer!'

Abigail lunged to grab her by the hair, but Deb

slashed wildly with the razor and felt it meet flesh. Abigail fell back. Blood flowered on the fabric of her sleeve. A splatter of dark on the pillow.

A moment of horrified silence. 'Vixen! You too.' Abigail pressed her other hand to her right arm. Her voice was loud in the small room. 'I see. Piet's trick – the razor.' Her voice dropped. 'Do it then, you are younger and stronger. What chance has an old woman against you?'

Deb shrank back, the pillow pressed to her heart. She felt the wooden rail of the bedhead dig in her back. She would not fall for Abigail's tricks. 'No, I know enough of you to know you're not as weak as you—'

A swoop like a hunting owl. Deb saw the blade just in time and rolled aside. The edge of Abigail's knife cut into the timber rail. Deb threw the pillow at her and leapt out of the room. Jamming her shoulder against the door to keep Abigail locked in, she pushed with all her strength. Abigail was stronger. It inched open. Deb pressed a moment more then let it go and turned and ran across the hallway and into the parlour. She dare not turn. A second might mean Abigail's blade would reach her. She made a dash for the door to the stairs.

The bolt was on.

Should have left it off, she thought. Her shaking fingers fumbled to free it, but it was stubborn and stiff. She tried to get a grip on it, her sweating fingers sliding on the metal knob. She had to find another way out.

No time. Abigail was behind her.

She turned back, held out the razor before her. 'Leave me be!' she cried.

Determination lit Abigail's eyes before the blade

flashed, but Deb was ready; she dodged to the side. Abigail's arm hit the door and her shoulder followed with a judder. The knife fell to the ground.

With a cry of frustration, Abigail stooped to retrieve it, stretching out her hand, but pain made her clumsy and slow. Deb took advantage, whipped behind her, touched the razor to her cheek.

She felt Abigail freeze, swallow.

Deb kicked Abigail's blade out of reach and bent the razor close to Abigail's eyes. 'Be still!' she said, hoisting Abigail's blood-soaked arm up behind her back. 'Listen to me, or I'll cut your face so deep you'll never work again.'

Deb brought the quivering edge of the razor close to her throat.

Abigail repressed a whimper.

'You've ruined me,' Deb said. 'I never wanted to do this, to *be* this. You trained me to it. If I'm good at it, you've only yourself to blame.'

'So you're to kill me. Why wait?' Abigail feigned nonchalance. 'I beg you, make it quick.'

Deb placed the metal edge on the thin skin of Abigail's neck, but it twitched away as her hand refused to press.

Abigail sensed it, turned her head. 'Did I teach you nothing? If you don't dispatch me, Piet will kill you.'

Deb kept the razor at her throat. 'We can outwit Piet. You want rid of it all, and so do I. I don't want to be watching my back every minute. It's not beyond us both, is it, to think of something?'

'So take the knife from my throat.'

'I don't trust you,' Deb said, tightening the grip on her arm.

'Nor I you, Deb dear.'

Deb felt a sneaking admiration for her bravery. 'So

there, we are equal. But there is no one else to help us.'

Abigail was silent. Under Deb's fingers, blood stuck Abigail's sleeve to her arm in a dark wet stain.

In a sudden movement Deb let her go, dived for the other razor and scooped it up. She circled Abigail at a safe distance, both weapons before her. 'You're bleeding. You weren't quick enough. It's only a matter of time; if not me, then some other girl will end it. Piet thinks you're finished, too old to be useful. But we could work together.'

Abigail got unsteadily to her feet. A nick on her neck dripped a runnel of blood. 'What for, if I'm finished?'

'We are women, not supposed to be able to think or to reason, yet I know you to be one of the cleverest people I've ever met. You would be dead by now if you were not.'

'You flatter me.' She scrutinised Deb, but did not move to the door. 'What would be the point?'

'I need you. We need each other. To stop.'

Cradling her injured arm, Abigail propped herself against the wall. 'Suppose I was to think about it. Piet's men know about you, know about both of us. They'd soon find us. They would not be as merciful as you.'

'Only Tromp knows of me. Maybe some of his confederates,' Deb said. 'But they only know me by the name of "Viola". I've never met anyone in person but Piet.'

'Viola.' She barked a laugh. 'Prettier name than Dr Allbarn.' She paused. 'I have met some of Piet's Dutch friends, years ago, but none of them were big fish. The Dutch keep us isolated deliberately, in case something goes wrong.'

Deb saw her thinking, the twitch of her gaze.

'The London spies would be nothing without Piet. He controls the network.' Abigail paused, looked down at her slashed sleeve, the sticky red stain. She swayed and put a hand to the wall.

'Just think,' Deb appealed to her, 'we could help each other. Find a way out of this. I'm sick of being fearful every moment. I want friends, a proper home. You could have the life you want, with Lord Bruncker.'

His name made Abigail's shoulders slump. 'Roses round the door too, I suppose. I was like you once. Had dreams. Lord B wanted to marry me. Me!' She shook her head, as if she could not believe it. She took a step nearer, examined Deb's face again through naked eyes. 'You're right, I am tired of all of this. Too tired. Have you ever been to Piet's house?'

'No, never. I have to send messages through the King's post, to a Mr Johnson, at a holding address – Noon Street – as you do.'

'We could watch his contact at Noon Street, trail him. I followed a man once – the fool looked all around but never saw me. I was in plain view, but they just don't expect a woman.'

'What are you saying?'

'The idea of giving Piet a draught of his own physic is appealing.'

Deb was wary. Abigail seemed to be actually considering it. But she still did not trust her. Deb's body was tense, poised, ready to run or to fight.

Abigail drew herself up. 'Are you serious about us working together? With your help it might just be possible.'

'You mean, hand him over to the authorities?'

'No. Not that. We could be traced that way. We

could finish him. The spy's way. Where no one sees.'

Deb shook her head.

'Such a squeamish little flower. Did you tell Piet about Berenger and his little wife?' Deb lowered her gaze. 'I'll bet they have holes in the skull by now, thanks to you.'

The thought shocked her. It couldn't be true. 'I didn't know, I didn't think …'

'Piet's not safe unless he's dead. We have to make sure. And be certain the finger points away from us.' Abigail sighed. 'It's all right. You can leave that side of it to me. But I'd need your help. The thought of never having to worry about Piet again has a certain charm. But I need to trust you.'

'And I you,' Deb said.

'Touché. Swear to me that you mean me no harm.'

'I swear.' There was only one way out. Deb took a deep breath, and sending up a silent prayer threw the weapons down towards Abigail. They clattered onto the floorboards and slid to her feet.

Abigail watched them skitter to rest. She looked back up. Her eyes had turned glassy. 'My God,' she whispered, 'you really meant it.'

Abigail knelt and reached for the razor and Deb's spine stiffened. But then Abigail slowly straightened, pressed it neatly closed with her thumb.

'Come,' she said, walking to the table, leaving the other one where it lay. 'Let's sit and see what we women can do.'

They talked through the night. By candlelight, Deb helped Abigail to bandage her arm and then to dress in one of her loosest gowns. The cut on her arm was a clean wound, not too deep, the one on her neck a mere scratch. Both women were girlish, giggling, as if an escape from the grim reaper had brought forth all the lightness in them. Neither went back to bed. Their new-found trust was still too fragile, too brittle for that.

'Did you ever find out anything more about your mother?' Abigail asked her, as they sat together to plan what they should do. It was not quite an apology, but Deb answered her as if it were.

'No. But I know where she is. Someone I know traced her. But I wouldn't want her to know me now. She wouldn't want to see me like this ... doing this. What I had to do with Pepys, with Crawley ...'

'Are you ashamed?' Abigail poured a dribble of brandy from a flask and pushed the cup towards her. 'Mothers always love their children, no matter what the circumstances. You'll understand, when you have your own. I loved my daughter, even though I knew well enough what she was.'

Deb put down the cup and swivelled to look at her. 'I didn't know you had a daughter. Where is she? Why haven't I ever met her?'

'She's a whore,' Abigail said bluntly. 'Was. She's dead.' The words were cast before her like stones. 'May, last year.'

Deb did not speak, but laid a comforting hand on hers.

'I miss her so ...' Abigail's mouth trembled and she began to shake with a great tremor. 'Don't look at me. Don't look!' She stood, pressed her hands to her eyes, but the tears came in a tide no sea defences could stem. A great wash of sobbing and keening, like the worst of winter storms.

Deb stood and tried to gather her in, to comfort her, but Abigail shrugged her away, hid her face, as if emotion was something no one should see. She clutched her arms around herself, locked into her own tight circle of grief. All Deb could do was watch helplessly in the flickering light until it blew itself out and the tears abated.

'Here. Brandy.' Deb thrust her cup into her hand.

'Can't seem to take it in, even now, that she's gone. Still worry that she'll wake up one day with a man who'll beat her black and blue. Stupid, isn't it? She's dead of the pox nearly a year, and I still fear for her like I used to. Still wake wondering where she is.' Abigail slumped into a chair, put her elbows on the table, leaning her head into her hands.

Deb reached out to gently rub her shoulder.

She turned. 'It's why I did it, the business with Piet, spying on Lord B. Right to the end I had such dreams for her, to get her out of Clement's Yard, to buy her a little house somewhere, give her a place to go and have a chance. A better chance than I ever had.'

'What happened?'

'She didn't want my money. She had too much pride. Wanted to make her own way. I had to stand by, watch her waste her goddamned life. If you'd seen her ... she was only young ... her pride finally ate her to death.'

'Oh, Abigail—'

'You can't live their lives for them. Your mother will want to see you. The picture, your miniature, it's Lizzie Willet, isn't it? She's a good woman. She's seen a lot worse than you. She tried to help my Joan.'

'I know. Jem Wells told me she was teaching at a school for poor children.'

'She'll be glad you're still alive to tell the tale. That's all that matters. Life. That blood still beats in your heart. I used to think life was cheap, but that was only because I didn't really feel the true cost of it, hadn't understood the pain of losing someone. When we're free of Piet, go and find Lizzie, tell her you did what you had to because you had no choice – just as she did, just as I did. Anyone who lives in Clement's Yard has to understand.'

Hoof beats, and the rumble of wheels outside.

The birds were just beginning to twitter their dawn chorus. Abigail went to the window and peered down into the dark. 'It's my carriage, come to take me to the docks.'

'You can't go. Like you said, Piet or his men might be waiting for you and Berenger there.'

'I know. You should have been more careful with your mouth. First law of espionage. A single word in the wrong ear can mean life or death. Go down and send the carriage away. Then we'll make a proper plan.'

Deb watched in fascination as Abigail calmly primed her pistol with powder and shot.

For her own part, she wrote a note to Piet: "*It's done. Viola.*" Then she went out at the first glimmer of dawn and sent a beggar-boy runner with the message, told him to deliver it to Mr Johnson at Noon Street. She watched with trepidation as the boy ran off down the street, the letter trailing a long red ribbon attached with sealing wax.

The wheels were set in motion now and there was no going back. Deb had a sudden urge to stop it all, this tomfool plan. To go back to yesterday, back even before that, to when the world was safe and she was full of bright-eyed optimism. But it was too late. Dressed in one of Deb's nondescript cloaks, Abigail had already crept down the gantry steps, and through the back alleys to fetch a hired gig.

Chapter Fifty

ABIGAIL DROVE DOWN LONG LANE straight to Noon Street and tethered the horse and gig to a hitching post by the Priory of St Bartholomew's. From there she walked briskly alongside the Priory walls, before taking up a position behind them to watch the house. Here, the stone was black and gritty under her touch, and had crumbled to give her a good view of the street. The Priory walls had protected this area from the Great Fire, and now she was grateful for their shelter. From here, she kept her eyes fixed on the house with the apothecary's pestle and mortar sign.

After only fifteen minutes she was gratified to see the messenger boy arrive, and a bespectacled man in a nightshirt take the beribboned letter. His expression said he did not like being woken so early. Less than a half-hour later, the same man came out, this time fully dressed in coat and breeches, coughing plumes of breath into the chill.

Abigail recognised the red flapping ribbon as he went, and followed him surreptitiously on foot along Cock Lane, past the Fortune of War Tavern, and down Farringdon Street. The linkman turned once to look over his shoulder but ignored her. She smiled to herself; women were invisible. She tailed him for only a few more streets, to Bear Alley and a busy baker's shop with rooms above. It was one of the few shops trading, for now it was light, there would be no respectable man dared lift a finger, for it was the Lord's Day, and all must rest.

The smell of baking hot cross buns made her stomach growl, but the man went round to the side alley, knocked a rhythmic four knocks on a peeling, smoke-stained green door.

In this area the houses had survived the fire and were cramped together, leaning in towards each other. A shutter swung open. Piet's tall figure appeared as a dark shadow at the upstairs casement. So this was his hidey-hole, right in plain view.

Abigail held her breath, pressed her back into the shadows of the doorway of the butcher's shop opposite, not daring to move. Just the sight of him gave her a tight feeling in her throat. The linkman held up the letter to Piet as a signal to get him to open up. Abigail ducked her head further under the hood of her cloak, grateful that the sun was not yet over the tops of the houses. A few minutes later the bespectacled man sauntered back out onto the street without the letter.

Abigail had seen what she needed to see. She cut back by Smithfield, and fetched the horse and gig. Deb was waiting, dressed respectably in a hat and cloak as Abigail reined the horse to a stop outside the house in Whetstone Park.

'Ready?'

Deb climbed in.

An hour later, the gig was standing close to the bear-baiting ring, and Abigail waited by the butcher's on the corner of Bear Alley, her shoulders and jaw stiff with tension. Deb knocked on the green door, exactly as she had instructed her to do.

Steady, girl, Abigail willed her. *Don't lose your courage.*

The shutter at Piet's window opened a crack. Abigail held her breath. She moved herself further round the corner out of sight. Piet mustn't see her. She had to do this right, for Deb's sake. Under her cloak, the flintlock pistol was a cold weight. Despite the chill, her palms were wet, slippery. She clutched the grip of the gun tighter, her eyes fixed on Deb's neat grey back.

There was a rumble behind her, and she stepped to the side in annoyance as an enormous stinking cart lumbered up to the butcher's shop. Two men hauled out the bad meat from the shop in a hurry, for it was after the curfew call, when all must be peace and tranquillity. The stink of rancid meat and offal made her almost gag.

But then she breathed out, took advantage of it and moved where the driver's seat would mask her from the buildings. *Good.* Now she was closer. In range. A fly settled on her shoulder but she dare not move. Under her cloak, she slid the pistol to full-cock.

Deb listened. The wood under her knuckles had sounded uncommonly loud. She licked her lips, wishing she could run. But Abigail would be watching her every move, and she could not back out now. When Piet's spider-like silhouette appeared at the window, she lifted her hand in greeting, smiled, and pointed to the papers she was holding. She could not see Piet's expression, but waited, shivering, hoping he could not see her hand shaking.

Sure enough, the door opened a crack. Her eyes

were level with the metal buttons on his coat.

'How did you get this address?' he said.

She fought back her fear. 'In her things.'

He frowned down at her. At the eye contact, her stomach liquefied.

'My man brought me the message,' he said. 'You had no need to come. And one of my men will collect and clear up ... if that's what is worrying you.' He was about to shut the door – she must stop him, keep him there.

'I brought these.' She held out some letters. 'They were in her things, too. I wasn't sure ... I just thought you might want them.' She sidestepped just out of his reach, away from, and to one side of the door. What was Abigail doing? What if Abigail had left her, double-crossed her? In the distance a cock crew.

Piet leaned out, holding the door open with an elbow, to take hold of the sheaf she offered him.

But at the last moment he seemed to sense something amiss. His eyes flicked right and left, before his arm snaked out like quicksilver to hook her under her chin. A sudden jerk on her gullet.

'What's this?' he hissed in her ear.

'Nothing.' She tried to speak, but he was hauling her backwards by the neck and the words were strangled in her throat. She grabbed for the door jamb. One thing she knew with certainty, once inside his house she might as well carve her own tombstone – she'd never come out. Her fingernails dug into the wood and her heels tried to gain purchase on the cracks between the flagstones. Abigail. Where was she? She could not see her.

Her fingers strained to keep hold, but they were slipping, slipping. In a moment the door would be shut to the world and she would be beyond anyone's help.

In desperation, she let go. In one swift movement she pulled the hatpin from her hat, stabbed it hard behind her. A Dutch curse – an explosion of consonants. Piet's hand loosened to go to his face. With an almighty twist, she dived forward and to the side.

A blast – so much of a shock she was momentarily stuck to the spot. Piet crumpled before her, his eyes wide, hands clutched to his chest, as if he might be able to claw the wound back together. His legs buckled, but he grappled for the door handle to keep himself upright. His hands were too slippery with blood. A groan, then his hand slid from the handle, and he slumped, a soft, heavy weight, like a sack of grain, half over the threshold. The hole in his ribs shone wet and black.

Deb coughed through the welter of smoke and sulphur.

'Hurry!' Abigail's voice galvanised Deb into motion.

She scrambled to her feet.

Abigail took hold of her arm. 'The gig's round the corner,' she said, setting off at a run.

Deb stumbled after her, and Abigail jerked the folding steps of the gig down, and Deb leapt in. The acrid smell of powder was still in her nose and the horse trod skittish and wild-eyed in its traces.

More gunshots. But no, it was the crack of the whip and Abigail setting the horse galloping.

Shutters banged open as people looked out, roused from their lying-in, bleary-eyed, to see what the disturbance was.

Lord have mercy, Lord have mercy.

They hied away, taking a twisting route through the narrow alleyways of the northern quarter, where there were still buildings to hide them, squeezing by parked delivery carts. A milkmaid jumped back out of their path. The city flew past in a rattling of iron wheels and blurred buildings, until the horse suddenly slowed and stopped and Deb was thrown forward. She was still clinging to the bloodied hatpin. She looked at it in horror and flung it away.

They were at the back of the Navy Offices, near the Three Tuns on Crutched Friars. Of course – Lord Bruncker's; the safest place for Abigail to be, a place where he would provide an alibi. Deb got out, panic making her pant for breath. Abigail almost fell from the driver's seat. She was white as whey and clutching her bad arm. The sun shone its pale orb above the houses.

'Lord Bruncker's papers, that you were copying,' Abigail said, with great effort. 'The ones I brought home to Whetstone Park a few days ago. We forgot them. They need to get back to his desk before he misses them. And there were others, plans of the docks from Crawley, navy minutes ... so many things ... besides, they'll go into Noon Street, and then to Bear Alley to make enquiries. I don't know whether Piet's clean, what's in his house, and we can't go back to check. Better bring all the papers back to me here. Soon as you can. And look for new lodgings. Clean it all out. Leave nothing to chance.'

Deb nodded. Her tongue felt detached from her thoughts.

'Is he dead?' Abigail asked, suddenly grasping her by the sleeve. 'Did we do it?'

'Yes,' Deb managed. 'He's not going to get up again.' The fact of it was just beginning to filter through. She swallowed, tasting bile in her throat.

Abigail seemed to read her thoughts. 'He would

have taken you in the end. In his world, unless you can become the hunter, you are always the prey.'

Deb reached out to bid her farewell, and to take the reins, but her knees trembled so violently she could hardly stand. Abigail embraced her tightly. The gesture was unexpected, but Deb did not resist. They held each other a moment in wordless comfort, and Deb could feel Abigail's heartbeat pulse through her back and into her hands. She caught the faint familiar aroma of lavender.

Abigail pulled away first. 'We must be careful. If I've learned anything, it's that this is the most dangerous time; if we relax our guard we might make mistakes. Promise me you won't forget. Anything from the navy has to go back somehow. Bring me everything from Whetstone Park that relates to Dr Allbarn or Viola so I can sort it. Scour the whole place. Thoroughness is essential.'

'I will, I promise.'

'Find another place to stay as soon as you are able. I'll pay off the landlord and forge you a good reference in a false name so you will be able to find a new position. Nobody need ever know we were associates.'

'What about you?'

'I'll stay here a while, just as I usually do, tell Lord B I'm feeling unwell, that I have cancelled my theatre tour and need to rest a little. Though I'll have to keep him out of my bed until my arm has healed.'

'I'm sorry.'

A loud clanging made Deb start and look wildly behind her.

'Only the end of curfew bell,' Abigail said. 'Take the gig back to Thames Street and find a way to get rid of it. You can walk from there, if you're quick, before the constables are out. When you get inside, make sure all the doors are locked.'

Deb squeezed her hands. 'Till later,' she said. 'Go safe.'

Abigail looked back at her with incredulity in her eyes. 'I can't believe it,' she said, 'that we've actually done it.'

As she went in through the gate, she turned, blew a kiss. It was a typically theatrical gesture and it made Deb smile. Deb blew one back and climbed onto the driving seat. She picked up the reins nervously. She hadn't driven anything bigger than a pony and trap since she was a child, and hoped the horse wouldn't sense her apprehension.

She glanced back at the solid outline of the Navy Buildings, the morning sun reflected at the windows, shining forth from the chambers where people like the Pepyses were just stirring, to wash themselves, toast their feet on last night's embers, go about their normal humdrum lives.

She remembered her first sight of Seething Lane, the day she arrived with Mr Batelier and Aunt Beth. Aunt Beth's words: *'Make sure you please Mr Pepys.'* It seemed so long ago, a lifetime ago.

It was no use thinking of that now. She flicked the reins as she'd seen Abigail do, and urged the horse into a trot.

Chapter Fify-one

AN INSISTENT CLANGING of bells woke Deb from her exhausted doze. She sat up on the bed, her heart beating too fast. She must have fallen asleep because she was curled on her side with her boots tangled in her skirts. The events of the dawn washed over her in an icy rush. Pray God the ostler would have found the horses and carriage in Thames Street; she felt sorry for that abandoned horse.

More bells in the distance.

Ten o'clock already.

Everything had changed, yet the room was just as it always was; the stripe of sunlight across the floor, her familiar cloak dangling over the chair. She hugged herself tight, unable to rid herself of the suffocating fear that closed around her.

When she'd returned earlier, she'd lit every single candle, all the sconces, all the rushlights, even in the daylight, but it hadn't been enough to dazzle her, to scour Piet's face from her mind. Had he deserved it? She didn't know. But she had sent him to his death. And the wound in his chest was fatal; she did not need to be a physician to know that. The memory of his expression as he tried to stitch his chest together with his fingers would not be shaken free.

She must make atonement for her sins, pray for Piet's soul. It was the least she could do. Sunday. She could make the eleven o'clock service. But she could not go to St Olave's – Crawley might be there, or Pepys, and she did not want a brush with either of them. She had a longing to see Jem Wells again, just to see his face, to bask in his goodness, to hear his blessing to the congregation. She knew she should not go near him, but he drew her. He need not see her, for it would be busy, and if she waited until the service had begun, she might be able to sneak in unseen. She would go there on the way to take everything to Abigail at Lord Bruncker's.

She hurried to wash, change her rumpled clothes, burn the bodice that was spotted with Piet's blood. She poked it into the fireplace, turned it as it glowed into ash, breaking it up until she was sure no trace remained. Abigail had not told her to burn the papers; did not trust her enough, she guessed. Probably needed to check them first, to return what was needed to Bruncker and the offices.

Deb went through the chambers with a hawk-like eye picking up anything that might have come from the Treasury, shoving it all into a leather bag. She untied the pillowslip beneath her skirts and drew out the batch of coded messages that Piet had sent her. She had been at pains never to leave Piet's letters in their chambers in case Abigail should find them, but now she knew Abigail would be reassured to see them all, to know that she was hiding nothing from her.

The only documents she kept back were her collection of Pepys' diary pages. These she still kept hidden beneath the folds of her skirts, and those only because she did not want to risk bringing more pain to that household if someone found them.

She didn't want Jem to spot her in the congregation, so she tied a kerchief round her neck, before coiling her long curls under a hat and swinging one of Abigail's dark unfamiliar cloaks over her dress. She curved her shoulders, jutted her chin. Abigail had taught her about disguise; she knew now that it was not just the clothes she needed to change, but her whole way of being in her body.

Her blurred reflection in the window, with its shifting face, reminded her of the gypsy, their strange encounter on Norwood Common. The woman had been right; the dark had drawn her in after all. She turned cold. She no longer recognised herself. Her father used to say that all life was predestined, that God had given everyone a role and they must play it out, even if it was the role of evil.

Another wave of panic and remorse forced her down the stairs and out into the chill air. When she arrived at the church there was a queue outside to go in, and she kept her head down and joined a threadbare family in the crush of people on the back benches. It was Dr Thurlow preaching, but she soon saw Jem – he was to read from the lectern and help with the communion.

She listened intently to the rector's words, about the ability of Jesus Christ to resurrect even the blackest soul in the same way as He himself had been resurrected. Still, she could not bring herself to participate in the communion. The words 'The body of Christ, the blood of Christ' were too resonant for her to bear.

'Lord have mercy, Lord have mercy.' Her prayers were so fervent that she stayed on her knees a little longer than her neighbours. When she came to rise, Jem was

staring straight at her, eyes questioning. Deb looked
hurriedly away and tried to squeeze out from her pew,
but the congregation were shaking hands, wishing each
other good day, and the family were blocking her in,
oblivious to her frantic 'excuse me's.

She glanced up. Jem was pushing his way out
through the side door. Desperate to get away before
he could stop her, Deb picked up her bag, then,
apologising, forced her way past elbows and walking
canes and voluminous skirts.

When she arrived at the front door, he was already
waiting. He caught her by the arm. 'Please, Miss
Willet, just a few moments of your time.'

'I'm in a hurry.'

'Just a few moments. We can walk in the
churchyard where we won't be disturbed. I'm quite
safe, you know. I won't bite.' His attempt at levity was
replaced by a face so earnest she could not resist.
'Please. I need to talk to you about Lizzie.'

She wanted to leave, but his words made it
impossible. They walked in silence until they passed
through the gates and onto the central path. She saw
him cast sidelong glances at her, until he found a
stone seat where they could sit.

'It's good to see you, Miss Willet. How is it with Dr
Allbarn?'

'It is well, thank you.' It was a wooden reply; she
did not dare look at him in case he should catch guilt
in her face. The grey slabbed tombs accused her.

'It's just, you don't look as happy as you did at the
Pepyses', and it bothers me.'

'It should not bother you.'

'But it does, because I care for you, because I still
think of you every minute. I think about the times
we used to walk out and look down over the bridge,

and how it felt to kiss you. I miss those times. When you came into church today it was like the light had come in with you.'

The light? Surely not? Caught off guard, she looked up and his eyes hooked hers.

She shook her head, 'Jem, I—'

'You know, I told Lizzie about you, despite your misgivings, and she would like to meet you. She is convinced you are her daughter. Why not just meet her? I can take you there myself if you would like to go.' He leaned closer towards her. 'Of course, I would not like to press you, but she is such a good woman, a kind soul, and it would mean so much for her to find the family she lost.'

'You don't understand. She wouldn't want this daughter.'

He took hold of her hand and pressed it. 'Don't be foolish. Of course she would, you're everything a mother could be proud of—'

'No.' She jumped up, as if scalded, her voice rising. 'You have no idea. If you did, you wouldn't want to know me.'

'Then give me the chance! I've thought about you every day for all these months, and I know you think well of me, too, or at least you used to.'

She turned her head away, afraid of her own emotion, but he tugged at her sleeve. 'Why must you shut me out, Miss Willet?' His eyes were soft and entreating.

Just for an instant, she grasped the possibility of collapsing into his arms, of letting go of the weight of it all. But at the last minute she wrenched herself away and the moment plummeted. 'Because I care for you ... leave me alone. Just leave me.'

She picked up her skirts and ran, blundering away

from him, through the double row of yew trees, between the upright stones of the wealthy dead. But she saw none of it, for it was not Jem she was running away from, but herself.

Jem watched her go, but did not follow. What had he said? She said she cared for him, yet then she'd fled. He couldn't think how he'd offended her. But Deb had changed since working at the Allbarns'. The girl who had laughed at his jests was gone and he wished he could get to the bottom of it. He pressed his forehead into his hands.

A leather bag was lying next to him on the bench – Miss Willet's bag. He grabbed it and shouted after her, ran helter-skelter down the path, but when he got past the church to the fork in the road there was no sign of her. He was already too late. But if she'd left it behind, then she might come back. He waited hopefully for a half-hour in the pale morning sun, but she did not return.

Still, it would give him another excuse to see her. He could send a note, ask her if he could call so he could return it to her. He wondered whether to look inside. His hand began to unbuckle the flap almost without thinking. But then he caught himself. It would be dishonest. He wrestled with his conscience a while before deciding that it would be a betrayal of her trust to look at her private things.

The ferryman held out his hand for his coin, and Deb clapped her hand to her mouth. Her bag. She searched around her feet in case she'd dropped it. She realised immediately what she'd done. She'd left it on the bench.

It was a disaster. She ran back to the park but Jem

was gone, and so was the bag. Breathless, clutching the stitch in her side, she returned to St Gabriel's, but it was locked. Heart full of foreboding, she tried the vicarage.

'Please, somebody come,' she whispered. She battered vainly at the door with her fists.

'He's gone out,' the neighbour said, from an upper window, his expression sour with disapproval under his slouched hat.

'Where?'

The neighbour shrugged.

'Had he a bag with him?' she asked, trying to stay calm. But no, the neighbour had noticed no bag, and shut the window with a slam.

Fortunately, her keys to Whetstone Park were on the belt around her waist, but she had no paper or a quill, and no money to buy writing materials, so she had to walk back to Whetstone Park before she was able to send Jem a note asking him if he had the bag. If so, she begged, would he meet her tomorrow at the evening service, and she'd fetch it?

If that bag fell into the wrong hands, then Abigail would be linked to Piet Groedecker and his death. And it would all be Deb's fault.

When the note arrived, Jem was relieved, and replied straight away to tell Deb that, of course, he would keep it safe and return it to her the next day. He hoped he would have another chance with her. But right now the bag was the least of his worries. Bart had gone out the previous night without a word and he hadn't come home.

Jem had heard him clanking about in the dark, and when he went to ask what he was doing at this hour, Bart had snapped at him and told him to go back to bed. Jem could tell by his brother's behaviour that something untoward was happening – Bart had girded on his sword and buckler, and his pistol was in his belt. Not only that, but he was obviously dressed in somebody else's fine suit of clothes, despite hiding it under his thick dark cloak.

Bart's talk of armed rebellion had given Jem an uneasy feeling. By lunchtime, when Bart still hadn't come home, Jem stopped off at the Black Bull tavern to see if he was there.

Crawley waved at him from a corner by the fire to take a drink with him. 'It's on me. I'm going to ask my girl for her hand in marriage,' he said, 'so it could be my lucky day.'

'My thanks. Who's the girl?' he asked.

'I think you met her – remember, she used to be Mr Pepys' maid – a little peach she is. We've been seeing quite a lot of each other.'

'You don't mean Miss Willet?' The room became blurred.

'The same. Mind you, she's not let me have much of a slap and tickle yet, so I reckon a betrothal might loosen her up. I know she likes me, but she's quite hoity-toity, and her employer doesn't let her out much, so I've had to take it slow.'

Jem stared down into his beer, his thoughts reeling. So that was it. That was what had been the matter. She was already promised to Crawley. He couldn't imagine them together. He took a sidelong glance at Crawley's pug-like face and greasy hair. What could she see in him? He took a gulp of beer, but it could not drown his disappointment, a sensation so tender he could not swallow. He spat the beer back into the tankard.

'Aren't you going to congratulate me?'

Jem curbed the urge to punch the self-satisfied bastard in the face. 'Sorry, Crawley, I'm a bit distracted. It's my brother, you see. He didn't come home last night. I've been everywhere, but I can't find any sign of him. I thought he might be in here. He's got himself involved with a bad crowd – they were planning something. I worry he might have got himself into trouble.'

'Bet it's the trouble at the docks at Chatham. Chaps I work with at the Navy Office had an emergency meeting this morning. Mennes was all of a lather over it. I kept my ear to the door to see what was going on.'

'Did they?' Jem was only half-listening, his mind was still on Deb.

'A skirmish, it seems. A set-up. Rebels planning an attack on the shipyard. It's all undercover, and nobody's supposed to know.' Crawley tapped his arm, whispered, 'But I'll tell you, because you're a friend.'

Jem stiffened, instantly wide awake. Rebels. A shipyard. It sounded too familiar. 'What else?'

'King's men have been drafted in as reinforcements. They've had a tip-off and they're after someone called Tom Player ... oh, and another one from the gunpowder works – Skinner, was it? Anyway, there's going to be a rout. Gunpowder's involved somehow. Could be a spectacle, eh?'

Jem grabbed his arm. 'Skinner, did you say?'

'Do you know him?' Crawley pursed his lips, shook his head. 'Looks bad. If your brother's gone in with him I wouldn't fancy his chances. They'll likely shoot the rebels on the spot. Or maybe they'll wait – public execution.'

Jem's face turned grey. He would wager his life it was those two that Bart had gone to meet yesterday.

'You're sure? Sure it was Player and Skinner?'

Crawley nodded. His eyes lit up at Jem's horrified expression. He licked his lips. 'Looks like you'll be needing a lawyer. Or an undertaker.'

Jem stood up, looked vaguely around, as if he might run, but didn't know where. He'd got to stop them, warn Bart somehow.

'You'll never get there in time,' Crawley said, plainly enjoying the spectacle of Jem's distress. 'It's a half-day's ride, and whatever it is, it's planned for sundown.'

Jem did not wait to hear more, but swiped up his hat and ran out, boots slithering on the cobbles. He had to warn Bart that the King's men were on the way.

A hurried scout around in the stables at the back, and ... saints be praised! Someone's horse, and still saddled. *Hope it's Crawley's nag,* he thought. Serve him right.

Jem dug his heels in the horse's flanks and set off at a wild gallop. His legs were unused to riding, and after ten miles on the Upnor road his thighs ached like the devil, but he dare not slow. The terrain was rough but marked by a well-ridden path through the wooded 'hundreds' of Northfleet and on through marshes to Rochester where he was finally able to water the sweating horse. He threw water over his own face, and risked a drink from the spring that fed the trough. He dare not tarry, despite his shaking legs; the sky threatened rain and he feared he had already taken too long.

Long before he arrived at the dock gate he could see the buildings and masts on the horizon, and, across the river, the fort. A group of men were assembling there and boats were being made ready. From Jem's vantage point they looked like little black rats. The feathers in their cocked hats identified them easily as the King's troops. He wiped his sweating hands on the horse's mane. A few boats bearing soldiers were already halfway across. 'Please God, let me be in time,' he prayed.

As he galloped up to the gate, the heavens opened in an almighty downpour – so heavy he could hardly see where he was riding. At the gate, he slid down and landed with both feet in a slime of mud. Water slopped up his boots. One of the two guards demanded his papers.

'Curate, is that right?' One of them gave a cursory glance at them.

'Yes, but don't keep me. I'm to give prayers to a dying man,' he said. It was half-true, he thought. If he did not get there in time Bart would be as good as dead. The King's men would arrest him for treason against the Crown.

'Not one of the inspectors is it?'

'Might be, someone with the falling sickness, they said.'

'Long as it's not catching, eh?' They passed his dripping papers back and waved him through. He dragged the horse by the reins behind him, but it was reluctant to move and he was getting more and more soaked. He lost patience and threw the reins round a post and picked his way down the treacherous slope towards the jutting masts and grey water. The muddy paths were slick with wet, and rain bounced off his shoulders. All sane men had retreated to shelter.

Jem looked left and right but could see no sign of Bart or of his friends, Player and Skinner. He peered through the blur of rain at the big ship in front of him. About twenty yards away the street erupted with men, all running towards him. He stopped, unsure what was happening, why they were running.

A blast like a clap of thunder shook the ground, followed by a searing white flash and a boom that seemed to come from inside his chest. Instinctively he ducked, put his hands over his head. Nails and bolts and splinters of wood rained down around him.

Bart. He had to find Bart.

He ran down the hill. The ship belched orange flame from a gaping hole in the hull. The shock of the noise meant he couldn't think, but he was aware of men running past him, in the opposite direction, away from the blast, and then the King's men looming up through the blizzard of rain. The noise of the fire split the sky. A musket ball rebounded from a building to his left. Men were streaming from the buildings now to see what was going on.

'Run, man!' shouted someone from behind them, and another man cannoned into his back. Jem fell, winded. He was disorientated. Feet splashed past him, and a man tripped over him and sprawled facedown before heaving himself up and running away. Jem struggled to upright.

A rough hand grabbed him, 'What the hell …?'

It was Bart, his hair plastered to his scalp, dragging him up by the arm so hard Jem thought his shoulder would leave its socket. 'This way!' Bart shouted, gesturing frantically for him to follow. He sprinted up the hill away from the river, but Jem's legs were weary from riding and the ground was too slippery. His boots skidded in the mud.

There was a yank on his coat, hands pulled on his waist and a militia man pinned him to the ground, a musket muzzle jammed against his temple. 'I've caught one of them,' yelled the soldier. Others came panting up and stood over him in a circle. They hauled him to his feet and one of them punched him in the eye.

'That's for pretending to be a man of the church.'

The second blow took the world to black.

Chapter Fifty-two

Dᴇʙ ᴡᴀꜱ ᴡᴇᴀʀʏ. She had gone to St Gabriel's as Jem asked, to meet him and collect her bag, but he was not there. Dr Thurlow was apologetic, but could supply no answers. Neither was Jem at home. The neighbour said that he often went over to the chapel at White Hall to meet with his friends, so the next day she set off in the bluster to walk the few miles there to see if she could find him. Two sleepless nights had passed since Piet's death, and that morning a note had arrived from Abigail to say she was laying low at Bruncker's and his Lordship was searching everywhere for his missing papers. Why hadn't she brought them? Where was she?

Deb's skirts blew flat to her legs, making her aware of the papers beneath. She must find Jem and that bag. On the way, she stopped at St Paul's Walk to buy a pamphlet with the latest news – to see if Piet's body had been found. It was a peculiar feeling to be free of him, to have made a truce with Abigail. She still felt hunted, and could not stop looking over her shoulder – it was a habit that was not easy to drop.

The finding of the body was news already, in the small print beneath some explosion at the docks. The fact that Mr Johnson's lodgings showed no sign of his apothecary business was made much of, and speculation that he was a Catholic spy was already rife. Deb scanned down, combing the words. A 'mystery woman' it said. She tensed, but then her shoulders relaxed when she realised nobody had a good description. One said: 'a woman in a dark hat', another 'a woman in a hooded cloak'. Nobody had seen faces. It was inconclusive. Nobody thought of *two* women.

She crammed into the crowded ferry to White Hall and pored over every word in case any hint could lead them to her or Abigail, but there was nothing. She found her way to the chapel, still pondering the printed words, when a familiar voice reached her ears – Mr Pepys, regaling Will Hewer in his usual manner.

He spotted Deb straight away, though Will had not, and, anxious to avoid him, she hurriedly followed two elderly matrons who were going down into the lobby of the chapel. There, the women met up with a well-dressed gentleman who was obviously waiting for them. Deb glanced behind, to check Mr Pepys had not followed, then asked if they knew the curate, Jeremiah Wells.

The gentleman was most polite, said 'yes', he was often there, but that he had not seen him there that day. Disappointed, she took her leave of them and was about to mount the stairs again when Mr Pepys came puffing down towards her, all of a fluster.

'Saints be praised, if it isn't little Deb,' he said. 'How are you?' His face glowed red, his hands pulling nervously on his waistcoat pocket flaps.

She was not quick enough to avoid him, and found herself with her back to a wall.

'Well,' she said, guardedly, 'but you must excuse me, I'm—'

'We miss you at home. I mean, I miss you. Our little talks, seeing you about the place. I still think of you, Deb. My heart is not mended. It was Elisabeth made me write, and now there's no one to talk books with, and I know you'd be interested to see my latest purchases—'

'I have little time for reading now,' she replied curtly.

'Still, you'd like to see them, wouldn't you? I tell you, the bindings are exquisite, hand-tooled calfskin, gold leaf ...' He closed in on her a little more. He seemed so large and solid, the coat of stiff wine-coloured velvet, his polished patent shoes almost too dainty to support his bulk. He looked down on her, his eyes beseeching.

'My life is very different now,' she said.

'But still time for old friends, eh?'

He put a hand on her shoulder but she shrugged it away, ignoring his pleading expression. 'Pardon me, Mr Pepys, but I must be going, my employer—'

'Is it far? Can I order you a hackney? Are you still at Allbarn's?'

'No, no need, it's only a few minutes.'

'If you have a day off, we can meet again—'

'Best not, Elisabeth ...'

'I suppose not.' He took up a lock of her hair, rubbed it between finger and thumb. 'Still as pretty, my little Deb. Can't we arrange something?'

'Isn't that Will, coming down the stairs?'

Mr Pepys leapt away from her, eyes anxiously searching the lobby. Deb slipped to the side as he turned. When she glanced back over her shoulder he took a couple of steps after her, but she did not wait – she just hitched up her skirts and ran.

It felt strange to ignore him. He still seemed like

her employer. But she was impatient; she had more important things to worry about than Mr Pepys, like the death of Piet Groedecker and tracking down Jem Wells and that bag.

Jem shifted against his shackles to try to ease his stomach. Two more days had passed, and he had eaten nothing but swill. His insides contracted against his ribs with what felt like an audible suck. Forced to kneel on the filthy floor by his iron bonds, he feared catching some pestilence; though now, he thought, it would scarcely matter.

He could not summon a mood for prayer. He closed his eyes tight, cast his mind to God, but the ensuing silence only conjured up his past sins. Little failings, that seemed so small at the time, loomed large; things like not visiting his mother enough, or his harsh words with Bart.

Never mind God, he was his own judge, and he could find far too many reasons why God should ignore his pleas now. He still could not quite believe it, that he was to die. He hadn't had time to find out what life was all about, let alone death, and he couldn't imagine a heaven; it was too far a jump from where he was now.

He hadn't had to wait long to find out his fate. The assizes had fallen, unfortunately for him, on Tuesday, and his trial, too politically sensitive for the public's ears, had taken place hurriedly behind closed doors. It had been woefully short. The magistrate had produced evidence in the form of some letters that they said they had found at his house.

It was all fabricated, of course. How could people make up such outright falsehoods? He protested most vehemently to anyone who would listen, and equally vehemently to those who would not. At the trial, he knew it was not helping his cause to rail and shout, but could not help himself. He supposed that calling the magistrate a 'deluded fool' hadn't helped. He was branded a traitor and the verdict was a foregone conclusion. The sentence – death by hanging. But not even a clean death. His body was to be mangled into four quarters and he was to be made a public example, presumably to prevent any further such rebellions.

His usual ebullient good humour ebbed away and he was frightened at the smallness of the man that was left. He thanked God he was sparing Bart this, about as often as he cursed him for leaving him to rot here with not so much as a word.

Now he just longed for it to be over. What use was it to starve him here, when his death could be arranged so quickly? A bit of rope and a chair. But he knew the answer. The crowd would want their entertainment. On Friday he'd be put in the condemned hold, and when they finally hammered off the shackles he would have to shake the hand of the hangman. Not as a courtesy, but a way of assessing the length of rope needed to hang him. Then would come the two-and-a-half mile drag on the horse-hitched trundle, past the hollow peal of St Sepulchre's bell, to the triple tree at Tyburn.

It was this journey he feared most of all. He would be weaker by then, more afraid. He would have to summon his strength and somehow die with dignity, as an innocent man should. The jeers of the crowd would be the last sound he would hear. He hoped Deborah Willet, at least, would not be amongst them.

Abigail barely moved from her curtained bed, telling Lord B she was suffering with a cold. It explained her red eyes and nose, for she was shaken by uncontrollable bouts of sobbing, intermingled with an exhaustion that made her legs as heavy as tombstones. Grief for Joan, mingled with relief that, at last, nobody was watching her. Today was the first day she was out of bed and she almost cheered when Deb finally appeared at Lord Bruncker's door, though of course she was careful to hide her thankfulness to see her.

The sensation of relief was short-lived though, when Deb explained that Jem Wells, a curate no less, was now in possession of all the documents from Whetstone Park. She'd spent the last few days trying to track him down. The tension bristled through Abigail's body, shooting along its familiar pathways, knotting her shoulders and stomach.

She sat down hard on the chair, pinching the top of her nose between finger and thumb in disbelief. She cursed herself. She should have asked Deb to burn it all, but she hadn't trusted her enough. And she'd wanted to check Deb's thoroughness, that she was not concealing anything against her.

'Where is this godforsaken curate now?' she asked wearily.

'I don't know,' Deb said, sitting down opposite her on a leather-topped stool. 'Nobody's seen him for days. My guess is that he's probably just been called away, maybe has duties in another parish.'

'Last night Lord B was looking for an inventory. It was one I took to Whetstone Park last week,' Abigail said. 'Turned the house half upside down looking for it. Has this man taken the bag with him?'

'I don't know. It's probably in his house somewhere.'

'Can't you get in and see?'

'Not easily, I checked. He lodges right on the main

thoroughfare in full view,' Deb said. 'A break-in would be too difficult. And I went to his parish, and I even sent a boy, to enquire at the school where he does charitable work. But I think he'll keep the bag safe and not look inside. After all, he's a curate. He won't snoop.'

'Of course he will. It's human nature.'

'He won't,' Deb said, 'because he knows it's mine and we trust each other. I'm worried ... he was going to return it, but something's stopped him ...'

'You should have come straight here.'

'Anyway,' Deb said defiantly, 'so far nobody has come knocking on my door.'

'That doesn't mean they won't. Clergymen ...' Abigail said, sighing. 'Never trust them. They're the worst. More priests in the bawdyhouses than anyone else. Have you found different lodgings?'

'There hasn't been time. The bag seemed more important. But I told Poole we could no longer employ her.'

'Does she know anything?'

'No. But she did not seem surprised,' Deb said. 'She said you knew where to find her when it had all blown over.'

'She's been in this situation before, that's why. She knows I value her discretion. But I trust you've told this curate nothing about us, about what we do?'

'No.' Deb shook her head. 'He thinks I'm just a maidservant.'

Abigail saw the way Deb's eyes would not meet hers, realised there must be some attraction between Deb and this man. She stood up and gestured at the portrait of Lord Bruncker in its gilded frame. 'Look at him. Handsome devil, isn't he? I fancied I was in love once. This curate – have you fallen for him?'

Deb joined her in front of the portrait. 'Jem's too respectable for me. It wouldn't be a suitable match.'

Abigail blinked, taken aback. It was a long time since she'd heard those words. What was 'respectable? Or 'suitable?' There would be few who could match Deb Willet for intelligence, or courage. 'Don't be too sure,' Abigail said. 'They're never as lily white as they pretend – nobody is.' She turned away from the portrait and poured them both a glass of Madeira from a decanter. 'My first husband was a well-respected army officer on the outside, until he got a bottle in his hand.' She held up the glass ruefully, before swallowing the liquid.

'Is he still alive?' Deb asked. 'Is that why you haven't married Lord Bruncker?'

'No. He's dead. John was twenty-nine years older than me when we married. An old man.' She paused, remembering. 'I was his second wife. It suited John, for I was heir to the Clere fortune and, at twelve years old, too young to understand what marriage meant. He ravaged my fortune in less than ten years, and abandoned me when it ran out. But he was already a ruin of a man. The old King's execution – he could never get over it. He was Cromwell's cousin.'

'You don't mean the late Lord Protector?'

'The same. The family used to be called Cromwell, but he had to change his name to Williams. When they wanted to kill the King, he tried to persuade his cousin to show mercy. Of course, you know the result.' She put down the glass and sat down, her legs were weak again. These days she seemed to have little stamina.

Deb passed over her own glass, which was untouched. 'So what happened to him then?'

Abigail sighed. 'After that, John was unwelcome in

any society – the Cromwells' or the King's. We were pariahs everywhere we went. We went into hiding to Holland. That's where I met Piet.'

Deb came to sit close to her. 'Did you know he was a spy?'

'Not then. My husband was losing his wits; he couldn't hold his drink, and that meant money slipped through his fingers like water. We were destitute, couldn't afford to eat, and Piet, knowing I could speak a little French, suggested I should act as a go-between between the Dutch and the French. He meant spying, of course.'

'So why did you come to England?

'To deliver some papers. It was on my way to England by ship that I gave birth to Joan.' Abigail closed her eyes a moment, to shut out the memory of the pain and the heaving of the sea. 'But when I looked into her face – so tiny, so innocent … in that moment I decided I could never go back to Holland. I wanted to give my daughter a better life than I'd had, set her a good example.' She paused, pressed a hand to her mouth to stop the sob that was rising. It was a moment before she spoke. 'I failed.'

'No. She chose the life she wanted. And she knew you loved her, at the last.' Deb took her by the hand.

Abigail didn't withdraw. They sat a while before she squeezed it and said, 'We understand each other. Bring the bag as soon as you get it. It makes me nervous not knowing who's reading those papers.'

'I will.' Deb went to fetch her cloak. 'Abigail, I hate to ask, but there's something else. I wondered if you could perhaps give me a loan …'

'Oh, Lord. You're right. I should have thought. I'm afraid you're on your own. Piet's was my only income and I gave all my silver coin to Lord B to keep up the pretence of a wealthy widow. He thinks I have money. It's one of my attractions. Takes more than love or beauty to bind a man to you, remember that. Money is power. So if there's one thing I've learnt, it's that if you don't care for them, make them pay. And if you do care for them, make them pay just the same.'

'What little money I had was all in that bag. I have nothing else valuable I can sell. I'd hoped—'

'Sorry, Deb, I'm down to my last farthing, though you're welcome to that. Oh, but wait—'

An idea. She took out her calfskin purse from her bag and tipped it into her hand. Two tokens and the brooch she sometimes wore at her throat. She held this out.

'Take the brooch. It's the last of my valuables. Lord B gave me it the first time I ... did him a favour. You can sell it.'

'I can't do that. It's too easily traced. It will link us together.' Deb shook her head.

She was right, Abigail realised. She should have thought of that herself. She had taught her well. To mask her feelings of pride, she turned with sudden impatience. 'Why are you wasting time talking to me? You should still be out searching for your Romeo. And as soon as you find him, for God's sake, bring me that bag.'

Deb had been relying on money from Abigail. Without it, how could she eat, let alone change lodgings? Abigail's reaction to her losing the bag had been less violent than she had anticipated. The sting had gone from their relationship, and she sensed a genuine partnership. Now Abigail's guard was down, Deb sensed her hidden softness, a glimpse of girlhood underneath her hard façade.

But she worried what had happened to Jem – whether he really had gone away, or whether he had given her up altogether. Talking about him to Abigail had made her heart full of longing. It was odd that he had not written to her, to apologise for not coming to their meeting. Perhaps she had offended him too much and he had changed his mind. She hurried on to escape the thought and its accompanying pain. She was just passing down Holborn Hill past the water conduit, when a coach slowed beside her.

She glanced in through the window, but looked away hurriedly. Mr Pepys. He was everywhere. Damn. He'd seen her. She pretended not to have noticed him and hurried on up the hill towards Smithfield. The coach rumbled along, keeping pace with her, and when she got to the end of the street he alighted and stood in her path.

'Deb, my dear! The very person. I tracked you down! Will Hewer confessed to me where you lodge in Whetstone Park and I was just on my way to see you.'

But she had no time to digest this, as he had taken hold of her arm. 'Come along, this way, there's a little alehouse there.' He set off briskly before she could protest and swept her into the dim interior of the tavern, pushing her ahead of him into a dark corner. He summoned the taverner to light a candle, though it was still bright outside. The thought came that perhaps she might persuade him to a loan.

'I wanted to show you my new books.' He took out his latest acquisitions, talking all the while as if to stop speaking might lay bare the awkwardness between them. He did not meet her eyes, but set out the books in a row before her.

'I can't stay long,' she said, aware that she was

- 430 -

jammed against the wall now he had slipped in beside her.

'Just a few minutes. You'll love these,' he said.

He pointed out the fine embossing, the marbled paper and the ornate capitals. 'Come closer,' he said, drawing her up to him with his hand around her shoulder.

She regretted now even coming inside, but the trouble with Mr Pepys was that he was hard to resist. With him, it was like trying to stop a runaway carriage. It blundered on, taking all before it. And after her recent experiences, he seemed mild, with not an ounce of malice in him.

'I'm hungry. Are you hungry, Deb? I'll order something.' He shouted the taverner over and sent him to fetch two pies, and just the thought of them made Deb's mouth water. One little pie could not hurt. She'd be careful, keep her wits about her.

As they ate, he told her about the wedding between Jane and Tom, and it was so good to hear of them, and slowly, with the warmth of the food, she began to relax, until Mr Pepys began to ponder over Jane and Tom's wedding night, and his hand crept around under her arm to rest on her thigh. She leaned away from him.

'It's so nice to see you. Remember when we played "hunt the key"?' he said. 'Is there a little kiss for Sam, Deb?'

She did not have to do this any more, she realised. He was no longer her employer. In an instant she saw herself as if from a great distance, saw what she had become. There was power in being a whore. She thought of Abigail's words of not an hour earlier: *If you don't care ... make them pay*.

'Now, Mr Pepys, you know if you want a kiss, you

will have to give me something.' She deliberately took on the teasing tone she used to use with him.

'What shall I give you? Perhaps one of my books, though I should be loath to—'

'Sixpence would do.' There. It was out.

He stopped talking, and his eyes widened in surprise.

'No. Don't be a goose. I can't give you money, not like ...'

'Like a common whore? Why not?' Anger rushed up like a red heat. 'You want my favours, don't you, so why not be honest? And I'll bet I've to be quiet about it, too, so that Elisabeth won't suspect. Well, silence must be paid for.'

He frowned, shook his head. 'What's happened to my little Deb? So hard, so—'

'I've grown up, Mr Pepys. You don't employ me, can no longer order me. If you want your kiss, it will be sixpence, and sixpence for my silence.'

He stared a moment as if she'd slapped him, and then he reached into his pocket. He took out two gold 'angels' and tossed them onto the table. Twenty shillings. It was an enormous amount, enough for two pairs of stockings of real silk.

'If you need money, then I have plenty,' he said. 'You need only ask. Take it as a gift. Now let us say no more about this foolish idea.' He took hold of her hand and squeezed it in his plump palm.

She swallowed, thought of Jem, and a wave of guilt washed over her. But she had no idea where Jem had gone. Perhaps, even now, he was going through the papers in her bag. He was a thoughtful man. Perhaps he did not come to meet her because he had realised the significance of the papers. Would he tell anyone? She might need to pay to get away. Money could buy her a path out of trouble.

Pepys squeezed her hand again and Deb stared at the glinting gold on the table. Abigail was right. If she was going to do this, she would be in control and she would be rightly recompensed.

Deb reached for the money and tucked the heavy coins into the pocket in her skirts. 'Forty kisses, then for twenty shillings,' she said. Like Judas's silver.

He started to protest, but anxious to get it done and get away, she pulled him towards her and brought her mouth up to his. His hands went to both breasts, but she pushed him away. 'No. Not that. Just kisses. Touching costs more.'

She kissed him quickly, short sharp pecks on the mouth, keeping count up to sixteen until he thrust her away.

'Stop!' he said. 'That was not what I meant. Where is the old Deb?'

She shook her head, unable to speak. It was a question she kept asking herself, and it brought with it a pain deep in her chest.

He sighed, gathered his books, irritation pushing his mouth into a pout. 'I can't stay. I have an appointment to keep. But we need to straighten this out, because you dishonour yourself. Will you meet me again?'

'No,' she said, 'I don't think so.'

'You still owe me,' he said, eyes too bright and glassy, the bulge in his breeches too proud.

'Will you pay then,' she said, summoning her strength, 'for me to keep my silence?'

He shook his head, sighed. 'If I must. But I never thought it would come to this, not with my little Deb, not with my peach.'

'This same time again tomorrow?' she asked, her voice brisk.

'If that's how it's to be, meet me in the Hall at Westminster. There's a room I can hire.' He stood up and bowed. He had never bowed to her before. It looked odd, and as he scattered more coins on the counter for the cellarman, she saw him suddenly differently, as a sad middle-aged man, like a hollow gourd with a need to stuff himself up, to preen and prattle to keep everyone away from seeing the little mouse inside.

Poor Elisabeth. He would always be wanting someone to make the mouse feel like a man.

Now Deb had money she hailed a hackney to get away as quickly as possible. Although Pepys had not touched a single inch of naked skin, she still felt dirty. First thing she would do would be to boil water and scrub herself all over. Her hand closed over the gold in her pocket. That amount would keep her a few weeks, buy bread and beer, provide a deposit for new lodgings and time to search for another position, though Elisabeth's paltry reference would not be much assistance. She should have reminded Abigail about her promise to write her a new one.

She did not want to meet Mr Pepys again. He would demand more, and the thought of it turned her stomach the way milk turns sour. Soon as she could, she would leave London, go to another town. Back to Bristol, perhaps. Somewhere far away from here, where she could make a new start. Perhaps Hester would be able to join her. Hester. Oh my Lord. What would she think of her, if she knew?

She alighted and paid the driver, and was just about to put a key in the door when she heard someone call her name. 'Miss Willet!'

Her heart jolted, and from habit she whipped

around. A man was waving to her. She recognised the well-muscled figure of Bart, Jem's brother. Her first thought was that he might be returning her bag, but she could see no sign of it. He ran up, slid to a standstill before her. 'Have you heard?'

'What?'

'It's not good news,' he was panting from exertion, 'but I thought you should know. Jem thought a lot of you. He wouldn't stop talking about you. But it's taken me a long time to find where you live.' He was embarrassed, reluctant.

'What? Tell me.'

'He's in gaol. Not his fault. Don't think ill of him. The neighbour says a bunch of men came to search our lodgings.'

'Why? What's happened?' Deb shook her head. 'He kept to the church rule. What's he supposed to have done?'

'It's nothing to do with the church. He got caught up in a skirmish at the docks. There was an explosion and ... well, they think he had something to do with it.'

Deb was sorting the pieces of the puzzle. The docks – the plot against the King; that was information she knew all about, from maps and documents she'd copied for Abigail. The plot that some foolish rebels were still intent on. She had a sudden flash of insight – Abigail must have sold this intelligence to the Crown. But what had this to do with Jem?

'They've put him in the Clink,' Bart said.

'It's a mistake. If he hasn't done anything wrong then they'll let him go, won't they? Why haven't they let him go?'

Bart's face was miserable. 'I don't know. It was my fault. It all went wrong ... he tried to tell me, but I wouldn't listen to reason. I was angry and vengeful and just wanted to *do* something. It had already been postponed once. It was a good plan, and I thought we could do it, even without the Dutch ... Player and Skinner and a good number of us. But this time it never even got started ... the rain was pelting down, we could hardly see straight, and then, suddenly, as we were setting the fuse, armed troops crashed in on us, shouting and waving muskets. Someone had betrayed us. We panicked, scattered, bolted for our lives. But Player had already lit the fuse and ... God, splinters and nails flying everywhere ...'

'What's this to do with Jem?'

'He was there, in the yard. Still don't know what the hell he was doing there. Maybe he'd come to help us.' Bart lifted his shoulders in a gesture of defeat. 'I did try, Miss Willet. I grabbed him, pulled him after me, but he got left behind. Next thing I knew they'd arrested him. Lord Bruncker accused him of spying on his papers in his office, and now they're saying they've found a bag of letters at our lodgings. Letters that don't look good.'

'What do you mean?'

'Correspondence stolen from the Navy Offices, and names that link him to our plot and some Dutchman that was shot. The one talked of in the broadsides. But I know bully-all about any of that. There was no such bag. It sounds like a trumped-up charge to me.'

Deb swayed slightly on her feet. Lord have mercy. Her bag. They'd found her bag. Jem must have taken it home. 'I'll just have to sit a moment,' she said, letting herself sink onto the cold stone of the mounting block.

'Sorry, miss, it's a bit of a shock, I know. Have you any smelling salts?'

'Upstairs,' she said weakly. 'But no, don't go. Tell me, what's this about letters?'

'I don't know, maybe it's just a rumour, but I got it from Crawley, clerk at the Treasury. I know he's a mouth like a sewer, but he's usually got a sixth sense for trouble.'

Crawley. Yes, it was just the sort of news he'd revel in. She rallied herself enough to ask, 'What are the charges?'

'Treason. Spiery. Attempted rebellion, murder and overthrow of the King. It's horseshit. You know him, Miss Willet. He wouldn't even squash a flea. It's me that's the bad one. It's all my fault.' He rubbed his hands through his hair, his big face creased with worry. 'I'm the one who's got him into trouble, and I don't know what to do, how to get him out.'

The prickle of guilt made Deb look at her feet. 'Have you seen him?'

He shook his head. 'No visitors – it's too serious for that. It's a hanging offence. I've just heard; he's to go to the scaffold Friday, the day after tomorrow. They want a scapegoat, a deterrent.'

'No.' She couldn't take it in. 'Where are you staying?'

'Rooms at the Black Bull. I daren't go home or they'll arrest me, too. We're all underground, all of us that had a hand in it. Skinner, Player, Bolton. We're working out what to do, but the others won't let me bleat because it puts their necks on the line, too.' He glanced over his shoulder.

It was then that she noticed another man, a small balding fellow in a long coat, watching them intently from the corner of the street, a pistol held loosely in his hand.

'They wouldn't let me come alone,' he said,

ruefully, 'in case I was tempted to go and give myself up. They reckon they'd torture the names out of me, see. They're happy –so long as he's the only one who got caught and they're laying it all on him, 'cause he knows nothing. But I thought you might want to go and see him ...'

'Yes, yes. I'll do that.' Her thoughts whirled; she couldn't order them.

The balding man began to approach, pistol raised, gesturing at Bart to leave.

'Sorry, got to go,' Bart said. He crushed her hand as if to press all his emotion into her palm. 'If you see him, tell him ... tell him, I'm sorry.'

When he'd gone, Deb hauled herself up the stairs and slumped in the chair by the window. She had never seen a hanging, but she knew from printed broadsides what it entailed: the humiliation, the mutilation afterwards. The thought made her head feel like it was full of feathers.

She could not let them do that to him.

Jem's face was stuck in her mind. His throaty laugh echoed in her memory, the sound of his footsteps as he walked alongside her, his eyes fixed on her face, as if she were the only thing worth looking at in the world.

Her heart ached as if it had been trampled by a carthorse, a pain so intense she could hardly breathe.

I love him, she thought in wonderment.

She looked up at the carved wooden angel on its nail above the door. It seemed so long since that Christmas, since that kiss. She unhooked it, clasped the smooth wood to her breast as she sank to her knees and sent up a prayer. At the end of it, she knew only one thing.

She would have to confess. Tell them they were her papers, that it was she who had spied for the Dutch, she who had killed Piet.

But it was not so simple. There was Abigail to consider. She could not betray Abigail, not now. If she was to do this, then she would have to pretend it was she alone who fired the shot that killed Piet. If they questioned her, she would have to be strong, and keep her counsel.

All night long, she stayed awake, pacing the room, seeing Jem's tawny eyes in her mind. To make a plausible account she would need to plan exactly what she would say. Finally, she took out paper and quill. She must be meticulous. She recalled precisely what was in the bag, made notes in her neat hand of all the implications. Finally, her story was ready.

Jem was the wrong man; he had picked up her bag in all innocence.

In the morning she dressed carefully in her blue taffeta bodice and skirt. For when would she wear it again if not now? Then she sat down to write to Jem. It was a love letter, the first and last she would ever write, so she explained it all, held nothing back, told him why she could not be there waiting for him when they let him go free.

> *"Please, I beg you, look after Hester, take her to Lizzie, and whatever you do, you must shield her from the worst of the scandal."*

When she had finished, she wrote the words:

*"I never meant to have such a
life. I meant to be better than
this. I'm sorry. Wherever I am
when you read this, pray for me*

She reached into her pocket and took the razor
from its ivory case to shear a lock of hair. After she
folded the curl inside the parchment, she heated the
wax and sealed the letter.

It was done. The act of confessing released a great
weight from her, as if, for the first time in her life, she
was truly herself.

Chapter Fifty-three

DEB HASTENED TO SOUTHWARK and the Clink, to try to bribe her way in to see Jem, or at the very least to pass him the letter, but Bart had been right, the place was a fortress and she was forcibly turned away at the gatehouse. Heart beating loud in her ears, she hurried back to Jem's house, kissed the letter and pushed it under the door. But she did not tarry, for she had to see the magistrate. Despite her urgent entreaties, she was told he was out, and she made the first appointment she could – for four in the afternoon.

A whole morning wasted. Thursday – and time was running out. Jem was still in gaol and she was no further forward. She brushed away tears of frustration with the back of her hand.

There was nothing for it but to return home, but with every hour her courage faltered as the terror of what her confession might mean grew. She could not settle, and strange chills flowed in her veins; when she tried to eat, her hands shook with apprehension, so finally, after the twelve o'clock bell, she resolved to sit outside the magistrate's office. She could not bear it, any more waiting. She picked up her cloak.

The noise of the door knocker made Deb start.

Not now.

Her heart leapt, though; maybe it was Bart to say they'd let Jem go? She peered out of the window but could see no one, just the brilliant blue of the sky, the passing, dissolving clouds. She was momentarily transfixed. So many days where she had not noticed that blue. And now so few left.

The knocker again. When she opened the door, a woman was standing there, right under the lintel. A woman in brown, a little shorter than she was, a woman whose arms were reaching out towards her.

Deb's knees gave way. The world seemed to fold inwards towards her heart.

Lizzie caught her and held her up. 'Deborah.'

The sound of her voice unleashed a tide of emotion so overwhelming Deb could not speak, but she struggled to detach herself from her mother's embrace.

Stunned, the words finally came. 'No,' she said. 'Not now. Please, you can't come now. It's too late.' She tried to barge past, but Lizzie caught her again, took hold of her by the waist.

'Don't. I know you are angry, you have every right to be so, but I only want you to listen. I can't bear it if you turn me away.'

It was the smell of her, that familiar smell of comfort. Deb could not move.

'There, my sugarplum.' Her mother's arms gathered her in close to her chest. Those words she'd used when Deb was small. Deb's shoulders heaved, but she refused to cry. She hardened herself, quashed the tears quickly. She was not a child to be cajoled, but a woman. And she would not be bent from her purpose.

'I've missed you all so much,' Lizzie said, her voice cracking. She touched Deb's face in wonder.

'And do you think we did not miss you? Every single day we hoped for a word, a note, anything at all. But you sent us nothing.'

'I tried to—'

'No. We managed all this time without you and we don't need you now.' She read the passing years in her mother's face, time's imprint in the wrinkles round her eyes, in the greying hair. 'I'm a grown woman, Mama. Look at me, I grew up without you.' Deb saw her mother's face crumple, and instantly regretted her words.

'I'm sorry,' Lizzie said. 'I see it now. It was wrong of me to hope you'd forgive me. You're right. I should not expect anything, not after ... I'll go now, it was a mistake me coming ...'She shook her head, wrapped her cloak tighter, and stumbled away, round the corner of the tannery.

Deb groaned. She could not bear it. 'Wait!' she shouted. When she rounded the corner, her mother was huddled against the wall. She looked so vulnerable that before Deb knew it she'd taken her arm and pulled her over to comfort her.

After they had held each other for a long stretch, Lizzie said, 'Lord, what a beauty you've grown into ... Deb, can we go in, out of the view of the street?'

'I can't,' Deb said. 'I have to go, and when I do I won't be coming back. I have to see the magistrate.'

'What do you mean? Are you in trouble? Come, love, tell me.'

Deb struggled to make an answer, but could not. Nor could she walk away and leave her mother standing alone on the street.

Seeming to sense this, Lizzie took charge, guided Deb through the gaping door and upstairs, and bade her sit. Deb saw Lizzie's eyes take in the letter addressed to Hester, which was still propped upon the table.

'Have you any liquor?' Lizzie asked.

'In the cupboard, if there's any left.' Deb was suddenly drained, as if her whole body had turned to ice.

'Whatever it is, it will wait an hour so that we can talk,' Lizzie said. She fetched two glasses and shared out the brandy, passing the biggest glass to Deb. The sight of her mother moving purposefully about the room as she always used to at their childhood home was so familiar and yet so strange. The brandy burned her throat, but Lizzie swallowed hers down and Deb did the same.

'Your father would not let me see you,' Lizzie said. 'I wrote, but I knew he did not let you receive my letters as I had no reply. I kept writing even so, it was all I could do.'

'We never got those letters. Why did you leave us? It was cruel.'

'I had no choice. When Goody Bradshaw handed me your brother, Thomas – something was not right. He was blue and sickly, his spine was bent, his skin not grown properly over it. And his hair was red as a fox, just like his father's.'

'Who?' Deb whispered.

'Our neighbour, John Blakeney.' Lizzie shook her head sadly.

'John Blakeney?' Deb remembered a red-haired, arrogant man on a big roan hunter.

'Oh, Deb, I was so stupid. I thought to pass the baby off as one of your father's, but as soon as I saw him I knew there would be trouble. But Thomas was so tiny and so weak, Goody Bradshaw had to slap the breath into him. The sound of his screaming was terrible.' Lizzie's face sagged with the memory of it, and she held up her hands in a gesture of hopelessness. 'Your father came running, thinking Goody Bradshaw was harming his babe, but when he saw Thomas, he was repulsed by him. He would not even touch him.

'"That's not my child," he said. "Whose child is it?" and I tried to convince him, "Yours, sir," but of course he would not believe it. I was foolish. I lied, told him my grandmother was ruddy-haired, but of course he could not countenance it.'

Lizzie's words flowed fast, like a waterfall. Deb could not take it all in.

'He wanted me to leave Thomas out on the moor to die,' Lizzie said, 'but I refused. "Get rid of him," he said. But Thomas was my son, too. He was so small, so helpless. How could I leave him?'

'What happened to him? Where is he?'

'The Great Fire took him. The smoke. I picked him up and we ran for our lives, but I couldn't save him. You see, he never thrived, needed constant mothering, even when he should walk and talk, he never did. But do you know, his eyes were wise, like an old soul. Through all his pain, when he looked up at me, so dependent, so trusting, I learned then what love was. Not Blakeney. No, that wasn't love, just passion. But a mother's love for a child ... well, it was the greatest lesson in my life. I have never regretted my decision. Except, of course, for you. And since then I have begged and begged your father to give me news of you, but he never would. He took my boys to Ireland, and he would never let me visit, nor say where you girls had gone. Tell me, Hester, is she ...?'

'Hester's well. At school in Bow. Aunt Beth brought us up.'

'Beth? But I wrote to Beth to ask after you. I had no reply. The hard-hearted—'

'We used to play a game, that you'd just gone out to the shops, and soon you'd come back for us, but no matter how often we played it, you never came.'

'Oh, love.' Lizzie took hold of her hand. 'I was so young and foolish. And after Thomas was born I was half-mad, what with the pain of childbed ... unable to think properly. My heart broke over Hester, she was so little—'

'Mama, promise you'll go and find Hester. She'll need you when I ... when I do what I have to do.' She realised all at once that she would never see Hester grown-up, would never see her married, would never see her bear children.

'What is this? Don't look so sad. We have found each other at last.'

'You must forget this daughter,' she said. And Deb told her everything, about her time at the Pepyses', about Abigail Williams and about Piet's death. She spoke low, looking down, fearful of what her mother might think. When she came to Jem's arrest, the charges against him and the bag of letters, she said, 'They'll hang me once I tell them they are my letters; that it was I who passed their secrets to their enemies, the Dutch.'

Lizzie stood and pressed her face into her hands. 'This is my fault. If you had had a mother to guide you, then maybe you wouldn't have needed to rely on Abigail Williams. I can scarce believe it, that it was she who has caused all this. Though I always suspected there was more to Abigail than she let me see. I should have—'

'Don't blame yourself. It wouldn't have made an ounce of difference.'

'But I should have been there to help you, to stop you from—'

'Abigail was just saving her own skin. We understand one another now.' Deb stood and wiped her cheeks with the backs of her palms. They were wet; she had not realised. 'And I must hurry, Mama, I have to be at the magistrate at four, to plead for Jem.'

'No. there must be some other way. I won't allow it.' Lizzie tried to keep hold of her hand, but Deb pulled it out of reach. 'Please,' Lizzie implored, 'Jem would not want you to do this for him. A boy came with a message for him, but he hadn't come to the school as he usually did. I was worried. So I came to see if I could find him here. And truth be told, I couldn't wait a moment longer to see if it was really you, if it was really my Deborah. And now I'm to lose you again? Don't do this, I can't—'

'Would you have someone else die because of my misdeeds?' Deb shook herself free.

'This is madness! I won't let you go,' Lizzie said, gripping her again by the arm.

'You must. You must pretend you never found me. Jem is a good friend to you, too. Think of him.'

'Don't do that, talk about it as if I'm choosing—'

Deb wrenched away. 'I have to do it, Mama. It's the right thing.'

'It's too much for me, to find you and lose you in one day. And Jem wouldn't want it.' Lizzie shook her head. 'He'd want you to live. He loves you, he told me so.'

The words dropped like flares. All of a sudden she could not stand to wait a moment more. 'All the more reason. I will go, Mama, whatever you say. Don't try to stop me.' She took a deep breath, walked to the door, dared not look back.

At the magistrate's, a thickset serving man told Lizzie to wait outside, and Deb's last sight of her was sitting white-faced, but poised, her hands pulling on a kerchief. She had followed Deb silently all the way.

The magistrate's chamber was a dark, box-like room with a narrow window. A scold's bridle and a cudgel hung on the back of the door. The magistrate was flanked by two heavyweight men in court livery; their short daggers, and the pistols lodged in their belts, told her these were his bodyguards. The magistrate himself, Justice Pembroke, was a thin, pinch-faced man in threadbare doublet and long woollen breeches. He looked at Deb with a resigned sigh.

'Name?'

'Deborah Willet.'

'Business?'

'I've come about Mr Wells.'

'Jeremiah Wells again.' He raised his eyebrows at his companions in annoyance. 'Should have guessed.' He flipped open a ledger and eyed the previous entry. 'Oh, God, I hate these cases. It's always the same.' Another heavy sigh before he looked up at Deb. 'Well, it's no use. His brother has been here already trying to claim *he* was the one at fault. Now you. But you're wasting your time. If he's innocent, I'm a pickled pig. Too much evidence against him, and nothing you can do will save him, so you might as well just go home quietly and—'

Deb had heard enough. 'You've got to listen. He's the wrong man, I can prove it—'

'Stop protesting, Miss Willet,' the magistrate said, holding up his hand. The two men stepped forward to her side of the desk; meat and muscle that took up most of the available space. 'You were not at the docks when they arrested him, you were not the one found running away from the scene of the explosion; he was. Mr Wells has been tried in the proper way, and whatever you wish to say will make not a speck of difference now.'

'But, sir, he's innocent, I swear it.' She leaned forward to grip the edge of the desk, brought reason to her voice. 'The letters you found are mine. The ones in the leather bag. And I was the one who took the documents from Lord Bruncker and Mr Pepys. Mr Wells knows nothing about it.'

The magistrate looked right and left at his companions and they suppressed smiles.

'Lord Bruncker swore under oath that he saw Mr Wells snooping in his office, perusing the papers on his desk,' Justice Pembroke said. 'How do you answer that?'

'He must be mistaken. If you'd just listen a moment, I'd be able to tell you all the papers in the bag are—'

'No, Miss Willet, Lord Bruncker was quite definite. You waste your breath. It's all water under the bridge now. I know you think you are helping him, but we have this same little play every week, sweethearts claiming that they are at fault. I don't know why they do it, never does anyone any good – never has once, in all my days in the law.' He coughed wheezily, poured himself a cup of water. 'The papers were things a maid would know nothing about.'

'But I do,' she said eagerly. 'I know about the code.' At last, they might listen. 'The papers dated March, from the Treasury, that's Shelton's method. And I know how every single one of them—'

But her words were stopped as one arm was seized from behind. She strained against it. 'No! Hear me out.' The magistrate's face was impassive. He bent to pick up a quill, began to write.

Deb held tight to the table as if it were a raft. 'Please, he really is innocent, I can prove it, just bring me the bag, and I'll—'

A hand seized her free arm and hauled her backwards, the table leg scraped, and water slopped from the cup. A curse of annoyance from the magistrate, before her fingers let go and a hand that smelled of salt sweat came over her mouth. An animal rage seized her so she cried out as they pulled her, kicking, from the room and tumbled her into the street.

'Don't hurt her!'Lizzie cried. Deb landed heavily on the ground with a crack to her elbow that made her dizzy.

She struggled to sit up. They had to believe her. She must go back. But this time Lizzie restrained her. The two men had barred the door and had their pistols cocked at the ready.

'Thank God,' Lizzie said, trying to fold her arms around her to comfort her. 'I thought you'd not come out of there.'

'They won't listen.' Deb could scarce believe it. 'I tried to tell them but they just laughed.' A sob burst through. 'What am I to do? They say he'll hang tomorrow.'

Lizzie knelt next to her, grasped Deb by the shoulders. 'Hush. Don't take on so. We'll get Jem out somehow. There's got to be a way.'

'What will I do? They won't hear the truth even

when it's right there in front of them. How will I live with it if they hang him?'

'Here, dry your eyes.' Lizzie handed Deb a kerchief already damp with her own tears. 'We need to think calmly. Let's walk.' She helped her down the street, holding Deb's shaking body upright, her arm tight in hers. 'You need someone with influence. What about Mr Pepys? Can't you talk to him?'

'I'm too embarrassed, he offered me money and I—' Deb stopped dead.

'What is it?'

'Wait a minute. I have to think.' There was a glimmer of a possibility, like a light through a crack in the door. 'The pages from his diary.'

'What? Jem kept a diary?'

'No. Mr Pepys. It's too long to explain ... I stole Pepys' diary. He complains about the King, writes down his frauds, his mistresses ... I could tell Pepys I'll print them.'

Lizzie's reply was instantaneous. 'No. He'll report you for theft of his papers, and theft from your employer is still a capital offence. Think, Deborah. There'll be no chance of leniency with a man like him—'

'Don't you understand? This is my fault. If I hang, then it's only what I deserve. I killed someone, Mama. Or as good as ... but Jem, he's done nothing, knows nothing of any of it. Without the evidence from my bag, maybe they would have let him go.'

'But Pepys'll be incensed that you spied on him. What man wants to be made to look a fool by a woman, especially his maid? He'll have to see punishment done, to keep his face.'

'I think Mr Pepys will listen to me, at least if I can get him to meet me. He's got a soft feeling for me, and you're right – he's a man of influence, with Bruncker and with the courts. I don't care for myself. I'll take the risk. Don't you see?' She grabbed hold of Lizzie's shoulders. 'It could be Jem's salvation. I can't bear the idea of him waiting there, unable to understand, wondering why no one speaks up for him.'

'If you think … I see your heart's set on it, though it grieves me. I'll come with you.'

'No, if I'm to try it, it's better that I go alone. But you can deliver the message.'

Deb took out a stub of graphite from her purse and a scrap of paper and scribbled an urgent note asking Mr Pepys to meet her in an hour at the tavern where they'd last met.

'Please, Mama, hurry,' she said. 'Take a hackney. Fast as you can – take this to his office at Seething Lane, tell him it's urgent. I'll be waiting.'

Chapter Fifty-four

DEB PACED UP AND DOWN the main thoroughfare, scanning the passing faces. The clocks had already chimed four but there was still no sign of Pepys. *Please God, make him come*, she thought. She could not bear to be still, but turned about and about, hearing the ring of the metal tips of her shoes on the cobbles. The sun was getting lower in the sky, her shadow lengthening into a dark needle. The sight filled her with despair. There were only hours left; soon, night would fall and it would be too late.

But at the end of the alley a familiar figure was hurrying towards her, his face anxious instead of beaming with his usual genial good humour. Deb sagged with relief.

'What's the matter? Has Elisabeth found out about our meeting?' Mr Pepys' usually red face was pale as dough.

'Is there somewhere private we can go?' she asked.

'This way,' he said, 'in the tavern. They have chambers to let. I'll get a key.' He was almost hopping from foot to foot. 'Follow me.'

The landlord asked no questions, and Deb got the impression Pepys had taken a private chamber before.

He unlocked the door and stood aside for her to

go through. The 'chamber' was more like a closet, poky, and empty except for a lopsided bed which keeled to one side and was obviously broken. Pepys produced a taper and struck a flint; lit a rushlight which struggled to give off as much light as it did smoke.

'Sorry about the place,' he said, 'but at least we'll be out of view. What's amiss? Has Elisabeth—'

'It's all right,' she said. 'Elisabeth knows nothing. I sent that message just to bring you.'

He exhaled, smiled knowingly and reached out towards her. 'That's the way, is it? You naughty—'

She stepped away. 'I've not come for that,' she said, and unhooked the shutter on the window to flood the room with evening light.

'Then what?' He frowned. 'I've had to get a hackney over here, and it was a mighty fuss. I can pay,' he said hopefully. 'Sixpence a kiss, was it?' He smiled and began to fumble in his pockets.

'Give me the key to this place,' she said. She would need to be sure she could buy time to get away, if she needed to. Once he knew about the diary, she could not risk being held there, for Jem's sake. She would lock Pepys in, if necessary.

'Oh, that little game! Delightful! Here it is.' He held it out on his palm but when she reached for it, he closed his fist.

Frustrated, she put a boot on the bed, hitched up her skirt, and brought out one of the sheets she'd copied from his diary. She shook it before him. 'Do you know what this is?'

He was still smiling as he tried to see.

'It's a sheet transcribed word for word from your diary. Give me the key and you can have it back. Otherwise, I will send it to a printer I know.'

His mouth fell open. 'What's this?' He moved closer to see the sheet. 'Are you jesting? It's not mine,' he bluffed. 'You're making it up.'

'Look closer,' she said, holding the paper tight in her hands.

He tried to take it from her but she held on, began to read aloud from the entry before her.

> *"He tells me that my Lady Castlemaine, however, is a mortal enemy to the Duke of Buckingham, which I understand not; but, it seems, she is disgusted with his greatness, and his ill-usage of her. That the King was drunk at Saxam with Sedley, Buckhurst and company, the night that Lord Arlington arrived, and would not give him audience, or could not which is true, for it was the night that I was there, and saw the King go up to his chamber, and was told that the King had been drinking—"*

'I never wrote that. You can't say I did.' His eyes bulged with indignation, his neck suffusing red.

'You know you did. Twenty-third of October last year. And fortunately for me, the public are only too willing to believe a story like mine.'

'Did you do this … this copying at my house?' His voice was smaller now.

'The key,' she demanded, standing her ground.

Without a word he thrust her the key, and she gave

him the paper. He squinted down at it, then brought it up close to his vision. 'Damned eyes,' he said. But when he looked up, his face had drained of colour. 'You stupid girl! You could have ruined me. If anyone at the Treasury got a-hold of this it could have been the end of my career. You have no idea what you are playing with ... it, it—'

'Oh, but I do,' she said calmly. 'That's why I have copies of the rest.'

'But it's not important,' he said, desperately. 'Surely you didn't think it true? It was just a little entertainment, a fiction, something I write for my own pleasure ...'

'Your truth is the most dangerous sort – the one laced with seams of falsehood. But I don't suppose the King will care which parts are true and which false.'

Mr Pepys put his hand to his forehead and sat down gingerly on the broken bed, which cracked ominously under his weight. 'What do you want?' he asked bitterly. 'I see you want something. I'll set you up somewhere, if that's what you're after.'

She almost laughed. 'No, a favour, that's all. I have your papers safe and you will get them back if you will help me.'

'How do I know you have them?'

'Do you really want me to publish your underhand dealings over the prize ships, your opinions on Clarendon, your liaisons with Doll Powell and Betty Martin?'

'You've read them all?' His hand came to his mouth.

'Of course. You left them where anyone with an ounce of wit could find them.'

'I didn't think you could read shorthand.' He

seemed amazed. 'Fancy that, my little Deb able to read shorthand.'

'You showed me how to read it yourself, surely you remember? *Tell, till, toll—*'

'Yes, but I didn't think you'd be able to—'

'You thought me too stupid to decipher it, I daresay.' She laughed, shook her head sadly. 'You only see what you want to see. You're blind, but it's not your eyes that are the trouble. There's a lot you don't know about me, Mr Pepys. A lot you don't know because you never asked.'

He got to his feet, squared his shoulders. For the first time he addressed her as an equal. 'You've betrayed me. I want those papers. Every last one. How much?'

'No, not money. You can't buy everything and everyone, Mr Pepys.' She told him succinctly about the charges against Jem Wells and where he was being held. 'You must get him out. There's no time to lose. If he hangs, then so will you, I swear. Here's what you must do – you must say you sent him to Chatham on an errand for you, with papers from your office.'

'How do you know all this?'

'That is my business. But I know Jeremiah Wells is a good man, and knows nothing of these crimes. Tell them that the leather bag used in the evidence, and the documents within, are yours.' Which was true, she thought. Some of them were his.

'You want me to perjure myself for a traitor? But I don't know about these papers, what they are, what I'm agreeing to.' He was flustered, unable to be still.

'Do you want the copies of your diary back, Mr Pepys? It's your choice.'

'Wait. This Jeremiah Wells, his name's devilish familiar.' He put a finger to his mouth before exclaiming, 'I remember him! Came about those damned sailors and their pay. What's he to you?'

'He's innocent of the charges, Mr Pepys, but I cannot convince them. Women have no influence, as you well know. Only a man of standing can sway their opinion. Someone well respected, like you.' The flattery seemed to mollify him. He stood up, turned his puppy-dog eyes on her again.

'Will you marry him?'

'Perhaps. If he asks.'

'I can't believe it – my little Deb.' He shook his head mournfully.

'If we are to do business, it can be Miss Willet from now on. What is it to be? Will you go now and tell them, or shall I find myself a good printer?'

'I gave you my heart,' he said.

'I never asked for it.' She hardened herself. 'Your decision, Mr Pepys.'

With a sudden movement he turned back, shook the paper at her in a temper. 'God alive! You know which it's to be. You know a damned sight too much. If I do as you ask, when can I have the papers back?'

'As soon as I see for myself that Jem Wells has gone free and that he has the bag of documents from his lodgings in his hands. I will leave the shorthand copies then in a parcel for you at Lord Bruncker's office.'

'Lord Bruncker? What has he to do with this?' His eyes flared with fear.

'Nothing. Do as I say and all will be well.' She gave him precise instructions, checked he understood. She felt her own power then – the power of her own intelligence commanding his respect. 'I suppose I need not tell you that writing anything of this matter in your diary is inadvisable. In fact, I'd weigh up the consequences of keeping such a diary altogether. What if Elisabeth were to read it?'

He paced the small room, still reluctant to go. 'You know, I could report you to the magistrate for trying to pervert the course of justice.' It was a feeble attempt, and she could see from his plaintive eyes that he knew it.

'You won't. Not if you want your business to stay off the broadsheets. You condemned yourself in your own words, Mr Pepys, not mine. Go now, unless you would like me to lock you in while you think about it.'

'Not even one kiss?'

He was incorrigible. Would he never give up? She frowned.

'I suppose not.' He shrugged. She watched him stuff his paper into his pocket and hurry from the room. Deb's knees buckled and she let herself sag to the floor, pressing her hands together in wordless payer. Had she done enough, or would he send the King's men after her to arrest her and forcibly take back his papers?

'Please, God, let him do it,' she said.

Chapter Fifty-five

THE MORNING OF THE HANGING, Jem was ready. They
had given him a Bible, and though he could not see
in the gloom to read it, just the feeling of its thick
leather spine in his hands bolstered his strength. He
prayed for Bart and for his mother and hoped for a
wet day, a day which would keep the crowds away.
Thoughts of Deborah Willet made him hug his own
thin chest. She'd been lucky. Perhaps it had been for
the best that she'd chosen Hal Crawley and not him.
At least Crawley would be alive. She'd be a widow to
a traitor if she'd chosen him, and who could live with
that kind of shame?

The noise of chains rattling and the key in the
padlock rippled a shudder through him. He made a
last-minute wordless prayer for salvation, over the
ring of the gaoler hammering off the shackles.

'Come on, Padre, out you go.' The gaoler beckoned
him towards the door, holding it wide.

'Are there many gathered?' he asked.

'It's your lucky day. You must have friends in high
places. Being a curate and all!' He laughed. 'It's been
called off, hasn't it? You're free to go.' He thrust his
coat towards him.

'What?'

- 460 -

'You can go. Never happened afore, not in all my born days. It's on account of Mr Pepys. Told the magistrate you had nothing to do with it, didn't he? It's all been hushed up. Gave me a sovereign too, to keep dumb.'

'Mr Pepys?'

'Samuel Pepys –from the Navy Treasury. Says he sent you to the docks. Like you said, you were trying to stop the rebels, weren't you? Pepys said the bag was his, not yours at all.'

'What bag?'

'This one.' The man thrust the bag into his hands.

It was Deb's bag, the one he'd meant to return. Jem could make no sense of it. Last time he'd seen the thing, it was on his table at home. He looked at it in astonishment. 'But I've never seen Mr Pepys, I mean ...' He could not fathom what was going on, but realised if he wanted to get out alive, it was best to keep his mouth shut.

The gaoler was still holding the door. Jem did not need more encouragement. He thrust his arms into his coat sleeves and, clutching the bag, reeled down the stone corridor and out into the fresh air. He'd imagined the day to be grey and wet, but it was brilliant with sunshine, the sky the perfect pale blue of a blackbird's egg.

He almost ran across the street, his eyes watering with the brightness and with relief. He felt in his jacket pocket and his hands closed around his door keys. Then he really did believe it.

He crunched down on his knees and kissed the pavement. 'Thanks be to God!' he yelled.

Several passers-by smiled in an amused kind of way, obviously thinking he was touched by bedlam with his filthy unshaven face and wild eyes.

He jumped onto a ferry, and fortunately the ferryman was an acquaintance and after looking at him askance, let him owe the fare. Jem slapped him on the shoulder so hard that the poor man almost toppled overboard. Jem inhaled the greasy stink of the river with relish. A quarter hour later and he bounced down the street and let himself in at home, feeling the beautiful familiar smoothness of his door handle, the glorious tufty bristles of the doormat under his boots. There were letters addressed to him that had been pushed under the door. Time enough for those later. He picked them up and carried them into his chamber.

Ah, the scent of home – warm floorboards, musty tobacco, candle wax. But the room was all awry, as if some fight had gone on there. The drawers were out of the desk, the wooden cupboard open, his papers and books scattered everywhere. People had been here, searching, he realised. He called out for Bart, but was unsurprised when no answer came. Bart's room was empty, the bed unmade, the water in the washbowl rancid and full of scum; the same as the day he left, as if Bart had just got out of bed and left in a hurry. He, too, must have been gone all this while, since the fight at the docks. He hoped Bart was safe and not in prison, too. He stared at the cup of ale on the table, which had grown a froth of green mould.

Perhaps the letters might tell him. But first he needed a hot wash, and to fetch food. Jem put the letters down unread and laid wood for a fire. Then he must go to Mr Pepys and thank him. Find out why he'd done this for him, and what he'd said, discover what had happened to Bart. While the water heated, he found a few coins in the pocket of his other breeches and went to the corner to the bread shop. His hands trembled as he ate, cramming the crumbs into his mouth, but he could not force much down. He was all a-jangle, filled with the sheer excitement of being alive.

When he had peeled off his filthy clothes, washed and eaten, he was so sleepy it was all he could do not to put his lolling head down on the table right there. But first he must find out about Bart. He picked up the letters, scanned them for his brother's hand. One arrested his attention. His heart leapt in his chest. It was Deb Willet's handwriting. He broke the seal and took out the letter.

It took him a while to read it because it was a long letter, a letter that seemed to be a confession. He scanned it once. Twice. A third time. He could not take it in. She was telling him that she was responsible for his arrest; that she was a spy for the Dutch and she was going to admit her guilt to the magistrate. She bid him *adieu*, and the letter avowed her love for him.

'*With my heartfelt love and deepest regard*,' she had written. The words danced inside him, making his legs feel flimsy as straw. He picked up the lock of her soft hair from the table where it had fallen, stroked it with his fingers, ran his thumb over the red ribbon which was holding it together. He blinked, unable to make proper sense of the information, as if his mind was too slow to believe it, his heart too eager to feel.

She had confessed to this for him, and even now she might be on the way to the Clink, the place he had just now escaped with such joy and freedom. He didn't understand. Where was Pepys in all this? Surely it was he who had fetched him free, not Deb? The bag must hold a clue. He unbuckled it, spread out the contents.

Plans of the docks, letters with official navy seals, illegible documents in some sort of code. Memoranda from the Cabinet in shorthand about navy policy. He ran his hands over them in astonishment. Deb had been harbouring all this information. It must be true. She really *was* involved in some sort of espionage.

The vision he had of Deb Willet as a ministering angel dissolved, to be replaced with a new, slightly frightening picture. He picked up her letter again, full of wonder. Here it was in her own hand, that she had saved him by sacrificing herself. His elation that she cared was doused by the realisation of what that meant for her. He let out a groan of despair. They'd hang her.

He dragged himself to his feet as if drunk. Wherever she was he had to find her. He blundered outside, hailing a hackney by standing in the street and waving his arms until one stopped.

'Whetstone Park,' he said. 'Across the bridge. Gallop.'

When the house was in sight he jumped from the carriage door as it was still moving, narrowly missing its flapping edge, and threw his last coins at the driver's feet. 'Turn around and wait for me,' he yelled.

At the battering on the door, Lizzie threw open the window. 'Who's there?' she called.

'Lizzie! Is that you?' Jem's voice.

'Jem! I'm coming down.'

A few moments later Lizzie slid back the bolt.

'Where is she?' Jem said, grasping her by the shoulder.

'It's all right, she's safe. They wouldn't listen to her. She went to Pepys, persuaded him to speak for you.'

'But how? I don't understand.'

'Are you angry with her?'

'Good Lord, no. I just want to see her. She wrote to me, she said—'

'Then come on in. I'll take your hackney and go on home now, back to Lukenor Lane. There'll be a welcome for you both there, and a hot supper later, if you'll join me.'

She embraced him briefly, whispered 'She's waiting upstairs', and slipped away. She was giving them time, he realised, time alone.

Deb heard his voice outside. She knew its tone and the rhythm of his speech. She looked out of the window to see the top of his auburn head, and it was such a dear sight she thought she might faint. Moments later, she heard his footsteps on the stairs and she held her breath, tried to be calm. But as the door opened and as she saw Jem's worried expression, she couldn't help herself – she took a few steps towards him, her eyes full of questions.

He was still a moment, looking at her as if to take her all in. Then his arms came out to hold her. She let herself be pressed against his chest with a great sob.

'Dearest Deb,' he soothed. 'You can see my neck is still the same length, thanks to you.'

'Oh, Jem,' she said. 'Thank God. They nearly killed you, and I'm the one to blame. My bag ... if it hadn't been for that, they would've had to let you go.'

'But you went to sacrifice your own life for mine. I can't take it in, that you cared so much. It makes me humble.'

'They wouldn't believe me. They think women are feeble-minded, not supposed to be capable of such things.'

'They are fools then.'

She pulled away from him. 'I'm not so noble. Don't think of me falsely, I have had enough of that. I persuaded Mr Pepys to put in a word for you. He owed me a favour. I don't want you to be under any illusions. I did spy for the Dutch. I did ... unspeakable things. Be careful, Jem. I'm not the woman you thought I was.'

'You gave me my life back, and I'm still trying to understand it, who you are, but I ... well, I want to try. To get to know you, the whole of you, not just the parts strangers see.'

'I deceived you,' she said. 'I need your pardon. And you need to know about—'

He put his hand to her lips. 'I fell for you the very first time I met you, kicking the devil out of that big white dog. I should've known then you were a woman to be reckoned with.'

'But did you not look in the bag—?'

'Hush, be quiet and let me kiss you.' He pulled her closer. Deb let his warm lips touch hers and his arms wrapped tight around her back to draw her in.

Finally, Jem spoke. 'I can't promise you a house like Seething Lane.'

'The less like Seething Lane, the better.'

The rapping at the door made Deb almost shoot out of her shoes.

'Don't answer it,' he said.

'Deb! Deb? Is there anyone there?' A female voice. They heard the door open and hurried footsteps tapping up the stairs, before Hester burst in on them.

'It's taken me days to find you!' Hester glared at Deb accusingly from under her fashionable hat. 'I had to stay with Lavinia's uncle and it was ... where are all the servants?' She looked around in astonishment at the bare room, at Jem's arm on Deb's. 'I've left school. I couldn't stand it another minute, and you're not to send me back.' She frowned, wrinkled her nose. 'Do you live here? Is *he* Dr Allbarn?'

'No, no. Dr Allbarn left,' Deb said. 'Let me introduce ... Jeremiah Wells.' She glanced at Jem, whose grin almost split his face. 'Jem, this is Hester, my sister.'

He made a small bow. 'So pleased to meet you at last,' he said, in his most charming voice.

Hester's mouth fell open. She took a few steps back. For once, she was lost for words.

'Won't Lizzie be surprised to see her?' Jem said to Deb, squeezing her around the waist.

'Who's Lizzie?' Hester asked. 'I don't understand. I don't remember any Lizzie.'

Jem turned to Deb and they laughed. 'You will,' he said.

Epilogue

Elisabeth Pepys was mightily pleased with her shiny new coach. She sat back in upholstered comfort to admire the view and the springing up of Wren's new buildings from the ashes of old London. As they clopped through the streets, the new coach drew the envious eyes of her neighbours. Of course, she knew she was only allowed it because Sam was trying to appease her and make amends for the whole sorry business with Deb. Last night he'd been positively loving, and today he'd offered to drive with her to call on Mr Coventry, hoping to impress him with their grand appearance, but unfortunately, Coventry was out.

'I thought we might take a ship to France, dear,' Sam said, 'as you are so keen to return there. Your brother can come with us, and we can visit some of your old haunts. It would improve my French. Maybe we could look at the cathedrals, see the sights of Paris, the great paintings and buildings.'

Or likely the docks, she thought, if you have your way. But Sam really was trying hard. He disliked her brother, Balty, with a passion, she knew, so it was good of him to invite him.

She reached out to take her husband by the hand.

'Thank you. Will it not be a terrible expense?'

'Yes, but it's no more than you deserve.' He looked at her ruefully.

'I know.'

'I'll make it up to you, I promise.'

She sniffed, but it was a pleased sort of a sniff. She knew better than to expect him to apologise, but there was an honesty in his look that was different from before. She leaned back against the green leather seat, still cool with him.

'I have a yearning to get away from England,' he said, 'away from the Treasury and the court. Lately I have felt ... oppressed. I need to get a breath of air.' And there was a tinge of sadness in his expression that made her think that it was not England that bothered him, but his own mind, his own self.

It touched her. She lifted his hand, placed a kiss there. 'I shall look forward to it. It's a fine idea, Sam.'

He held her gaze a moment. 'And you are a fine wife.'

Passing through London that night, if you were to peep through the window of Seething Lane, you would see Mr and Mrs Pepys at home. She has a French romance open on her lap and is staring into the fire, dreaming of the dressmakers in the fashionable leafy quarters of Paris. In the study, Mr Pepys is on his hands and knees with a cloth tape, measuring for more bookcases. He stands up, pulls his waistcoat straight, and trots over to the desk where a dish of half-eaten bread and herring has just called for his attention.

In another part of the Navy Building, close by, Abigail Williams takes Lord Bruncker's wig and, patting it fondly, puts it on its stand. She climbs back into the four-poster, rolling up her petticoat to show him the embroidered tops of her stockings, and he reaches for her before they disappear under the heap of silk counterpane. For a few moments, the silk heaves and rolls like waves on the sea, until it gently subsides to stillness.

Passing by Lukenor Lane, through the window of a tavern in Clement's Yard, the candles on the table are flickering low, illuminating four plates bearing the remains of a pease pudding. Lizzie Willet leans close to a pink-cheeked Hester, who is explaining something, gesturing animatedly with her hands. Every now and then Hester looks up to see her mother still listening, head tilted to one side, eyebrows raised, a surprised smile on her face. Jem Wells, his long hair tied in a black sash, has his back to the window. If you were to wait a little longer, you would see Jem put his arm around Deb Willet's shoulder and pull her close, as if he might kiss her.

Deb turns, looks through her own reflection, into the night outside, her face caught in the light for just an instant, before her hand flashes up, and she closes the curtain on the dark.

Postscript

On 31st May 1669, shortly after his last recorded meeting with Deb, Samuel Pepys wrote his last diary entry. In this final entry he says his eyesight is failing, and tells the reader, with his eye firmly on posterity, that he will ask his clerks to help him keep the diary, but to *'be contented to set down no more than is fit for them and all the world to know; if there be any thing, which cannot be much, now my amours to Deb are past.'*

Sadly, Elisabeth Pepys died from a fever on November 10, 1669. She had recently returned from a sightseeing tour of France with her husband.

In 1673 a fire began in Lord Brunker's apartment and burned down the offices of the Navy Board and Pepys' house. Pepys narrowly managed to save his diaries and books. Abigail Williams was responsible for starting the blaze in her closet.

According to research by Dr Loveman at the University of Leicester, Jeremiah Wells and Deborah Willet were married in January 1670 in Chelmsford. He went on to work for Pepys as ship's chaplain on the ships *Dover* and *Resolution*. The couple had two daughters, Deborah and Elizabeth. Mrs Deborah Wells died in 1678 at the age of 27, and her husband Jeremiah only eighteen months later at the age of 31.

Historical Notes

SAMUEL PEPYS' REMARKABLE DIARY has fascinated me for many years. While researching my other novels set in the seventeenth century, I referred to it for those small details about the Restoration period which could only come from a man who recorded it for us, as it happened, through his own eyes. But every time I used the diary I became intrigued by the shadowy female figures that Pepys mentions only in passing: Elisabeth Pepys, referred to only as 'my wife', and Deborah Willet, whom he calls 'Deb', the girl who stole his heart. I wondered what their view of events would be, but it was quite a few years before I thought of actually using the diary more directly, to spark a novel of its own.

Researching Deb Willet, I discovered that she was not the unlettered maid she is usually made out to be, but as well-educated as her mistress, and that the fact that she had been schooled was one of the reasons she was chosen as a companion for Elisabeth. A maid's subservience to an employer demands a certain reticence, an ability to be on the fringes of things, to watch and listen. I realised an intelligent woman in her position could be useful to those who wished to know more about the affairs of the navy, so the idea of a novel, with Deb at its centre, was born.

Constructing a novel around the diary was both a

joy and a headache for a fiction writer. Pepys gives us such a wealth of detail that cannot be circumvented. For example, I could not manipulate the weather to heighten an emotional scene, and I had to deal with the problem of periods in the diary where Pepys is frustratingly silent in terms of Deb's story. However, Deb must have had a vibrant life between his mentions of her, though there is little evidence surviving of her life. I am grateful to Dr Kate Loveman, whose research into Deb Willet's family, and what happened to her after she left Seething Lane was invaluable to this novel. Filling gaps is what a historical fiction writer loves, and I have made full use of them, though I have been careful to ensure Deb's story coheres with Pepys' recording of the events of the diary.

Espionage

My main source of reference for this novel has been Pepys' diary itself in various editions. The online versions are particularly good as they contain useful and insightful comments from Pepys' cognoscenti, as well as the actual text. My secondary reference work was the excellent *Intelligence and Espionage in the Reign of Charles II* by Alan Marshall. In this period, England as a nation was still awash with religious dissenters, and with different factions nursing various grievances left over from the Civil Wars. Marshall's description of a country riddled with plots both real and fake, the one often indistinguishable from the other, guided the construction of the espionage subplot. The seventeenth-century poet, Dryden, expressed the feeling of the nation very well when he said:

> *"Plots true or false are necessary
> things,
> To raise up commonwealths and
> ruin kings."*

There is no doubt that after the first Dutch war there was massive distrust of the fragile treaty with the Dutch. They were still being blamed – along with God's vengeance – for the Great Fire, and Marshall gives us strong evidence of the Low Countries as a refuge for English rebels of all persuasions. Perhaps my character Bart might have found his way there.

Morality

Our views on morality and sexual conduct have moved on since Pepys' day. What was considered perfectly acceptable in the seventeenth century is totally unacceptable now. A Deb of today certainly would not have put up with her employer's harassment. Pepys in my novel could easily have been a monster, but he is regarded everywhere with such affection – rightly or wrongly – that to paint this view of him would have caused great resistance in a reader who has turned to this novel because it features him.

From Pepys' diary we can read that, just like today, a simplistic view cannot suffice, as within the diary itself we see conflicted views of what constituted moral behaviour – Pepys' remorse and feelings for his wife when he has strayed, Elisabeth's disdain for the behaviour of 'Madam' Williams. Whether or not I have successfully picked my way across this quagmire of sexual abuse versus the historical mores of the time is something I hope my readers will discuss between themselves.

Names and Dates

Many of Deb Willet's family were called Elizabeth – her mother and both aunts, and to make it even more confusing Mrs Pepys was also an Elizabeth. I have used different diminutives or spellings to try to make it clear who is who. I was juggling with this when I realised I also had the confusion of Wells, Williams and Willet as surnames – all unavoidable as they were real people.

Certain names of people and places are as in the diary, rather than in more modern usage, for example 'Lord Bruncker' rather than Brouncker, and 'White Hall' rather than Whitehall.

The dates of the novel refer to the Julian Calendar, so that those who wish might cross-reference my novel with the diary and read Samuel Pepys' actual words on the events taking place. These dates do not necessarily concord with the modern Gregorian Calendar. Also, in those days, the New Year did not officially start until 25th March, but Pepys does refer to the idea of January as the beginning of the year in the diary, so for the purposes of this novel, I have kept to our familiar New Year's Day as the start of the year.

Language and Pepys' diary

I have picked out certain phrases and adjectives from Pepys' diary to aid authenticity, particularly in my imaginings of his dialogue. Pepys used shorthand to write his diary, and for the past two centuries scholars have been attempting to produce an 'English' version that translates every mark accurately. The reader should be aware that the online shorthand translations of his diary were made in the Victorian era and are therefore somewhat archaic translations. The standard translation now is by Robert Latham and William Matthews (1970–83) and is available via academic institutions.

I have tried to be accurate as far as the diary is concerned and to use what reference material I could find to support my story, though I am quite sure it is apparent to the reader that there is a very large dollop of fiction in with the fact! I am not a historian but a storyteller, so for historical errors or inaccuracies in this book, I apologise in advance, and I am always happy to hear from readers who have better knowledge or expertise in areas or subjects I do not know. I have had great fun reimagining the world of Pepys' diary, and can only hope that Mr Pepys, with his love of the theatre and books, would have been mightily entertained.

Selected Further Reading

Samuel Pepys: The Unequalled Self – Claire Tomalin
Intelligence and Espionage in the Reign of Charles II – Alan Marshall
Voices from the World of Samuel Pepys – Jonathan Bastable
The Illustrated Pepys – Ed. Robert Latham
Young Mr Pepys – John Hearsey
Restoration London – Liza Picard
The Weaker Vessel – Antonia Fraser
Early Modern England: A Social History – J. A. Sharpe
Nell Gwyn – Charles Beauclerk
Transformations of Love: The friendship of John Evelyn and Margaret Godolphin – Frances Harris
Mrs Pepys: Her book – Marjorie Astin (fiction)
The Journal of Mrs Pepys – Sara George (fiction)
The Diary of Samuel Pepys: BBC Radio 4 drama – Hattie Naylor (audio)

Acknowledgements

My thanks to Phil Gyford who set up the splendid website, www.pepysdiary.com, and all the knowledgeable commenters on his site. Dr Kate Loveman was kind enough to read the manuscript for obvious anachronisms. Thanks to Alis Hawkins and Tim Stretton who advised me on earlier drafts, and all the Macmillan New Writers for their support. Special mention must go to Richard Sheehan for his editorial advice, and to Jay Dixon, my editor at Accent Press, whose suggestions and comments have made this a stronger novel. As always, my heartfelt thanks go to my husband John, who acted as first reader, chief chef, and giver of ever-sensible advice.

Thank you, the reader.
If you'd like to find out more about my books you can find me at www.deborahswift.com
Or follow me on Twitter @swiftstory

5. Abigail Williams was a real person, and there is speculation she was a spy, like Aphra Behn, the well-known dramatist. What does Abigail contribute to the story? How much is Deb a reflection of Abigail, and how is she different?

6. Deb says that Pepys describes her as something 'quite *other*'. When a diarist describes a real person how does this differ from a portrayal within a biography or a novel?

Reading Group Questions

1. What did you think of the character of Mr Pepys? Did he have any redeeming characteristics, and if so, what were they?

2. Deb reads Pepys' private diary in the novel. Did you think this was a betrayal of trust? Have you ever kept a diary, and how would it make you feel if someone else read it?

3. Diaries are supposed to be the honest reflections of daily life. Do you think this is always the case? Do diarists only have a limited view of the truth? Were you surprised by what might have gone on 'between the lines' of Pepys' diary?

4. Have you read any other diaries which have given you an insight into history, and how important were these in our understanding of historical events?